The Artificial Man and Other Stories

More Belt Revivals

Poor White by Sherwood Anderson

Main-Travelled Roads by Hamlin Garland

The History of the Standard Oil Company by Ida Tarbell

The Damnation of Theron Ware by Harold Frederic

Stories of Ohio by William Dean Howells

The Marrow of Tradition by Charles W. Chesnutt

The Artificial Man and Other Stories

Clare Winger Harris

First Belt Publishing Edition 2019
ISBN: 978-1-948742-32-0

Belt Publishing
3143 West 33rd Street, Cleveland, Ohio 44019
www.beltpublishing.com

Book design by Meredith Pangrace
Cover by David Wilson

contents

introduction

I'm standing in front of a house outside Cleveland, half-waiting for a spaceship to arrive. When it finally appears, blotting out the sky, I will crane my neck and stare at its sleek, impossible angles. People will shout, point, and run.

But I don't see it.

Instead, the house at 1652 Lincoln Avenue sits quiet. It was built in 1917 of stone brick with a front porch. The house is a duplex, split in two by an interior wall I can only imagine. There is a single dormer window sticking out from the attic, perched towards the sky. There is a big tree on the left, whose tips are already turning to fire, here in the September sun. The front door is closed.

When I asked to organize a new edition of Clare Winger Harris's stories, I knew I wanted to see the place she once lived in Lakewood, Ohio. But as I stare at her old house, I see little in the way of connection. There is some old grating and windowsills that may have survived the century, but that's about it. The old bones are there, but the paint is new.

People still live here, but there is no one home, so I don't push it. What's to push, anyway? This wasn't William Faulkner's house. Or Emily

Dickinson's. It didn't belong to Langston Hughes, who went to high school in Cleveland. No, this was the house of Clare Winger Harris, who wrote weird science fiction in the early decades of the twentieth century. If I rang the bell and announced that, like I was some door-to-door literary merit salesman, I can easily guess the reply:

Who?

It's a fair response, especially for a woman author who wrote in a marginal genre in cheap magazines. That is why I wanted to write something here that wasn't the usual elevation of her work. I don't want to tell you what to think of her stories; I just want you to read them. Instead, I want to tell you about her.

I circle around again, looking at the cracks and corners. I again hope for some unexplainable trans-temporal event, a sudden fold in space-time from which Ms. Harris would appear, stepping through a shimmering tunnel with Mary Poppins-like authority to answer my questions in full.

I then realize that the people who live here now, whoever they are, might have one of those security cameras to guard against people stealing their Amazon packages. As I duck behind the dashboard, I think about what Clare might think of such an invention. I think of similar things possibly inside this house: phones, computers, microwaves, and televisions; pads and tablets and smart things you can shout at. In a way then, she was here in full.

I look again. Maybe instead of an alien ship I can I hear the three baby boys she raised here, something we have in common. I can see her husband Frank, hat in hand, out the front door and on to his job as an engineer at American Monorail. I can almost see the postman come to the door. All writers, regardless of decade, wait for the mail.

But I still can't see her. I can't see Clare. But she's inside. I know it. I can hear the typing.

If I had a future-o-scope or a time-televisor (the Golden Age of science fiction had singularly practical terms for these things) and could look ahead to the next several months as I researched Clare's life, I would have seen that I would soon reveal, in this introduction, an important unpublished story of hers and a whole chapter of her life that had never been written about, among other things.

But that is yet to come.

Claire Marie Winger was born on January 18, 1891, in the county seat of Freeport, Illinois, to Mary Porter 'May' Stover and Frank Stover Winger, an electrical engineer. Frank was related to Mary; he was a Stover on his mother's side. Clare had a brother, Stover Carl Winger, born 1893, who was named after their mother's wealthy father, Daniel Carl "D. C." Stover, founder of the Stover Engine Works. After their children were born and raised, Clare's parents divorced.

In 1910, Clare graduated from Chicago's Lake View High School and went to Smith College with a bright future ahead of her. While at school, Clare met Frank Clyde Harris, a veteran of World War I who worked as an engineer designing heavy armor plating. He might have seemed very familiar to her. Clare dropped out and they married in 1912 in Chicago. The newlyweds traveled to Europe before relocating cross-country as Frank finished his Master's in architectural engineering. During these years, Clare had three sons: Clyde Winger (1915), Donald Stover (1916), and Lynn Thackrey (1918).

In 1917, Clare's father published a novel with the fantastical title of *The Wizard of the Island; or, The Vindication of Prof. Waldinger*. How did an electrical engineer become drawn to science fiction? He most certainly read the best trade magazine on the subject, *The Electrical Experimenter*, which later became *Science and Invention.* In addition to publishing circuit diagrams, editor Hugo Gernsback pontificated on all kinds of bizarre, theoretical inventions like the "thought telegrapher" and "television." He also advocated for a new type of literary genre called "Scientifiction" that used scientific fact as the basis for imaginative stories.

In 1923, Clare wrote her first and only published novel, the classically-themed *Persephone of Eleusis: A Romance of Ancient Greece* through the Boston-based Stratford Company. Three years later, *Weird Tales Magazine* published her story "A Runaway World" in its July issue. Attributed to "Mrs. F. C. Harris," it is the first American science-fiction story by a woman using her own name.

The realm that Clare was publishing in was a decidedly strange one. Though writers had been publishing weird science stories since Mary Shelley's *Frankenstein; or, The Modern Prometheus* in 1818, it wasn't until the advent of the pulp magazines that the genre became popular. The pulps, with names like *Amazing Stories* and *Science Wonder Stories,* were aimed at the youngish reader with their fully painted covers, spot illustrations, and dense stories printed on cheap paper. They had letter columns where readers could offer critique and exchange letters in a kind of early typeset Internet. Many of these early letter writers rose up into significant and lucrative roles as writers, editors, and publishers. Science fiction was embraced, and then run, by its first-contact fans.

In June 1927, while Clare was living in Lakewood, *Amazing Stories* ran a writing contest cooked up by Gernsback, who had now fully embraced science fiction publishing. Clare entered, along with three hundred and fifty-eight other people, with her environmental space opera "The Fate of the Poseidonia," in which Earth's water supply is stolen by opportunistic Martians. Clare won third place for her story (with a female lead) and signed it "Clare Winger Harris."

In announcing the winners, Gernsback, whose earlier editorials probably influenced Clare's father, gave praise couched in the cultural moment:

That the third prize winner should prove to be a woman was one of the surprises of the contest, for, as a rule, women do not make good scientification writers, because their education and general tendencies on scientific matters are usually limited. But the exception, as usual, proves the rule, the exception in this case being extraordinarily impressive.

The prize opened doors for Clare. She published extensively in the pulps for the next three years, especially for Gernsback. These stories, reprinted in this volume, run the gamut of quaint, thrilling, and terrifying. I will not spoil your experience by summarizing them here. Read them. You are so close. Trust me.

Her story "The Ape Cycle" in the May 1930 issue of *Science Wonder Quarterly* is generally considered her last. It might also be a largely unacknowledged source for a popular media franchise, but I will let you judge that for yourself. Then suddenly, at age thirty-nine, Clare stopped. Someone even wrote into *Amazing Stories* in late 1930 and asked, "What happened to Clare Winger Harris? I've missed her . . ." Every single account of her life says that she quit to focus on raising her children.

When Clare quit, her popularity was so great that her name was regularly being used on covers as advertising. She could have, like her peers, gone on to write novels, comic books, or even for the screen. But she walked away. Or did she?

In the early thirties, after "The Ape Cycle," a fan of Clare's from the east side of Cleveland wrote her a fan letter. He gushed about her work. He said that he was working on his own magazine with his best friend and would like her to submit to it. He was in high school.

Clare might have smiled at this request, which might be why she sent a story. It appeared in 1933 in the fifth and last issue of a stapled, mimeographed pamphlet called *Science Fiction* that had a print run of maybe—maybe—fifty issues. The boy who wrote her was Jerry Siegel and his friend was Joe Shuster. In a couple of years, they would go on to create Superman, the most recognized science fiction character on the planet.

I am very pleased that we have that story, titled "The Vibrometer," collected here for the first time since that small self-published magazine. Special thanks to comics scholar Dr. Thomas Andrae for his generous gift of this time-lost story. Its existence shows how influential Clare was to the next generation of science fiction writers, even those creating the perfect fictional hero. She was often a teacher. One of her most enduring legacies, also reprinted here, is a letter she wrote for the August 1931 issue of *Wonder Stories*. In it, she lists possible science fiction plots for writers like Jerry Siegel and others, including "Interplanetary space travel," "Adventures on other worlds," and "The creation of synthetic life." Hopeful writers tore this out and followed it. You can still follow them today. I have endeavored to follow them here.

Clare and Frank eventually divorced, and Clare moved out west. In an April 10, 1960, interview with the *Plain Dealer*'s Jane Scott, Frank Harris looks back on his life in Cleveland, where he stayed after the divorce. His monorail company was integral to the war effort and he was now—in 1960—worth six million dollars. Frank, still a workaholic, doesn't mention Clare. He says his hobbies are collecting oriental art with his new wife, whom he met on a golf course. He is also proud of his children: Clyde develops missile systems, Don is an engineer in Indiana, and Lynn is a research writer for the government in California. Some later accounts of Clare's life claim that Frank, as the fully realized technological man of the future, was an inspiration for her own work.

Though Clare disappeared from the writing life, her stories were reprinted with great regularity in other sci-fi mags, though with similar biographical blurbs. In 1947, she self-published a collection of her short stories titled *Away from the Here and Now: Stories in Pseudo-Science* from Dorrance Press without any introduction. Other reprints and inclusions by fans and scholars followed, from Richard A. Lupoff and Lisa Yaszek, among others. She was recently included in a 2018 summertime exhibit at the Pasadena Museum of History celebrating science fiction authors in the area.

Every single published account of Clare Winger Harris ends that she stopped writing, raised her family, and died in 1968. Some go so far as to say she had no living relatives.

She left only her stories behind.

But for someone who wrote about spaceships, cyborgs, and ape-men, such an ending is, if we're being truthful, a little unsatisfactory.

For several months, I try in vain to locate relatives of Clare Winger Harris. I finally give up. I send a last, desperate Facebook message to someone named Dan. He writes back and says he is part of the larger Harris family, but doesn't know anything. I give up again. The following Monday, I get a call. I almost don't answer until I see the glowing words "California."

"Hello," I say.

"Hi." A pause. "It's Don Harris. I got your number from my nephew. You wanted to talk about Clare?"

When Don was twelve or thirteen years old, he remembers visiting the Brookmore Apartments, an elegant, four-story brick building in

Old Town Pasadena. Don went there to visit his grandmother. When he entered her one-room apartment, he was always struck by one inescapable fact: it was filled to the top with books.

"You could tell she was smart," Don says.

Donald Lynn Harris visited his grandmother every couple of months. She shared books with him on Tibetan Buddhism and Rosicrucianism. She was analytic, but also philosophical. Don remembers one time she gave him a book by Manley P. Hall, the metaphysical thinker and occultist whom Clare knew. It sparked quite an interest in him. One time, she gave him her own book of stories. He remembers reading part of it.

"Clare was brusque and businesslike," Don says. "But she was nice to me. She would have been a bad grandma for a young child, but she was a good one for an older person."

Years later, Don and his family crowded around the computer and started typing the names of relatives into a search engine. They were astounded when Clare's name filled the results.

"There was nothing about my grandfather Frank," Don says. "We thought he was more famous than her."

When I ask why they divorced, there is a pause.

"We have a whole family of eccentrics," Don says, laughing. They stayed together until their kids were fully grown, but their personalities were just too similar. Grandfather wanted to be chief of the roost. He was a big man—six feet, eight inches tall. His sons saw him as overwhelmingly powerful.

"But he was gentle with me," Don remembers. "He gave me some Chinese art once."

Don recalls that Clare didn't have a lot. Sometimes, when she needed extra money, she would work the switchboard at the Brookmore, plugging wires in and out. She was supposed to inherit a great deal of money from D. C. Stover, but by the time it eventually reached her, the estate had been plundered. Others tried to warn her of this, but she was reluctant to believe it. She was a loner.

"They found her in the hall," Don says. It was October 26, 1968. She was seventy-seven. "I'm not sure any of us knew what it was. A heart attack? She didn't waste away. She was very healthy."

All three of her sons came to California for the funeral. There was the elder Don, who flew missions in World War II. There were rumors he had flown over Dresden. Someone whispered that during one flight, one of his copilots got hit and had his head severed. Don flew back with it in the plane with him.

"He came back darker," says Don, who was named after him.

Lynn was a Marine who came back with a little bag of gold teeth. He showed them to Don. Lynn was very close to Clare. But he was always getting into trouble, says Don. He lived in the Yucatan and she had to bail him out of various problems. When Clare died, Lynn was accused by the family of looting her apartment.

"He took the TV," Don says. "I have some stuff of hers, mostly books. She didn't have much. She was relatively reclusive."

When I ask if the family was influenced by her work, or at least the spirit of it, Don says that his dad was the biggest fan. Clyde Harris was a physics nerd who worked on heat-seeking missile systems. Don, a liberal, would often argue with his dad and try to guess at his various projects, which were classified. His dad would often cave, and they would argue about the ethics of it all.

"It was all in good fun," says Don.

After his dad died, Don traveled to Nepal with his wife. They went to Lumbini, the windswept birthplace of the Buddha. Don attributes his interest in Buddhism to his grandmother Clare, who he said was one of the first in southern California to embrace it.

Don takes a breath that I can hear over the phone. He explains to me that he saw something very strange on that trip. Something weird.

"There was a dog," he says. "Only I looked into his face and I saw my dad. I can't explain it. But I saw it. My dad told me something then, just by looking at me. I had a big change after that."

Donald Lynn Harris is the grandson of Clare Winger Harris and lives in a house in the California woods. When he was younger, he was into drag racing. He joined the Back to the Land movement, bought land, and set up probably the first solar panels in the county. He started small-scale hydro systems to encourage renewable energy resources. He set up similar systems in Nicaragua, where he met Benjamin Linder, the American engineer who was murdered by the Contras in 1987. Infuriated, Don became vocal and political, drawing the attention of the government. Years later, he would end up, for a moment, on a long list of suspects in the Unabomber case. Don laughs when he tells me this. He is still very political but gives me the advice to choose my battles. But, he says, thinking aloud "the older I get, my belief system means more to me than my own aging body."

Don must radiate out from his remote home to get a good wireless signal. I picture him under an open sky, his voice beaming through the ether like the radio waves in his grandmother's stories. He wouldn't have it any other way, living along the outer rim of society, even though it's getting a little harder to chop his own wood.

Don has no children. His wife of forty-two years recently passed away. When I offer my condolences, he tells me it's okay.

"We believe in other dimensions," he says, using the present tense. "So, keep an open mind," he tells me, cheerily and full of wonder.

"We believe in that stuff."

Brad Ricca
September 2018

The Artificial Man and Other Stories

The Artificial Man

I.

In the annals of surgery no case has ever left quite as horrible an impression upon the public as did that of George Gregory, a student of Austin College. Young Gregory was equally proficient in scholastic and athletic work, having been for two years captain of the football team, and for one year a marked success in intercollegiate debates. No student of the senior class of Austin or Decker will ever forget his masterful arguments in the question:—"Resolved that bodily perfection is a result of right thinking." Gregory gave every promise of being one of the masterful minds of the age; and if masterful in this instance means dominating, he was that— and more. Alas that his brilliant mentality was destined to degradation through the physical body—but that is my story.

It was the Thanksgiving game that proved the beginning of George's downfall. Warned by friends that he would be wise to desist from the more dangerous physical sports, he laughingly—though with unquestionable sincerity—referred to the context of his famous debate, declaring that a correct mental attitude toward life—he had this point down to a mathematical correctness—rendered physical disasters impossible. His sincerity in believing this was laudable, and so far his credence had stood him in good stead. No one who saw his well-proportioned six-foot figure making its way through the opponents' lines, could doubt that the science of thinking rightly was favorably exemplified in young Gregory.

But can thinking be an exact science? Before the close of that Thanksgiving game George was carried unconscious from the field, and in two days his right leg was amputated just below the hip.

During the days of his convalescence two bedside visitors brightened the weary hours spent upon the hospital cot. They were David Bell, a medical student, and Rosalind Nelson, the girl whom George had loved since his freshman year.

"I say, Rosalind," he ventured one day as she sat by his bedside. "It's too bad to think of you ever being tied up to a cripple. I'm willing to step aside—can't do it gracefully of course with only one leg—but I mean it, my dear girl. You don't want only part of a husband!"

Rosalind smiled affectionately. "George, don't think for a minute that it matters to me. You're still you, and I love you, dear. Can't you believe that? The loss of a bodily member doesn't alter your identity."

"That's just what gets me," responded her lover with a puzzled frown. "I have always believed, and do now, that the mental and physical are so closely related as to be inseparable. I think it is Browning who says, 'We know not whether soul helps body more than body helps soul.' They develop together, and if either is injured the other is harmed. Losing part of my body has made me lose part of my soul. I'm not what I was. My mental attitude has changed as a result of this abominable catastrophe. I'm no longer so confident. I feel myself slipping and I—oh it is unbearable!"

Rosalind endeavored to the best of her ability to reassure the unfortunate man, but he sank into a despondent mood, and seeing that her efforts at cheering him were unavailing, she arose and left him.

In the outer hall she met Bell on his way to visit the sick man. He noticed her troubled mien and asked if George were not so well today.

"Yes, David," she replied, a quiver in her voice, "the wound is healing nicely, but he is so morose. He has a notion—oh how can I tell it—a sort of feeling that some of his mental poise and confidence have gone with his lost limb. You will soon be a graduate physician, won't you assure him that his fears are groundless?"

"I don't know but that his case is one for the minister or psychologist rather than the medical man," answered Bell. "His physical wound is healing, but it seems his mental wound is not. However, I will do my best, not only for your sake, Rosalind, but because I am interested in the happiness of my old college chum."

Rosalind smiled her gratitude and turned abruptly away to hide the tears that she had held back as long as possible.

Five months passed, and with the aid of a crutch George made excellent headway in overcoming the difficulties of locomotion. If David and Rosalind noticed a subtle change in the disposition and character of their mutual friend, they made no further reference to it.

II.
A Transformation

At length came a day when in the company of both of these faithful friends George Gregory announced his intention of using an artificial limb instead of a crutch. His sweetheart voiced immediate remonstrance.

"No, George, I'd rather see you walking with the visible aid of a crutch than to think of your using an artificial leg. Somehow it seems like hypocrisy, a kind of appearing to be what you aren't. I know my idea is poorly expressed, but that's the way I feel about it."

A peculiar light came into Gregory's eyes, a light that neither friend had ever seen there before. He straightened visibly, almost without the aid of his crutch.

"I'll walk yet as well as any one and maybe it will give me back my mental confidence. My mind shall triumph over my body as well as it ever did!"

The artificial leg was duly applied to the hip stump, and it really was amazing to observe the rapidity with which Gregory mastered the art of using it proficiently. Anyone unacquainted with his deformity would never have realized that he did not possess two normal legs.

And then came the automobile accident a week before the time set for the Nelson-Gregory nuptials. How George Gregory's car was struck by an oncoming truck, reduced to a junk-heap, and George thrown into a ditch, so that the arm finally required amputation, never will be known, for George had always been a careful driver. Even with his artificial leg he declared he had no difficulty in putting on the brake. The fall had, as was proved later, caused also internal injuries so that some of the bodily organs did not function properly.

The months that followed were to all who were closely concerned with the accident, like a descent into Hades. Dr. Bell, serving as an intern in the Good Samaritan Hospital, devoted himself untiringly to the tragic case of George Gregory. A world famous specialist was summoned in consultation concerning the internal injuries sustained by Gregory. Very little hope was held out for the life of the unfortunate man, although there was one chance: an artificial kidney. The vigorous constitution of the invalid came to his rescue. He not only survived the operation but seemed to be in the best of health afterward.

And it is not to be wondered that Rosalind began to doubt whether her love for George Gregory could remain the same as before. Thrown constantly as she was in the company of Dr. David Bell, observing his devoted care and interest in George, she began to compare, or rather to contrast, the two men. George's rapid deterioration was no longer a possible flight of the imagination. It was an actuality. It was no longer possible to overlook the meaning behind his words.

"God expresses Himself through the physical world," he said when the three were together at George's apartment on Kenneth Drive. "He is a Spirit, but He makes Himself manifest in the perfection of a physical world. As much of physical perfection as I have lost, that much of God or Goodness has left me and there are no two ways about it."

Remonstrance was useless, so convinced was the invalid that his theories were correct. Also in his mind there grew steadily an ever increasing dislike for the friend of his college days, the doctor. He could no longer be blind to the fact that it was a struggle for Rosalind to be loyal to him. He was also aware of the growing affection that existed between David and Rosalind. From a dislike his feelings gradually changed to those of implacable hatred for his former chum.

III.

The Parting

At length after weary days and nights of indecision Rosalind came to the conclusion that she could not marry George Gregory. She longed to tell David of her feelings, but could not because she was conscious of her love for the young doctor. The subject of marriage had not been mentioned by either George or Rosalind since the second accident, but instinctively the girl felt that her lover's previous offer at the time of his lost leg, to release her from their engagement, was not to be renewed; though he must have known that his qualifications as a husband were now fewer than they could possibly have been before.

The moment that Rosalind had dreaded came at last. They were strolling together one evening toward the outskirts of the town. The moon softened, with its silvery glow, objects that in the glare of noon stood out in too bold relief. As they left the highway for the river-path George said:

"Let us set a day for the wedding. I've waited long enough." As he spoke he put around her waist an arm, not one with which nature had equipped him, but one so cunningly wrought that a casual observer would never have known. But Rosalind knew! She shuddered, and in that act, George Gregory knew that his doom was sealed.

"I can't marry you, George," she pleaded in a hoarse, unnatural voice. "I am sorry that it is so, but I cannot do it."

The man laughed and the tones chilled the heart of the girl. "You said once that my identity remained, no matter what the physical imperfections of my body. Now you deny it!" His voice rose in his excitement.

"Listen, oh George," she cried now thoroughly panic-stricken. "You are yourself allowing your mental attitude toward life to be altered. You have admitted it. Had you remained unchanged mentally, I truly believe your physical difference would not have mattered. I loved you for what you were, but, George, you are so changed!"

"Yes, I am changed," he shrieked, "but my desires and passions are no different, unless intensification indicates a difference."

He reached toward her, but adept as he was in the use of his two artificial limbs, she eluded his grasp and was off with a bound up the rough river-path and toward the highway. She heard distinctly the sound of pursuit. Could he outrun her handicapped as he was?

Once he fell, and the sound of muttered oaths came to her ears. On and on she flew, not daring to look back though she suspected that he was gaining. Just within the border of the town where the houses were somewhat scattered he caught her and simultaneously she fainted away.

When consciousness returned a dear familiar face was bent near her own. With a sob of joy she put her arms about David's neck, and in a few endearing words they plighted their troth.

David, on his way back from a professional call, where he was substituting for old Dr. Amos, who was ill, had witnessed from a distance the two running figures. Before he arrived upon the spot with his car, the pursuing form had overtaken the other.

To rescue a maiden from the arms of her lover seemed a very peculiar service to render—but one look into the eyes of George Gregory proved to the doctor beyond the question of a doubt that he was not dealing with a sane man. The contest was an unequal one, though the agility displayed by the cripple would have done credit to a normal man of more than average prowess. David tried to reason with his antagonist, but the use of logic at that time was unavailing. It was a hard struggle, but George was finally willing to admit himself defeated.

IV.
A Man Obsessed

About three months following this incident Dr. Bell (now in possession of the office of the late Dr. Amos) was about to lock up after the afternoon consultations when he heard the approach of a belated visitor in the hall. Looking up he beheld Gregory who passed quickly through the waiting room and into the inner office, closing the door behind him. The peculiar look of a fanatic, that had become more marked since his second accident, was evident now as he seated himself and turned wild eyes to the doctor.

"Don't be scared, doc," he jeered at sight of Bell's white drawn face. "I didn't come to blame you for winning Rosalind's love, though I confess the thought of your wedding next week goes considerably against the grain. I came for another purpose and I want you to help me."

He rose now and advanced toward the physician. The latter observed the perfect mastery of the artificial limbs, a mastery that proved how well the brain can be trained to control nerves and muscles under unusual conditions. Was all the effort of this brain being turned in that direction to the detriment of a well-balanced reasoning power?

"Here's my proposition, Bell," the words jangled harshly, bringing to a swift conclusion the doctor's thoughts regarding the changed mental status of his one-time friend. "I have decided what I want done. I'll admit that what I'm about to tell you will prove I have a mental quirk which, by the way, corresponds to my physical quirks, but this thing has become an obsession with me."

The speaker leaned forward and held the other's attention with a steady gaze. He then resumed, "I am going to try out an experiment, or rather have it tried out on me, for I shall be a passive factor in this case. I am going to find out how much of this mortal coil I can shuffle off and still maintain my personal identity as a piece of humanity here on Earth. In other words, as much of my body as can be removed and substituted by artificial parts, I wish to have done."

During Gregory's recital David's eyes had dilated in horror, and he unconsciously recoiled from his visitor until the width of the room was between them. Not a word could he utter. The seconds ticked away on the little ebony clock on the desk and still the two men regarded each other with unquestionable antagonism.

"Well, will you do it, Bell?" The man pointed significantly to the surgical instruments and the operating table. "I have ample means to pay you handsomely. I'm going to find out about this mortal body and its relation to the soul before I die. You've robbed me of one desire of my heart, but this you shall grant!"

At last Bell spoke, and with the sound of his voice his courage returned. "George, whether you believe it or not, you are a madman and I refuse to comply with your request. If, as you yourself maintain, with the loss of every bodily member, your mental and spiritual powers have waned, what in heaven's name, tell me, would you be with only enough of your body left to chain your spirit to Earth? I will not aid you in this mad project of yours. Go, or shall I have you taken to the hospital for the insane?"

George Gregory saw that further persuasion was useless. He walked toward the outer office but at the doorway he turned and faced Bell. "There are other surgeons in the world, and mark my words, I shall find out yet by how slender a thread body and soul can hang together."

V.
The Artificial Man

Five years passed. David Bell married Rosalind Nelson and built up a splendid reputation as a surgeon. Nothing had been heard in those years of George Gregory. His memory passed as an evil dream and his name was never mentioned. Then one day (it was shortly after the erection of the new county hospital) David and a young intern by the name of Lucius Stevens were putting away the instruments after an operation, when they felt rather than heard the approach of an individual. Turning, they beheld the unfamiliar form of a stranger. He was a little under average height. A cap covered the upper portion of his face and a long loose overcoat concealed most of his figure.

"What can we do for you, stranger?" asked Dr. Bell of the silent figure in the door.

"Stranger!" exclaimed the hollow, metallic voice that issued from somewhere beneath the visor of the cap. "I am no stranger, though possibly you do not recognize me. Do you remember your rival George Gregory, Dr. David Bell? I am he."

"You—it is impossible," exclaimed the amazed doctor. "Gregory was a tall man, altogether different in appearance. You—"

"Nevertheless I tell you I am George Gregory and I have come to settle old accounts with you. Clear out," he shouted to the frightened Stevens. "My trouble is not with you."

Lucius lost no time in following the stranger's suggestion. After his departure the two men in the operating room faced each other for some moments in silence.

"Before I have done with you," came the metallic tones again, "I will explain a few things that may puzzle you."

Here he walked to the office door, locked it and put the key into the overcoat pocket. "Now, sit down, David Bell, don't be in a hurry, for you are not going to leave this room alive. I promise you that, and I am accustomed to doing what I promise."

Bell did as he was bade. The curiosity of his analytical mind was aroused and he wished to find out more about this stranger whose identity he could in no way associate with Gregory. Fascinated, he watched while the man removed his cap and overcoat, and then before David's startled gaze the newcomer placed his right hand to his left shoulder and with a slight manipulation removed the left arm which he propped up in the chair nearest him. He then seated himself and proceeded to dismember himself until naught but a torso, head and one arm remained, all of which were scarred with countless incisions. A mirthless laugh jarred to the depths the doctor's overwrought nerves. The features of the intruder were not recognizable as those of his former friend, Gregory. There was no nose, only two nostrils flat upon the surface of the face. The head was bald and earless, the mouth a toothless gap.

A shudder of disgust went through David, and again the dry laugh of this monstrosity echoed through the room.

"I'm not exactly pretty, eh? But I'm finding out what I wanted to know. After I left you five years ago I went to a famous German surgeon and put my plea to him. He was as interested as I in the experiment, and you see the result. The operations required a period of two years in order to give nature a chance to have the body recuperate in the interim between experiments. As you see me now I am without any parts except those absolutely essential to life. One exception to this however, are my eyes. I did not yet wish to be shut off from the outer world by all of the senses. The artificial internal organs I dare not remove as I do my appendages for they are necessary to my life. The crowning operation of all was a pump replacing my heart. This pump is a simple double valve mechanism which circulates the small amount of blood required for my torso, head and arm. Look here!"

As he spoke he proceeded to reattach the artificial members. After he had again thus assumed semblance to human form he called attention to something David had not noticed before, a flat object lying upon his chest.

"This is the control board," he explained. "With the exception of the right arm I now move my body by electricity. The batteries are concealed within a hollow below the hip of my right leg. Behold in me an artificial man who lives and breathes and has his being with a minimum of mortal flesh! My various parts can be mended and replaced as you would repair the parts of your automobile."

During Gregory's recital David had not withdrawn his fascinated but horrified eyes from the mechanical man. Invulnerable and almost immortal, this creature was existing as a menace to mankind, a self-made Frankenstein. When he was again complete he stood before David, a triumphant gleam in the eyes which alone, unchanged physically, were yet scarcely recognizable as Gregory's, for the soul that peered through these windows was transformed.

In the gathering gloom Bell could see the automaton staring at him. He moved slowly toward a window hoping to elude his antagonist by a sudden exit in that direction, but Gregory crept toward him with a clocklike precision in his movements. The doctor noticed that the right hand was kept busy manipulating the control board at his chest. If this were the case, the interloper possessed only one free arm, but little had Bell reckoned on the prowess of that left arm! Like the grip of a vise the metallic fingers clutched at his throat. One thought pervaded his mind. If he could get that right hand away from the control and damage the connections to the various appendages and organs! But he soon realized how futile were his weaponless hands against the invulnerable body of his adversary. Down, down, those relentless claws bore him. The darkness fell about him like a heavy curtain. A throbbing in his temples that sounded like a distant pounding. Then oblivion.

VI.
The Thread Snaps

When David Bell regained consciousness he was lying in his bed. The bright sunlight shining through the curtains made delicate traceries across the counterpane. His first thought was that this was heaven by contrast to the events of his last conscious moments. Surely that was an angel hovering above him! No—at least not in the ethereal sense—but an angel nevertheless, for it was Rosalind, her sweet face beaming with love and solicitude.

"Mr. Stevens and I have been watching by your side for hours, David dear," she said as she placed a cool hand upon his brow. "You have him to thank for saving your life, not only at the time of the attack, but during the uncertain hours that have followed."

David turned grateful eyes toward his rescuer.

"Tell me about it, Lucius," he said quietly.

Stevens seated himself in a chair by the bedside and proceeded with this narrative.

"After that demon you called Gregory ordered me from the room, Dr. Bell, I turned over in my mind what had better be done to save you from his vengeance. I thought it advisable to say nothing at the time to Mrs. Bell because I did not wish to alarm her unnecessarily, but I knew that when I forced entrance into the room, it must be with adequate assistance, and within a very short period of time. I made my way to the office as quickly as I could without arousing suspicion. Miss Cullis was at the desk. Knowing I could rely on her natural calmness of demeanor and self-possession, I told her briefly of the danger which threatened you, then I phoned police headquarters. Before ten minutes were over Copeland and Knowles had arrived armed with automatics and crowbars. I carried an axe. Cautiously we made our way to the door of the operating room and stood without, listening. We heard no sounds of voices and Copeland wanted to force entrance immediately, but I held him in temporary restraint. I wanted to obtain some cue as to conditions on the other side of the door before taking drastic measures. But thanks to Copeland's impatience we broke down the door and saw—I shall never forget the sight till my dying day—that fiend of hell with his talons gripping your throat. He was evidently somewhat deaf for he heard no motion of our approach. We closed in on him from the rear, but he swung around with such force in that left arm that we all went down like tenpins. Knowles, as soon as he was on his feet again, struck him several times with the bar, but his efforts were wasted, for he might as well have rained blows upon a stone wall. Copeland aimed for his head in which he knew was encased a mortal brain, but that blow was avoided by the monster's ever active legs and arms. I was reserving my axe for a telling stroke, when it came upon me with sudden clarity of understanding, that the man governed his movements by manipulating the fingers of his right hand upon a place of control at his breast. His right arm and the switchboard! These were the vulnerable parts. At last I had found the heel of Achilles!

"While Gregory was occupied with his other two antagonists I dealt a sudden stroke with the axe at his right hand, but missed, the weapon falling heavily upon his chest. My first emotion was disappointment at having missed my mark but in another second I realized that the blow had disabled him. The left arm hung useless at his side, but what prowess it lacked was made up in the increased activity of the legs. He ran, and never have I seen such speed. He would have made Atlanta resemble a snail! However, three against one put the odds too heavily in our favor. Between lurches and thrusts at the flying figure I managed to convey to the two policemen my discovery in regard to his mortal points, and we soon had his trusty right arm disabled. The rest was comparatively easy. We dismembered him. We did not want to kill him, but it was soon apparent to us that the damage done to the control board would prove fatal. He wanted to speak, but his voice was faint, and stooping I could hardly get the words.

"'Tell David,' he said, 'that I've been wrong, dead wrong ever since I was carried off the field in that football game. I had been right at first.

Mental perfection does make the physical harmonious, and with the right mental attitude after that accident, I could have risen above the physical handicap. It was not the physical loss of my leg that brought me to this. *It was the mind that allowed it to do so.* Tell David and Rosalind I am sorry for the past, and I wish them much happiness for the future!' Those were his last words."

David Bell and his wife looked at each other with tear-dimmed eyes.

Next day the "slender thread" which had held George Gregory to this world was laid in its last resting place, but the soul which had realized and repented of its error, who knows whither it went?

The Fifth Dimension

I.

"Why, this has happened before!" I cried as I poured my husband a third cup of coffee.

John laid down the morning paper and roared with laughter.

"I'll say it has, and it's liable to happen again tomorrow morning! Did you ever know me to drink fewer than three cups of coffee at breakfast, Ellen?"

"Oh, you don't know what I mean," I responded, a trifle irritably. "I have reference to that feeling that we all have occasionally; that the identical set of circumstances that surround us has existed before in some remote eon of time."

"Fiddlesticks!" ejaculated John as he set down his empty coffee cup and folded his napkin. "I'm going to get my car started, as it takes so long these cold mornings."

In which unsympathetic mood he donned hat and overcoat and disappeared through the kitchen door. A second later his head was thrust through the reopened door, and a jovial smile spread over his features.

"Say, Ellen, it strikes me as I go out to get the old bus that this has happened before," he called back to me.

"Something else will strike you," I cried, playfully picking up an empty cup.

He dodged in mock consternation, then his face grew earnest.

"But seriously, my dear girl," he said, "I hope you aren't getting to believe in all that rot about soul transmigration. Surely you don't think your personality has been previously decked in other corporeal trappings, do you?"

"No," I replied, "I do not believe that. I have always been myself, and you will always be yourself (stubborn as ever)! My explanation of the oft-repeated phenomenon that my life has been lived before exactly as I live it now lies solely in the theory that time, which is the fourth dimension, is, like space, curved, and travels in great cycles. You cannot conceive of either the end of space or time. The law of the universe, as illustrated by the movements of the stars and planets and the endless motion of the molecules and atoms and the whirling of the electrons, proves that orbital motion is a cosmic law and that all things return eventually to their starting point. And so, in the vast cycles of time and space, we repeat our existence upon this earth, and I claim that occasionally a fleeting memory of previous cycles thrusts itself into our consciousness."

"Too deep for me," said John with a shrug. "I must get down to the office and, by the way, an apple pie for dinner tonight would be greatly appreciated! I haven't had any for a long time."

"Do you like my apple pies, John?" I asked smiling.

"Do I? You are an expert at it. I suppose," he added as he all but disappeared through the crack of the door as it stood slightly ajar, "the infinite number of times that you have baked apple pies in previous cycles of existence has made you adept in that line!"

The door closed and he was gone.

Dear John! Of course he understood the theory as well as I did, but he was forced out among associates in the business world and it was essential that his mind be continually occupied with the practical affairs of life. Dreamers might be vouchsafed glimpses of the truth, but did such visions always prove beneficial? There was no doubting that John was a greater success in life than I, whether he grasped the significance of certain cosmic truths or not!

"After all," I mused, "the difference between the great and the small, the infinite and the finite, right and wrong, good and evil, is sometimes one of degree and not of quality. The most difficult is simple if we follow the rules. The people who make a muddle of their lives have deliberately, though unknowingly, chosen the harder way. They are law-breakers, not necessarily in our legal sense, but they are transgressors of Universal Law. Had they simply worked in harmony with the Law, success would have come easily."

"I have not always worked in harmony with the Law," I thought. "None of us have. Do I, now in this cycle of time, possess the ability to change errors performed in previous eons, or am I a mere puppet, destined to a certain definite course of action throughout eternity? Was Henley right or wrong when he wrote, 'I am the master of my fate, the captain of my soul?'"

I believed in the cycle theory of time, and yet in it I saw no hope for changing the errors of the past. My theory was a death blow to progress and evolution!

II.

I had just slipped my last pie into the oven and glanced casually out of the kitchen window when I spied my neighbor, Mrs. Maxwell, on her cinder path between her house and the garage. Suddenly I had the same sensation that I had experienced at breakfast, "This *has* happened before. I *know* it."

Then, like a flash, before a seeming darkness obliterated my fleeting memory, came the warning to my consciousness that Mrs. Maxwell ought not to enter her garage. I took a step toward the door with the intention of calling to Mrs. Maxwell. There was plenty of time; the path was long and she was not a third of the way to the garage. I watched her, my heart thumping wildly. She had stopped to pick up a scrap of paper. I took another step toward the door, then paused.

"Oh, what's the use," I argued, "she'd think I was crazy to run out there and attempt to keep her from her errand to her garage. I wonder why I have had two sensations of this memory enigma today! Often they are weeks, even months, apart."

Resolutely I turned and left the kitchen, intending to finish my remaining housework. I reached the first landing of the stairs when the sound of an explosion that rocked the house to its foundation caused me to start in wild-eyed terror. In a panic of fearful premonition I rushed to a south window. The Maxwell garage was a mass of roaring flames!

"It is fate, fate," I groaned in my anguish. "There is no hope! We mortals cannot escape. The cycles of time like the wheels of the ancient Juggernaut ruthlessly grind us to our destruction and *there is no hope!*"

It seemed that for months after Mrs. Maxwell's funeral I could not rise above a sense of despondency. A hopelessness was ever present in my consciousness, and nothing I did seemed worth the effort. Finally realizing that my present mental state must not continue, I plunged into domestic and social duties with a vim that was most unusual for me.

Not once during many months following the Maxwell tragedy had I experienced a single recurrence of my unaccountable memory flashes. Then one day the sensation returned.

III.

John was ready to make a business trip to the south and had purchased his railroad ticket early in the afternoon. The train was scheduled to leave town at 8:15 p.m. The supper dishes had just been cleared away and John had hurried upstairs to pack his grip, when the feeling that this had all happened before came upon me, more realistically than I had ever before experienced it, and this time it was accompanied by a premonition of the same nature as that which had warned me of Mrs. Maxwell's fatal trip to her garage.

I lost no time in hurrying up to John's room, where I found him sorting over the things to take with him on his trip.

"John, don't go this evening," I said, trying to keep my voice steady. "There is a morning train at 11:53. Can't you take that instead of going tonight?"

My husband carefully tucked his hairbrush into his satchel, and for a moment deigned me no reply.

"I'm afraid to have you go tonight, John," I continued. "I've had a—a—sort of warning. You know what I mean."

John closed and locked his grip. "Are you afraid here alone?" he asked, after what seemed an interminable silence.

"No. It's not for myself that I fear danger, but for you. Won't you defer your trip?" I persisted.

"Now see here, Ellen," John responded with a show of irritation, "I've already bought my ticket and laid my plans for meeting Hopkins in Atlanta on Friday and I can't and won't stop because of some fool notion of yours. I had supposed you had forgotten about this fourth dimension time-cycle business!" He picked up his satchel. "But whether you've forgotten it or not, the 8:15 sees me ensconced on my way to Georgia."

"But, John dear," I cried in desperation, "remember the Maxwell affair. If I had only obeyed my impulse to rush out and warn poor Mrs. Maxwell, she would be living now!"

John paused and looked at me as if considering, but it was only for a second; then he resumed his descent of the stairs.

"No," he said, "I've got to be in Atlanta on Friday or stand a chance of losing one of the biggest orders we've had in months."

Then it seemed as though something snapped in my brain and I heard my voice as though it were another's coming from a distance, "The Juggernaut, Fate, grinds mortals beneath its wheels and *there is no hope.*"

I soon became conscious of the fact that I was sobbing hysterically and that John was holding me in his arms.

"Ellen, Ellen," his dear voice was saying. "I'm going to fool Fate a trick and let Hopkins wait. I leave tomorrow at 11:53. Let's see what's on the radio for the rest of the evening."

I gazed at him with incredulity. "Oh, John," I cried ecstatically, "do you think we can prove that the cycles of time are not inexorable?"

"We can at least give the theory a fair trial," he said smiling.

IV.

I poured John his third cup of coffee, but did *not* feel that it had happened before! A mild thump on the front porch informed me that the morning paper had arrived. I brought it in and laid it in front of John, then I fled to the kitchen, where the odor of burning toast apprised me of the fact that I was much needed. Returning with the scraped toast, I seated myself opposite John for the purpose of resuming my breakfast.

"What news?" I asked casually.

For answer John handed me the paper and pointed mutely to an enormous headline. His face was ashen and his hand trembled.

With a sinking sensation I read the large letters: "Head-on collision demolishes engines and cars, and kills seventy persons."

"John," I gasped, "is it—was it—the 8:15?"

His voice was husky with pent emotion.

"Ellen, it was the 8:15, and I have been on it in the other cycles of time. I know it now."

I gazed at him incredulously for a moment, and then half in fun, half seriously, I said, "John, you are now living on borrowed time!"

He smiled a little wanly.

"Not exactly that, dear," he said, "but my mind has been doing some rapid thinking since I saw those headlines, and I believe I have a solution to your ever-puzzling problem of the fourth dimension, time."

"If you can prove my time-cycles are not incompatible with progress, evolution, and growth," I cried eagerly, "you will make me the happiest woman on Earth!"

"Wouldn't a new fur coat delight you more?" he asked teasingly.

"Well, that would help some," I admitted, "but tell me what makes you believe that evolution and progress are fact, despite the eon-worn ruts of the cycles of time?"

"The fifth dimension," he replied in a quiet voice.

"The fifth dimension?" I echoed, puzzled.

"Which is simply this, Ellen. There is a general progression of the Universe over and above the cycles of time which renders each cycle a little in advance of the previous one. We see and recognize this truth daily in the phenomena of humanity. Every baby born starts life a little in advance, materially and mentally, of its father. This process is very slow and we call it evolution, but it is a perceptible progress nevertheless. It may be aptly likened to the whorls of a spring as compared to a mere flat coil or wire. The earth follows an orbit around the sun, and every year it is in the same relative position with regard to the sun as it was the previous year. It has completed one of its countless cycles. But you know as well as I do that the sun and the earth, as well as the other planets, are *all* farther along in space together. There is a general progression of twelve miles a second on some vaster orbit. This general progression, then, is analogous to our possibility of change and growth; the power to better our conditions; in other words, it is a fifth dimension."

"The wheels of the Juggernaut can be turned aside," I said reverently, "and *there is hope.*"

A Runaway World

I.

The laboratory of Henry Shipley was a conglomeration of test tubes, bottles, mysterious physical and chemical appliances and papers covered with indecipherable script. The man himself was in no angelic mood as he sat at his desk and surveyed the hopeless litter about him. His years may have numbered five and thirty, but young though he was, no man excelled him in his chosen profession.

"Curse that maid!" he muttered in exasperation. "If she possessed even an ordinary amount of intelligence she could tidy up this place and still leave my notes and paraphernalia intact. As it is I can't find the account of that important nitrogen experiment."

At this moment a loud knock at the door put an abrupt end to further soliloquy. In response to Shipley's curt "come in," the door opened and a stranger, possibly ten years older than Shipley, entered. The newcomer surveyed the young scientist through piercing eyes of nondescript hue. The outline of mouth and chin was only faintly suggested through a Vandyke beard.

Something in the new arrival's gaze did not encourage speech, so Shipley mutely pointed to a chair, and upon perceiving that the seat was covered with papers, hastened to clear them away.

"Have I the honor of addressing Henry Shipley, authority on atomic energy?" asked the man, seating himself, apparently unmindful of the younger man's confusion.

"I am Henry Shipley, but as to being an authority—"

The stranger raised a deprecating hand, "Never mind. We can dispense with the modesty, Mr. Shipley. I have come upon a matter of worldwide importance. Possibly you have heard of me. La Rue is my name; Leon La Rue."

Henry Shipley's eyes grew wide with astonishment.

"Indeed I am honored by the visit of so renowned a scientist," he cried with genuine enthusiasm.

"It is nothing," said La Rue. "I love my work."

"You and John Olmstead," said Shipley, "have given humanity a clearer conception of the universe about us in the past hundred years than any others have done. Here it is now the year 2026 AD and we have established by radio regular communication with Mars, Venus, two of the moons of Jupiter, and recently it has been broadcast that messages are being received from outside our solar system, communications from interstellar space! Is that true?"

"It is," replied La Rue. "During the past six months my worthy colleague, Jules Nichol, and I have received messages (some of them not very intelligible) from two planets that revolve around one of the nearer suns. These messages have required years to reach us, although they travel at an inconceivable rate of speed."

"How do you manage to carry on intelligent communication? Surely the languages must be very strange," said the thoroughly interested Shipley.

"We begin all intercourse through the principles of mathematics," replied the Frenchman with a smile, "for by those exact principles God's universe is controlled. Those rules never fail. You know the principles of mathematics were discovered by man, not invented by him. This, then, is the basis of our code, always, and it never fails to bring intelligent responses from other planets whose inhabitants have arrived at an understanding equal to or surpassing that of ourselves. It is not a stretch of imagination to believe that we may some day receive a message from somewhere in space that was sent out millions of years ago, and likewise we can comprehend the possibility of messages which we are now sending into the all-pervading ether, reaching some remote world eons in the future."

"It is indeed a fascinating subject," mused Henry Shipley, "but mine has an equal attraction. While you reach out among the stars, I delve down amid the protons and electrons. And who, my dear fellow, in this day of scientific advancement, can say that they are not identical except for size? Planets revolve about their suns, electrons around their protons; the infinite, the infinitesimal! What distinguishes them?"

The older man leaned forward, a white hand clutching the cluttered desk.

"What distinguishes them, you ask?" he muttered hoarsely. "This and this alone: *time,* the fourth dimension!"

The two men gazed at one another in profound silence, then La Rue continued, his voice once more back to normal: "You said a moment ago that my planetary systems and your atoms were identical except for one thing—the fourth dimension. In my supra-world of infinite bigness our sun, one million times as big as this Earth, gigantic Jupiter, and all the other planets in our little system, would seem as small as an atom, a thing invisible even in the most powerful microscope. Your infra-world would be like a single atom with electrons revolving around it, compared to our solar system, sun and planets. I believe the invisible atom is another universe with its central sun and revolving planets, and there also exists a supra-universe in which our sun, the Earth, and all the planets are only an atom. But the fourth dimension!"

La Rue picked up a minute speck of dust from the table and regarded it a moment in silence, then he went on: "Who knows but that this tiny particle of matter which I hold may contain a universe in that infra-world, and that during our conversation eons may have passed to the possible inhabitants of the planets therein? So we come to the fact that time is the fourth dimension. Let me read you what a scientist of an earlier day has written, a man who was so far ahead of his time that he was wholly unappreciated:

"'If you lived on a planet infinitesimally small, or infinitely big, you would not know the difference. Time and space are, after all, purely relative. If at midnight tonight, all things, including ourselves and our measuring instruments, were reduced in size one thousand times, we should be left quite unaware of any such change.'

"But I wish to read you a message which I received at my radio station on the Eiffel Tower at Paris."

La Rue produced a paper from a pocket and read the following radiogram from Mars:

"'A most horrible catastrophe is befalling us. We are leaving the solar system! The sun grows daily smaller. Soon we shall be plunged in eternal gloom. The cold is becoming unbearable!'"

When the Frenchman had finished reading he continued addressing the physicist: "A few astronomers are aware of the departure of Mars from the system, but are keeping it from the public temporarily. What do you think of this whole business, Shipley?"

"The phenomenon is quite clear," the latter replied. "Some intelligent beings in this vaster cosmos or supra-universe, in which we are but a molecule, have begun an experiment which is a common one in chemistry, an experiment in which one or two electrons in each atom are torn away, resulting, as you already know, in the formation of a new element. Their experiment will cause a rearrangement in our universe."

"Yes," smiled La Rue significantly, "every time we perform a similar experiment, millions of planets leave their suns in that next smaller cosmos or infra-world. But why isn't it commoner even around us?"

"That is where the time element comes in," answered his friend. "Think of the rarity of such an experiment upon a particular molecule or group of molecules, and you will plainly see why it has never happened in all the eons of time that our universe has passed through."

There was a moment's silence as both men realized their human inability to grasp even a vague conception of the idea of relativity. This silence was broken by the foreigner, who spoke in eager accents: "Will you not, my friend, return with me to Paris? And together at my radio station we will listen to the messages from the truant Mars."

II.

The radio station of La Rue was the most interesting place Shipley had ever visited. Here were perfected instruments of television. An observer from this tower could both see and hear any place on the globe. As yet, seeing beyond our Earth had not been scientifically perfected.

La Rue had been eager to hear from his assistants any further messages from Mars. These could have been forwarded to him when he was in the States, but he preferred to wait until his return to his beloved station. There was nothing startlingly new in any of the communications. All showed despair regarding the Martians' ability to survive, with their rare atmosphere, the cold of outer space. As the planet retreated and was lost to view even by the most powerful telescopes, the messages grew fainter, and finally ceased altogether.

By this time alarm had spread beyond scientific circles. Every serious-minded being upon the globe sought for a plausible explanation of the phenomenon.

"Now is the time for your revelation," urged La Rue. "Tell the world what you told me."

But the world at large did not approve of Henry Shipley's theory. People did not arrive at any unanimous decision. The opinion was prevalent that Mars had become so wicked and had come so near to fathoming the Creator's secrets, that it was banished into outer darkness as a punishment.

"Its fate should," they said, "prove a warning to Earth."

The scientists smiled at this interpretation. As a body of enlightened and religious men they knew that God does not object to His Truth being known, that only by a knowledge of the Truth can we become fully conscious of His will concerning us.

The frivolous, pleasure-seeking, self-centered world soon forgot the fate of the ruddy planet, and then—but that is my story!

III.

It was five months to the day after the radios had first broadcast the startling news that Mars was no longer revolving around the sun that I, James Griffin, sat at breakfast with my wife and two children, Eleanor and Jimmy, Jr. I am not and never have been an astronomical man. Mundane affairs have always kept me too busy for stargazing, so it is not to be wondered at that the news of Mars' departure did not deeply concern me. But the whole affair was, much to my chagrin, indirectly the cause of a dreadful blunder at the office.

"Mars was closer to the sun than we are," I had remarked one day to Zutell, my assistant at the office, "but I'll bet the old war-planet is getting pretty well cooled off by now."

Zutell looked at me with a peculiar expression which I haven't forgotten to this day.

"Mars closer to the sun than Earth?" he ejaculated. "Why, man alive, didn't you know Mars's' orbit is more remote from the sun than ours?"

His manner was extraordinarily convincing, and inwardly I was mortified at my ignorance.

"It is not!" I declared stubbornly, then added weakly, "Anyhow, what difference does it make?"

His glance of amused condescension stung my pride, and from that time on his already too sufficient self-confidence increased. In his presence I seemed to be suffering from an inferiority complex. I laid the entire blame for my loss of self-confidence upon the truant Mars, and secretly wished the ruddy planet all kinds of bad luck.

But to return to the breakfast table. My wife, Vera, poured me a second cup of coffee and remarked sweetly, "The Zutells are coming over this morning, since it is a holiday, dear, to listen to the radio and see in the new televisio. You know President Bedford is to address the nation from the newly completed capitol building, which will be seen for the first time in the televisio. If you like, I'll ask the Mardens, too. You seem to like them so much."

"Hang it all," I said irritably, "can't you leave the Zutells out of it? Ed's forever rubbing in something about Jupiter or Venus, now that Mars is gone. He's an insufferable bore!"

"Why, Jim," cried Vera, half laughing, "as sure as fate I do believe you're jealous, just because—"

"Jealous!" I burst out. "Jealous of him? Why, I can show him cards and spades—"

"I know you can. That's just it," laughed Vera; "that's just why it's so funny to have you care because you didn't know about Mars. It's much more important that you know more about cost-accounting than Ed does."

Vera was right, as usual, and I rewarded her with a kiss, just as Junior screamed that Archie Zutell was coming across the lawn to play with him and Eleanor.

"Well, you kids clear out of here," I said, "and play outside if we grown-ups are expected to see anything of the president and hear his address, and Jimmy, don't let Archie put anything over on you. Stick up for your rights."

I imagined Vera smiled a little indulgently, and I didn't like it.

"Well, at any rate," I said, "I do like young Marden and his bride. There's a fellow that really is an astronomer, but he never shoots off his mouth about it in inappropriate places."

Truth was, Marden held a high college degree in astronomy and taught the subject in our local college. Just across the street from our residence, which faced the beautiful campus, stood the observatory on a picturesque elevation. Many summer evenings since my deplorable error in regard to Mars I had visited the observatory with Oscar Marden and learned much that was interesting about the starry host.

The breakfast dishes cleared away, Vera and I seated ourselves at our televisio that worked in combination with the radio. It was the envy of the neighborhood, there being but three others in the entire town that could compare with it. There was yet half an hour before the president's address was scheduled to commence. We turned on the electricity. Vice-president Ellsworth was speaking. We gazed into the great oval mirror and saw that he was in the private office of his own residence. A door opened behind him and a tall man entered the room, lifted his hand in dignified salutation, and smiled at his unseen spectators. Then in clear resonant tones he began addressing his invisible audience in a preliminary talk preceding the one to be delivered from the new capitol steps.

At this point the Mardens and Zutells arrived, and after exchange of a few pleasantries, were comfortably seated pending the main address of the morning.

"Citizens of the Republic of the United Americas," began President Bedford.

I reached for the dials, and with a slight manipulation the man's voice was as clear as if he talked with us in the room. I turned another dial, and the hazy outlines were cleared, bringing the tall, manly form into correct perspective. Behind him rose the massive columns of the new capitol building in Central America.

The address, an exceptionally inspiring one, continued while the six of us in our midwestern town were seeing and hearing with millions of others throughout the country, a man thousands of miles away. The day had commenced cloudy, but ere long the sun was shining with dazzling splendor. Meanwhile the president continued to speak in simple but eloquent style of the future of our great republic. So engrossed were we six, and undoubtedly millions of others upon two continents, to say nothing of the scattered radio audience throughout the world, that for some time we had failed to notice the decreasing light. Mrs. Zutell had been the first to make the casual remark that it was clouding up again, but a rather curt acknowledgment of her comment on the part of the rest of us had discouraged further attempts at conversation.

Not long afterward the front door burst open and the three children rushed in, making all attempts of the elders to listen to the address futile.

"Mamma, it is getting darker and colder," exclaimed Eleanor. "We want our wraps on."

"Put on the light!" cried Jimmy, suiting the action to the word.

With the flood of light any growing apprehension that we may have felt diminished, but as we looked through the windows we noticed that outside it was dusk though the time was but 10:00 a.m.

Our faces looked strangely drawn and haggard, but it was the expression on young Marden's face that caught and held my attention. I believe as I review those dreadful times in my mind, that Oscar Marden knew then what ailed this old world of ours, but he said not a word at that time.

We turned our faces to the televisio again and were amazed at the scene which was there presented. President Bedford had ceased speaking and was engaged in earnest conversation with other men who had joined him. The growing darkness outside the capitol made it difficult to distinguish our leader's figure among the others, who in ever-growing numbers thronged the steps of the great edifice. Presently the president again turned to the invisible millions seated behind their radios and televisios, and spoke. His voice was calm, as befitted the leader of so great a nation, but it was fraught with an emotion that did not escape observing watchers and listeners.

"Tune in your instruments to Paris," said the great man. "The noted astronomer, La Rue, has something of importance to tell us. Do this at once," he added, and his voice took on a somewhat sterner quality.

I arose somewhat shakily, and fumbled futilely with the dials.

"Put on more speed there, Griffin," said Marden.

It was the first time I had ever heard him speak in any other than a courteous manner, and I realized he was greatly perturbed. I fumbled awhile longer until Ed Zutell spoke up.

"Can I help you, Jim?" he asked.

"Only by shutting up and staying that way," I growled, at the same time giving a vicious twist to the stubborn long-distance dial.

In a little while I had it: Paris, France, observatory of Leon La Rue. We all instantly recognized the bearded Frenchman of astronomical fame; he who with Henry Shipley had informed the world of the fate of Mars. He was speaking in his quick, decisive way with many gesticulations.

"I repeat for the benefit of any tardy listeners that Earth is about to suffer the fate of Mars. I will take no time for any scientific explanations. You have had those in the past and many of you have scoffed at them. It is enough to tell you positively that we are leaving the sun at a terrific rate of speed and are plunging into the void of the great Universe. What will be the end no man knows. Our fate rests in the hands of God.

"Now hear, my friends, and I hope the whole world is listening to what I say: Choose wisely for quarters where you will have a large supply of food, water and fuel (whether you use atomic energy, electricity, oil, or even the old-fashioned coal). I advise all electrical power stations to be used as stations of supply, and the men working there will be the real heroes who will save the members of their respective communities. Those who possess atomic heat machines are indeed fortunate. There is no time for detailed directions. Go—and may your conduct be such that it will be for the future salvation of the human race in this crisis."

The picture faded, leaving us staring with white faces at one another.

"I'll get the children," screamed Vera, but I caught her *arm*.

"You'll do nothing of the kind. We must not any of us be separated. The children will return when they are thoroughly cold."

My prediction was correct. The words had scarcely left my lips when the three ran into the hall crying. It was growing insufferably cold. We all realized that. We rushed about in addle-pated fashion, all talking at once, grabbing up this and that until we were acting like so many demented creatures.

Suddenly a voice, loud and stern, brought us to our senses. It was young Marden who was speaking.

"We are all acting like fools," he cried. "With your permission I will tell you what to do if you want to live awhile longer."

His self-control had a quieting effect upon the rest of us. He continued in lower tones, but with an undeniable air of mastery, "My observatory across the street is the place for our hibernation. It is heated by atomic energy, so there will be no danger of a fuel shortage. Ed, will you and Mrs. Zutell bring from your home in your car all the provisions you have available at once? Jim" (I rather winced at being addressed in so familiar a manner by a man younger in years than myself, but upon this occasion my superior), "you and Mrs. Griffin load your car with all your available food. I was going to add that you buy more, but an inevitable stampede at the groceries might make that inadvisable at present. My wife and I will bring all the concentrated food we have on hand—enough for two or three years, I think, if carefully used. Kiddies," he said to the three who stood looking from one to the other of us in uncomprehending terror, "gather together all the coats and wraps you find here in the Griffin house!"

A new respect for this man possessed me as we all set about carrying out his orders.

"You watch the children and gather together provisions," I called to Vera. "I am going to see if I can't get more from the store. We must have more concentrated and condensed foods than we are in the habit of keeping on hand for daily use. Such foods will furnish a maximum amount of nourishment with a minimum bulk."

IV.

I opened the door but returned immediately for my overcoat. The breath of winter was out-of-doors, though it was the month of June. The streets were lighted, and in the imperfect glow I could see panicky figures flitting to and fro. I hurried toward the square, which was exactly what everyone else seemed to be doing. A man bumped my elbow. Each of us turned and regarded the other with wide eyes. I recognized Sam McSween.

"My God, Griffin," he cried, "what does it all mean? Ella's been laid up for a week—no food, and I thought I'd—"

I left him to relate his woes to the next passerby. My goal was Barnes's Cash Grocery. There was a mob inside the store, but old man Barnes, his son and daughter and two extra clerks were serving the crowd as quickly as possible. Guy Barnes's nasal tones reached my ears as I stood shivering in the doorway.

"No—terms are strictly cash—friends."

"Cash!" bawled a voice near my ear. "What good will cash do you, pard, in the place we're all headed for?"

"I have cash, Guy. Gimme ten dollars' worth o' canned goods and make it snappy," yelled another.

Petty thievery was rife, but no one was vested with authority to attempt to stop it. One thought actuated all: to get food, either by fair means or foul.

At length I found myself near the counter frantically waving in the air a ten-dollar bill and two ones.

"You've always let me have credit for a month or two at a time, Guy," I said coaxingly.

The old grocer shook his head in a determined manner. "Cash is the surest way to distribute this stuff fairly. The bank's open, Jim, but the mob's worse there than here, they tell me."

I shrugged my shoulders in resignation. "Give me ten dollars' worth of condensed milk, meat tablets, some fruits and vegetables."

He handed me my great basket of groceries and I forced a passage through the crowd and gained the street. There were fewer people on the square than there had been an hour earlier. On their faces had settled a grim resignation that was more tragic than the first fright had been.

On the corner of Franklin and Main Streets I met little Dora Schofield, a playmate of Eleanor's. She was crying pitifully, and the hands that held her market basket were purple with the cold that grew more intense every moment.

"Where are you going, Dora?" I asked.

"Mother's ill and I am going to Barnes's grocery store for her," replied the little girl.

"You can never get in there," I said. My heart was wrung at the sight of the pathetic little figure. "Put your basket down and I'll fill it for you. Then you can hurry right back to mother."

She ceased her crying and did as I bade her. I filled her smaller basket from my own.

"Now hurry home," I cried, "and tell your mother not to let you out again."

I had a walk of five blocks before me. I hurried on with other scurrying figures through the deepening gloom. I lifted my eyes to the sky and surveyed the black vault above. It was noon, and yet it had every appearance of night. Suddenly I stopped and gazed fixedly at a heavenly body, the strangest I had ever seen. It did not seem to be a star, nor was it the moon, for it was scarcely a quarter the size of the full moon.

"Can it be a comet?" I asked, half aloud.

Then with a shock I realized it was our sun, which we were leaving at an inconceivably rapid rate. The thought appalled me, and I stood for some seconds overwhelmed by the realization of what had occurred.

"I suppose Venus will give us a passing thought, as we did Mars, if she even—"

My train of thoughts came to an abrupt conclusion as I became aware of a menacing figure approaching me from Brigham Street. I tried to proceed, assuming a jaunty air, though my emotions certainly belied my mien. I had recognized Carl Hovarder, a typical town bully with whom I had had a previous unfortunate encounter when serving on a civic improvement committee.

"Drop them groceries and don't take all day to do it neither," demanded Hovarder, coming to a full stop and eyeing me pugnaciously.

"This is night, not day, Carl," I replied quietly.

"Don't you 'Carl' me!" roared the bully. "Hand over that grub, and I don't mean maybe!"

I stooped to place the basket of provisions upon the walk between us, but at the same time I seized a can. As Carl bent to pick up the basket I threw the can with all the strength I possessed full at his head. He crumbled up with a groan and I snatched the precious burden and fled. When I was a block away I looked back and saw him rise and stoop uncertainly. He was picking up the can with which I had hit him. I did not begrudge him the food contained therein. That can had done me more good than it could ever possibly do Carl Hovarder.

The last lap of my journey proved the most tedious, for I was suffering with cold, and depressed at the fate of humanity, but at last I spied the observatory.

V.

The grassy knoll upon which this edifice stood had an elevation of about twenty feet and the building itself was not less than forty feet high, so that an observer at the telescope had an unobstructed view of the heavens. The lower floor was equipped as a chemical laboratory, and in its two large rooms college classes had met during the school term in chemistry and astronomy. The second story, I thought, could be used as sleeping quarters for the nine souls who felt certain the observatory would eventually be their mausoleum.

"All in?" I shouted as I ran into the building and slammed the door behind me. How welcome was the warmth that enveloped me!

"Yes, we're all in, and I suspect you are, too, judging from appearances," laughed Vera.

I looked from one to another of the little group and somehow I felt that though each tried to smile bravely, grim tragedy was stalking in our midst.

Late in the afternoon I thought of our radio and televisio, and decided to run over to the house and get them. The streets were deserted and covered with several inches of snow, and the cold was intenser than I had ever experienced. A few yards from the observatory lay a dark object. I investigated and found it to be a dog frozen as stiff as though carved from wood, and that in a few hours! My lungs were aching now as I looked across the street at our home, and though I wanted the instruments badly I valued life more highly. I turned and retraced my steps to the observatory.

The men were disappointed that we were to be so cut off from communication with the outside world, but the essentials of life were of primary importance. We swallowed our disappointment then and many times in the future when from time to time we missed the luxuries of modern life to which we had been accustomed.

Later, while the children were being put to bed, we men ascended the steps to the telescope room where we gazed ruefully at the diminishing disk of the luminary that had given life to this old earth of ours for millions of years.

"I suppose that's the way old Sol looked to the Martians before the days of our system's disruption," commented Ed with a side glance in my direction.

"The inhabitants of Mars saw a larger orb in their heavens than that," replied Oscar, adjusting the instrument. "We are well beyond the confines of our solar system. What do you see there, boys?"

We looked alternatively through the eyepiece and beheld a bright star slightly smaller than our once glorious sun now appeared to be.

"That is Pluto," explained Marden, "the outermost planet of the system."

"So we are entering the unknown! Whither are we bound, Marden?" I cried, suddenly overwhelmed with the awfulness of it all.

The young astronomer shrugged his shoulders. "I do not know. But we shall not be the only dead world hurtling through space! The void is full of them. I think it was Tennyson who wrote—"

"Never mind Tennyson!" I fairly shrieked. "Tell me, do you think this is the—the end?"

He nodded thoughtfully and then repeated: "Lord Tennyson wrote, 'Many a planet by many a sun may roll with the dust of a vanished race.'"

"Say, this is as cheerful as a funeral service," said Zutell. "I'm going down with the women. I can hear them laughing together. They've got more grit and pluck than we have. You two old pessimists can go on with your calamity-howling. I'm going to get a few smiles yet before I look like a piece of refrigerator meat."

"Ed's right for once," I laughed. "We can't help matters this way."

VI.

I should gain nothing by a detailed account of the flight of Earth through interplanetary space. Seconds, minutes, hours, days, weeks and months lost their significance to the isolated inhabitants of a world that had gone astray. Since time had always been reckoned by the movements of the Earth in relation to the sun, there was no way to ascertain the correct passage of time. True, a few watches among the members of our group aided in determining approximately the passage of time in accordance with the old standards to which we had been accustomed. How we missed the light of day, no being can imagine who has never experienced what we lived through.

"Is the moon still with us?" I asked one time of Marden.

"I cannot ascertain definitely," he replied. "With no sunlight to reflect to Earth from its surface, it has eluded my observation so far, but I have imagined a number of times that a dark object passes periodically between us and the stars. I shall soon have my observations checked up, however. How I do miss radio communication, for doubtless such questions are being discussed over the air pro and con! We are still turning on our axis, but once in every twenty-seven hours instead of twenty-four. I don't understand it!"

Oscar spent virtually all his time in the observatory. He did not always reward the rest of us with his discoveries there, as he was naturally taciturn. When he spoke it was usually because he had something really worthwhile to tell us.

"You remember I told you that the Earth continued to rotate, though slowly, on its axis even though it no longer revolved around the sun," he said on the day we completed approximately five months of our interstellar wandering. "I also told you that should such a calamity befall the Earth as its failing to rotate, the waters would pile up and cover the continents. I have not told you before, but I have calculated that Earth is gradually ceasing to rotate. However, we need not fear the oceans, for they are solid ice. I may also add that with this decrease in our rate of rotation there is a great acceleration in our onward flight. In less than a month we shall be plunging straight forward at many times our present rate of speed."

It was as Oscar Marden had predicted, and in a few weeks the positions of the heavenly bodies showed that Earth was hurtling straight onward at the speed of light. At the end of two years our provisions were running very low in spite of the scanty rations which we had allowed. The telescope had become our only solace for lonely hours, and through its gigantic lens we became aware of what the future held for us. I flatter myself that I was the first to whom Oscar revealed his fearful discovery.

"Tell me what you see," he said, resigning his seat at the eyepiece to me.

"I see a very large star," I replied, "considerably larger than any near it."

He nodded. "I will tell you something that need not be mentioned to the seven below, Jim, because I can trust you to keep your head. For some weeks past I have known that we are headed for that star as straight as a die!"

I must have paled, for he glanced at me apprehensively and added, "Don't allow yourself to worry. Remember, complete resignation to whatever fate is in store for us is the only way to meet natural catastrophes."

"Yes," I agreed. "Man may be the master of his own fate as regards his relation to his fellowmen, but he has no hand in an affair like this!"

"None whatever," smiled Marden, and I thought it seemed the very nicest smile in the world, except possibly Vera's.

"If we are destined to plunge headlong into this sun that lies directly in our path, and is undoubtedly what is drawing us onward, you may rest assured that human suffering will be less prolonged than if we pass this sun and continue to fathom the abyss of the eternal ether. If we were to plunge into it, the Earth would become a gaseous mass."

"Tell me," I pleaded, "is it because we are not rotating, that we are threatened with this awful disaster?"

"Yes, I believe so," he answered slowly. "If we had continued to rotate we might have escaped the powerful drawing force of this sun."

VII.

Since young Marden had taken me into his confidence I spent many hours of each waking period, for one could not call them days, at his side studying the star which grew steadily brighter. I believe as I look back through the years of my life that the increasing magnitude of that star was the most appalling and ominous sight I had ever beheld. Many were the times that in dreams I saw the earth rushing into the blazing hell. I invariably awoke with a scream, and covered with perspiration. I sat, it seems, for days at a time watching it, fascinated as if under the hypnotic influence of an evil eye. Finally its presence could no longer be kept a secret from the others who saw outside the windows the brightness that increased as time went on.

Printed indelibly on my memory was our first excursion out of doors after three years of confinement. Walking warily along the deserted streets, we were reminded of the ancient cities of Herculaneum and Pompeii. It was not ashes and lava that had worked the doom of hundreds of human beings; the destroyer in this case was intangible, but nevertheless potent. Many silent huddled forms were seen here and there, bringing tears to our eyes as we recognized this friend and that; but the greatest tragedies were in the homes where many whole families were discovered grouped together around whatever source of heat they had temporarily relied upon for warmth. We learned that none who had depended upon coal had survived the frigidity, and in some instances starvation had wiped out entire households.

The scene which was the greatest shock to the reconnoitering party was that staged in Guy Barnes's store. The old grocer had been game to the end, and his body was found behind the counter, where he had apparently been overcome by the intensity of the cold during his labors for his fellowmen. The last overwhelming cold had descended so swiftly that many had been unable to reach shelter in time.

Next came the sad task of burying our dead. Prompt action was necessary, for the ever-growing disk of the great sun hastened the process of decay. The simplest of ceremonies were all that could be employed by men and women struggling to return the living world to pre-catastrophic normality.

The sun grew terrible to behold, as large in diameter as our old sun. Still it seemed good to be once more in the open! The children scampered about, and Ed and I had a race to the square and back. Scorch to death we might in a very short time, but it was certainly a pleasant thing to spend a few days in this solar glow which we had been denied so long.

Came a time when we could no longer be ignorant of the fact that it was growing uncomfortably warm. Finally we decided to do as everyone else was doing; pack up our earthly possessions and move to a part of the Earth's surface where the heat was not so direct.

Ed came over, mopping his forehead with his handkerchief.

"You folks about ready?" he queried. "We're all packed up. The Mardens are going in our car."

I walked to the door and gazed across the seared landscape toward the mammoth fiery orb. Suddenly I gave a startled cry. The new sun was not in its accustomed place in the heavens. It was several degrees lower down, and to the east!

"Look!" I cried, pointing with trembling finger. "My God—do you see?"

I think Ed concluded I had gone insane, but he followed the direction of my gaze.

"Jim, old fellow, you're right," he ejaculated, "as sure as Mars was farther from the sun than we were, that sun is setting, which means—"

"That we are rotating on our axis and probably revolving around the new sun," I finished triumphantly. "But we are turning from east to west instead of from west to east as formerly. If the whole world wasn't temperate nowadays I should think I had been imbibing some of the poisonous drink of our ancestors!"

VIII.

That evening the townspeople who had not already migrated to cooler regions held a jubilee in Central Park Square. The principal speaker of the evening was Oscar Marden, who explained to the people what capers our planet had been cutting during the past three years. After his address I noticed that he kept gazing skyward as if unable to bring his attention to Earth.

"Say, will you come to the observatory with me now?" he asked as I was talking to a group of friends shortly afterward.

"I'll be right along," I replied.

Scarcely half a block away we saw Ed Zutell going in the general direction of home.

"Do we want him?" I asked, not a little annoyed. "Can't we beat it up an alley? I'd like this conference alone, for I know by your manner you have something important to tell me."

"In the last part of what you say you are right," responded Marden, "but in the first part, wrong. I do want Ed, for I have something to show him, too."

When the three of us were again in the familiar setting of the past three years, Marden gazed for quite some time at the heavens through the great instrument. Finally he turned to us with a wry smile on his lips and a twinkle in his eyes.

"Just take a peep, boys, and tell me what you see." He strove in vain to conceal his amusement.

We both agreed that we saw a rather reddish star.

"That 'reddish star,'" said Oscar, impressively, "is our old friend, Mars, and he is revolving in an orbit between us and the sun!"

Ed and I looked at each other speechlessly for some seconds; then without a word Ed dropped on his knees before me in something of the fashion of an Arab bowing toward Mecca.

"What's the big idea?" I asked, not a little frightened, for I wondered if the confinement of the years had crazed him.

Oscar was laughing so that he had to hold on to the telescope for support, so I concluded there was nothing very radically amiss in the situation.

"I am worshiping a god," said Ed, "for so I would call anyone who can move the planets about so that they line up in accordance with his conceptions of the way they ought to do."

"I'd like to take the credit," I laughed, then more seriously, "but a higher authority than mine has charge of the movements of the planets."

"Well, it certainly is uncanny how you have your way in everything," grumbled Ed.

IX.

There is little more to tell. The world soon adjusted itself to its new environment. People became accustomed to seeing the sun rise in the west and set in the east.

Vera was ineffably delighted with the new system of time which was necessitated by the increased orbit of Earth. Inasmuch as it now required a trifle over two years for our planet to make a journey once around the new sun, Vera figured that she was less than half her former age, and this new method of figuring, I may add, others of her sex were not slow to adopt.

The huge sun rendered Earth habitable clear to the poles, and strange to say, it caused very little increase of heat in the tropics. Astronomers proved that, though a big sun, it was not as hot a one, for it was in the later stages of the cooling-off process to which all suns eventually come. Two planets had already been journeying around the giant sun before the advent of Mars and Earth, and what they thought of the intrusion of the two strange worlds was before long made evident through radio communication.

To the astronomers of this new era the welkin presented a fascinating opportunity for studying new neighbors in space.

And thus the chemical experiment of the superpeople of that vaster cosmos was finished.

The Fate of
the *Poseidonia*

I.

The first moment I laid eyes on Martell I took a great dislike to the man. There sprang up between us an antagonism that as far as he was concerned might have remained passive, but which circumstances forced into activity on my side.

How distinctly I recall the occasion of our meeting at the home of Professor Stearns, head of the astronomy department of Austin College. The address which the professor proposed giving before the Mentor Club, of which I was a member, was to be on the subject of the planet, Mars. The spacious front rooms of the Stearns home were crowded for the occasion with rows of chairs, and at the end of the double parlors a screen was erected for the purpose of presenting telescopic views of the ruddy planet in its various aspects.

As I entered the parlor after shaking hands with my hostess, I felt, rather than saw, an unfamiliar presence, and the impression I received involuntarily was that of antipathy. What I saw was the professor himself engaged in earnest conversation with a stranger. Intuitively I knew that from the latter emanated the hostility of which I was definitely conscious.

He was a man of slightly less than average height. At once I noticed that he did not appear exactly normal physically and yet I could not ascertain in what way he was deficient. It was not until I had passed the entire evening in his company that I was fully aware of his bodily peculiarities. Perhaps the most striking characteristic was the swarthy, coppery hue of his flesh that was not unlike that of an American Indian. His chest and shoulders seemed abnormally developed, his limbs and features extremely slender in proportion. Another peculiar individuality was the wearing of a skullcap pulled well down over his forehead.

Professor Stearns caught my eye, and with a friendly nod indicated his desire that I meet the new arrival.

"Glad to see you, Mr. Gregory," he said warmly as he clasped my hand. "I want you to meet Mr. Martell, a stranger in our town, but a kindred spirit, in that he is interested in astronomy and particularly in the subject of my lecture this evening."

I extended my hand to Mr. Martell and imagined that he responded to my salutation somewhat reluctantly. Immediately I knew why. The texture of the skin was most unusual. For want of a better simile, I shall say that it felt not unlike a fine, dry sponge. I do not believe that I betrayed any visible surprise, though inwardly my whole being revolted. The deep, close-set eyes of the stranger seemed searching me for any manifestation of antipathy, but I congratulate myself that my outward poise was undisturbed by the strange encounter.

The guests assembled, and I discovered to my chagrin that I was seated next to the stranger, Martell. Suddenly the lights were extinguished preparatory to the presentation of the lantern-slides. The darkness that enveloped us was intense. Supreme horror gripped me when I presently became conscious of two faint phosphorescent lights to my right. There could be no mistaking their origin. They were the eyes of Martell and they were regarding me with an enigmatical stare. Fascinated, I gazed back into those diabolical orbs with an emotion akin to terror. I felt that I should shriek and then attack their owner. But at the precise moment when my usually steady nerves threatened to betray me, the twin lights vanished. A second later the lantern light flashed on the screen. I stole a furtive glance in the direction of Martell. He was sitting with his eyes closed.

"The planet Mars should be of particular interest to us," began Professor Stearns, "not only because of its relative proximity to us, but because of the fact that there are visible upon its surface undeniable evidences of the handiwork of man, and I am inclined to believe in the existence of mankind there not unlike the humanity of the earth."

The discourse proceeded uninterruptedly. The audience remained quiet and attentive, for Professor Stearns possessed the faculty of holding his listeners spellbound. A large map of one hemisphere of Mars was thrown on the screen, and simultaneously the stranger Martell drew in his breath sharply with a faint whistling sound.

The professor continued, "Friends, do you observe that the outstanding physical difference between Mars and Terra appears to be in the relative distribution of land and water? On our own globe the terrestrial parts lie as distinct entities surrounded by the vast aqueous portions, whereas on Mars the land and water are so intermingled by gulfs, bays, capes and peninsulas that it requires careful study to ascertain for a certainty which is which. It is my opinion, and I do not hold it alone, for much discussion with my worthy colleagues has made it obvious that the peculiar land contours are due to the fact that water is becoming a very scarce commodity on our neighboring planet. Much of what is now land is merely the exposed portions of the one-time ocean bed, the precious life-giving fluid now occupying only the lowest depressions. We may conclude that the telescopic eye, when turned on Mars, sees a waning world, the habitat of a people struggling desperately and vainly for existence, with inevitable extermination facing them in the not far distant future. What will they do? If they are no farther advanced in the evolutionary stage than a carrot or a jellyfish, they will ultimately succumb to fate, but if they are men and women such as you and I, they will fight for the continuity of their race. I am inclined to the opinion that the Martians will not die without putting up a brave struggle, which will result in the prolongation of their existence, but not in their complete salvation."

Professor Stearns paused. "Are there any questions?" he asked.

I was about to speak when the voice of Martell boomed in my ear, startling me.

"In regard to the map, professor," he said, "I believe that gulf which lies farthest south is not a gulf at all but is a part of the land portion surrounding it. I think you credit the poor dying planet with even more water than it actually has!"

"It is possible and even probable that I have erred," replied the learned man, "and I am sorry indeed if that gulf is to be withdrawn from the credit of the Martians, for the future must look very black."

"Just suppose," resumed Martell, leaning toward the lecturer with interested mien, "that the Martians were the possessors of an intelligence equal to that of terrestrials, what might they do to save themselves from total extinction? In other words to bring it home to us more realistically, what would *we* do were we threatened with a like disaster?"

"That is a very difficult question to answer, and one upon which merely an opinion could be ventured," smiled Professor Stearns. "'Necessity is the mother of invention,' and in our case without the likelihood of the existence of the mother, we can hardly hazard a guess as to the nature of the offspring. But always, as Terra's resources have diminished, the mind of man has discovered substitutes. There has always been a way out, and let us hope our brave planetary neighbors will succeed in solving their problem."

"Let us hope so indeed," echoed the voice of Martell.

II.

At the time of my story in the winter of 1954–55, I was still unmarried and was living in a private hotel on East Ferguson Avenue, where I enjoyed the comforts of well-furnished bachelor quarters. To my neighbors I paid little or no attention, absorbed in my work during the day and paying court to Margaret Landon in the evenings.

I was not a little surprised upon one occasion, as I stepped into the corridor, to see a strange yet familiar figure in the hotel locking the door of the apartment adjoining my own. Almost instantly I recognized Martell, on whom I had not laid eyes since the meeting some weeks previous at the home of Professor Stearns. He evinced no more pleasure at our meeting than I did, and after the exchange of a few cursory remarks from which I learned that he was my new neighbor, we went our respective ways.

I thought no more of the meeting, and as I am not blessed or cursed (as the case may be) with a natural curiosity concerning the affairs of those about me, I seldom met Martell, and upon the rare occasions when I did, we confined our remarks to that ever-convenient topic, the weather.

Between Margaret and myself there seemed to be growing an inexplicable estrangement that increased as time went on, but it was not until after five repeated futile efforts to spend an evening in her company that I suspected the presence of a rival. Imagine my surprise and my chagrin to discover that rival in the person of my neighbor, Martell! I saw them together at the theatre and wondered, even with all due modesty, what there was in the ungainly figure and peculiar character of Martell to attract a beautiful and refined girl of Margaret Landon's type. But attract her he did, for it was plainly evident, as I watched them with the eyes of a jealous lover, that Margaret was fascinated by the personality of her escort.

In sullen rage I went to Margaret a few days later, expressing my opinion of her new admirer in derogatory epithets. She gave me calm and dignified attention until I had exhausted my vocabulary voicing my ideas of Martell, then she made reply in Martell's defense.

"Aside from personal appearance, Mr. Martell is a forceful and interesting character, and I refuse to allow you to dictate to me who my associates are to be. There is no reason why we three cannot all be friends."

"Martell hates me as I hate him," I replied with smoldering resentment. "That is sufficient reason why we three cannot all be friends."

"I think you must be mistaken," she replied curtly. "Mr. Martell praises your qualities as a neighbor and comments not infrequently on your excellent virtue of attending strictly to your own business."

I left Margaret's presence in a downhearted mood.

"So Martell appreciates my lack of inquisitiveness, does he?" I mused as later I reviewed mentally the closing words of Margaret, and right then and there doubts and suspicions arose in my mind. If self-absorption was an appreciable quality as far as Martell was concerned, there was reason for his esteem of that phase of my character. I had discovered the presence of a mystery; Martell had something to conceal!

It was New Year's Day, not January 1 as they had it in the old days, but the extra New Year's Day that was sandwiched as a separate entity between two years. This new chronological reckoning had been put into use in 1950. The calendar had previously contained twelve months in length from twenty-eight to thirty-one days, but with the addition of a new month and the adoption of a uniformity of twenty-eight days for all months and the interpolation of an isolated New Year's Day, the world's system of chronology was greatly simplified. It was, as I say, on New Year's Day that I arose later than usual and dressed myself. The buzzing monotone of a voice from Martell's room annoyed me. Could he be talking over the telephone to Margaret? Right then and there I stooped to the performance of a deed of which I did not think myself capable. Ineffable curiosity converted me into a spy and an eavesdropper. I dropped to my knees and peered through the keyhole. I was rewarded with an unobstructed profile view of Martell seated at a low desk on which stood a peculiar cubical mechanism measuring on each edge six or seven inches. Above it hovered a tenuous vapor and from it issued strange sounds, occasionally interrupted by remarks from Martell, uttered in an unknown tongue. Good heavens! Was this a new-fangled radio that communicated with the spirit-world? For only in such a way could I explain the peculiar vapor that enveloped the tiny machine. Television had been perfected, but as yet no instrument had been invented which delivered messages from the "unknown bourne!"

I crouched in my undignified position until it was with difficulty that I arose, at the same time that Martell shut off the mysterious contrivance. Could Margaret be involved in any diabolical schemes? The very suggestion caused me to break out in a cold sweat. Surely Margaret, the very personification of innocence and purity, could be no partner in any nefarious undertaking! I resolved to call her up. She answered the phone and I thought her voice showed agitation.

"Margaret, this is George," I said. "Are you all right?"

She answered faintly in the affirmative.

"May I come over at once?" I pled. "I have something important to tell you."

To my surprise she consented, and I lost no time in speeding my volplane to her home. With no introductory remarks, I plunged right into a narrative of the peculiar and suspicious actions of Martell, and ended by begging her to discontinue her association with him. Ever well poised and with a girlish dignity that was irresistibly charming, Margaret quietly thanked me for my solicitude for her well-being but assured me that there was nothing to fear from Martell. It was like beating against a brick wall to obtain any satisfaction from her, so I returned to my lonely room, there to brood in solitude over the unhappy change that Martell had brought into my life.

Once again I gazed through the tiny aperture. My neighbor was nowhere to be seen, but on the desk stood that which I mentally termed the devil-machine. The subtle mist that had previously hovered above it was wanting.

The next day upon arising I was drawn as by a magnet toward the keyhole, but my amazement knew no bounds when I discovered that it had been plugged from the other side, and my vision completely barred!

"Well, I guess it serves me right," I muttered in my chagrin. "I ought to keep out of other people's private affairs. But," I added as an afterthought in feeble defense of my actions, "my motive is to save Margaret from that scoundrel." And such I wanted to prove him to be before it was too late!

III.

The sixth of April, 1955, was a memorable day in the annals of history, especially to the inhabitants of Pacific coast cities throughout the world. Radios buzzed with the alarming and mystifying news that just overnight the ocean line had receded several feet. What cataclysm of nature could have caused the disappearance of thousands of tons of water inside of twenty-four hours? Scientists ventured the explanation that internal disturbances must have resulted in the opening of vast submarine fissures into which the sea had poured.

This explanation, stupendous as it was, sounded plausible enough and was accepted by the world at large, which was too busy accumulating gold and silver to worry over the loss of nearly a million tons of water. How little we then realized that the relative importance of gold and water was destined to be reversed, and that man was to have forced upon him a new conception of values which would bring to him a complete realization of his former erroneous ideas.

May and June passed, marking little change in the drab monotony that had settled into my life since Margaret Landon had ceased to care for me. One afternoon early in July I received a telephone call from Margaret. Her voice betrayed an agitated state of mind, and sorry though I was that she was troubled, it pleased me that she had turned to me in her despair. Hope sprang anew in my breast, and I told her I would be over at once.

I was admitted by the taciturn housekeeper and ushered into the library where Margaret rose to greet me as I entered. There were traces of tears in her lovely eyes. She extended both hands to me in a gesture of spontaneity that had been wholly lacking in her attitude toward me ever since the advent of Martell. In the role of protector and adviser, I felt that I was about to be reinstated in her regard.

But my joy was short-lived as I beheld a recumbent figure on the great davenport and recognized it instantly as that of Martell. So he was in the game after all! Margaret had summoned me because her lover was in danger! I turned to go but felt a restraining hand.

"Wait, George," the girl pled. "The doctor will be here any minute."

"Then let the doctor attend to him," I replied coldly. "I know nothing of the art of healing."

"I know, George," Margaret persisted, "but he mentioned you before he lost consciousness and I think he wants to speak to you. Won't you wait, please?"

I paused, hesitant at the supplicating tones of her whom I loved, but at that moment the maid announced the doctor, and I made a hasty exit.

Needless to say I experienced a sense of guilt as I returned to my rooms.

"But," I argued as I seated myself comfortably before my radio, "a rejected lover would have to be a very magnanimous specimen of humanity to go running about doing favors for a rival. What do the pair of them take me for anyway—a fool?"

I rather enjoyed a consciousness of righteous indignation, but disturbing visions of Margaret gave me an uncomfortable feeling that there was much about the affair that was incomprehensible to me.

"The transatlantic passenger plane, *Pegasus*, has mysteriously disappeared," said the voice of the news announcer. "One member of her crew has been picked up who tells such a weird, fantastic tale that it has not received credence. According to his story the *Pegasus* was winging its way across mid-ocean last night keeping an even elevation of three thousand feet, when, without any warning, the machine started straight up. Some force outside of itself was drawing it up, but whither? The rescued mechanic, the only one of all the fated ship's passengers, possessed the presence of mind to manipulate his parachute, and thus descended in safety before the air became too rare to breathe, and before he and the parachute could be attracted upwards. He stoutly maintains that the plane could not have fallen later without his knowledge. Scouting planes, boats and submarines sent out this morning verify his seemingly mad narration. Not a vestige of the *Pegasus* is to be found above, on the surface or below the water. Is this tragedy in any way connected with the lowering of the ocean level? Has someone a theory? In the face of such an inexplicable enigma the government will listen to the advancement of any theories in the hope of solving the mystery. Too many times in the past have so-called level-headed people failed to give ear to the warnings of theorists and dreamers, but now we know that the latter are often the possessors of a sixth sense that enables them to see that to which the bulk of mankind is blind."

I was awed by the fate of the *Pegasus*. I had had two flights in the wonderful machine myself three years ago, and I knew that it was the last word in luxuriant air travel.

How long I sat listening to brief news bulletins and witnessing scenic flashes of world affairs I do not know, but there suddenly came to my mind and persisted in staying there a very disquieting thought. Several times I dismissed it as unworthy of any consideration, but it continued with unmitigating tenacity.

After an hour of mental pros and cons I called up the hotel office.

"This is Mr. Gregory in Suite 307," I strove to keep my voice steady. "Mr. Martell of 309 is ill at the house of a friend. He wishes me to have some of his belongings taken to him. May I have the key to his rooms?"

There was a pause that to me seemed interminable, then the voice of the clerk, "Certainly, Mr. Gregory, I'll send a boy up with it at once."

I felt like a culprit of the deepest dye as I entered Martell's suite a few moments later and gazed about me. I knew I might expect interference from any quarter at any moment, so I wasted no time in a general survey of the apartment, but proceeded at once to the object of my visit. The tiny machine which I now perceived was more intricate than I had supposed from my previous observations through the keyhole, stood in its accustomed place upon the desk. It had four levers and a dial, and I decided to manipulate each of these in turn. I commenced with the one at my extreme left. For a moment apparently nothing happened, then I realized that above the machine a mist was forming.

At first it was faint and cloudy but the haziness quickly cleared, and before my startled vision a scene presented itself. I seemed to be inside a bamboo hut looking toward an opening which afforded a glimpse of a wave-washed sandy beach and a few palm trees silhouetted against the horizon. I could imagine myself on a desert isle. I gasped in astonishment, but it was nothing to the shock which was to follow. While my fascinated gaze dwelt on the scene before me, a shadow fell athwart the hut's entrance and the figure of a man came toward me. I uttered a hoarse cry. For a moment I thought I had been transplanted chronologically to the discovery of America, for the being who approached me bore a general resemblance to an Indian chief. From his forehead tall, white feathers stood erect. He was without clothing and his skin had a reddish cast that glistened with a coppery sheen in the sunlight. Where had I seen those features or similar ones recently. I had it! Martell! The Indian savage was a natural replica of the suave and civilized Martell, and yet was this man before me a savage? On the contrary, I noted that his features displayed a remarkably keen intelligence.

The stranger approached a table upon which I seemed to be, and raised his arms. A muffled cry escaped my lips! The feathers that I had supposed constituted his headdress were attached permanently along the upper portion of his arms to a point a little below each elbow. *They grew there.* This strange being had feathers instead of hair.

I do not know by what presence of mind I managed to return the lever to its original position, but I did, and sat weakly gazing vacantly at the air, where but a few seconds before a vivid tropic scene had been visible. Suddenly a low buzzing sound was heard. Only for an instant was I mystified, then I knew that the stranger of the desert sle was endeavoring to summon Martell.

Weak and dazed I waited until the buzzing had ceased and then I resolutely pulled the second of the four levers. At the inception of the experiment the same phenomena were repeated, but when a correct perspective was effected a very different scene was presented before my startled vision. This time I seemed to be in a luxuriant room filled with costly furnishings, but I had time only for a most fleeting glance, for a section of newspaper that had intercepted part of my view moved, and from behind its printed expanse emerged a being who bore a resemblance to Martell and the Indian of the desert island. It required but a second to turn off the mysterious connection, but that short time had been of sufficient duration to enable me to read the heading of the paper in the hands of a copper-hued man. It was *Die Münchene Zeitung.*

Still stupefied by the turn of events, it was with a certain degree of enjoyment that I continued to experiment with the devil-machine. I was startled when the same buzzing sound followed the disconnecting of the instrument.

I was about to manipulate the third lever when I became conscious of pacing footsteps in the outer hall. Was I arousing the suspicion of the hotel officials? Leaving my seat before the desk, I began to move about the room in semblance of gathering together Martell's required articles. Apparently satisfied, the footsteps retreated down the corridor and were soon inaudible.

Feverishly now I fumbled with the third lever. There was no time to lose and I was madly desirous of investigating all the possibilities of this new kind of television set. I had no doubt that I was on the track of a nefarious organization of spies, and I worked on in the self-termed capacity of a Sherlock Holmes.

The third lever revealed an apartment no less sumptuous than the German one had been. It appeared to be unoccupied for the present, and I had ample time to survey its expensive furnishings which had an oriental appearance. Through an open window at the far end of the room I glimpsed a mosque with domes and minarets. I could not ascertain for a certainty whether this was Turkey or India. It might have been any one of many eastern lands, I could not know. The fact that the occupant of this oriental apartment was temporarily absent made me desirous of learning more about it, but time was precious to me now, and I disconnected. No buzzing followed upon this occasion, which strengthened my belief that my lever manipulation sounded a similar buzzing that was audible in the various stations connected for the purpose of accomplishing some wicked scheme.

The fourth handle invited me to further investigation. I determined to go through with my secret research though I died in the effort. Just before my hand dropped, the buzzing commenced, and I perceived for the first time a faint glow near the lever of No. 4. I dared not investigate 4 at this time, for I did not wish it known that another than Martell was at this station. I thought of going on to dial 5, but an innate love of system forced me to risk a loss of time rather than to take them out of order. The buzzing continued for the usual duration of time, but I waited until it had apparently ceased entirely before I moved No. 4.

My soul rebelled at that which took form from the emanating mist. A face, another duplicate of Martell's, but if possible more cruel, confronted me, completely filling up the vaporous space, and two phosphorescent eyes seared a warning into my own. A nauseating sensation crept over me as my hand crept to the connecting part of No. 4. When every vestige of the menacing face had vanished, I arose weakly and took a few faltering steps around the room. A bell was ringing with great persistence from some other room. It was mine! It would be wise to answer it. I fairly flew back to my room and was rewarded by the sound of Margaret's voice with a note of petulance in it.

"Why didn't you answer, George? The phone rang several times."

"Couldn't. Was taking a bath," I lied.

"Mr. Martell is better," continued Margaret. "The doctor says there's no immediate danger."

There was a pause and the sound of a rasping voice a little away from the vicinity of the phone, and then Margaret's voice came again.

"Mr. Martell wants you to come over, George. He wants to see you."

"Tell him I have to dress after my bath, then I'll come," I answered.

IV.

There was not a moment to spare. I rushed back into Martell's room determined to see this thing through. I had never been subject to heart attacks, but certainly the suffocating sensation that possessed me could be attributed to no other cause.

A loud buzzing greeted my ears as soon as I had closed the door of Martell's suite. I looked toward the devil-machine. The four stations were buzzing at once! What was I to do? There was no light near dial 5, and that alone remained uninvestigated. My course of action was clear; try out No. 5 to my satisfaction, leave Martell's room and go to Margaret Landon's home as I had told her I would. They must not know what I had done. But it was inevitable that Martell would know when he got back to his infernal television and radio. *He must not get back!* Well, time enough to plan that later; now to the work of seeing No. 5.

When I turned the dial of No. 5 (for, as I have stated before, this was a dial instead of a lever) I was conscious of a peculiar sensation of distance. It fairly took my breath away. What remote part of the earth's surface would the last position reveal to me?

A sharp hissing sound accompanied the manipulation of No. 5 and the vaporous shroud was very slow in taking definite shape. When it was finally at rest, and it was apparent that it would not change further, the scene depicted was at first incomprehensible to me. I stared with bulging eyes and bated breath trying to read any meaning into the combinations of form and color that had taken shape before me.

In the light of what had since occurred, the facts of which are known throughout the world, I can lend my description a little intelligence borrowed, as it were, from the future. At the time of which I write, however, no such enlightenment was mine, and it must have been a matter of minutes before the slightest knowledge of the significance of the scene entered my uncomprehending brain.

My vantage point seemed to be slightly aerial, for I was looking down upon a scene possibly ninety feet below me. Arid red cliffs and promontories jutted over dry ravines and crevices. In the immediate foreground and also across a deep gully extended a comparatively level area which was the scene of some sort of activity. There was about it a vague suggestion of a shipyard, yet I saw no lumber, only great mountainous piles of dull metal, among which moved thousands of agile figures. They were men and women, but how strange they appeared! Their red bodies were minus clothing of any description and their heads and shoulders were covered with long white feathers that, when folded, draped the upper portions of their bodies like shawls. They were unquestionably of the same race as the desert island stranger—and Martell! At times the feathers of these strange people stood erect and spread out like a peacock's tail. I noticed that when spread in this fan-like fashion they facilitated locomotion.

I glanced toward the sun far to my right and wondered if I had gone crazy. I rubbed my hands across my eyes and peered again. Yes, it was our luminary, but it was little more than half its customary size! I watched it sinking with fascinated gaze. It vanished quickly beyond the red horizon and darkness descended with scarcely a moment of intervening twilight. It was only by the closest observation that I could perceive that I was still in communication with No. 5.

Presently the gloom was dissipated by a shaft of light from the opposite horizon whither the sun had disappeared, so rapidly that I could follow its movement across the sky; the moon hove into view. But wait, was it the moon? Its surface looked strangely unfamiliar, and it too seemed to have shrunk in size.

Spellbound, I watched the tiny moon glide across the heavens the while I listened to the clang of metal tools from the workers below. Again a bright light appeared on the horizon beyond the great metal bulks below me. The scene was rapidly being rendered visible by an orb that exceeded the sun in diameter. Then I knew. Great God! There were two moons traversing the welkin! My heart was pounding so loudly that it drowned out the sound of the metalworkers. I watched on, unconscious of the passage of time.

Voices shouted from below in great excitement. Events were evidently working up to some important climax while the little satellite passed from my line of vision and only the second large moon occupied the sky. Straight before me and low on the horizon it hung with its lower margin touching the cliffs. It was low enough now so that a few of the larger stars were becoming visible. One in particular attracted my gaze and held it. It was a great bluish-green star, and I noticed that the workers paused seemingly to gaze in silent admiration at its transcendent beauty. Then shout after shout arose from below and I gazed in bewilderment at the spectacle of the next few minutes, or was it hours?

A great spherical bulk hove in view from the right of my line of vision. It made me think of nothing so much as a gyroscope of gigantic proportions. It seemed to be made of the metal with which the workers were employed below, and as it gleamed in the deep blue of the sky it looked like a huge satellite. A band of red metal encircled it with points of the same at top and bottom. Numerous openings that resembled the portholes of an ocean liner appeared in the broad central band, from which extended metal points. I judged these were the "eyes" of the machine. But that which riveted my attention was an object that hung poised in the air below the mighty gyroscope, held in suspension by some mysterious force, probably magnetic in nature, evidently controlled in such a manner that at a certain point it was exactly counter-balanced by the gravitational pull. The lines of force apparently traveled from the poles of the mammoth sphere. But the object that depended in mid-air, as firm and rigid as though resting on terra-firma, was the missing *Pegasus*, the epitome of earthly scientific skill, but in the clutches of this unearthly looking marauder it looked like a fragile toy. Its wings were bent and twisted, giving it an uncanny resemblance to a bird in the claws of a cat.

In my spellbound contemplation of this new phenomenon I had temporarily forgotten the scene below, but suddenly a great cloud momentarily blotted out the moon, then another and another and another, in rapid succession. Huge bulks of aircraft were eclipsing the moon. Soon the scene was all but obliterated by the machines whose speed accelerated as they reached the upper air. On and on they sped in endless procession while the green star gazed serenely on! The green star, most sublime of the starry host! I loved its pale beauty, though I knew not why. Darkness. The moon had set, but I knew that those frightfully gigantic and ominous shapes still sped upward and onward. Whither?

The tiny moon again made its appearance, serving to reveal once more that endless aerial migration. Was it hours or days? I had lost all sense of the passage of time. The sound of rushing feet, succeeded by a pounding at the door, brought me back to my immediate surroundings.

I had the presence of mind to shut off the machine, then I arose and assumed a defensive attitude as the door opened and many figures confronted me. Foremost among them was Martell, his face white with rage, or was it fear?

"Officer, seize that man," he cried furiously. "I did not give him permission to spy in my room. He lied when he said that." Here Martell turned to the desk clerk who stood behind two policemen.

"Speaking of spying," I flung back at him, "Martell, you ought to know the meaning of that word. He's a spy himself," I cried to the two apparently unmoved officers. "Why he—he—" To continue was futile.

From their unsympathetic attitudes, I knew the odds were against me. I had lied, and I had been found in a man's private room without his permission. It would be a matter of time and patience before I could persuade the law that I had any justice on my side.

I was handcuffed and led toward the door just as a sharp pain like an icy clutch at my heart overcame me. I sank into oblivion.

V.

When I regained consciousness two days later I discovered that I was the sole occupant of a cell in the State Hospital for the Insane. Mortified to the extreme, I pled with the keeper to bring about my release, assuring him that I was unimpaired mentally.

"Sure, that's what they all say," the fellow remarked with a wry smile.

"But I must be freed," I reiterated impatiently, "I have a message of importance for the world. I must get into immediate communication with the Secretary of War."

"Yes, yes," agreed the keeper affably. "We'll let you see the Secretary of War when that fellow over there," he jerked his thumb in the direction of the cell opposite mine, "dies from drinking hemlock. He says he's Socrates, and every time he drinks a cup of milk he flops over, but he always revives."

I looked across the narrow hall into a pair of eyes that mirrored a deranged mind, then my gaze returned to the guard who was watching me narrowly. I turned away with a shrug of despair.

Later in the day the man appeared again, but I sat in sullen silence in a corner of my cell. Days passed in this manner until at last a plausible means of communication with the outside world occurred to me. I asked if my good friend Professor Stearns might be permitted to visit me. The guard replied that he believed it could be arranged for sometime the following week. It is a wonder I did not become demented, imprisoned as I was, in solitude, with the thoughts of the mysterious revelations haunting me continually.

One afternoon the keeper, passing by on one of his customary rounds, thrust a newspaper between the bars of my cell. I grabbed it eagerly and retired to read it.

The headlines smote my vision with an almost tactile force.

"Second Mysterious Recession of Ocean. The *Poseidonia* is lost!"

I continued to read the entire article, the letters of which blazed before my eyes like so many pinpoints of light.

"Ocean waters have again receded, this time in the Atlantic. Seismologists are at a loss to explain the mysterious cataclysm as no earth tremors have been registered. It is a little over three months since the supposed submarine fissures lowered the level of the Pacific Ocean several feet, and now the same calamity, only to a greater extent, has visited the Atlantic.

"The island of Madeira reports stranded fish upon her shores by the thousands, the decay of which threatens the health of the island's population. Two merchant vessels off the Azores, and one fifty miles out from Gibraltar, were found total wrecks. Another, the *Transatlantic*, reported a fearful agitation of the ocean depths, but seemed at a loss for a plausible explanation, as the sky was cloudless and no wind was blowing.

"'But despite this fact,' wired the *Transatlantic*, 'great waves all but capsized us. This marine disturbance lasted throughout the night.'

"The following wireless from the great ocean liner, *Poseidonia*, brings home to us the realization that Earth has been visited with a stupendous calamity. The *Poseidonia* was making her weekly trans-Atlantic trip between Europe and America, and was in mid-ocean at the time her message was flashed to the world.

"'A great cloud of flying objects of enormous proportions has just appeared in the sky, blotting out the light of the stars. No sound accompanies the approach of this strange fleet. In appearance the individual craft resemble mammoth balloons. The sky is black with them and in their vicinity the air is humid and oppressive, as though the atmosphere were saturated to the point of condensation. Everything is orderly. There are no collisions. Our captain has given orders for us to turn back toward Europe—we have turned, but the dark dirigibles are pursuing us. Their speed is unthinkable. Can the *Poseidonia*, doing a mere hundred miles an hour, escape? A huge craft is bearing down upon us from above and behind. There is no escape. Pandemonium reigns. The enemy—'

"Thus ends the tragic message from the brave wireless operator of the *Poseidonia*."

I threw down the paper and called loudly for the keeper. Socrates across the hall eyed me suspiciously. I was beginning to feel that perhaps the poor demented fellow had nothing on me; that I should soon be in actuality a raving maniac.

The keeper came in response to my call, entered my cell and patted my shoulders reassuringly.

"Never mind, old top," he said, "it isn't so bad as it seems."

"Now look here," I burst forth angrily, "I tell you I am *not insane!*" How futile my words sounded! "If you will send Professor Mortimer Stearns, teacher of astronomy at Austin, to me at once for an hour's talk, I'll prove to the world that I have not been demented.

"Professor Stearns is a very highly esteemed friend of mine," I continued, noting the suspicion depicted on his countenance. "If you wish, go to him first and find out his true opinion of me. I'll wager it will not be an uncomplimentary one!"

The man twisted his keys thoughtfully, and I uttered not a word, believing a silent demeanor most effective in the present crisis. After what seemed an eternity:

"All right," he said, "I'll see what can be done toward arranging a visit from Professor Mortimer Stearns as soon as possible."

I restrained my impulse toward a too effusive expression of gratitude as I realized that a quiet dignity prospered my cause more effectually.

The next morning at ten, after a constant vigil, I was rewarded with the most welcome sight of Professor Stearns striding down the hall in earnest conversation with the guard. He was the straw and I the drowning man, but would he prove a more substantial help than the proverbial straw? I surely hoped so.

A chair was brought for the professor and placed just outside my cell. I hastily drew my own near it.

"Well, this is indeed unfortunate," said Mortimer Stearns with some embarrassment, "and I sincerely hope you will soon be released."

"Unfortunate!" I echoed. "It is nothing short of a calamity."

My indignation voiced so vociferously startled the good professor and he shoved his chair almost imperceptibly away from the intervening bars. At the far end of the hall the keeper eyed me suspiciously. Hang it all, was my last resort going to fail me?

"Professor Stearns," I said earnestly, "will you try to give me an unbiased hearing? My situation is a desperate one, and it is necessary for someone to believe in me before I can render humanity the service it needs."

He responded to my appeal with something of his old sincerity that always endeared him to his associates.

"I shall be glad to hear your story, Gregory, and if I can render any service, I'll not hesitate—"

"That's splendid of you," I interrupted with emotion, "and now to my weird tale."

I related from the beginning, omitting no details, however trivial they may have seemed, the series of events that had brought me to my present predicament.

"And your conclusion?" queried the professor in strange, hollow tones.

"That Martian spies, one of whom is Martell, are superintending by radio and television, an unbelievably well-planned theft of Earth's water in order to replenish their own dry ocean beds!"

"Stupendous!" gasped Professor Stearns. "Something must be done to prevent another raid. Let's see," he mused, "the interval was three months before, was it not? Three months we shall have for bringing again into use the instruments of war that, praise God! have lain idle for many generations. It is the only way to deal with a formidable foe from outside."

VI.

Professor Stearns was gone, but there was hope in my heart in place of the former grim despair. When the guard handed the evening paper to me I amazed him with a grateful "thank you." But my joy was short-lived. Staring up at me from the printed passenger list of the ill-fated *Poseidonia* were the names of Mr. and Mrs. T. M. Landon and daughter, Margaret!

I know the guard classed me as one of the worst cases on record, but I felt that surely Fate had been unkind.

"A package for Mr. George Gregory," bawled a voice in the corridor.

Thanks to the influence of Professor Stearns, I was permitted to receive mail. When the guard saw that I preferred unwrapping it myself, he discreetly left me to the mystery of the missive.

A card just inside bore the few but significant words, "For Gregory in remembrance of Martell."

I suppressed an impulse to dash the accursed thing to the floor when I saw that it was Martell's radio and television instrument. Placing it upon the table I drew a chair up to it and turned each of the levers, but not one functioned. I manipulated the dial No. 5. The action was accompanied by the same hissing sound that had so startled my overwrought nerves upon the previous occasion. Slowly the wraithlike mist commenced the process of adjustment. Spellbound I watched the scene before my eyes.

Again I had the sensation of a lofty viewpoint. It was identical with the one I had previously held, but the scene—was it the same? It must be—and yet! The barren red soil was but faintly visible through a verdure. The towering rocky palisades that bordered the chasm were crowned with golden-roofed dwellings, or were they temples, for they were like the pure marble fanes of the ancient Greeks except in color. Down the steep slopes flowed streams of sparkling water that dashed with a merry sound to a canal below.

Gone were the thousands of beings and their metal aircraft, but seated on a grassy plot in the left foreground of the picture was a small group of the white-feathered, red-skinned inhabitants of this strange land. In the distance rose the temple-crowned crags. One figure alone stood, and with a magnificent gesture held arms aloft. The great corona of feathers spread, following the line of the arms like the open wings of a great eagle. The superb figure stood and gazed into the deep velvety blue of the sky, the others following the direction of their leader's gaze.

Involuntarily I too watched the welkin where now not even a moon was visible. Then within the range of my vision there moved a great object—the huge aerial gyroscope—and beneath it, dwarfed by its far greater bulk, hung a modern ocean liner, like a jewel from the neck of some gigantic ogre.

Great God—it was the *Poseidonia!* I knew now, in spite of the earthly appearance of the great ship, that it was no terrestrial scene upon which I gazed. I was beholding the victory of Martell, the Martian, who had filled his world's canals with water of Earth, and even borne away trophies of our civilization to exhibit to his fellow beings.

I closed my eyes to shut out the awful scene, and thought of Margaret, dead and yet aboard the liner, frozen in the absolute cold of outer space!

How long I sat stunned and horrified I do not know, but when I looked back for another last glimpse of the Martian landscape, I uttered a gasp of incredulity. A face filled the entire vaporous screen, the beloved features of Margaret Landon. She was speaking and her voice came over the distance like the memory of a sound that is not quite audible and yet very real to the person in whose mind it exists. It was more as if time divided us instead of space, yet I knew it was the latter, for while a few minutes of time came between us, millions of miles of space intervened!

"George," came the sweet, faraway voice, "I loved you, but you were so suspicious and jealous that I accepted the companionship of Martell, hoping to bring you to your senses. I did not know what an agency for evil he had established upon the earth. Forgive me, dear."

She smiled wistfully. "My parents perished with hundreds of others in the transportation of the *Poseidonia,* but Martell took me from the ship to the ether-craft for the journey, so that I alone was saved."

Her eyes filled with tears. "Do not mourn for me, George, for I shall take up the thread of life anew among these strange but beautiful surroundings. Mars is indeed lovely, but I will tell you of it later, for I cannot talk long now."

"I only want to say," she added hastily, "that Terra need fear Mars no more. There is a sufficiency of water now—and I will prevent any—"

She was gone, and in her stead was the leering, malevolent face of Martell. He was minus his skullcap, and his clipped feathers stood up like the ruff of an angry turkey-gobbler.

I reached instinctively for the dial, but before my hand touched it there came a sound, not unlike that of escaping steam, and instantaneously the picture vanished. I did not object to the disappearance of the Martian, but another fact did cause me regret; from that moment I was never able to view the ruddy planet through the agency of the little machine. All communication had been forever shut off by Martell.

Although many doubt the truth of my solution of the mystery of the disappearance of the *Pegasus* and of the *Poseidonia,* and are still searching beneath the ocean waves, I know that never will either of them be seen again on Earth.

The Menace
of Mars

I.

Professor Harley pointed to the steam that issued with a merry singing noise from the spout of the teakettle, then designated a glass of water that stood near, and lastly placed his hand upon a small cake of ice in a saucer on the table. Turning, he surveyed the class from over the tops of his horn-rimmed spectacles.

"Elementally speaking, they are the same, but they manifest differently. The molecules in the case of the former," he continued in pedantic discourse, "are in a state of violent agitation, rushing upward and outward. Their speed is terrific. Now in the case of the water, the molecular motion is less evident. The temperature is considerably lower and the molecular orbits are far more restricted, hence the manifestation in the liquid state. When we contemplate the last of the three states of H_2O, we find a solid of low temperature. In this cold, compact form there is still less freedom among the whirling molecules. Modern science tells us that the motion of molecules in the case of solid bodies is confined within so narrow a range that we cannot detect that they alter their places at all."

My eyes wandered involuntarily from the kettle, glass and saucer till they rested upon the very attractive daughter of Professor Harley who occupied a desk two rows ahead and one row to the right of my own. From where I sat, her bobbed bronze ringlets as they curled away from her ears and the nape of her neck, were far more interesting phenomena to me than steam, water and ice. Physics and chemistry were not to be mentioned in the same breath with Vivian Harley.

At the close of the class period, the professor read the following announcement, a copy of which had been posted on the bulletin board.

"As it will be an especially fine evening for astronomical observation, the college observatory will be open between eight and ten to any who may wish to view the heavens through the new telescope. Professor Aldrich will speak about the planets and stars in the field of the instrument."

I lost no time in finding out if Vivian Harley was to be at the observatory.

"I've got to go," she smiled ruefully. "Father insists upon it. I suppose you're going, Hildreth?"

"Yes, I'm majoring in the subject, you know," I replied. "Maybe I could give you some astronomical instruction that would be more interesting than the learned discourses of Professor Aldrich."

"I fear even you couldn't make it very interesting to me." Her words were curt, but her brown eyes were smiling. "You see I am very one-sided in my tastes, and I happen to be greatly interested in father's subject, chemistry. I'm majoring in that, you know, and maybe I could give you some chemical instruction that would prove more interesting than the learned discourses of Professor Harley!" she added with a twinkle in her eye.

"Chemistry and astronomy be hanged!" I ejaculated in semblance of great ferocity. "Your father wants you to be at the observatory tonight and I intend to be there, so I'll see you at eight."

I was climbing the steps to the telescope balcony at the appointed hour. The Professor of astronomy, surrounded by a group of some thirty students, was standing on the north side pointing out the constellation, Hercules, when I came up. It did not take me long, even in the dim starlight, to discern the form of Vivian Harley, as her eyes followed the direction of the learned man's finger with rapt gaze.

"She is interested in the subject," I said half aloud, "or else Professor Aldrich is proving more entertaining than usual."

I approached the dark group silhouetted against the interminable canopy of the heavens wherein blazoned the fiery host of suns innumerable. How insignificant seemed man, even as learned a man as Professor Aldrich, when one could lift the eyes but a little higher and behold with one glance mighty Vega, Altair and Deneb. Yet I knew in my heart that much as I loved my astronomical pursuits, a certain small figure in yonder group of humanity was dearer to me than all the suns that shine in the eternal ether.

"And so we believe there *is* an analogy between the universe of chemistry and that of the stars," the professor was saying. "Within a tiny scrap of matter lies hidden a whole atomic universe in ceaseless and terrific movement. This is infinite smallness, but we can comprehend the idea with finite minds. Let these finite minds of ours contemplate for a moment, infinite bigness. As everywhere throughout all space the conditions are repeated which we find within the atom, we can deduce therefrom that our own universe is an atom of infinite bigness in which atomic worlds and systems come and go and progress through space in orbital movement as do the electrons of infinite smallness in the atoms they go to build up."

"Our universe an atom!" I heard Vivian gasp as I approached her side.

Apparently the idea had never impressed her before. She turned to me and her eyes were wide with wonder.

"Of course," I smiled, "and the sun with his family of planets is an atom, and the same planets are electrons. That sort of connects up your chemistry and my astronomy. Isn't that so?"

She turned to me with a preoccupied air and said slowly, "It is stupendous—and so plausible!"

"Of course," I replied, "it proves more reasonable than the laws of Newton which are being replaced in part by those of Einstein."

The student group led by the instructor, entered the observatory and mounted the spiral stairs to the telescope room where we took turns viewing Saturn. While Vivian gazed upon the ringed planet, I approached Professor Aldrich with this question:

"Is it beyond the hope of man ever to ascertain of what gigantic body our universe is an atom? Man is given but a very vague conception of the scheme of things if he cannot conceive the niche in which he has a place."

The scholarly man smiled wistfully and said as he laid a hand upon my shoulder, "My lad, we can never know the billionth part of where we fit into God's great plan. Here we are isolated in the midst of Infinity by the limitations of our five senses. They present a mere crack through which we obtain but the faintest suggestion of what lies beyond."

"But," I persisted, "by the very analogy you suggested when out on the balcony, might man conceive the nature of the gigantic masterpiece of which he is an infinitesimal part?"

"I grasp the significance of your question," said the professor with growing enthusiasm. "Yes—we can surmise something of the nature of that great body in which Destiny has placed us. In fact we can *know* at least this much. *It is a gas.* The proportional distances between the atoms (or solar systems, since we are contemplating the vaster cosmos) and their inconceivable speed, indicates a gaseous constitution. That much knowledge is vouchsafed us!"

II.

Two years passed. I had graduated and become Professor Aldrich's assistant, teaching freshmen astronomy. It was Vivian Harley's senior year. She was majoring in chemistry to be her father's laboratory assistant, but thanks to the inspiration of that night at the observatory two years ago, she had minored in my subject, astronomy, and gave promise of being a worthy aide to her future husband as well as to her father. Yes, Vivian had promised to be mine after her graduation in June, and it was now April.

Late in the afternoon of April 17 (a never-to-be-forgotten-day in history) I was crossing the meadowlands between the low hills that surround the country estate of my maternal uncle, the late Senator Gilroy. His sudden death had brought relatives from all over the country to attend the funeral. Many had arrived by plane, for in the year 1958, travel by airplane was common.

I was, as I said, walking across the low meadows, entranced with the loveliness of nature, when I noticed a peculiar thing. The sun was very low over the hills, and I was cognizant of the fact that the setting sun always appears much larger than when it is higher in the heavens. But even the knowledge of this optical illusion could not satisfactorily account for the phenomenal enormity of the sun as it slowly sank to rest beyond the hills toward Pleasantown. The evening was uncommonly warm and I shed my coat and seated myself on the grassy mead, determined to enjoy a quiet evening amid rural surroundings, before returning to the companionship of friends and relatives at the Gilroy mansion.

It was during the magical moments between the setting of the sun and the appearance of the first stars, that I experienced an uncanny premonition of approaching disaster. I could attribute the foreboding to no physical discomfort other than to an increasing oppressiveness of the atmosphere, that was not unlike the sultriness of an approaching storm. I decided to watch for the appearance of the first star that should come into my range of vision over the western treetops.

"It will be Antares," I conjectured.

Then in far less time than is required to tell it, the sky clouded over and all prospective view of the heavens was temporarily denied me. The nightmare that followed beggars description. Why I was not drowned I do not know, for the flood of rain descended in torrents, striking my face with such force that I could scarcely breathe. After several hours, how many I do not know, for I had lost all track of the passage of time, I was wading more than knee-deep in a turbulent stream that was rapidly rising about me, while occasionally I was struck by floating debris as I strove in the Stygian darkness to make my way back to the house. Something soft brushed against my leg. It yielded to my touch. I strove to hold it, but the waters tore it from my grasp and it was gone.

Gradually the downpour abated and I believed I had nothing more to fear from overhead.

"This isn't so bad," I assured myself, speaking aloud and comforted by the sound of my voice. "I'll wait until the stars come out and they will guide me to the house."

Suddenly the waters began to swirl and eddy around me. They rose and fell like the waves of the sea; occasionally they reached neck-high and I nearly lost my footing.

"Thank God my feet are on terra-firma," I cried, "otherwise—"

The ground beneath me swayed. The waters rushed up to meet me. For the next few minutes I knew not sky from water nor water from ground. I felt as if I were revolving with a mill wheel, by far the greater part of which was under water.

At last I stood again waist-high in water, but Nature had ceased her havoc. Earth no longer quaked, waters were not rising, and a faint light was suffusing the black sky.

"If I find Antares now," I mused, "I can get my bearings and return to the house to see what has happened there."

A small area of the clouds was rapidly dispersing. I fixed my gaze upon it expectantly, but was not prepared for that which burst upon my vision. A great red ball of fire hung in the heavens. For a moment I thought it a toy balloon, but such a bauble on a night like this was incongruous. In appearance it was about an eighth the size of the full moon. The clouds continued to scatter until several other fiery balls, varying in red, blue and yellow light, were visible through the rift. Might it be that the inhabitants of Pleasantown were celebrating the cessation of the deluge in a most extraordinary manner? Still it seemed to me that sane human beings were likely at this moment to be engaged in reconstructive work instead of wasting valuable time and energy in making useless aerial toys.

After the appearance of a dozen or more, the gathering clouds again hid them from view, but I had had sufficient time to definitely locate the house, in the upper story of which lights now gleamed faintly.

I plowed my way through the water and finally dragged myself wearily upon the stone veranda which remained a good foot and a half above the flood. The sound of excited voices assailed my ears from the upper floor as I crossed the threshold.

"I just know it's the end of the world," shrilled the voice of Cousin Donna. "Poor dear Cousin Paul (Senator Gilroy) is the lucky one. He lived almost as long as we're going to, and he escaped doomsday!"

The reassuring tones of her husband, Miles Tracy, came next to my ears, as I stood in my drenched clothing at the foot of the stairs.

"What's worrying me is what's become of Cousin Hildreth. The last I saw of him he was setting out on a lonely hike, headed toward Pleasantown. I hinted he might want company, but he told me plainly that he preferred to be alone. Queer sort of chap, Hildreth. Is he that way because he's an astronomer or is he an astronomer because he's that way?"

"Which came first, the chicken or the egg?" laughed another male voice.

"But all joking aside," continued Miles, "we must send out a rescue party after Hildreth. The Lord only knows what happened to him during the climax of the earthquake!"

"Don't allow yourselves to become alarmed on my account," I called as I mounted the stairs and appeared before the astounded group in my wet clothing. "I've been taking a little swim and watching some toy balloons over Pleasantown."

Miles tapped his head significantly and looked from one to another of the members of the group as they crowded around me.

I was bombarded with questions from all sides, but Mrs. Gilroy insisted that I get into dry clothes at once before I attempt any narration of the events prior to and following the catastrophe.

III.

The rehearsal of events must have taken up the greater part of the night, but we retired eventually. When I awoke and looked at my watch, the hour hand pointed to ten. 10:00 a.m.! It was more like 10:00 p.m. and hot—I had never been as warm in my life. The thermometer by my door registered 94° F and the humidity was intolerable. My room faced the east, so I hastily threw up the shades to see why old Sol was not on duty.

The eastern horizon was a lurid red, as if many miles away a great conflagration raged. Even as I watched, the heavy clouds were partially dispelled, and a sight, the most awful, barring one, that these eyes have ever beheld, met my view. The sun, increased to mammoth size, hung between the horizon and zenith, a veritable hell of blazing fury. Was Earth plunging into the fiery orb of day? Was this Earth's ultimate doom, after the prediction of astronomers, myself included, that a frozen lifeless world would eventually swing around a rapidly cooling sun?

Intelligent radio communication was almost impossible, but the disconnected reports that came from time to time told of the tragic deaths of thousands upon thousands, who were unable to seek adequate protection from the scorching rays of the sun.

The guests of Gilroy manor passed the day in alternate panic and despondency. There is nothing to do in the face of natural calamities except to adjust oneself to them. Their incontestable force cannot be averted. The only thing that humanity could do during that first terrible day was to seek its cellars, if they were dry, and await the ultimate setting of the gigantic orb.

My thoughts constantly turned to Vivian. How much easier would have been this catastrophe, if we could have been together. Although I had complete confidence in Professor Harley's sane judgment under any circumstances, I desired nothing so much as to have my fiancée with me.

As the day wore on, passed in the relatively cool depths of the cellar for fear of further earthquakes, we noticed a buoyancy taking the place of the former heavy oppressiveness that had seemed to weigh us down. The sultriness had given way to a dryness, very hot to be sure, but much less unpleasant than the excessive humidity that had characterized the night, morning and early afternoon. So light and gay did we feel toward the sunset hour, that we indulged in music and dancing. Frivolous it may seem to read of it, but man is so constituted that he can mercifully relieve overstrained nerves with various forms of relaxation, though he may know that the stress of fear and worry has not permanently subsided. And if this narrative is to adhere strictly to the truth, I must not omit a few words in regard to the discovery of the late senator's private stock, which I think deserves as much credit for having relieved the mental strain of the day as any natural reaction might have done.

I can write of this in a perfectly unbiased manner, for I am a strict teetotaler, and this day spent in the subterranean depths of the Gilroy mansion was no exception to the rule. But as regards Miles Tracy, James Urban and even my ordinarily dignified Uncle Mark Atkins, I can make no such positive assertion, and even Donna was not above suspicion.

The first inkling I had of it all was when Donna appeared suddenly from some remote part of the basement. As I watched her, I thought we were having another earthquake.

"Say folks," she called as she approached the rest of us, "I just got weighed, and glory be—I've lost seventy-two pounds! It pays to try dieting for reducing. I told you, Marian (Mrs. Gilroy), you'd lose flesh if you cut out the starches."

The widow of the late senator recovered quickly from the shock of her guest's apparent loss of weight) and replied rather icily, "I think you'd better look at the scales again, Donna. There must be some mistake."

"'S'fact," this from Uncle Mark whose belligerent attitude signified all too plainly that he was prepared to back Donna up in her assertion in regard to her loss of weight.

"Come in and see the scales if you don't believe it!"

Glad of another diversion from our gloomy thoughts, we trooped into the little side room in the corner of which stood a weighing machine, the platform of which Donna quickly mounted. The rest of us crowded around the dial, and with Donna's and James's triumphant, "We told you so!" in our ears, observed that the pointer indicated that Donna, a woman of apparently more than average weight, tipped the scales at precisely seventy-six pounds!

There followed a series of experiments that resulted in the undeniable conclusion that each one of us weighed only a little more than half of his or her former weight!

"The machine is out of order," I explained, but in my heart I knew differently, though I would not vouchsafe to tell these people what I suspicioned of the truth at this time.

IV.

A few minutes later, Miles approached me in a confidential manner, and lowering his voice to a whisper said, "I swear I didn't drink enough to hurt a flea, but I'm sure seeing things! Since it is now nighttime, I went upstairs and out on the veranda thinking it might be cooler, but—I'm in no shape to be about! Guess I'll turn in and sleep it off."

He was quickly gone as I turned in alarm and saw his rapidly receding figure climbing the stairs. He did not seem intoxicated. His step was steady, but emotionally he was a wreck.

As I reached the entrance hall, he was still mounting the stairway to the sleep-rooms. Once I was minded to call and reassure him, but upon second thought decided to discover the cause for his consternation myself. I heard his bedroom door close; then I hurried to the front door and rushed out upon the porch.

I have said elsewhere in this narrative that the sight of the mammoth sun was the most awful, barring one, that I had ever beheld. This is the "barring one." The night was bright as day, not the dazzling splendor of brilliant sunlight, but the clear cold light as of a thousand moons, and that seemed to be literally what I beheld as I raised my eyes skyward.

Like one demented, I ran out into the open, regardless of the water that had receded to ankle depth, and gazed aloft with bulging eyes. The welkin was a crowded galaxy of heavenly bodies of vastly varying sizes and degrees of brilliancy. All the starry and planetary universe had marched up to us during the cataclysmic events of the last twenty-four hours, or so at least it seemed!

"Nevertheless it is what I vaguely suspected," I muttered to myself. "No wonder we weigh less with the counter-gravitational pull of the stars and planets!"

Few of the stars twinkled. They shone with the steady dazzling splendor of suns, and many heretofore unseen planets encircling them were visible with the naked eye. The moon was not visible, but Venus, an enormous silvery disc, four times the diameter of the old full moon, occupied her part of the western sky, and through her streaked cloudy veiling, I caught fleeting glimpses of mountain peaks that would dwarf into insignificance the Himalayas or the Alps.

Shooting stars and meteors were more frequent than I had ever known them to be heretofore. In the few moments that I stood dumb with amazement, a dozen or more fell within my immediate range of vision.

By this time I heard the voices of the Gilroy guests from the porch, and judging from the vociferous exclamations, they too were cognizant of the proximity of the stars and planets. I returned to the house only to be bombarded with questions regarding my opinion of the present state of the universe.

I had a theory, but so daring was it in its scope that I did not venture to voice it at this time.

"Let's get the radio and television into working order," I suggested. "We must learn something of the extent that this calamity has visited the earth."

With the very able assistance of Miles, who was finally fully convinced that he was not "seeing things" that were not an actuality, we succeeded in getting the radio into working order. There seemed to be nothing on the air but distress signals, but eventually through the staccato of one very remote but persistent call, we recognized the familiar voice of Professor Aldrich, whose reputation as an astronomer was without parallel in the country.

"—and so somewhere in that greater cosmos in which we are but an atom, has been experienced merely the transition of a substance from the gaseous, through the liquid to the solid state, but to us, the atom, it has been a phenomenon of such stupendous proportions that it is difficult for us to grasp the significance of it with our finite minds.

"Why has it never happened before? Simply because Time like Space, is purely relative, and a million years in the microcosmos may well be a second in the vaster universe, the macrocosmos, of which it forms so minute a part.

"And now we must turn our minds from the theoretical to the practical, for our time grows short. The proximity of the sun will make it impossible for humanity at present to inhabit any but the polar regions of Earth, and because we are already living in the northern hemisphere, I suggest that we at once move our entire population and all available food stuffs northward by airplanes. There have been appointed throughout the nation many local headquarters for the arrangement of details pertaining to the great flight, for these details apply to your local station."

There followed a list of service stations and other directions followed by the deep, well-modulated tones of the national broadcaster:

"Friends, Professor Harley, the nationally known chemist, will speak to you now for a few minutes."

Vivian's father! I approached the radio in order not to miss a single word, when suddenly, with a crackling and sputtering, the instrument went dead. There followed an hour of frantic endeavor to get it to function again, but it was all to no purpose. The requisite material for the repair work was not available.

Even if only secondhand information, Professor Harley's talk would have given me at least a remote idea of Vivian's experiences during the cataclysm; but I consoled myself with the happy prospect of being reunited with her at the north pole.

V.

On the beginning of the third day, after radio communication had ceased (as far as we were concerned), we were on comparatively dry ground. The food supply was low and we realized the immediate necessity of reaching the nearest airplane base, which was located at Chicago. The three small planes, that had brought the funeral guests to the Gilroy estate, sufficed to take them away together with the meager supply of provisions available, and shortly after noon my plane landed west of Chicago.

The reader may be able to form a vague conception of the united drawing force of the combined stars and planets that had marched toward us during those tragic days. We learned at Chicago that coasts all over the world had been alternately inundated and left high and dry by the waters which were subject to the pull of the heavenly bodies.

Four gigantic airships, each capable of carrying a thousand passengers (though for ordinary usage their capacity was limited to six hundred), were being rapidly filled under a great white canopy that had been erected for the purpose of cutting off some of the intolerable rays of the sun. Miles, Donna, Cousin Marian Gilroy and I ran up to the gangplank of the *Calvin Coolidge* just too late. A guard announced briskly that a thousand souls were already aboard the great round-the-world flyer, but that if we hurried we might board another. We raced to the nearest one several blocks away, and discovered it to be the ill-fated *Icarus* that, like its ancient namesake, fell into the sea with crippled wings, though this one, contrary to its namesake, had been salvaged from the deep, though with loss of life. It had on the whole suffered little from this mishap, and was now once more ready for service. Evidently the reputation of the *Icarus* was against it though, for it was not filling as rapidly as might be expected.

"Let's try to get aboard yonder ship," exclaimed Cousin Marian, pointing to where a beautiful ship, the color of summer skies, seemed to crouch ready for flight.

"It is the *Azuria*," said Miles, "the last word in speedy, luxuriant air travel."

But even as we turned our back to the *Icarus,* the humming of the *Azuria's* engines came to our ears. Then slowly and majestically she rose, her three decks a black swarm of humanity, and soon, too soon, her blue hulk was invisible against the azure of the sky.

"What is the name of the other ship?" I asked the officer at the gangplank of the *Icarus.*

"The *Celestia*," he replied, "but do not fear to board the *Icarus.* Since its overhauling, there is no safer airship."

We had no choice now but to cast our lot with the *Icarus.* I mopped my perspiring brow and leaned against the rail watching the workmen removing the canvas that protected the *Icarus* from the sun. I heard a voice at my elbow. It was Donna.

"The *Celestia* is coming this way. They are going to bring it alongside the *Icarus* before embarking."

Miles and Marian had joined us. They were watching for others of the recent group that had been at the Gilroy home, but I was ever searching for a possible glimpse of Vivian Harley, though I did not know whether she had left from Chicago or the Philadelphia base, being located very nearly midway between the two.

The *Celestia* approached as closely as the spread of its wings and ours permitted and a man on board called through a megaphone:

"The *Celestia* is carrying 1,137 people. Have you room for the surplus?"

The captain of the *Icarus* replied that we had, and would be glad to take 150 to 200 of the *Celestia*'s passengers. We waited, but there was no sign that such a transference would be made. The people aboard the *Celestia* were fearful of the reputation of the ill-named *Icarus*.

"Look," cried Donna excitedly, "there are Max and Ethel Sabin and Cousin James and Uncle Mark on the top deck of the *Celestia*!"

In vain did Donna, Miles, Marian and I try to persuade our late companions to join us in our airship. They remained obdurate to all our entreaties.

At last the gangplank was withdrawn and the *Celestia* winged her way skyward. The last we saw of her was a faint blur low on the northern horizon.

And last but not least, the *Icarus*, with 783 souls aboard, left the sun-dried earth far, far below and sought the relief of the cool, high altitudes.

Through the long hours of the night, while Mars and Jupiter looked as if they would fall from the sky and obliterate us, we sped toward Polaris, occasionally seeing on the 2,000 foot level below us great freight-flyers winging their way north and south like moving trucks of olden times, taking the paraphernalia of civilization to a new abode.

But we found ourselves in a dreadful predicament. The northernmost lands were submerged too far south for humanity to live with any degree of comfort. The north polar region was nothing but water, dotted with a few rapidly diminishing icebergs. And this was to be our home, the abode of man who had at one time conquered the earth! What had become of the conquest of which he once so proudly boasted?

VI.

Is it possible for you of the new era to form any conception of the first year spent in our polar abode? It was, of course, a period of reconstruction. Man built for himself vast floating cities, lived upon fish and synthetic foods and enjoyed a salubrious climate.

In vain did I search the floating islands of our northern world for my promised wife, Vivian Harley. Terror gripped my heart. Could she have been numbered among the victims of the *Celestia*? That great air liner, due no doubt to the fact that she had been greatly overloaded, had fallen into the Arctic Ocean where the northern coast of Greenland used to be. Not a trace of her has ever been found. Her fate should prove a constant reminder of the failure of fear and superstition against the triumph of reason.

But as soon as the luxury of radio communication could be indulged in, we of Polaria, as we named our combined north civilization, received a communication that was quite startling. The long summer days in which the sun never set during the early months of our sojourn in Polaria caused us to be a little neglectful of punctual hours for rising and retiring, though I doubt if we were any more deplorably negligent in this particular than were the Americans of the twentieth century, living where day and night were clearly defined. But one night, when the huge sun glowed on the eastern horizon, we Polarians who happened to be up and listening at that hour and tuned by chance to an exceptionally short wave length, heard the following message:

"This is Professor Richard Harley speaking over station OGICU. No, friends, I am not floating around the north pole just because it happened to be a few hundred miles nearer at the time of our catastrophe. I am living in a veritable Eden on terra firma, and this Eden is at the south pole! My opinion of folks who contrive, by years of unnecessary work, to save themselves a few hundred miles trip in a palatial air liner, would not sound well expressed publicly. The new garden of Eden is a paradise. No, I am not trying to sell real estate. There are comparatively few of us here, but we don't want all of you to come. Possibly by this time you have worked out a feasible program for making the north polar regions comfortably habitable, and I suggest that most of you stay where you are, but there is room for 200,000 more down here in Eden. When you get your television sets functioning and can get a glimpse of this Utopia, I'll warrant that the north polar region will be a deserted place.

"This is Richard Harley of station OGICU signing off till tomorrow at this time."

There was no mention of Vivian, of course, but she must be safe or her father would not have spoken in so light a vein. I wanted to leave immediately for the south pole, but Professor Aldrich would not hear of it.

"The beginning of the six months polar night is not far off," he explained in voicing his objection to my going, "and we astronomers must be ready to observe and record the new and amazing phenomena that the enlarged stars and planets will present to us."

The long night arrived, but it did not seem like night to us, for the moon, which is full and visible from the pole during the first part of the polar night, shed its cold, white, reflected light upon us. It occupied so large a portion of the sky that astronomical observations were limited exclusively to it. Many fascinating discoveries were made about our satellite, but as this story is not especially concerned with lunar problems, I shall pass on to the mid-winter observations, when Mars and Venus came within the scope of our vision.

I shall never forget the time that Professor Aldrich and I first studied Venus from our new vantage. Like a great silvery Chinese lantern, she seemed but a few rods away. Her light was far brighter than that shed by the moon in the olden days. Our telescope revealed evidences of a civilization that had been blighted by the universal catastrophe. There had been a civilization, but now there was no life. We searched the polar regions with the telescopic eye, thinking the Venerians would have done as we did, but all over the planet there was evident only a scorched devastation.

"Wait until we see Mars," said the professor encouragingly, "this cataclysm has surely improved the conditions of the Martians."

"I don't agree with you," I objected. "Whatever their previous condition, they were used to it. We cannot judge them by our standards. They are hotter than they were, and it stands to reason they are discomfited to as great an extent as we are."

"Possibly there is some truth in what you say," admitted the astronomer, "but I am inclined to believe this cosmic calamity will cause life to be more active on the red planet. But time will tell, and that time is not far off."

In the meanwhile television and radio had established regular communication between the north and the south, and it had been my great joy to see and speak with Vivian several times. I planned to leave for Eden as soon as the long night began in the Antarctic regions, for there were stars I wished to study in the skies above Eden. Flights between the poles even now were not infrequent, for many in Polaria were weary of water reflecting great balls of light, and longed for land

and daylight. And some in Eden, lured by the description of night in Polaria, flew northward.

VII.

Miles Tracy had become an astronomy enthusiast and was with me virtually all the time in the great Polaria observatory. He seemed never to weary of gazing at the planets. For weeks we had Mars under closest observation, but could detect no signs of life. This planet did not even present the possibility of life having ever existed previous to the change in the molecular structure of our universe from the gaseous to the solid state. The planet's surface presented only a conglomerate mass of crystalline reddish rock. On some parts of this strange world's surface, the sun's rays reflected ruby scintillations, in others great cracks and crevices suggested abysmal depths.

"Mars is deader than a doornail," remarked Miles upon one occasion as we studied alternately the physiography of the huge world that hovered so near us in space. "He is less interesting than Venus because he does not even grant us the privilege of studying a past civilization."

Professor Aldrich had entered the observatory in time to overhear Miles's remark, and he surprised us with these words:

"Do not be too sure that Mars is a dead world. Life may not always be vested with the attributes with which our existence clothes it. What is life anyway?" he asked, turning abruptly to Miles.

"Why—er—er—let me see. Life—er—shows action, it's energy," stammered Miles.

"Exactly as I thought," snapped Aldrich, "you do not know. What do you say it is, Hildreth?"

"Life is the sum total of our forces that resist death," I replied, vaguely recalling something learned in college.

The professor looked at me pityingly. "Not bad as far as it goes, but have you two ever really associated life with radiant energy?"

"Radiant energy and vital energy are two distinct processes," I said. "Life manifests the latter. The sun, a source of radiant energy, is not alive as we understand life, although it is active." I turned to Miles, who appeared rather nonplussed by our remarks.

"I believe, friends," said Professor Aldrich impressively, "that the primary function of the universe is *radiant energy.* Primeval matter must go on transforming itself into inert ash. This so-called inert ash, like the planet upon which we live, constitutes a very small portion of the universe. How great in size and number are the stars throughout space that are undergoing this transformation due to radiant energy? How small the inert matter upon which life, as we know it, can exist! Yet we lay such great stress upon vital energy, or life, which in every respect, in space, time and physical conditions, is limited to an inconceivably small corner of the universe. Primeval matter that is in the process of radioactivity is *really* life as the Creator meant it; this so-called life (vital energy) that exists in inert substance is merely a disease of old material after its radiant energy is spent. It is a sort of fungus that infests matter in its old age."

Miles and I were speechless. Was Professor Aldrich going mad that he could speak of life, which included man's soul and mind, in such derogatory terms? Had a "fungus growth" caused the evolution of an amoeba into a man? Had a "disease of old age" built up a civilization from primitive caveman communities to the vast cities of the twenty-first century?

The professor smiled at our horror. "I suppose you two and millions like you have always thought the sun was expending its radiant energy for the sole purpose of maintaining puny 'life' upon Earth and the other planets. But, my dear boys, many of the planets are not inhabited. Is the sun expending its energy in vain? Not a bit of it! It matters not whether the fungus grows. It may hang on where it can. It is secondary matter compared to radiant energy, the real universal life!"

We were glad when the professor's footsteps became inaudible as he left the observatory.

"Crazy as a loon," was Miles' comment. "I suppose the excitement of the past months has been too much for a man of his years."

VIII.

"Many a planet by many a sun
May roll with the dust of a vanished race,
Swallowed in Fastness, lost in Silence,
Drowned in the deeps of a meaningless Past."
    —Tennyson

Mars, dead, inert, beset by old age, and without even the "fungus growth" of Earth! Was it better off than Earth? Which planet consummated the Creator's plan?

Such were the puzzling and depressing thoughts that came to me some time later, when I sought the telescope alone, and ruefully viewed the planet that my imaginative mind had always depicted as teeming with intelligent, active, progressive life, exemplifying a civilization older and therefore farther advanced than ours. I had expected the eyepiece to reveal a prophetic vision of Earth many aeons in the future.

It did not take long for both Miles and myself to lose all interest in Mars, but not so Professor Aldrich. Hour after hour he sat gazing at the lifeless world. We soon learned to let him alone and avoid his cheerless discourse on "radiant energy" and "inert ash."

The comparatively few remaining inhabitants of Earth, with but few exceptions, took up their abodes alternately at the poles, when it was night for six months. Either polar circle was delightfully balmy, the temperature ideal during the night that had been unbearable in days of yore.

The mammoth sun had been visible on the horizon for a week, when one time, upon waking, I heard the sound of excited voices and rushed out of my tent, which was located near the edge of Aldrich Isle (the name given to the artificial, man-made floating island upon which a thousand of us lived). The *Azuria,* which had brought a number of people from Eden, was ready to return to the Antarctic, and her captain had decided to leave at once. It necessitated speed on our part, for Professor Aldrich was very anxious to begin a study of the southern heavens and did not want to wait another week for the arrival of another flyer.

Miles and Donna decided to join us, but Mrs. Gilroy enjoyed the presence of a number of congenial friends, with whom she preferred to remain and try out an Arctic summer.

A few hours later the flying palace, *Azuria,* had left the island-rafts of Polaria, headed due south, and six hours later the seared and lifeless plains of North America lay in panorama below her. Hour after hour I leaned on the rail of the lower deck and watched the great continent slip by beneath me as our flying machine sped along at the rate of 400 miles an hour. The thread of the nearly extinct Mississippi River showed faintly as we approached the Gulf of Mexico.

Over twelve hours after leaving Polaria we crossed the equator and for the next few hours the South American Andes marked our route toward the south.

It was during the hours of early morning, as we flew over the ruins of La Paz in Bolivia, that all who chanced to be watching the vanishing landscape turned questioning faces to one another and asked unanimously the same questions.

"Do you see the streak of living vegetation?" and "What is the cause of it when on either side lies sterility?"

Why the path of life through a world of death?

The sight was amazing and held everybody at the ship's rails spellbound. A straight path of green, ten or twelve miles in width, like a swath cut by some gigantic scythe, stretched from La Paz to Valparaiso. Every eye was fixed upon the miraculous sight and many explanations were ventured.

"Underground water that hasn't evaporated like the surface water," suggested one.

"Cool polar air currents," said another, and someone laughed.

"I saw something move among the greenery," exclaimed a girl, "but I couldn't tell whether it was a human being or an animal."

"Imagination," was someone's verdict, and the question of human or animal life was dropped.

In slightly over twenty-four hours after the *Azuria* had left Polaria, it came to rest in the semi-twilight in the land of Eden. We acknowledged from our first glimpse that the continent of the south had been aptly named. It was such a paradise as man has long dreamed of. There have been grander, more rugged scenes, but for sheer beauty, this Eden could scarcely have been surpassed by the original.

In the garden that surrounded the Harley home, Vivian was waiting for me, a rather pale and troubled Vivian, whom the events of the past months had impressed with awe and bewilderment.

Not long after our reunion, an early date was set for our wedding, but we were soon to realize the truth of Burns's words concerning "the best laid plans of mice and men."

IX.

Reports from mail and passenger planes verified the observations of the *Azuria* in regard to the fertile strip of land in South America, though, according to the latest news, the streak had shifted slightly westward. And now not even the brainiest individuals could venture an explanation concerning the puzzling green path extended from Georgetown to Buenos Aires.

One time I walked into the observatory for the purpose of making some private observation. I felt it was high time that Professor Aldrich relinquished the telescope to someone else. However, I did not wish to incur the enmity of the taciturn professor, for whom I felt an emotion akin to pity. I really feared that his constant dwelling upon the enigma of the uninhabited Mars was affecting his mind, so I approached him as tactfully as I could.

"Any signs of life on Mars, Professor?" I asked cheerfully, as I entered.

There was no answer and I felt indignation rising within me. I opened my mouth to voice my resentment, when he said abruptly:

"By 'sign of life,' I suppose, you mean movement, and to that I can assuredly answer in the negative, but life, intelligence or whatever you may choose to call it (the appellation is immaterial) may be evidenced in other ways, and I say to you now, as I shall soon state to the peoples of the two poles, that there *are* evidences of intelligence on Mars. Oh, I know what your reaction to my assertion will be," as I began to reply, "but I repeat, movement is not essential to intelligence throughout the Universe."

"Nevertheless," I said firmly, "there is no evidence of anything ever having been done by intelligent beings on that planet. It is nothing but a huge pile of reddish rock of a crystalline nature; nothing but 'inert ash!'"

I uttered the last two words somewhat sarcastically, and an amused smile played about the professor's thin lips.

"The term 'inert ash' is hardly applicable to our neighbor, Mars," he replied, "as you and the rest of the world will soon discover."

He left the observatory and I took my place at the eyepiece, which was directed, as I knew it would be, toward the red planet. There it hung in space, a mountainous mass of red rock crystal, traversed by straight chasms and fissures, no doubt its "canals." Desolation, silence, and a more monotonous landscape than that on the moon!

"If Mars isn't a dead world, one can expect life in a corpse," I muttered. "That's the deadest-looking scene I ever gazed upon!"

A few more minutes was all I could tolerate before shifting to a more interesting heavenly body. What fascination did Mars hold for Professor Aldrich week in, week out, for months at a time?

"Darn his silence," I blurted out, and then realized that the professor had returned and had evidently been observing me for some time.

"Locate Mars again," he said tersely.

I obeyed, for there was that in his expression that indicated he would not brook opposition.

"There is something the matter with the timing-gear," I said. "I cannot keep Mars in the center of observation without moving the telescope by hand. What's wrong?"

"Are you sure?" he snapped at me.

"Most assuredly. Let's get at it."

"We can do nothing now," he replied more quietly. "I have just heard by the latest radio news that seismologists have detected extensive earth tremors, presumably in the equatorial region of Earth. 'There is no great loss without some small gain,' so we can be pleased that there are no human beings on that portion of the globe to suffer from the quakes. Also, since the earthquakes, the green streak in South America is vanishing."

"That is small consolation," I made reply. "Our situation is lamentable, though we have made the best of it."

Professor Aldrich drew out his watch and, upon perceiving the time, crossed to the radio, with which the observatory was equipped, not only with receiving, but also with broadcasting apparatus.

"I am scheduled to speak in a half hour—will you—"

There came a crackling, splitting sound, followed by a roar. We reeled like drunken men, lost our footing completely, and slid together with all the loose paraphernalia to one side of the room. Well shaken up, but uninjured, we emerged not a moment too soon. With a thunder like the crack of doom, the great telescope, literally ripped from its foundation, fell where a few seconds before we had crouched helplessly. A second, splintering, cracking noise and the last I remember was the two of us catapulting through the broken floor into the story below.

X.

"Oh, father, he is regaining consciousness."

These were the first words to greet my ears after a blank period of insensibility. I opened my eyes to behold Vivian bending over me, her eyes alight with loving concern. I was comfortably tucked in a bed in the Harley home.

"Professor Aldrich?" I asked weakly.

As if in answer to my question, the professor's voice sounded loud and tense from the opposite side of the room. "This is Professor Aldrich speaking from station OGICU."

And while I listened to the voice of the companion of my misfortune, who had miraculously escaped with no injuries, Vivian and a nurse administered to my needs. As I ate my broth, I and the rest of a listening world heard the following from the lips of the greatest living astronomer :

"I have been severely criticized for maintaining too strict a silence; but it was my opinion that such criticism was less objectionable than the open derision that would have been mine had I ventured to voice my conjectures in the beginning. Your ridicule would have interfered with my observations and delayed the solution of the enigma, which solution I am about to give you now.

"First of all, know that Mars is a living world; vital, selfish, malignant! He is not vital in the sense that Earth is—(Earth, a huge ball of inert ash covered with human fungi). He is intelligent as a *whole,* as an *entity.* He is so old that if he ever possessed organisms creeping about his once inanimate core, they have undergone a transmutation from vital to radiant energy and are an integral part of his superb unity. Can you not, my friends, imagine evolution on a vast scale having proceeded so far that human activity as we know it will have ceased? Orderliness out of chaos (which is the goal of our activities now as expressed in our organization processes) attained even to the orderly and systematic arrangement of the atoms in his vast molecular structure! He has reached that perfect balance between cause and effect, toward which all struggle is directed. He is an example of a perfect state of equilibrium, or possibly

I should have used the past tense and said 'was,' for Mars, once sufficient unto himself, has been greatly discommoded by the recent alteration in the arrangement of the Universe. His adaptation to his environment previous to the cataclysm was perfect, but he has been thrown off his poise, so to speak, and has found it necessary to rehabituate himself.

"His first attempt to regain his former composure was by the expulsion of a protective ray against the rays of the sun. This ray nullified to a correct degree the intensified heat from our luminary. I discovered the existence of this ray whenever Earth lay between Mars and the sun. As its electrons swept past the surface of our globe they counteracted the solar rays affecting the earth, in just the same manner as they did for Mars, and in the wake of the ray, Earth blossomed as of yore. This was the path of verdure you beheld in South America.

"This Martian protective ray, while seemingly effective, has apparently not been wholly satisfactory to Mars. It may have required too much continued effort on his part. We cannot know. At any rate, Mars, the planet entity, has hit upon another solution to his difficulty, and briefly it is this."

I had finished my broth and was resting quietly with Vivian's hand in mine. Her father paced the floor with nervous strides, stopped presently and came over to the foot of my bed. He smiled from one to the other of us and then said:

"I am about to succeed Professor Aldrich at the microphone, so I'll be going now. You'll hear me presently."

"—these earthquakes," continued Professor Aldrich's voice from the radio loudspeaker, "are caused by a retardation in speed of Earth in its orbit around the sun. This slowing-up process has taken place gradually, but not so slowly that it failed to cause severe shocks to the world. This diminution in the speed of our planet around the sun is not directly due to the recent rearrangement of the Universe, but is caused by a force exerted upon the Earth by Mars. Earth is held in an intangible but powerful grip by the malignant planet, held as a shield between him and the flaming sun. We are now traveling in an orbit that keeps us serving in the capacity of a huge sunshade to the planet Mars, and it would seem that Mars is happy to have us render this service. It is evidently less of an effort to hold us thus than to continue the emission of the protective ray, for Mars travels in his orbit at approximately fifteen miles per second; Earth, eighteen miles per second, a rather small difference.

"What can we do in our present quandary? Absolutely nothing. It is seldom that man has faced a problem impossible of solution, but the scattered efforts of mankind cannot vie with a unit-intelligence such as belongs to Mars.

"And now, radio listeners, I will turn over the microphone to Professor Harley, who will throw more light from another angle upon this baffling mystery."

XI.

"Father's conception is mine," whispered Vivian, "and I think before he is finished, it will be yours."

I pressed her fingers with what newly acquired strength I possessed, and presently Professor Harley's voice came to us over the radio.

"Friends of the radio audience of Eden and Polaria. Professor Aldrich has explained to you the mystery of Mars. I will try to make clear to you the puzzling features of the cataclysmic events of the past year and a half. The idea is not original with me, for Professor Aldrich himself voiced this sentiment prior to our worldly catastrophe. The theory that our universe is an atom in a vast material substance is too generally accepted to require reiteration here. But as to the nature of that 'vast material substance,' no man except one has heretofore raised the slightest inquiry, it having been naturally supposed that such knowledge was beyond the ken of mere humanity. However, I believe there is no limit to the growth of man's knowledge, provided he obeys Nature's laws in attaining information. By comparisons of observations of the telescope and the microscope, we discover many startling analogies. The Universe, we find, approaches in constitution a gaseous substance rather than a liquid or a solid. The distance between our sun and the nearest fixed star is about 10^{18} cm, and this, when reduced in the same ratio, becomes 10^{-4} which is approximately the mean free path of a molecule in a somewhat attenuated gas. On the other hand, if we magnify the tiny world of the atom by the factor 10^{22}, leaving all the velocities unchanged, we should then cause an oxygen atom, or any similar atom, to become of the same size as the solar system, and its planetary electrons would closely resemble Neptune and Uranus both as regards size, distance from the center and period of rotation.

"Now in the face of this startling similarity, we ask, 'What happened to the molecule of gas in that unthinkably vast Cosmos in which we play so infinitesimal a part?'

"Simply this, friends, the gas became condensed to a liquid, passed completely through the fluid states into that of solidity. Steam to water, water to ice. That is the general explanation, though I doubt if the molecular constituency is our familiar H_2O.

"When the Universe was in the gaseous state, we had nothing to fear from Mars, but since the transition into solidity, he is uncomfortably close.

"'But,' I hear you ask, 'what additional harm can he do us by using our world as a shield between himself and the sun? The big catastrophe was not of his doing. The retardation in our orbital speed is a minor concern to Earth at present.'

"But is it? Do you relish being carried about in the clutches of a malign entity, subject to his cruel whimsicalities? Do you like being the particular helpless tool that will further his every diabolical design?

"Professor Aldrich has given me permission to announce to an unsuspecting world some of his most recent discoveries concerning Mars. Jupiter, who looks slightly larger than our moon appeared to us prior to the catastrophe, is undergoing a subtle change. The first thing Professor Aldrich noticed was the rapid growth of the large red area on the surface of Jupiter. This reddish band has always puzzled astronomers, and they have never known its exact nature, but since its recent rapid growth, it shows every evidence of being identical in nature with the substance of the planet Mars. All present indications are that before very long Jupiter will be a gigantic reproduction of Mars.

"Now the question is, 'Is this a form of colonization being practiced by Mars, or is it a change that Jupiter is undergoing as a whole?' At any rate, it can be considered as a form of conquest, for surely a planet is being conquered by another when it is being made over into that other's likeness. What capers will we be expected to cut, may I ask, if Jupiter chooses eventually to shift us about as he wills, and we become the bone of contention between two mighty worlds?"

XII.

It seemed to require an undue length of time for me to recover from the injuries sustained at the time of the earthquake, and the long

Antarctic day was far advanced before my marriage to Vivian took place. We planned to spend our honeymoon in Polaria, for I was receiving urgent requests by every mail from Professor Aldrich to join him at the observatory there.

One day in early February, Miles, Donna, Tracy, Vivian and I were passengers on the *Icarus,* headed for the north polar circle. As the great flyer winged its way across the ruins of the United States, we were drawn irresistibly to the rail of the low observation deck. Our altitude was so great that we could mark few details, though far ahead on the north horizon we could make out the Great Lakes district. Suddenly the ship swooped earthward, veered to one side, struggled ineffectually to right itself and continued a steady drop, though not at a falling rate. Vivian clung to my arm in terror; Donna fainted. Pandemonium reigned over the entire air-vessel. Was the *Icarus* to suffer the fate of its namesake after all?

A white-faced officer appeared on our deck just as the plane lurched violently to the other side, carrying terrified humanity with it.

"We are not falling," were his first somewhat reassuring words, "we're being pulled down by some force we can't throw off. The pilot says he can't change her course an iota. The engines are working to their utmost capacity, but they can't keep her in the air fifteen minutes!"

Something *must* be done. Several mechanics among the passengers offered their assistance, but soon all realized that it was beyond the reach of human skill to control the airship as formerly. She continued a steady slanting course earthward.

"I didn't know the Great Lakes were surrounded by reddish sand," exclaimed Vivian. "I don't remember having ever noticed any sand in that region before."

I strained my eyes for a minute scrutiny of the approaching landscape, and checked an exclamation of horror. Below us lay an area of crystalline rock exactly like what I had seen countless times through the big telescopes when I looked at Mars, and later at Jupiter!

"Vivian, Miles, Donna, wait right here!" I cried in tones husky with the terror I could no longer conceal.

There were but a few minutes left to us and I knew that time was our most precious possession. I rushed to the radio room, and to my amazement found the operator gathering his things together for flight.

"Have you sent out an S. O. S.?" I thundered at him.

"Yes," he replied.

"Did you follow up with details by radio?" I persisted.

"No. What good would it do? By the time—"

I did not wait to hear him through, but took my place at the instrument.

"This is Hildreth, on board the airship *Icarus*. We are being pulled slowly to earth into a Martian colony, latitude 45°, longitude 87°. Send help at once."

When I appeared again on deck, I must have had the appearance of a maniac, for they all backed away from me and shook their heads at one another.

"Jump," I cried, "everybody jump! Your parachutes will save you if you leap now. It is the *Menace of Mars!*"

"But, Hildreth, the ship is not actually falling," said the officer who had warned us in the first place. "We'll make a comfortable landing if a few more passengers don't go crazy and lose their heads."

There was no time to argue. I turned to Vivian. "You understand, don't you, dear?"

For answer she ran to the rail and leaped nimbly over the side. I followed her with anxious eyes. Her parachute was bearing her gently below.

"I'm with you, Hildreth," cried Miles. "Come on, Donna."

"Not on your life," screamed his irate wife. "I'll not follow the dictates of a crazy man!"

"Crazy or not crazy, over you go!" I exclaimed, and raising her bodily, flung her free of the ship's edge.

Miles and I followed immediately, for there wasn't a moment to spare. Already the ruddy gleam of the Martian crystals covered the north horizon like an undulating sea of blood, and ever closer to the crimson line approached the fated *Icarus*.

Our parachutes brought us down on the sunbaked earth, where a scene of desolation greeted our eyes. Heretofore our vantage point had always been aerial, but here we were in the midst of a scene that might have been taken from Dante's *Inferno*, with nothing but the clothes on our backs, and we could easily have dispensed with them, so terrifically hot was it on this barren desert. But with little thought at the present as to our own difficulties, we turned fascinated eyes to the descending airship. By this time it must be over the edge of the red border. Suddenly a lone figure separated itself from the great plane and fell like a drop of water from a bucket; then another and another. The first to fall was running our way with superhuman speed, and as he approached we saw that it was the officer who had warned us. His face was livid with terror and he was inarticulate. And now we observed that as the others leaped and landed, they did not rise as he had done, but remained, transformed into red rock, retaining the postures they had unconsciously assumed upon landing on the mysterious substance beneath.

Rooted to the spot in abject horror, we saw the *Icarus* land, and then where it had been but a moment before, an air-navigator of inestimable beauty and utility, it lay a conglomerate mass of— Martian consciousness.

At the sight, Waite, the officer, found his voice:

"Run south as fast as you can, all of you! It is spreading in every direction but north."

His words were true. In two minutes we noticed that the blood-red metamorphosis was coming our way, and as it crept along, all the sunbaked ruins at its edge became transformed into its own likeness. The Martian curse was going to take the world and every living creature on it!

Five beings fled southward in a panic lest the Martian menace overtake them. Tired and footsore, we still sped on, for when we stopped to rest the distance between us and our pursuer grew less. We dared not rest!

"Did you notice its northern boundary was the lake?" asked Officer Waite. "I think water puts at least a temporary end to its advance. Surely we'll come to a river and—"

I shook my head dubiously. "The rivers have dried up long ago."

It was getting dark, but even with the abating of the terrific heat of the sun, we had about reached the limit of endurance. We staggered on in drunken fashion, ready to succumb to the fate that seemed inevitable.

"Do you—suppose the red death is—worse than—this headlong flight—when we're nearly dead?" gasped Vivian.

"I don't know," replied Miles, "but I don't propose to merge my consciousness with that of Mars. I don't think it's death we'd suffer, but a sort of annexation to the awful entity that seems to reach out after the whole solar system."

"It's been coming faster since the sun set," declared Donna. "The sun seemed to retard its activities."

Donna had spoken truly. Run as fast as we could, we seemed able to keep only an even distance between us and the onrushing tide of horror.

"This can't keep on indefinitely," cried Waite. "I'm through. Wish I'd stayed with the ship. When I'm part of what's after us, I suppose I'll do my infinitesimal bit to catch you folks, but—I'm not going any farther."

Remonstrance was useless. The four of us dragged onward. We knew we would go on until sheer exhaustion ended our flight.

At this juncture I recognized a change in the landscape ahead of us. A rocky ridge lay across our path, and as we approached, we saw that it was the bank of a river, and to our amazement there was water, though many feet below its normal level.

"We'll try this," I said with decision. "It may be our end, but if we press on we can't last many hours longer."

"Unless an airship comes to our aid in response to the S.O.S.," said Donna.

I shook my head. "That is too big a chance to take. Into the river, all of you!"

We found, to our satisfaction, that the water was in no place above our heads and in most places scarcely knee-deep. It was apparent that soon no river water would remain as such in the temperate and tropic zones, but the deepest, widest rivers had not yet vanished entirely.

It was a brave stand, and we stood defiantly with faces toward the north—waiting.

Then out of the night a crimson band, stretching from east to west, grew wider as we watched, and the starlight reflected from its many shining apexes gleamed like a myriad of baneful eyes in the nocturnal gloom.

Presently a dark object leaped from the bank and stood for a second, a black mysterious silhouette against the oncoming crystalline tide.

"Waite!" I shouted.

"Not on your life! I won't wait for anybody."

In another second our companion, whom we had given up for lost, joined us in the river.

"It won't be long now," he said, as he sank to a sitting posture in the warm water of the river. "I could scarcely keep ahead of it."

And with Waite's last word, the Menace was at the river's edge. With ineffable relief we saw that the water laved the strange substance and receded unharmed by the contact. So here at least was temporary respite!

In a few minutes, sitting propped back to back, we were asleep in the middle of the river.

XIII.

Who was the first to waken in the morning I do not know. It seemed we simultaneously became conscious of the growing heat of the fierce sun that blazed like a vast conflagration in the east. Hungry we were, but not thirsty. We thanked heaven for an ever available supply of drinking water. The red rocky northern embankment lay like some huge beast of the jungle, waiting for an opportune moment to spring upon its prey. The first question at issue was whether to venture southward from our watery haven after our long night's rest. Donna and Vivian were in favor of moving onward, for the very sight of the red Menace gave them the "creeps." But the men did not share their opinion. We expected hourly, yes, any moment, the appearance of a rescuing airship which would soon put many miles between ourselves and the evil entity that was gradually transforming a planet into itself.

A cry from Officer Waite caused us to turn with apprehension toward the north bank, but we soon saw our error in direction. Waite was pointing to the west, a direction in which we had least interest, for the sun flamed in the east and our rescue plane was expected from the south. Nevertheless, our lack of observation of the unexpected quarter might have been our undoing, for creeping steadily toward us from the west and on the *south* side of the river were the red crystals of Mars!

Suddenly a series of shrill whistling notes pierced the stillness about us. Again and again the staccato tones stabbed the death-like silence of the scene. Uncomprehending, we huddled together and peered futilely toward the blazing orb that nearly blinded us, and in whose heat we suffered intolerably. A moment later a familiar whirring sound apprised us of the proximity of an airliner whose presence we could not see because of the glaring brilliancy of the sun.

Waite and I looked at each other dazedly, and then slowly a look of dawning comprehension spread over Waite's features.

"Code," he whispered fiercely. "Listen!"

The whistling notes *were* code and soon, out of the previously mysterious sounds, an intelligible message came to us.

"Leave river and run southeast as fast as possible. If we approach any nearer we feel the drawing power of the red Menace, which seems to act with magnetic force upon the metal parts of our ship."

Not a moment was wasted in carrying out the orders of the rescue plane. We climbed up the south bank and fled with all possible speed in the direction indicated. And it was indeed necessary that we hurry, for the long red glittering line from the west seemed bearing down on us with incredible rapidity.

"Vivian, don't look back so much," I warned her. "It interferes with your progress."

"I feel like Lot's wife," she said with a wan smile, "and I imagine my fate might not be very different, although this modern Sodom is somewhat livelier than the one of Biblical fame."

Soon the plane, a small one of twenty-passenger capacity, seemed almost above us and we expected to see it land, but it failed to do so, and again the shrill whistle-code startled us:

"You must run faster and farther. We are on the border of the Menace's zone of attraction."

After our fatiguing experience of yesterday, it seemed that we had already reached the limits of our physical endurance, but when one is racing with death, he draws upon his reserve forces, and can sometimes accomplish the well-nigh impossible. So it was with our little group of five souls racing over the rough, barren plain into the face of a mammoth sun, its rays death-dealing in their intensity.

The plane landed and waited for us to board it and soon we were flying south, putting many miles between us and our pursuer. As we had suspected, the Martian terror had followed the north bank of the river to a point far west, where the shallow water had entirely evaporated. Here it had crossed and spread like an infectious disease toward the sea, along the south bank. Thankful though we were to be rescued, we saw no hope of saving the world at large. We took food and rest and returned to Eden to discuss with the leaders there what should be done. Professor Aldrich was at Polaria, and as a band of the living crystalline substance encircled the globe, our communication was necessarily confined to radio.

XIV.

What would have been the fate of the earth had she not been visited with another mysterious phenomenon can be imagined, for she was girdled on land by a great red belt of the Martian matter that was creeping stealthily over the landed area of the world. No human agency could have stopped it. But time soon proved that there was a Power to which even the Martian influence had to succumb.

Before we reached Eden, we were given a faint warning of what was to follow. The plane fought its way through a terrific gale and at one time had to land. The earthquakes that followed were so numerous and so violent that thousands of planes stayed aloft practically all the time to avoid the earth tremors that shook the planet to its core.

Then the deluge commenced and all planes had to descend, some with disastrous speed. As the downpour increased, the quakes subsided. Darkness covered the face of Earth, even in Eden, where it was presumably the time for the long days. There have been many varying expressions of opinion as to the length of time the surviving remnant of humanity was buffeted by the winds, shaken by the quakes and half-drowned by the floods, but the consensus of opinion is that it was about three days and four nights. And when the convulsions of nature stopped, we knew what glorious thing had taken place.

The following is part of the first radio speech broadcast by Professor Aldrich from Polaria, where he had been at the time of Nature's great readjustment.

"I now believe our Universe to be in a state of stability such as it has never enjoyed before. My observations of the relative distances between the stars convince me that it is now in the liquid state. Of course, in some chemical compounds, the liquid state is not the one most easily maintained at normal temperature, but for scientific reasons, too abstruse for me to enter into at this time, I believe the liquid state to be certainly more normal than the solid, and probably more so than the gaseous.

"Our sun, as the people of Eden can testify, is closer than of old, but from its recent escapade it has retreated with its accompanying planets half way back to its former status. We can truly say with the psalmist of old, 'The heavens declare His glory and the firmament showeth His handiwork.'

"The great upheavals, through which a few thousand of us have lived, were the act of Terra wrenching herself free from the grip of Mars, whose intangible power was forced to relax with the liquefying of the Universe. Neither I nor any other mortal living can rest assured of the stability of the Universe even now, but, from the terrestrial standpoint, the arrangement will be ideal. The habitable portions of the globe will be somewhat shifted, but certainly there will be no great inconvenience to man. The only uninhabited area will be the torrid zone. Polaria and Eden will continue to flourish, but before we can occupy the north temperate zone, the Menace must be conquered."

XV.

Miles, Officer Waite and I felt an irresistible urge to be of the investigating party sent out to see what progress Mars had made on our planet. Our request to be part of a scouting party of fifteen in a small plane was granted.

We proceeded cautiously, keeping a sharp lookout toward the north, watching for a fearful red horizon that would warn us of the danger. By late afternoon, South America was rapidly vanishing beneath us. Had the Isthmus of Panama proved sufficient protection? Was yonder red line along the gulf coast proof that the continent of North America was a Martian colony?

The *Lindbergh* was pointed slightly west of north, flying high, but cautiously. We were on the alert to detect the slightest deviation from a straight horizontal course. We did not propose to suffer the fate of the *Icarus* if it were humanly possible to prevent it. The red horizon still threatened us, but we felt no undue terrestrial pull.

Finally a laugh from Messer, one of the crew, brought an inquiry from each of us, to which he replied:

"It is nothing but the glow of sunset, proving what overactive imaginations can do!"

We laughed rather sheepishly, but were secretly satisfied that we had erred on the side of over-precaution.

With the coming of night and the corresponding drop of temperature, we decided to make a landing on the ground, inhospitable though it was, and start again in the morning, when we could better see what lay ahead and beneath us. Much of the land was under water from the recent deluge, but we succeeded in finding a location high and dry enough to accommodate us for the night. We took turns keeping a lookout for the creeping danger from the north, but throughout the night those on guard saw nothing.

Scarcely was the first streak of dawn visible in the east than we were off once more, flying as slowly as possible and keeping an even altitude of 1,500 feet.

I think every one of us saw it at the same instant, so intently were we watching for the first indication of the awful presence.

"Any downward pull?" Waite's words snapped the ominous silence.

"Not a bit," the pilot responded.

"Funny. We felt it before this with the *Icarus.*"

"Remember the *Lindbergh* has no exposed metal on her under surface," said the pilot. "We figured that would make a difference."

"That's right, but go easy," admonished Waite, whose recent harrowing experience with the red Menace made him over-cautious.

All eyes were on the red boundary, the line of demarcation between Life and Death as we thought.

"Funny, but that line is not advancing one iota," declared Miles Tracy. "I've been gauging it by certain landmarks."

"It is deliberately waiting to lure us on to destruction," was the pilot's verdict,

"Easy now! Let's land," called Waite. "We can't find out its purpose from the air."

At a distance of a half mile south of the red line, the *Lindbergh* landed, and its crew proceeded cautiously toward the seemingly frozen waves of blood.

"I call this area the Red Sea," I suggested, to relieve the awful tension of the situation.

"A frozen sea of blood!" cried Messer in an awed voice. "What if it is the life-blood of all the inhabitants of Mars from time immemorial, crystallized into an evil entity!"

No one heeded Messer's fantastic utterance. In an unwavering line we marched steadily and silently on, even as the Menace had done before, though each man knew that should the waiting Intelligence from Mars choose to advance toward us, we should have no recourse but flight. And now we were scarcely a stone's throw away. On and on, and we stood at the brink of my so-called Red Sea, and still we lived!

"It looks the same," cried Waite, "but what's the matter with it?"

As he finished speaking, he picked up a stone and threw it onto the red. And now we stood agape, for the rock was not converted by the infectious touch of the red Menace. Instead it sank within an oozy, jelly-like substance that offered no resistance to its weight. A gasp of incredulous relief burst from the lips of each member of the party as it dawned upon all that the mysterious substance was no longer a crystal, and was impotent for evil.

"I guess the floods put it out of commission," remarked Miles. "Thank God it was vulnerable!"

I stooped to examine the substance. It resembled nothing so much as red Vaseline. I hastily filled an empty matchbox with the innocuous matter, intending to give it a chemical analysis at my convenience.

XVI.

No untoward incident marked our return to Eden with the glad news that the Martian invasion was ineffectual. The next day I analyzed the small quantity of the Martian substance I had brought with me from the lakes district, and found it to be pure protoplasm, the essence of life in matter! I put it in a glass receptacle with the idea of keeping it as a souvenir and possibly of experimenting further with it, and left the laboratory.

In the dead of the night an unearthly howl reverberated through the house. I recognized it as issuing from the throat of Duffer, the German police dog belonging to Professor Harley.

"Old Duffer is equal to any occasion," I thought. "He will hold the assailant at bay until I get there."

With a reassuring word to Vivian, who had likewise wakened at Duffer's awful cry, I seized my automatic and searchlight. The perfectly apparent absence of further disturbance was less assuring than a commotion would have been. I cautiously pursued a direction whence Duffer's bark had first issued and discovered with fear and dread that I was going straight toward the laboratory. I flung open the door."

A red glassy mound was the first sight upon which my eyes fell. It was as if a sculptor had modeled Duffer from a ruby of colossal dimensions. The dog had been caught in flight and he stood facing me, a bloody statue of terrible beauty! All this I realized later, for at that time my eyes were holden to all except the dire aspects of the situation.

And now from the feet of Duffer the red crystalline substance was spreading; no longer red Vaseline, but hard crystals of igneous rock. Fan-shaped, it was emerging from the confines of its glass receptacle. Without thinking, I fired two shots into it, but merely with the result that the growth was accelerated. Then I bethought me of the temporary impotency of the horrible stuff when water was used on it.

There remained now but a narrow aisle between me and the wall, *en route* to the water faucet. With great agility, I ran and turned the tap. A growing pool at my feet kept me safe from the marauder, but I had no receptacle for water with which to dampen the ardor of the ambitious Menace!

At this moment Vivian and her father appeared in the doorway, too terrified to move, and still less to comprehend the unfamiliar situation.

"A hose," I screamed. "A hose or a tub. No, do not enter," as my father-in-law would have penetrated the barrier.

Without further hesitancy, he hastened to obey my request, and returning shortly with a few feet of hose, tossed it to me. It did not take long to reduce the crystalline protoplasm to its jelly-like state of inefficiency, and not before the area thus transformed measured approximately a square of ten feet. The red Menace, together with any portion of the laboratory that came into contact with it, was transported to the sea and dumped in. Not a trace was left in our part of the world. As for rendering ineffectual the red-landed girdle of the globe, it was necessary, we discovered by experiment, to wet its boundary line every week, if Nature through rain did not do so.

And since the recession of the sun, stars and planets, due to the liquid constituency of the Universe, North America is habitable up to within five miles of the dread line. The five-mile limit is advisable, because that represents the maximum distance that the Menace could spread in a night while an unconscious populace slept, ignorant of the encroaching peril.

Is Mars, the planet, conscious of his inability to convert Earth to his state? Many times I ponder over the peaceful effectuality of his conscious existence as he swings in space like a world. Is he better off— that is, is he more in tune with his environment than we poor strugglers of Earth? I wonder.

A Certain
Soldier

I.

I met Lee Clayton in Rome. The attraction was a mutual one, for we discovered that we had much in common; both students of history, fond of travel, and possessing an insatiable thirst for the uncovering of forgotten and apparently insignificant historical data that might throw light upon questions of dispute.

At the end of three weeks we had covered the city of the seven hills from the Flaminian to the Appian Way, reveling especially in those relics that gave us any knowledge of the dead past. Dead? Can the past ever really die? I believed, and I think my friend Clayton agreed with me, that the past lives today. It is immortal, but in its changed form it is manifest in influence and posterity. These two in a stream of continuity render the antiquity of Rome a vital fact in the twentieth century AD

One warm evening Clayton and I returned to the hotel veranda after an interesting day among the ruins of the Roman Forum. To our ears came the characteristic sounds of Italian life: a snatch of song in melodious tenor, a sharp staccato exclamation, the rumble of cab wheels over cobblestones, and the occasional bleating of goats whose milk supplied the native quarter. To our right the yellow thread of the Tiber was faintly visible.

Clayton smiled understandingly and waved a hand toward the streets below as he sank luxuriously into a comfortable chair.

"Great thing for a rest, Ebson," he remarked. "It's a change from the hurry and bustle of the average American city. I like it."

"Yes," I agreed, "and a change always means rest. Although we are both young, we've been living strenuously in a modern business world, and can't help appreciating the contrast."

We sat for some time in silence, the while I noticed Clayton's features displaying a growing pensive mood. His former joviality was disappearing. I made no attempt to encourage conversation, for I felt that it would come when the time was ripe.

"Friend Ebson," said Lee Clayton at length, dropping his listless mien and leaning toward me, "for many years the repetition of a certain dream has troubled me. The vision first appeared when I was in high school and followed me throughout my entire college career, its vividness increasing with the passing of the years. It pertains to the solution of the mystery surrounding the ambiguous expression in the Greek, Latin and Jewish scripts where the incendiary of the temple of Jerusalem is invariably referred to as 'a certain soldier.' In my constantly recurring dream I seem continually on the verge of discovering the identity of this 'certain soldier,' but always I awake just before solving the mystery. My trip upon this occasion to the Eternal City is to find out, if possible, who threw the flaming torch into the temple at Jerusalem when the legions of Titus took the city of the Jews. If it is ever possible to bring my haunting dream to a consummation, it should be here amid the relics of its original enactment."

I must have gazed at him incredulously, for he continued hastily, "In all sincerity I mean what I say, my friend. Either here or in Jerusalem I should be able to ascertain the identity of that 'certain soldier' who threw a lighted torch into a window of the sanctuary. Why, man alive, think of the responsibility of that act!"

Had the heat of a semi-tropic sun or the fatigue of daily sightseeing affected my friend's mind? I hesitated before voicing a mild rebuke, and in that moment of pause the spirit of adventure, tempered with tolerance for the incomprehensible whims of another, possessed me. My answer must have surprised him.

"There's a quest worthy of some time and effort!" I answered with more enthusiasm than I really felt. "The *Forum Romanum* has already disclosed to us a few of its secrets, and why not this one? We'll show the world yet that Tacitus and Josephus and a few others of the ancients didn't get exactly the right dope on all this."

My light mood did not affect Clayton. He continued seriously, his eyes showing a dreamy expression.

"You remember the historians, Josephus and Tacitus, were both contemporaries of Titus—and this 'certain soldier.' They had firsthand evidence and certainly ought to have been more explicit in their details. As a matter of fact," he added, "they are more evasive in their narrations of the events connected with the siege of Jerusalem, of which they must have been eyewitnesses, than they are regarding historical occurrences preceding their era."

"Yes, that is strange," I agreed. "How do you account for it?"

Clayton was about to reply when I noticed a pallor spread over his features and he leaned forward with eyes intent upon the hotel entrance. Following the direction of his gaze I saw the well-tailored back of a gentleman disappearing through the doorway. I turned with a glance of inquiry to my friend. His manner showed agitation, and I did not press him for the explanation, which I knew would be forthcoming shortly.

"That man," Clayton explained in a husky voice, "is an enemy—and possibly not without reason," he added reflectively. "Two years ago I was fortunate enough to win as my wife the girl whom we both loved. Shortly afterward the company in which we were both financially interested elected me to the presidency, a position to which each of us had aspired. Since that time my dear wife died—but the business concern in which that man and I are mutually interested is prospering. Although my two victories have been won solely by fair means, the man whom you saw disappearing within the doorway has proved a determined enemy whose obsession is to avenge his defeat in love and war."

I was a little disquieted, though I sought to cover my uneasiness with cheering words.

"Never mind, old chap. We are living in the twentieth century. No one can stoop to revenge in these days and get away with it. Now if we were living in 70 AD, for instance, you might have cause for alarm. Life was held pretty cheap at the time Titus laid siege to Jerusalem, and one had to live warily, but things are different now."

He smiled wanly. "Speaking of Titus, let's begin tomorrow to solve the mystery of the 'certain soldier.'"

"Agreed!" I replied heartily. "I'm in my element when it comes to finding an explanation for the inexplicable."

II.

Sleep seemed to have forsaken me completely that night. The full moon shining in at my window caused me to abandon all further thought of rest. I arose, dressed myself and stood gazing out across the silvery landscape. The moonlight softened objects below that in the glare of day stood out in too bold relief.

I stood for some time in a troubled and hesitant mood.

"Why not?" I exclaimed, half aloud.

Once resolved upon my course of action I sought the streets below without eliciting any surprise from the sleepy concierge at the desk. The streets were silent and deserted, the pavement echoing with the ring of my footfall until it seemed to me that all Rome must be apprised of my nocturnal sally. Soon I spied the ancient grandeur of the Colosseum as it rose tier on tier above the stone ruins and cypress trees that nestled in its shadow. I was approaching the familiar territory of the once busy mart of ancient Rome. The Arch of Constantine rose before me, sublime in its architectural beauty. Then I turned fascinated eyes down to the ruins of the Forum, which lie several feet below the level of the present city.

I know it was surprise, though not untinged with fear, that possessed me as I became aware of the presence of another figure not fifty feet ahead of me. It was that of a man, and he was agilely descending the steps to the lower level. I instantly recognized Lee Clayton and watched him with fascinated gaze. What could the man be doing alone among silent ruins in the dead of the night? Then I thought of myself and my own intentions and I nearly laughed aloud. Well, I would not spy on my friend! I quickened my pace with the intention of making my presence known, when further progress was arrested by the changed demeanor of Lee Clayton.

No longer did he walk as a man alone, but rather as one who wends his way in and out among a crowd. Occasionally he paused and gazed fixedly at some object apparently visible to him, then his head turned as though following the course of something in motion.

The effect was most uncanny, and I pinched myself to make certain I was not asleep. The somnambulist, if he were such, strode with dignity in the direction of the triumphal Arch of Titus, and there he paused. Strange words were wafted to my ears, phrases in an unknown tongue. Unknown. Had I studied Latin for six years not to recognize it when I heard it, even in this fashion? Occasionally Clayton paused, apparently to lay his hand upon the shoulder of an invisible associate. Some of the things he thought he heard were mirth-provoking, and his laughter rang out weirdly shrill in the white silence around us.

"Jumping Johosophat!" I exclaimed, wiping my perspiring brow with my handkerchief. "That's a wow of a dream all right!"

He must have heard me, for he looked in my direction and smiled as if in friendly greeting. Tremblingly I smiled back. I racked my brain for one intelligent sentence in Latin.

"'All Gaul is divided into three parts' won't do upon this occasion," I mumbled disconsolately.

The only other words that came to my muddled brain were the Latin version of "Twinkle, twinkle, little star." I tried them and was greeted with a burst of uproarious laughter from Clayton, the incongruity of which at this time caused me to tremble with fear. He said something about *vinum nimium,* and then turned his attention to the Arch of Titus, talking off and on the while as if engaged in conversation with many around him.

For an hour the apparent monologue continued while I stood spellbound. Finally he turned abruptly and proceeded in the direction of the Colosseum. He strode so rapidly that I had difficulty in keeping a desirable distance behind him. I intended to see that he returned without harm to his rooms at the hotel.

At the foot of the flight of steps leading to the level of present-day Rome, Clayton paused and passed a hand across his brow. He gazed about him in apparent bewilderment and proceeded thereafter with the air of a man in solitude.

Thinking that possibly the knowledge of a witness might cause him some embarrassment I did not make my presence manifest, but allowed him to retire to his apartment before entering the hotel myself.

Was the true explanation of Lee Clayton's night expedition in any way connected with the puzzling dream of which he had told me? Sleep claimed me for the few hours that remained until dawn.

III.

The following morning found me in bed at a late hour. My vigilance of the previous night had been more fatiguing than I had at the time realized. I lay for some time pondering the enigma of my friend's behavior. Should I feign ignorance of the occurrence in the Forum, or would it be best to inform Lee Clayton of what I knew? Unable to decide the better course to pursue, I dressed and hastened down to breakfast.

Clayton was breakfasting alone in a far corner of the dining room. As I took the chair opposite him he looked up with a smile of recognition and passed across the table to me an open volume which he had been perusing, pointing to a paragraph therein.

"Hebrew!" I ejaculated. "I'm sorry, but I don't know a word of it."

"Then here is a rather free translation of it," he replied, "but I regret that you cannot read the original. Some of the author's thought is always lost in the process of translation."

I accepted the proffered script and read the following:

"The secret of the identity of a certain soldier who fired the sanctuary of the holy temple of the Jews lies buried in his bosom. An associate, upon threat of exposure, bids him make record of his deed. This he has done, but so obscurely that nearly twenty centuries shall pass before the mystery shall be made clear."

"Well, that's beginning to get close," I commented, returning the paper to Lee. "Who was the old fellow that wrote that?" indicating the volume.

"That is not known," Lee Clayton replied, turning to the title page. "It seems to be merely a collection of anonymous Hebrew manuscripts published by a German house in the early part of the sixteenth century."

"But why all the secrecy?" I asked. "The 'certain soldier' was merely fulfilling destiny when he obeyed an impulse to fire the sanctuary."

Young Lee Clayton shot me a swift, searching glance.

"If you believe so," he said quietly, "I will not gainsay, but if you want my personal opinion, the 'certain soldier' was, as indeed all of us are, the captain of his own soul. He was entirely responsible for his deed. You know Shakespeare wrote:

"'The fault, dear Brutus, is not in our stars,

But in ourselves, that we are underlings.'"

"What if he did?" I admitted, warming to the argument. "But if I remember rightly he is also responsible for these words:

"'There's a divinity that shapes our ends,

Rough-hew them how we will.'

How do you reconcile the two?"

Clayton laughed pleasantly. "It seems to be a case of 'pay your money and take your choice,' friend Ebson, and my choice is made and is unchangeable."

"I admire you for your convictions," I said heartily. "I confess my own are not so unshakable."

He smiled a little pensively, then remarked, "And because I believe this 'certain soldier' to have been entirely responsible for his act of desecration, I wish to ascertain his identity. And now I am going to a curio-shop which I chanced upon yesterday. Will you come too?"

I readily consented, and together we wended our way through the busy streets of modern Rome.

Not far from the Piazza de Spania, near the end of a short and narrow street lined with native bazaars and stalls, is a curio-shop of one Antonio Salvucci, dealer in antiques. Although the place was far from cleanly and had a very cluttered appearance, it was not wholly lacking in charm. The proprietor appeared from the rear of the shop as we entered and eyed us appraisingly.

"The American gentlemen wish some Roman antiques?" questioned the Italian eagerly.

"Just looking, Mr. Salvucci," replied Clayton, and aside to me: "The museums have most of the genuine antiques, but occasionally one can pick up something good for very little money."

We walked about the little store looking at and inquiring about various objects. Most of the curios were relics of Coptic art that had been found in and about the catacombs where the early Christians had met secretly to escape persecution. Occasionally an object that dated back to the Republic was seen, but the majority were identified in some way with the period of Rome's downfall when attacked by the tribes from the north.

"Have you any relic of the time of Vespasian or Titus?" asked Clayton, coming at last to the subject that was nearest his heart.

"Titus—Titus," repeated the foreigner as if trying to recall some long-forgotten fact. "Wait, I see."

He vanished through a rear door, but reappeared some minutes later bearing in his arms a miniature restoration of the famous Arch of Titus which had been erected in honor of the Roman conquest of Jerusalem in 70 AD. This facsimile was two feet at its greatest length, and the other dimensions were proportional.

We were delighted with our find, but feigned indifference. I perceived, though, that it was all Lee could do to keep his hands off it.

"What price do you ask?" I inquired casually.

"Twenty-five dollars," answered the Italian promptly.

"Nothing doing," I replied, turning toward the door, "I'll give you five for it."

"Oh—but, *signor,* I have four *bambini.* I must make a living," he pleaded with characteristic Italian pathos.

"I'll give you ten," said Clayton somewhat harshly.

The sale was eventually consummated at the sixteen-dollar figure, and we bore our trophy away with exultation.

Back in the hotel and safely ensconced in Lee Clayton's rooms we studied the little arch minutely. It was a very perfect reproduction in Pentelic marble like the original, and showed a faithfulness to detail that was nothing short of marvelous.

There were the faces in bas-relief of Titus, the son of the Emperor Vespasian; a number of triumphant Roman warriors; a line of Jews in bondage; and a reproduction of the seven golden candlesticks which had been seized from the Holy of Holies when the temple at Jerusalem was plundered. The chiseling of the faces was unique, each one displaying its characteristic individuality.

"Do you notice," I observed, "that the sculptor has differentiated between the Jews and the Romans? The facial characteristics of each race are quite in evidence."

"Yes—only—hold on a minute, Ebson!" cried Lee in excitement. "He's made one error. Unless I'm very much mistaken he's got a Jew among the victorious Romans!"

"To be sure!" I exclaimed, my excitement equaling his own. "That figure near the middle certainly belongs to the conquered race. But there were Jews who were Roman citizens," I added; "and the chances are they were even more numerous in 70 than in 40 AD."

"That is very true," Lee answered a little abstractedly, I thought, "but it is very poor taste for the artist to be so realistic in a symbolic creation where comparatively few figures are represented. I think he showed decidedly bad judgment—unless," he added, "the Jew in question was a man of considerable importance."

"That explanation sounds plausible to me," I said. "The torchbearer is undoubtedly a man of fame whose portrait is indispensable to an accurate depiction of the triumphal entry into Rome."

IV.

Night and a full moon shedding its ethereal light across the eternal city prove a combination irresistible to lovers of beauty and romance.

Lee Clayton and I left the hotel at sundown and wandered on the Roman Campagna, amid the venerable quietude of its ilex and cypress trees. The beauty and serenity of the scene were not likely to be soon forgotten. When the moon hung low we returned to the city seeking that part which is rich in historic associations. We saw splashing fountains, old altars, partly demolished statues of ancient origin, picturesque arches and shattered pillars, their outlines softened and half concealed by flowers and vines.

After the moon had disappeared we retraced our steps to the hotel. I had just locked my door preparatory to retiring for the night when I was forcibly impressed with a possible solution to the enigma of the Roman soldier who was a Jew! I unlocked my door, locking it again behind me, and stepped into the hall. There was light in Lee's room and the door was slightly ajar. I rapped lightly but received no response. Upon the center table stood the small replica of the famous arch, and it seemed to me as I gazed ruefully at it that the handsome features of the mysterious Roman Jew regarded me with amusement not untouched with contempt.

I left the room and descended to the first floor.

"Did Mr. Clayton leave the hotel?" I inquired of the desk clerk.

"He passed this way just a moment ago," the man replied.

My mind was made up. Without a moment's hesitation I left the hotel and stepped into the quiet of a semi-tropic night. I discerned the figure of my friend as I had seen him upon the previous night, striding rapidly toward the site of the Forum of ancient Rome.

But his pace was too rapid for me, and I knew that unless I dashed madly after him, running the risk of arousing suspicion, I could not hope to catch up with him. Instinctively I retraced the route of the night before. In a breathless condition I espied the familiar ruins of the great Colosseum and the arch of the first Christian emperor, Constantine, flanking the mammoth pit of the ancient Forum wherein clustered pillars, like tombstones of a bygone age, gleamed palely.

Fatigued to the point of exhaustion I seated myself on a boulder and mopped my perspiring brow. The night seemed to be growing warmer—and a faint glow of suffused light pervaded the landscape.

"But the moon set an hour ago," I murmured in bewilderment.

Then I stared with gaping mouth and bulging eyes. The Arch of Constantine was growing hazy and transparent while I gazed. I turned to the Colosseum and saw that the familiar sloping sides where Time had put its stamp of demolition were fast fading away and in their stead the outline of the vast arena became more distinct in its pristine splendor.

"Merciful heaven—am I going mad?" I exclaimed, passing a hand across my eyes in perplexity.

When I looked again for the Arch of Constantine, it was gone! Something seemed to snap in my brain, and then—

V.

"By the Gods, Pliny, you are missing the fun. Our new emperor, Titus, is marching with the legions through the triumphal arch which is just completed. His route is through the Forum, as it was nine years ago upon his return from Jerusalem while his father, Vespasian, yet wore the purple."

I looked up from the rock upon which I was seated to see a familiar face regarding me affectionately.

"I shouldn't want to miss that, Quintilian," I replied in the fluent Latin in which he had addressed me.

I cast a hurried glance at my attire, thinking how incongruous a figure I must appear in a suit of the twentieth century. But my alarm was short-lived, for I perceived that a spotless toga draped my body in graceful folds.

My companion plucked my sleeve, and I arose and turned toward the Forum.

"See," exclaimed Quintilian, "the soldiers are already passing the Temple of Vesta. Hurry!"

Stretching before me beneath an azure sky lay the busy Roman marketplace of the First Century, its pure marble fanes and statues reflecting the brilliance of a mid-afternoon sun. Throngs of white-robed people intermingled with young men in military accouterments who were scattered singly and in groups about the great mart.

My sensation was a most peculiar one. While I recognized my identity as Paul Ebson, of Cleveland, Ohio, at the same time I was cognizant that as I stood here with my good friend Quintilian, the famous rhetorician, I was Pliny the Elder, noted naturalist of Rome.

We forced our way through the crowd and stood before a statue of two figures, symbolic of the conquest of Judea by Rome; as beautiful a piece of statuary as I had ever seen, comparable to the works of the most noted Greek sculptors rather than to this decadent period of Roman art. Alas that the twentieth century had never seen even a remnant of this masterpiece of sculptural art!

I was about to comment upon this creation when the cheers of the populace directed my attention to the approaching procession, at the head of which, mounted upon a richly caparisoned steed, rode young Titus, emperor of Rome. He was followed by a bodyguard of stalwart men. Following this came a cohort of Roman soldiers, and immediately behind, long lines of captive Jews, eight abreast, their heads bowed to the yokes of the conquerors. Then followed the legions of Rome, their spears and shields clattering rhythmically as they marched toward the great triumphal Arch of Titus.

A youth of eighteen years came up to my side and greeted me with a friendly salutation. He was my nephew, Pliny the Younger, who shared with me the joys of scientific research.

"Uncle," he cried, his eyes sparkling with excitement, "I wish I had been old enough to have gone with the legions of Titus to Jerusalem like Flavius over there; but see, they have passed through the arch and some of the soldiers are rejoining the rest of us. Look, here comes Tacitus. Isn't he handsome?"

I looked at the stalwart young soldier who was nearing our group. Yes, it was Tacitus, who, though young, was establishing for himself quite a reputation as an historian.

"Tacitus—Tacitus," I repeated under my breath, but I knew that the youthful historian and soldier was Lee Clayton.

Tacitus regarded me with an enigmatical smile.

"Is your ire still aroused, Pliny, that the portrait of my fellow historian appears upon the arch and mine does not?" he asked. Then he added, "You must remember that his years number more than mine and that his reputation in the chosen profession of both of us is already established."

"I know that, my dear Tacitus," I replied, "but I am convinced that your narratives adhere more strictly to historical facts than do those of your Jewish rival, and what is more, I don't like a man who can take part in the overthrow of his own people."

Tacitus smiled. "I don't believe the possibility of my becoming his professional rival is worrying Josephus so much as the fact that the fair Julia has consented to become my wife. You know he sought her hand after the death of his Jewish wife, Vashti. His failure in love has embittered him. We have been doing a little work jointly in preparing an accurate chronicle of the siege of Jerusalem. I asked him if he knew who threw the lighted torch into the window of the sanctuary of the temple, as I thought the act of sufficient importance to warrant minute detail in narration, but he was evasive upon the subject, finally remarking that the expression 'a certain soldier' was sufficient information to hand down to posterity; that the deed and not the doer was in this case of paramount importance."

"Well, Tacitus," I said, "I admire your love of truth and detail and I will do what I can to assist in procuring for you the identity of this 'certain soldier.'"

VI.

Our little group of four moved slowly toward the Arch of Titus while around us surged the Roman populace. As we walked we were greeted by friends on this side and that. At length we stood facing the great arch through which the legions of Titus had but recently filed. How familiar it looked! And there in the foreground, sculptured among surrounding notables of pure Roman blood, was the face of Josephus with the same expression of mockery.

I tore my attention from the arch to the scene in the Forum. The crowds were thinning as the shadows lengthened. I became aware of another presence, and turning I encountered the ironic gaze of the historian Josephus. I recognized him to be a man of extraordinary intellect. His lofty brow and thoughtful eyes indicated that. Still there was something about the man I did not like and I was forced to confess to myself that the feeling was inexplicable.

"Well met, Pliny," Josephus said in salutation. "I hear you leave on the morrow for Pompeii. Give my regards to Lucius Sulla and tell him that I will myself be in Pompeii by the ides of next month. And here is my fellow historian Tacitus," he continued, smiling upon the younger man with a patronizing air. "How goes the account of the siege?"

"I am still wanting to put a name in the place of 'a certain soldier,'" Tacitus replied. "Future generations will not tolerate ambiguity."

Josephus shrugged his shoulders and pointed with a smile toward the portrait upon the arch. "Quite an honor for an insignificant soldier, don't you think, my friends?"

"I am of the opinion that your part in the siege may not have been as insignificant as you would like to have us believe," I said.

"What do you mean?" Josephus demanded, his brow clouding.

I did not reply at once, for Quintilian was excusing himself to go to his home. Pliny the Younger was off for the new Colosseum, which had been but recently completed.

When they were out of hearing, Josephus repeated his question with glowering mien, then recalling suddenly the presence of Tacitus, controlled his anger with effort. I knew that he would vouchsafe no information in the presence of his rival historian.

I shot a significant glance into the eyes of my dear friend Tacitus, and remarked casually, "By the way, Tacitus, is it not the fair Julia's daily custom to ride in the vicinity of the Colosseum toward sundown in the chariot of her father, Agricola?"

"You have spoken truly, Pliny. I am to meet her at the hour of sundown by the Golden House of Nero," the young man replied.

"I will say farewell, Tacitus," I called after him, "for I may not see you again until my return from Pompeii."

The latter's reference to Julia did not improve the temper of the Jewish historian, who turned to me with a third repetition of his question.

"I will ask you, Josephus," I replied quietly, "why the portrait of 'a certain soldier' who ignites the sanctuary of his own besieged people is not important enough to appear on a triumphal arch. But there is one objection, his name should appear in the written chronicle."

The historian trembled with mingled fear and rage and his voice was thick as he answered, "Do you dare to identify me with that accursed 'certain soldier?'"

I looked sternly at the wretched man through narrowed eyes and said, "Josephus, if you will write a confession of your deed you will find favor with the Gods, and posterity will hold your records in good repute."

"And what if I have already revealed in writing the name of the soldier who was moved by a divine impulse to throw a lighted torch into the window of the sanctuary?" he asked mockingly.

"Divine impulse!" I exclaimed. "Would you consider it a divine impulse were I suddenly to seize a bar and demolish the sculptural figure of yonder smirking Jew who aids in the overthrow of his people?"

His apparent terror wrung my heart.

"But your confession," I urged in gentler tones. "Where is the written chronicle you mentioned in which 'a certain soldier' is named?"

"In my bosom the secret lies, Pliny, and there it shall stay—yes, it shall be unrevealed till twenty centuries have rolled by. Historians are sometimes permitted glimpses of the future as well as of the past!"

I lunged toward him, but he fled, his prophetic words ringing in my ears. I stood alone in the Roman Forum before the Arch of Titus, gazing at the smug countenance of the sculptured Josephus that seemed gloating over the secret within its breast.

Within its breast!

"By all the immortal Gods," I cried, "I understand the words of Josephus, 'In my bosom the secret lies.'"

Impetuously I picked up a blunt bar that lay on the ground a few feet away, and cast a hurried glance around me. From behind the Temple of Jupiter Stator a figure was approaching. I recognized it as that of Tacitus returning from his ride with Julia. I lifted the bar for a shattering stroke that did not fall.

The beautiful arch was aging before my eyes. Corners were becoming worn away, inscriptions grew faint, and in some instances were completely obliterated. Weeds and the creepers of vines clambered over the surface, and many of the chiseled features were chipped or worn smooth by the fingers of Time. The face of Josephus was gone completely. For all posterity might know, a typically Roman visage could have topped those shoulders.

I stood aghast, but with undiminished ardor commenced to knock away the marble folds that covered the breast of Josephus. Then I felt a restraining hand on my arm, and a voice: "Not that, friend Ebson! One does not wantonly destroy the relics of ancient art."

I turned and gazed full into the face of Lee Clayton. "But it is in there," I exclaimed, "the proof of the identity of 'a certain soldier!'"

He looked at me uncomprehendingly. A first gleam of early dawn stole across the city and found its way into the midst of the monuments and pillars that now give but a vague conception of the glory that was Rome when she was mistress of the world.

"The truth is in there," I asseverated, "and the twenty centuries have expired. Come, let us see?"

I seized the bar once again for a telling stroke, but instead dropped it helplessly at my feet as I became aware of the figure of a man observing us with penetrating gaze through the arch.

"Josephus!" I muttered hoarsely.

"That is Joseph Pollard," Lee whispered hurriedly in my ear. "It is he, my enemy, of whom I told you yesterday."

"Nevertheless, behold the 'certain soldier,'" I cried triumphantly.

"You are both insane somnambulists!" shrilled the voice of Joseph Pollard, "and if either of you dares to deface this arch, I shall report you to the authorities."

There was a ring of triumph in his voice and a gleam of malice in his eyes as he strode through the arch toward us. I caught the glitter of steel as he came through on our side of the monument. Then a distant shout, followed by a confused jargon and the sound of hurrying footsteps, dragged our attention to the approach of two officers who ran up to Pollard and seized him.

"You are under arrest," said one of the policemen, "for entering a hotel guest's room and destroying his property."

Clayton and I left Pollard in the safe hands of the officers and returned to the hotel. We repaired at once to Lee's room. There, strewn on the table and floor, were minute fragments of what had once been a miniature likeness of the Arch of Titus. I commenced picking the pieces off the floor and Lee proceeded to clear up the fragments from the table, where they lay scattered across the books and papers which in his hurry he had left opened and thrown about.

A sudden exclamation brought me hurriedly to his side. He was staring with bulging eyes at a page of Latin wherein the words *miles certus* seemed to jump up out of the text to meet us, and immediately above the inscription, laid by the careful hand of Fate, was a fragment of the tiny arch; the breast and head of Josephus!

"The twenty centuries are passed," I said, "and the prophecy is fulfilled. Josephus was right, though he did all within his power to prevent its accomplishment. He was unconsciously a tool in the hands of Fate."

After a silence of some moments I asked, "Why didn't Tacitus correct his version of 'a certain soldier?' Pliny intended to tell him the revelation of Josephus and that would have made it unnecessary for two thousand years to pass before its becoming known."

Lee Clayton smiled. "If you will look up Pliny the Elder in the encyclopedia, you will learn that he died at Pompeii in the famous eruption of Mt. Vesuvius in 79 AD."

The Miracle of
the Lily

I.
The Passing of a Kingdom

Since the comparatively recent resumé of the ancient order of agriculture, I, Nathano, have been asked to set down the extraordinary events of the past two thousand years, at the beginning of which time the supremacy of man, chief of the mammals, threatened to come to an untimely end.

Ever since the dawn of life upon this globe, life, which it seemed had crept from the slime of the sea, only two great types had been the rulers: the reptiles and the mammals. The former held undisputed sway for eons, but gave way eventually before the smaller, but intellectually superior mammals. Man himself, the supreme example of the ability of life to govern and control inanimate matter, was master of the world with apparently none to dispute his right. Yet, so blinded was he with pride over the continued exercise of his power on Earth over other lower types of mammals and the nearly extinct reptiles, that he failed to notice the slow but steady rise of another branch of life, different from his own; smaller, it is true, but no smaller than he had been in comparison with the mighty reptilian monsters that roamed the swamps in Mesozoic times.

These new enemies of man, though seldom attacking him personally, threatened his downfall by destroying his chief means of sustenance, so that by the close of the twentieth century, strange and daring projects were laid before the various governments of the world with an idea of fighting man's insect enemies to the finish. These pests were growing in size, multiplying so rapidly and destroying so much vegetation, that eventually no plants would be left to sustain human life. Humanity suddenly woke to the realization that it might suffer the fate of the nearly extinct reptiles. Would mankind be able to prevent the encroachment of the insects? And at last man *knew* that unless drastic measures were taken *at once*, a third great class of life was on the brink of terrestrial sovereignty.

Of course no great changes in development come suddenly. Slow evolutionary progress had brought us up to the point, where, with the application of outside pressure, we were ready to handle a situation, that, a century before, would have overwhelmed us.

I reproduce here in part a lecture delivered by a great American scientist, a talk which, sent by radio throughout the world, changed the destiny of mankind: but whether for good or for evil I will leave you to judge at the conclusion of this story.

"Only in comparatively recent times has man succeeded in conquering natural enemies; flood, storm, inclemency of climate, distance, and now we face an encroaching menace to the whole of humanity. Have we learned more and more of truth and of the laws that control matter only to succumb to the first real danger that threatens us with extermination? Surely, no matter what the cost, you will rally to the solution of our problem, and I believe, friends, that I have discovered the answer to the enigma.

"I know that many of you, like my friend Professor Fair, will believe my ideas too extreme, but I am convinced that unless you are willing to put behind you those notions which are old and not utilitarian, you cannot hope to cope with the present situation.

"Already, in the past few decades, you have realized the utter futility of encumbering yourselves with superfluous possessions that had no useful virtue, but which, for various sentimental reasons, you continued to hoard, thus lessening the degree of your life's efficiency by using for it time and attention that should have been applied to the practical work of life's accomplishments. You have given these things up slowly, but I am now going to ask you to relinquish the rest of them *quickly;* everything that interferes in any way with the immediate disposal of our enemies, the insects."

At this point, it seems that my worthy ancestor, Professor Fair, objected to the scientist's words, asserting that efficiency at the expense of some of the sentimental virtues was undesirable and not conducive to happiness, the real goal of man. The scientist, in his turn, argued that happiness was available only through a perfect adaptability to one's environment, and that efficiency *sans* love, mercy and the softer sentiments was the shortcut to human bliss.

It took a number of years for the scientist to put over his scheme of salvation, but in the end he succeeded, not so much from the persuasiveness of his words, as because prompt action of some sort was necessary. There was not enough food to feed the people of the earth. Fruit and vegetables were becoming a thing of the past. Too much protein food in the form of meat and fish was injuring the race, and at last the people realized that, for fruits and vegetables, or their nutritive equivalent, they must turn from the field to the laboratory; from the farmer to the chemist. Synthetic food was the solution to the problem. There was no longer any use in planting and caring for foodstuffs destined to become the nourishment of man's most deadly enemy.

The last planting took place in 2900, but there was no harvest, the voracious insects took every green shoot as soon as it appeared, and even trees, that had previously withstood the attacks of the huge insects, were by this time, stripped of every vestige of greenery.

The vegetable world suddenly ceased to exist. Over the barren plains which had been gradually filling with vast cities, man-made fires brought devastation to every living bit of greenery, so that in all the world there was no food for the insect pests.

II.
Man or Insect?

Extract from the diary of Delfair, a descendant of Professor Fair, who had opposed the daring scientist:

From the borders of the great state-city of Iowa, I was witness to the passing of one of the great kingdoms of Earth—the vegetable, and I cannot find words to express the grief that overwhelms me as I write of its demise, for I loved all growing things. Many of us realized that Earth was no longer beautiful; but if beauty meant death, better life in the sterility of the metropolis.

The viciousness of the thwarted insects was a menace that we had foreseen and yet failed to take into adequate account. On the city-state borderland, life is constantly imperiled by the attacks of well organized bodies of our dreaded foe.

(*Note:* The organization that now exists among the ants, bees and other insects, testifies to the possibility of the development of military tactics among them in the centuries to come.)

Robbed of their source of food, they have become emboldened to such an extent that they will take any risks to carry human beings away for food, and after one of their well organized raids, the toll of human life is appalling.

But the great chemical laboratories where our synthetic food is made, and our oxygen plants, we thought were impregnable to their attacks. In that we were mistaken.

Let me say briefly that since the destruction of all vegetation which furnished a part of the oxygen essential to human life, it became necessary to manufacture this gas artificially for general diffusion through the atmosphere.

I was flying to my work, which is in Oxygen Plant No. 21, when I noticed a peculiar thing on the upper speedway near Food Plant No. 3,439. Although it was night, the various levels of the state-city were illuminated as brightly as by day. A pleasure vehicle was going with prodigious speed westward. I looked after it in amazement. It was unquestionably the car of Eric, my co-worker at Oxygen Plant No. 21. I recognized the gay color of its body, but to verify my suspicions beyond the question of a doubt, I turned my volplane in pursuit and made out the familiar license number. What was Eric doing away from the plant before I had arrived to relieve him from duty?

In hot pursuit, I sped above the car to the very border of the state-city, wondering what unheard-of errand took him to the land of the enemy, for the car came to a sudden stop at the edge of what had once been an agricultural area. Miles ahead of me stretched an enormous expanse of black sterility; at my back was the teeming metropolis, five levels high—if one counted the hangar-level, which did not cover the residence sections.

I had not long to wait, for almost immediately my friend appeared. What a sight he presented to my incredulous gaze! He was literally covered from head to foot with the two-inch ants, that next to the beetles, had proved the greatest menace in their attacks upon humanity. With wild incoherent cries he fled over the rock and stubble-burned earth.

As soon as my stunned senses permitted, I swooped down toward him to effect a rescue, but even as my plane touched the barren earth, I saw that I was too late, for he fell, borne down by the vicious attacks of his myriad foes. I knew it was useless for me to set foot upon the ground, for my fate would be that of Eric. I rose ten feet and seizing my poison-gas weapon, let its contents out upon the tiny black evil things that swarmed below. I did not bother with my mask, for I planned to rise immediately, and it was not a moment too soon. From across the wasteland, a dark cloud eclipsed the stars and I saw coming toward me a horde of flying ants interspersed with larger flying insects, all bent upon my annihilation. I now took my mask and prepared to turn more gas upon my pursuers, but alas, I had used every atom of it in my attack upon the non-flying ants! I had no recourse but flight, and to this I immediately resorted, knowing that I could outdistance my pursuers.

When I could no longer see them, I removed my gas mask. A suffocating sensation seized me. I could not breathe! How high had I flown in my endeavor to escape the flying ants? I leaned over the side of my plane, expecting to see the city far, far below me. What was my utter amazement when I discovered that I was scarcely a thousand feet high! It was not altitude that was depriving me of the life-giving oxygen.

A drop of three hundred feet showed me inert specks of humanity lying about the streets. Then I knew; *the oxygen plant was not in operation!* In another minute I had on my oxygen mask, which was attached to a small portable tank for emergency use, and I rushed for the vicinity of the plant. There I witnessed the first signs of life. Men equipped with oxygen masks were trying to force entrance into the locked building. Being an employee, I possessed knowledge of the combination of the great lock, and I opened the door, only to be greeted by a swarm of ants that commenced a concerted attack upon us.

The floor seemed to be covered with a moving black rug, the corner nearest the door appearing to unravel as we entered, and it was but a few seconds before we were covered with the clinging, biting creatures, who fought with a supernatural energy born of despair. Two very active ants succeeded in getting under my helmet. The bite of their sharp mandibles and the effect of their poisonous formic acid became intolerable. Did I dare remove my mask while the air about me was foul with the gas discharged from the weapons of my allies? While I felt the attacks elsewhere upon my body gradually diminishing as the insects succumbed to the deadly fumes, the two upon my face waxed more vicious under the protection of my mask. One at each eye, they were trying to blind me. The pain was unbearable. Better the suffocating death-gas than the torture of lacerated eyes! Frantically I removed the headgear and tore at the shiny black fiends. Strange to tell, I discovered that I could breathe near the vicinity of the great oxygen tanks, where enough oxygen lingered to support life at least temporarily. The two vicious insects, no longer protected by my gas mask, scurried from me like rats from a sinking ship and disappeared behind the oxygen tanks.

This attack of our enemies, though unsuccessful on their part, was dire in its significance, for it had shown more cunning and ingenuity than anything that had ever preceded it. Heretofore, their onslaughts had been confined to direct attacks upon us personally or upon the synthetic-food laboratories, but in this last raid they had shown an amazing cleverness that portended future disaster, unless they were checked at once. It was obvious they had ingeniously planned to smother us by the suspension of work at the oxygen plant, knowing that they themselves could exist in an atmosphere containing a greater percentage of carbon dioxide. Their scheme, then, was to raid our laboratories for food.

III.
Lucanus the Last
A Continuation of Delfair's Account

Although it was evident that the cessation of all plant life spelled inevitable doom for the insect inhabitants of Earth, their extermination did not follow as rapidly as one might have supposed. There were years of internecine warfare. The insects continued to thrive, though in decreasing numbers, upon stolen laboratory foods, bodies of human-beings and finally upon each other; at first capturing enemy species and at last even resorting to a cannibalistic procedure. Their rapacity grew in inverse proportion to their waning numbers, until the meeting of even an isolated insect might mean death, unless one were equipped with poison gas and prepared to use it upon a second's notice.

I am an old man now, though I have not yet lived quite two centuries, but I am happy in the knowledge that I have lived to see the last living insect which was held in captivity. It was an excellent specimen of the stag-beetle (*Lucanus*) and the years have testified that it was the sole survivor of a form of life that might have succeeded man upon this planet. This beetle was caught weeks after we had previously seen what was supposed to be the last living thing upon the globe, barring man and the sea life. Untiring search for years has failed to reveal any more insects, so that at last man rests secure in the knowledge that he is monarch of all he surveys.

I have heard that long, long ago man used to gaze with a fearful fascination upon the reptilian creatures which he displaced, and just so did he view this lone specimen of a type of life that might have covered the face of the earth, but for man's ingenuity.

It was this unholy lure that drew me one day to view the captive beetle in his cage in district 404 at Universapolis. I was amazed at the size of the creature, for it looked larger than when I had seen it by television, but I reasoned that upon that occasion there had been no object near with which to compare its size. True, the broadcaster had announced its dimensions, but the statistics concretely given had failed to register a perfect realization of its prodigious proportions.

As I approached the cage, the creature was lying with its dorsal covering toward me and I judged it measured fourteen inches from one extremity to the other. Its smooth horny sheath gleamed in the bright artificial light. (It was confined on the third level.) As I stood there, mentally conjuring a picture of a world overrun with billions of such creatures as the one before me, the keeper approached the cage with a meal-portion of synthetic food. Although the food has no odor, the beetle sensed the man's approach, for it rose on its jointed legs and came toward us, its hornlike prongs moving threateningly; then apparently remembering its confinement, and the impotency of an attack, it subsided and quickly ate the food which had been placed within its prison.

The food consumed, it lifted itself to its hind legs, partially supported by a box, and turned its great eyes upon me. I had never been regarded with such utter malevolence before. The detestation was almost tangible and I shuddered involuntarily. As plainly as if he spoke, I knew that Lucanus was perfectly cognizant of the situation and in his gaze I read the concentrated hate of an entire defeated race.

I had no desire to gloat over his misfortune, rather a great pity toward him welled up within me. I pictured myself alone, the last of my kind, held up for ridicule before the swarming hordes of insects who had conquered my people, and I knew that life would no longer be worth the living.

Whether he sensed my pity or not I do not know, but he continued to survey me with unmitigated rage, as if he would convey to me the information that his was an implacable hatred that would outlast eternity.

Not long after this he died, and a world long since intolerant of ceremony surprised itself by interring the beetle's remains in a golden casket, accompanied by much pomp and splendor.

I have lived many long years since that memorable event, and undoubtedly my days here are numbered, but I can pass on happily, convinced that in this sphere man's conquest of his environment is supreme.

IV.
Efficiency Maximum

In a direct line of descent from Professor Fair and Delfair, the author of the preceding chapter, comes Thanor whose journal is given in this chapter:

Am I a true product of the year 2928? Sometimes I am convinced that I am hopelessly old-fashioned, an anachronism, that should have existed a thousand years ago. In no other way can I account for the dissatisfaction I feel in a world where efficiency has at last reached a maximum.

I am told that I spring from a line of ancestors who were not readily acclimated to changing conditions. I love beauty, yet I see none of it here. There are many who think our lofty buildings that tower two and three thousand feet into the air are beautiful, but while they are architectural splendors, they do not represent the kind of loveliness I crave. Only when I visit the sea do I feel any satisfaction for a certain yearning in my soul. The ocean alone shows the handiwork of God. The land bears evidence only of man.

As I read back through the diaries of my sentimental ancestors I find occasional glowing descriptions of the world that was; the world before the insects menaced human existence. Trees, plants and flowers brought delight into the lives of people as they wandered among them in vast open spaces, I am told, where the earth was soft beneath the feet, and flying creatures, called birds, sang among the greenery. True, I learn that many people had not enough to eat, and that uncontrollable passions governed them, but I do believe it must have been more interesting than this methodical, unemotional existence. I cannot understand why many people were poor, for I am told that Nature as manifested in the vegetable kingdom was very prolific; so much so that year after year quantities of food rotted on the ground. The fault, I find by my reading, was not with Nature but with man's economic system which is now perfect, though this perfection really brings few of us happiness, I think.

Now there is no waste; all is converted into food. Long ago men learned how to reduce all matter to its constituent elements, of which there are nearly a hundred in number, and from them to rebuild compounds for food. The old axiom that nothing is created or destroyed, but merely changed from one form to another, has stood the test of ages. Man, as the agent of God, has simply performed the miracle of transmutation himself instead of waiting for natural forces to accomplish it as in the old days.

At first humanity was horrified when it was decreed that it must relinquish its dead to the laboratory. For too many eons had man closely associated the soul and body, failing to comprehend the body as merely a material agent, through which the spirit functioned. When man knew at last of the eternal qualities of spirit, he ceased to regard the discarded body with reverential awe, and saw in it only the same molecular constituents which comprised all matter about him. He recognized only material basically the same as that of stone or metal; material to be reduced to its atomic elements and rebuilt into matter that would render service to living humanity; that portion of matter wherein spirit functions.

The drab monotony of life is appalling. Is it possible that man had reached his height a thousand years ago and should have been willing to resign Earth's sovereignty to a coming order of creatures destined to be man's worthy successor in the eons to come? It seems that life is interesting only when there is a struggle, a goal to be reached through an evolutionary process. Once the goal is attained, all progress ceases. The huge reptiles of preglacial ages rose to supremacy by virtue of their great size, and yet was it not the excessive bulk of those creatures that finally wiped them out of existence? Nature, it seems, avoids extremes. She allows the fantastic to develop for awhile and then wipes the slate clean for a new order of development. Is it not conceivable that man could destroy himself through excessive development of his nervous system, and give place for the future evolution of a comparatively simple form of life, such as the insects were at man's height of development? This, it seems to me, was the great plan; a scheme with which man dared to interfere and for which he is now paying by the boredom of existence.

The earth's population is decreasing so rapidly that I fear another thousand years will see a lifeless planet hurtling through space. It seems to me that only a miracle will save us now.

V.
The Year 3928
The Original Writer, Nathano, Resumes the Narrative

My ancestor, Thanor, of ten centuries ago, according to the records he gave to my great grandfather, seems to voice the general despair of humanity which, bad enough in his times, has reached the nth power in my day. A soulless world is gradually dying from self-inflicted boredom.

As I have ascertained from the perusal of the journals of my forebears, even antedating the extermination of the insects, I come of a stock that clings with sentimental tenacity to the things that made life worthwhile in the old days. If the world at large knew of my emotional musings concerning past ages, it would scarcely tolerate me, but surrounded by my thought-insulator, I often indulge in what fancies I will, and such meditation, coupled with a love for a few ancient relics from the past, have led me to a most amazing discovery.

Several months ago I found among my family relics a golden receptacle two feet long, one and a half in width and one in depth, which I found, upon opening, to contain many tiny square compartments, each filled with minute objects of slightly varying size, texture and color.

"Not sand!" I exclaimed as I closely examined the little particles of matter.

Food? After eating some, I was convinced that their nutritive value was small in comparison with a similar quantity of the products of our laboratories. What were the mysterious objects?

Just as I was about to close the lid again, convinced that I had one over-sentimental ancestor, whose gift to posterity was absolutely useless, my pocket-radio buzzed and the voice of my friend, Stentor, the interplanetary broadcaster, issued from the tiny instrument.

"If you're going to be home this afternoon," said Stentor, "I'll skate over. I have some interesting news."

I consented, for I thought I would share my "find" with this friend whom I loved above all others, but before he arrived I had again hidden my golden chest, for I had decided to await the development of events before sharing its mysterious secret with another. It was well that I did this, for Stentor was so filled with the importance of his own news that he could have given me little attention at first.

"Well, what is your interesting news?" I asked after he was comfortably seated in my adjustable chair.

"You'd never guess," he replied with irritating leisureliness.

"Does it pertain to Mars or Venus?" I queried. "What news of our neighbor planets?"

"You may know it has nothing to do with the self-satisfied Martians," answered the broadcaster, "but the Venusians have a very serious problem confronting them. It is in connection with the same old difficulty they have had ever since interplanetary radio was developed forty years ago. You remember, that, in their second communication with us, they told us of their continual warfare on insect pests that were destroying all vegetable food? Well, last night after general broadcasting had ceased, I was surprised to hear the voice of the Venusian broadcaster. He is suggesting that we get up a scientific expedition to Venus to help the natives of the unfortunate planet solve their insect problem as we did ours. He says the Martians turn a deaf ear to their plea for help, but he expects sympathy and assistance from Earth who has so recently solved these problems for herself."

I was dumbfounded at Stentor's news.

"But the Venusians are farther advanced mechanically than we," I objected, "though they are behind us in the natural sciences. They could much more easily solve the difficulties of space-flying than we could."

"That is true," agreed Stentor, "but if we are to render them material aid in freeing their world from devastating insects, we must get to Venus. The past four decades have proved that we cannot help them merely by verbal instructions."

"Now, last night," Stentor continued, with warming enthusiasm, "Wanyana, the Venusian broadcaster, informed me that scientists on Venus are developing interplanetary television. This, if successful, will prove highly beneficial in facilitating communication, and it may even do away with the necessity of interplanetary travel, which I think is centuries ahead of us yet."

"Television, though so common here on Earth and on Venus, has seemed an impossibility across the ethereal void," I said, "but if it becomes a reality, I believe it will be the Venusians who will take the initiative, though of course they will be helpless without our friendly cooperation. In return for the mechanical instructions they have given us from time to time, I think it no more than right that we should try to give them all the help possible in freeing their world, as ours has been freed, of the insects that threaten their very existence. Personally, therefore, I hope it can be done through radio and television rather than by personal excursions."

"I believe you are right," he admitted, "but I hope we can be of service to them soon. Ever since I have served in the capacity of official interplanetary broadcaster, I have liked the spirit of good fellowship shown by the Venusians through their spokesman, Wanyana. The impression is favorable in contrast to the superciliousness of the inhabitants of Mars."

We conversed for some time, but at length he rose to take his leave. It was then I ventured to broach the subject that was uppermost in my thoughts.

"I want to show you something, Stentor," I said, going into an adjoining room for my precious box and returning shortly with it. "A relic from the days of an ancestor named Delfair, who lived at the time the last insect, a beetle, was kept in captivity. Judging from his personal account, Delfair was fully aware of the significance of the changing times in which he lived, and contrary to the majority of his contemporaries, possessed a sentimentality of soul that has proved an historical asset to future generations. Look, my friend, these he left to posterity!"

I deposited the heavy casket on a table between us and lifted the lid, revealing to Stentor the mystifying particles.

The face of Stentor was eloquent of astonishment. Not unnaturally his mind took somewhat the same route as mine had followed previously, though he added atomic-power-units to the list of possibilities. He shook his head in perplexity.

"*Whatever* they are, there must have been a real purpose behind their preservation," he said at last. "You say this old Delfair witnessed the passing of the insects? What sort of a fellow was he? Likely to be up to any tricks?"

"Not at all," I asserted rather indignantly, "he seemed a very serious minded chap; worked in an oxygen-plant and took an active part in the last warfare between men and insects."

Suddenly Stentor stooped over and scooped up some of the minute particles into the palm of his hand—and then he uttered a maniacal shriek and flung them into the air.

"Great God, man, do you know what they are?" he screamed, shaking violently.

"No, I do not," I replied quietly, with an attempt at dignity I did not feel.

"Insect eggs!" he cried, and shuddering with terror, he made for the door.

I caught him on the threshold and pulled him forcibly back into the room.

"Now see here," I said sternly, "not a word of this to anyone. Do you understand? I will test out your theory in every possible way but I want no public interference."

At first he was obstinate, but finally yielded to threats when supplications were impotent.

"I will test them," I said, "and will endeavor to keep hatchings under absolute control, should they prove to be what you suspect."

It was time for the evening broadcast, so he left, promising to keep our secret and leaving me regretting that I had taken another into my confidence.

VI. The Miracle

For days following my unfortunate experience with Stentor, I experimented upon the tiny objects that had so terrified him. I subjected them to various tests for the purpose of ascertaining whether or not they bore evidence of life, whether in egg, pupa or larva stages of development. And to all my experiments, there was but one answer. No life was manifest. Yet I was not satisfied, for chemical tests showed that they were composed of organic matter. Here was an inexplicable enigma! Many times I was on the verge of consigning the entire contents of the chest to the flames. I seemed to see in my mind's eye the world again overridden with insects, and that calamity due to the indiscretions of one man! My next impulse was to turn over my problem to scientists, when a suspicion of the truth dawned upon me. These were seeds, the germs of plant life, and they might grow. But alas, where? Over all the earth man has spread his artificial dominion. The state-city has been succeeded by what could be termed the nation-city, for one great floor of concrete or rock covers the country.

I resolved to try an experiment, the far-reaching influence of which I did not at that time suspect. Beneath the lowest level of the community edifice in which I dwell, I removed, by means of a small atomic excavator, a slab of concrete large enough to admit my body. I let myself down into the hole and felt my feet resting on a soft dark substance that I knew to be dirt. I hastily filled a box of this, and after replacing the concrete slab, returned to my room, where I proceeded to plant a variety of the seeds.

Being a product of an age when practically to wish for a thing in a material sense is to have it, I experienced the greatest impatience, while waiting for any evidences of plant life to become manifest. Daily, yes hourly, I watched the soil for signs of a type of life long since departed from the earth, and was about convinced that the germ of life could not have survived the centuries, when a tiny blade of green proved to me that a miracle, more wonderful to me than the works of man through the ages, was taking place before my eyes. This was an enigma so complex and yet so simple, that one recognized in it a direct revelation of Nature.

Daily and weekly I watched in secret the botanical miracle. It was my one obsession. I was amazed at the fascination it held for me—a man who viewed the marvels of the thirty-fourth century with unemotional complacency. It showed me that Nature is manifest in the simple things which mankind has chosen to ignore.

Then one morning, when I awoke, a white blossom displayed its immaculate beauty and sent forth its delicate fragrance into the air. The lily, a symbol of new life, resurrection! I felt within me the stirring of strange emotions I had long believed dead in the bosom of man. But the message must not be for me alone. As of old, the lily would be the symbol of life for all!

With trembling hands, I carried my precious burden to a front window where it might be witnessed by all who passed by. The first day there were few who saw it, for only rarely do men and women walk; they usually ride in speeding vehicles of one kind or another, or employ electric skates, a delightful means of locomotion, which gives the body some exercise. The fourth city level, which is reserved for skaters and pedestrians, is kept in a smooth glass-like condition. And so it was only the occasional pedestrian, walking on the outer border of the fourth level, upon which my window faced, who first carried the news of the growing plant to the world, and it was not long before it was necessary for civic authorities to disperse the crowds that thronged to my window for a glimpse of a miracle in green and white.

When I showed my beautiful plant to Stentor, he was most profuse in his apology and came to my rooms every day to watch it unfold and develop, but the majority of people, long used to business-like efficiency, were intolerant of the sentimental emotions that swayed a small minority, and I was commanded to dispose of the lily. But a figurative seed had been planted in the human heart, a seed that could not be disposed of so readily, and this seed ripened and grew until it finally bore fruit.

VII. Ex Terreno

It is a very different picture of humanity that I paint ten years after the last entry in my diary. My new vocation is farming, but it is farming on a far more intensive scale than had been done two thousand years ago. Our crops never fail, for temperatures and rainfall are regulated artificially. But we attribute our success principally to the total absence of insect pests. Our small agricultural areas dot the country like the parks of ancient days and supply us with a type of food, no more nourishing, but more appetizing than that produced in the laboratories. Truly we are living in a marvelous age! If the earth is ours completely, why may we not turn our thoughts toward the other planets in our solar system? For the past ten or eleven years the Venusians have repeatedly urged us to come and assist them in their battle for life. I believe it is our duty to help them.

Tomorrow will be a great day for us and especially for Stentor, as the new interplanetary television is to be tested, and it is possible that for the first time in history, we shall see our neighbors in the infinity of space. Although the people of Venus were about a thousand years behind us in many respects, they have made wonderful progress with radio and television. We have been in radio communication with them for the last half century and they shared with us the joy of the establishment of our Eden. They have always been greatly interested in hearing Stentor tell the story of our subjugation of the insects that threatened to wipe us out of existence, for they have exactly that problem to solve now; judging from their reports, we fear that theirs is a losing battle. Tomorrow we shall converse face to face with the Venusians! It will be an event second in importance only to the first radio communications interchanged fifty years ago. Stentor's excitement exceeds that displayed at the time of the discovery of the seeds.

Well it is over and the experiment was a success, but alas for the revelation!

The great assembly halls all over the continent were packed with humanity eager to catch a first glimpse of the Venusians. Prior to the test, we sent our message of friendship and goodwill by radio, and received a reciprocal one from our interplanetary neighbors. Alas, we were ignorant at that time! Then the television receiving apparatus was put into operation, and we sat with breathless interest, our eyes intent upon the crystal screen before us. I sat near Stentor and noted the feverish ardor with which he watched for the first glimpse of Wanyana.

At first hazy mist-like spectres seemed to glide across the screen. We knew these figures were not in correct perspective. Finally, one object gradually became more opaque, its outlines could be seen clearly. Then across that vast assemblage, as well as thousands of others throughout the world, there swept a wave of speechless horror, as its full significance burst upon mankind.

The figure that stood facing us was a huge six-legged beetle, not identical in every detail with our earthly enemies of past years, but unmistakably an insect of gigantic proportions! Of course it could not see us, for our broadcaster was not to appear until afterward, but it spoke, and we had to close our eyes to convince ourselves that it was the familiar voice of Wanyana, the leading Venusian radio broadcaster. Stentor grabbed my arm, uttered an inarticulate cry and would have fallen but for my timely support.

"Friends of Earth, as you call your world," began the object of horror, "this is a momentous occasion in the annals of the twin planets, and we are looking forward to seeing one of you, and preferably Stentor, for the first time, as you are now viewing one of us. We have listened many times, with interest, to your story of the insect pests which threatened to follow you as lords of your planet. As you have often heard us tell, we are likewise molested with insects. Our fight is a losing one, unless we can soon exterminate them."

Suddenly, the Venusian was joined by another being, a colossal ant, who bore in his fore-legs a tiny light-colored object which he handed to the beetle-announcer, who took it and held it forward for our closer inspection. It seemed to be a tiny ape, but was so small we could not ascertain for a certainty. We were convinced, however, that it was a mammalian creature, an "insect" pest of Venus. Yet in it we recognized rudimentary man as we know him on Earth!

There was no question as to the direction in which sympathies instinctively turned, yet reason told us that our pity should be given to the intelligent reigning race who had risen to its present mental attainment through eons of time. By some quirk or freak of nature, way back in the beginning, life had developed in the form of insects instead of mammals. Or (the thought was repellant) had insects in the past succeeded in displacing mammals, as they might have done here on Earth?

There was no more television that night. Stentor would not appear, so disturbed was he by the sight of the Venusians, but in the morning, he talked to them by radio and explained the very natural antipathy we experienced in seeing them or in having them see us.

Now they no longer urge us to construct etherships and go to help them dispose of their "insects." I think they are afraid of us, and their very fear has aroused in mankind an unholy desire to conquer them.

I am against it. Have we not had enough of war in the past? We have subdued our own world and should be content with that, instead of seeking new worlds to conquer. But life is too easy here. I can plainly see that. Much as he may seem to dislike it, man is not happy, unless he has some enemy to overcome, some difficulty to surmount.

Alas my greatest fears for man were groundless!

A short time ago, when I went out into my field to see how my crops were faring, I found a six-pronged beetle voraciously eating. No—man will not need to go to Venus to fight "insects."

The Evolutionary Monstrosity

I.

"I believe you three fellows are going to startle the world yet," Professor Lewis of the biology department of our college remarked when we three students, who had termed ourselves the triumvirate, gathered in the laboratory at the close of class. "Marston, what was that theory of evolution you hinted at just before the bell rang? It sounded interesting."

Ted Marston laughed in a slightly embarrassed manner, though modesty was not ordinarily an outstanding attribute of Ted's character. His environment, judging from the little information we were able to glean from time to time, had been one of poverty and squalor. He was working his way through college and had proved a credit to that institution.

"Oh, it's a little far-fetched, professor, and I'm afraid my two high-brow pals here will think I'm cuckoo," and he tapped his head significantly, "but the idea's been grinding away in my brain for several days now."

"Out with it, Ted," said Irwin Staley jocosely. "Remember this triumvirate holds no secrets from itself. All thoughts are shared."

Irwin was the son of a wealthy New York broker and had been raised with every luxury that the modern age was capable of producing. His was a brilliant mind, too, but it somehow lacked the initiative that necessity had instilled into the being of Theodore Marston.

"Well if you insist," replied Ted more seriously. "It's something like this. I wonder if evolution isn't the result of a certain bacterial growth which slowly and continuously changes the cellular structure of living organisms, causing the formation of new tissue and organs, and breaking down the old."

"Poppycock and fiddlesticks!" ejaculated Professor Lewis. "Environment must also play a part in evolutionary change, for evolution is adaptability to environment, and Darwin was right in his theory of the survival of the fittest."

I'll admit I was dumbfounded by Marston's assertion, but not so Irwin Staley.

"Ted," he cried with enthusiasm, "you've got the right dope. It sounds so reasonable. But can you prove it?"

"I sure will," he answered, "if only for the satisfaction of convincing these doubting Thomases," indicating the professor and myself, who looked our incredulity.

"The only way you can prove it," I said, "is to develop specimens more rapidly than environment could possibly change them."

"That is precisely what I intend to do," he said.

II.

I, Frank Caldwell, could boast of no extremes either in environment or heredity. My people were middle class, my father being a factory owner in a small town in Iowa. My collegiate rank was slightly above the average, though I showed a decided preference for biology, in which study my two friends excelled.

Following graduation I became Professor Lewis's assistant, after the position had been refused by Marston. It seems the enthusiasm which Ted Marston felt had been shared, as I feared, by Irwin Staley, who placed at his chum's disposal ample funds for the purpose of developing his theory of evolution. Thus the "triumvirate" dwindled temporarily to two, while I, troubled with no new, fanciful idea, taught my classes with no inkling of what was to come.

One warm day in June at the close of the school year, I received a letter from Ted and Irwin, who were at the latter's specially equipped laboratory, endeavoring to carry out Ted's great scheme for proving to the world the primary causes of evolutionary changes in mankind.

The letter ran as follows:

"Dear Frank:

"A meeting of the triumvirate is called for the first possible moment you can get there. We want you in on this. We are in a position to convince you whether you will or no! You can be of real assistance to us in the carrying out of our plans. Don't delay.

"Ted and Irwin."

I had vaguely planned a European trip for the summer, but abandoned the rather hazy idea upon receipt of my friend's letter. My curiosity was unquestionably aroused. Had the two succeeded in isolating the "evolutionary germ" and in putting their theory to a test? It seemed incredible and yet strange things have happened.

Wonderingly, and not wholly without excitement, I presented myself at the Staley mansion, which stood secluded in the center of a twenty-acre estate. I was surprised to have the door opened, not by a servant, but by Mrs. Staley herself, and I could tell at once by her manner that something was the matter.

Irwin had always been proud of his mother, and justifiably so, for she was a woman of keen intellect and young in appearance for her years. She was obviously nervous as she bade me be seated for a moment, before going out to the laboratory on the rear of the estate. We exchanged a few pleasantries, but I felt that she wanted to approach me upon what was a vital subject to her, but that she lacked the courage to do so. I finally decided to "break the ice" myself.

"How are Irwin and Ted getting along with their experiments?" I asked. I knew the subject had to be broached, painful though it was.

She looked away with a quick, nervous movement that had something of fear in it, then she seemed to gain control of herself.

"Frank," she said earnestly, "can't you stop them? It is my opinion they are guilty of great desecration. One cannot so distort God's laws without evil results."

At once my old habit of defending my friends came to the front.

"But is it distortion?" I countered. "They are breaking no natural laws. They are merely speeding them up. Where would we be today, Mrs. Staley, had we failed to speed up and control the use of electricity? Left to its natural manifestations, it would not turn the wheels of our machinery nor send our voices to remote parts of the world."

"Well, I do not know," she said miserably, "but I cannot feel that it is right."

Suddenly she stiffened and gave vent to a muffled scream. "It is coming. I can feel it near!"

Before I had time to question her meaning, I felt, rather than saw, a malign presence in the room. I turned from the woman who was now frightened into speechlessness to gaze down into a pair of evil eyes a few inches above the floor.

"My God, what is it?" I cried, sharing her terror in spite of myself.

My fright seemed to cause her to find voice, and she replied, scarcely above a whisper, "It was once my beautiful tabby cat, Cutey."

"Cutey!" I gasped. "What a name for *that!*"

I have always been very fond of cats, and at one time was nicknamed "old maid" because of the fondness I showed for the species. But this unnamable horror! It stood upright on two clumsily padded feet. Furless, its flesh the color of a decaying corpse, it seemed to me a miniature ghoul. The lidless eyes stared up into mine with an implacable hatred. But it was what I presume had once been whiskers that held my half-reluctant, half-fascinated attention. They bristled separately, as though imbued with individual volition.

Suddenly a shrill, whining voice spoke and I forced my eyes whence it came. It issued from the tiny, malformed object on the rug; from the travesty on feline beauty as we know it.

"You are wanted in the laboratory. Come at once."

Yes, that hairless, furless object, no bigger than a mouse, that stood on two feet and gazed at me with deep malevolence, had issued a command, and I could do naught but obey!

I turned to Mrs. Staley, but she was sitting with her head buried in her arms, so I silently left her and followed "Cutey" from the room.

As I entered the reception hall I heard the approach of a light footfall. I must have jumped unknowingly, for my nerves were ajangle after the experience of the last few minutes, and a peal of merry laughter tore my eyes from Cutey.

A girl was standing at the foot of the stairs regarding me with a quizzical smile. My first impression of her was that she was beautifully and expensively clothed, and I am not a man who ordinarily observes clothes before people. In this particular instance, however, the clothes really possessed more personality than their wearer. The girl was pretty in an insipid, baby-doll way. I knew at once that she was Irwin's sister, for she was a feminine counterpart of her brother, minus Irwin's attractive personality.

"Isn't Cutey a dear?" she asked with a giggle.

"I don't quite agree with you—er—Miss Staley, I presume?" I asked, stepping toward her.

"Yes, I'm Irwin's kid sister, and I suppose you're Frank Caldwell. Irwin's mentioned you so often. But I don't see why you don't like Cutey. She's quite intelligent, you know."

"Ye—es, I don't dispute that Miss Staley, but she seems to lack some necessary qualities to make her attractive," I said, and to myself I thought, "and so does a certain young lady!"

"Your mother seems genuinely distressed over this evolution business, Miss Staley, and well she may be. I think it has gone too far," I continued.

"Gone too far!" she echoed. "Why it's only just begun, and by the way, call me Dot and I'll call you Frank. It's easier."

"Why what else have Irwin and Ted done along this line?" I asked, ignoring her remark.

"It isn't Irwin," she corrected. "It's Ted," and at the mention of the latter's name she smiled simperingly, I suppose to give me the impression that there was an understanding between them.

"Well he's welcome to her," I thought. Aloud I said, "It seems to me your mother's feelings should be considered in this matter and I know she disapproves."

"Oh, mother's so fussy," she replied as she tripped to the full-length mirror and surveyed herself critically but with very evident ultimate approval. "Ted is really doing something wonderful for humanity, you know. At least that's what he says, and I like to believe him."

Suddenly I looked toward Cutey, my gaze drawn in that direction involuntarily. The round, blinkless eyes of the cat (if I can call it such) were regarding me with impelling magnetism, and all the long whiskers were pointed toward me. With a brief "good-bye" to Dorothy Staley, I opened the door and followed the feline horror into the open. As I shut the door behind me, I heard Mrs. Staley call her daughter to her.

III.

"If I could but kill it!" I thought as I followed the thing along the flower-bordered path. "Is it a representation of the future? God forbid the development of such life upon this globe! It would seem that the evolutionary processes minus the modification of environmental influences point toward retrogression instead of progress. Man dare not tamper with God's plan of a general, slow uplift for all humanity."

At length the laboratory appeared ahead of me and I hurried toward it, with something of joy at the prospect of meeting my old chums once more. Forgotten for the moment was the diminutive horror that had once been a cat, as I eagerly grasped a hand of Ted and of Irwin, who drew me into the building with many expressions of cordiality.

"Quite some workshop, eh?" queried Ted with an air of pardonable pride.

"Indeed it is," I replied fervently. "I wish the college had half the equipment you've got here."

Irwin's brow puckered into a little frown. "I have neglected dear old Alma Mater. They would appreciate some more paraphernalia there, wouldn't they, Frank?"

"Indeed they would," I echoed heartily. "The department's running down, and poor Professor Lewis is about at his rope's end."

It was now Marston whose brow clouded, but not with remorse.

"Lay off the sentimental Alma Mater stuff, Irwin," he said. "They've got enough equipment there to educate the mediocre college boy. Your money and energy can do more good here."

I was not a little shocked at Ted's depreciative words; he who had always been such a loyal alumnus of the university! It displeased me to find none of the former joviality and loyalty that had characterized him in college days.

It was on the tip of my tongue to voice a protest against the preferable equipage of a private laboratory over that of a public institution, but on Irwin's account I stayed the impulse.

"Well," I said finally, in well-controlled tones, "how are the evolution bugs evolving?"

Ted and Irwin exchanged hasty glances, and I looked at Ted, for it was evident he was the spokesman and the mastermind.

"What did you think of Cutey, if I may answer your question with another?" Ted Marston asked with a half smile.

Immediately my indignation was aroused. I had presented one side of the argument to console Mrs. Staley, but it was the other side that I proposed to give to Marston.

"If you want my honest opinion," I said frigidly, "I think that what you are doing is the most hellish practice since the days of necromancy."

"And *that* from a member of the triumvirate, if you please!" said Ted smiling unpleasantly at Irwin.

Irwin Staley was obviously embarrassed and ill at ease. I had a feeling that he was "in deep" with Ted and couldn't get out, though why was a little hard to explain. The laboratory equipment was all his, and legally he could have kicked Ted out any time he chose, but morally he lacked the courage to do so. Ted and Irwin were living examples of mind over matter.

"Yes," I said, "and I am here to fight you to the finish if need be! Professor Lewis was right. Without the modifying and mollifying influence of a changing environment, evolution is a tool in the hands of the devil."

"I thought you never believed in his Satanic majesty," said Marston sarcastically.

"Nor do I now," I replied heatedly. "I have always maintained that evil was not a positive force, merely negative good; a misdirection, so to speak, of the same forces that can result in good. Just so is evolution a force for good if used as the Creator intended, but woe befall humanity if its laws are tampered with. Electricity is an example of a force that can benefit us or kill us, according as we obey or disobey its laws."

"Very well, Parson Caldwell," said Ted sneeringly, "granted there is some force to your argument, what are you going to do about it?"

"Be reasonable, Ted," I pleaded. "If you—"

"*Reasonable!*" he mocked. "What does the world know about reason? Since the days of Plato, Aristotle, Socrates and Anaxagoras have we advanced one iota in mentality? Answer me that! True we have invented machines, have increased our luxuries, but have we any purer logic or do we come any nearer to knowing the Why of God than some of the philosophers of 500 BC? Let us hope, my friend, that a rapid evolution will increase the reason in most of us!"

"But look at that—that—cat!" I finally found voice to say. "Isn't that thing a warning to you, Ted?"

"That cat, so far removed from your present state of evolution, is a shock to you merely because it is unfamiliar," he said quietly. "Had you progressed parallel to it, you would look upon it as a delightful pet."

"Pet be hanged!" I blurted forth. "If that object could ever be a pet, I'm going home to get a rattlesnake for company!"

"A very good idea! It would prove an excellent partnership," with which cutting words he arose and disappeared into an adjoining room.

"This situation is awful," I said to Irwin after the door had closed behind Marston. "Do you share his views, may I ask?"

Irwin Staley cleared his throat and glanced nervously toward the anteroom which closeted his companion.

"To tell the truth, Frank," he said huskily, "I think Ted is going a little too far. It was all immensely interesting for awhile. I didn't even mind Cutey as you seem to, but when he began introducing evolutionary bacteria into his own system to change the tissues and organs through the many stages of bacterial infection, I confess I began to feel that he had carried the matter to an extreme. He has seemed different ever since he commenced it."

"Good heavens!" I exclaimed. "How long ago was that?"

"Only a couple of weeks," came the reassuring reply, "and in very moderate doses, but just this morning he intimated a desire to speed up the process, as he is becoming impatient."

"Irwin, if I were you I'd clear out and let him alone, even though it might mean considerable financial loss," I admonished. "He is dangerous."

"I can't, Frank, that's the trouble. He wants me in his experiment."

I looked at him in exasperation. "You can't? Has the man any power over your will?"

"I believe he must have," Irwin mumbled pitifully, "for it seems I have to do his bidding."

I turned away in disgust.

"Count me out," I said harshly. "I believe I'll take my trip to Europe after all."

I walked down the path and he followed me, a forlorn, unhappy man. His courage seemed to return as he left the vicinity of the laboratory.

"I rather wish I could get out of this whole business," he said sheepishly. "I'd love to go to Europe with you."

"Come on, old boy," I said delightedly. "Can you be ready by Thursday? The boat actually sails Friday."

His eyes were wistful and he seemed almost persuaded when Ted Marston's voice called from the region of the laboratory, "Where on earth are you, Irwin? Come here. I need you for an experiment."

Instantly all the joy faded from Staley's countenance.

"Sorry, Frank, but I'll have to give up that trip. Some other time maybe," he muttered vaguely.

I stared mutely after him till he vanished behind the shrubbery at a turn in the path.

IV.

As luck would have it I learned upon my return that I had been granted a sabbatical year, and so instead of returning to my teaching that fall, it was not until a year from that autumn that I came back to the States and plunged immediately into college work. In the interim I had heard no word from Ted and Irwin. The following summer I planned to visit them, but the death of Professor Lewis shortly before the close of the school year necessitated my remaining and working at the college, for I had been appointed head of the department of biology to take Professor Lewis's place. I missed the kindly old man and hoped I should prove a worthy successor. Thus it was three years before I returned to the laboratory that stood upon the beautiful Staley estate.

I had read of the death of Mrs. Staley two years before, so I did not stop at the house as I had upon the previous occasion, but started immediately in the direction of the laboratory. As I approached, a strange sensation took possession of me. I had an irresistible desire to flee, and yet it was not exactly fear that possessed me. Imagine my amazement when I realized that *contrary to my will* I had turned my back upon the laboratory and was walking away with the intention of returning home!

I had reached a turn in the path when I was startled by a hoarse, inhuman cry. I turned to see a decrepit figure hurrying toward me in obvious distress. There was a vague familiarity in the uncouth stranger and I stood puzzled on the verge of discovering the elusive identity.

"Who are you?" I demanded in fearsome apprehension.

Before he could reply, he turned inexplicably about and retraced his steps toward the laboratory, and I, discovering my movements now unhampered, followed him with quickening pace. To the very threshold I followed, but the door closed with a loud bang between us, and again I felt powerless to enter. Whatever the force that controlled me now as it had a few moments before, it had ceased to act while the degenerate was returning to the building. I was confident that the control was from a source within the laboratory, and that mighty though it was, it was limited in its power of concentration to one subject at a time.

Surely here was a state of affairs that needed investigation, and yet I seemed powerless to act! I returned to college and pondered the situation. Should I return with an armed force or should I try it again alone?

Several days after this inexplicable occurrence I was the recipient of a letter from Dorothy Staley:

"Dear Mr. Caldwell:

"I heard recently that you are again in the States, and if it would not be too much trouble I should appreciate your coming here at once. Things have been going from bad to worse, and I am in serious trouble. May I count on your help?

"Dorothy Staley."

I confess I was puzzled. The letter did not seem like the product of the pen of the addlepated girl I had met three years before. Could three years, even of trouble, so tone down and change the frivolous maid whom I recalled with a feeling almost of disgust? Or was the author of the note someone who was trying to trick me by the use of the girl's name?

It was late afternoon as I approached the estate. The long line of poplars like sturdy sentinels seemed to guard the mansion from external danger, but what was symbolic of its protection against an encroaching menace within? As I mounted the veranda steps, the door opened—and Dorothy stood framed in the entryway. For a moment I discontinued my ascent of the steps and gazed speechlessly at her, for it seemed I had never seen this girl before—yet I knew it was Dorothy. What refining process had altered her nature and appearance so intrinsically? Trouble is the refiner's fire necessary for some natures, yet somehow this change in Dorothy was not so much one of degree as one of actual difference of quality.

"Mr. Caldwell," she said with a quiet, sad smile. "I sent for you because I believed you could help me as no one else in the world can."

"I am flattered, I assure you," I murmured as I followed her into the large gloomy interior and passed the long mirror, where, three years ago, she had primped herself so vainly.

When we were seated in the luxurious living room whose windows opened on a fountain outside, she began the explanation of her worry. Her beautiful face with its serious sincerity held my enraptured gaze as she talked.

"Things have advanced to a terrible state between Ted and Irwin, and even I—" she paused and glanced about her apprehensively, "am fearful of what the future has in store for us all. Ted has—" here she broke down completely and was unable to continue.

"Just what has Ted done?" I asked partly to relieve the embarrassing and distressing silence.

"I have not seen Ted in the last year," she replied, sitting up straight in her chair and making a renewed effort to control herself, "but I have heard of his progress through my brother, who is his helpless tool—and it is my understanding," she lowered her voice to a whisper, "that Ted has progressed (if one can call it progression) beyond any semblance to humanity as we know it!"

"Horrible!" I ejaculated, mentally recalling a certain example of feline evolution.

"I thought I loved him once," continued Dorothy, "but now I do not even respect him."

"No, I should think not," I replied dryly. "And it seems to me he should be made to relinquish his hold on Irwin. Maybe what he does to himself is his own business, but he should not be allowed to involve others."

"'Be allowed' is a strange term to be used in regard to Ted Marston," said the girl bitterly. "He is his own master. For some reason or other he will not allow me to see him, but sends Irwin to me with his messages. A week ago Irwin came to the house looking so wretched and miserable. I pleaded with him to force Ted to go away, but all I could get from him was, 'I can't, sis. I know it is unbelievable, but I've got to do what he says. He really is wonderful. If you knew him as I do, you would think so too.'

"I was sitting in this very chair, Fra—er, Mr. Caldwell, a week ago," the sweet voice went on, "during the conversation with my brother Irwin. He looked so unhappy, even while he praised Ted, that I knew his tongue belied his real feelings in the matter. Suddenly he told me very earnestly that Ted still loved me, but that he knew that two beings so far apart in evolutionary development would not be suited to one another, so he intended inoculating me with the germs in order to advance me to his stage of development. Then we two, he told me through Irwin, would rule the world! I was so horrified I found myself unable to move, and as I sat there stunned, Irwin quietly advanced and, without the slightest warning of what was to follow, plunged a hypodermic needle into my arm. I must have fainted, for the next I knew I was in bed and Cora, our maid, was moving about in my room. Strange to say I felt no ill effects; in fact, if there was any difference, I felt better, not physically so much as mentally. I seemed to understand things in a quiet, impersonal sort of way, and was, so to speak, above petty emotions and passions that had swayed me constantly prior to this experience. If this was evolution, I thought, it was very much to be desired and I wondered at Irwin's very apparent fear of Ted. Then that night Irwin came again, but this time he seemed different."

Two tears rolled down Dorothy's fair cheeks, but she continued with obvious effort.

"He told me that Ted was asleep, and that upon such rare occasions as he slept, he, Irwin, seemed free to follow the dictates of his own will. Previously he had found himself locked in, but upon this occasion he had escaped through an open window and a torn screen. He warned me earnestly not to allow him to inflict me again with the germs of evolution.

"'This dose, which was very light for the initial treatment, would have very little effect on the body tissues,' he told me, 'but each subsequent injection would cause such obvious change that in time one would be, as Ted is, unrecognizable as a human being!'

"I begged him to tell me what Ted looked like, but he only shuddered and turned away, and his last words were a repetition of his first, 'Don't let me administer to you any more germs of evolution.'

"That was a week ago and I have not seen him since—my own brother—yet I dare not seek him under these awful circumstances. I want to see that he is well, but I dread his approach for what it will mean to me. Can you help?"

Her last words expressed such utter anguish, I longed to put my arms about her and comfort her, but instead I merely said, "Dorothy, if I may be allowed to stay here until this danger that threatens you is put out of the way, I shall count it a very great privilege."

For answer she smiled a grateful acquiescence.

V.

"You may have the southwest bedroom during your stay here," Dorothy informed me. "Its windows overlook the laboratory, though the latter is so completely surrounded by trees and bushes that only its approximate locality can be detected."

A few minutes later I stood at a window of the beautiful room assigned to me and looked out across a veritable Eden; winding gravel paths, a splashing fountain, tall trees and clumps of bushes. And suddenly, with something like a shock, I knew that the large mass of vegetation at the far end of the estate hid from view the laboratory that housed my former friends.

"Former!" Was it true that I could no longer think of them as such?

"Such is the effect upon normal man of gross distortions of God's laws," I thought.

It was dusk by this time, and as I turned from my survey of the grounds below me to put on the light, I detected a movement in the shrubbery near the spot where the laboratory was hidden from view, and then much to my surprise, a figure emerged from the surrounding shadows. As it walked with a slouching posture and shuffling gait toward the house, along the flower-bordered path, I recognized with a disheartening shock Irwin Staley; no longer the aristocratic-appearing youth I had left three years ago, but a disheveled hobo with apparently one vague but persistent idea obsessing his mind.

I rushed to the door of my room, opened it and peered down the dimly lighted hallway. There was no one in sight, but I heard Dorothy moving about in the lower hall.

"Are you going to lock the house for the night?" I called to her from the top of the stairs.

"Yes," her sweet voice floated up to me. "I am on my way to the front door now."

Leaning over the broad banisters, I glimpsed her as she approached the door, but before she reached it, it was thrust open from the outside and Irwin staggered in. Her face, white with terror, Dorothy turned beseeching eyes in my direction and I lost no time in descending the stairs. Irwin looked at me with apparently no recognition. If his had been a one-track mind in college days, it was now even a narrow-gauge, one-track mind, for it seemed that no other idea entered his brain other than his mission in regard to his sister.

"Hey, sis," he said ignoring me as if I were nonexistent, and for ought I know, I may have been so to him, "Ted wants you to come out to the laboratory. He wants me to give you the evolutionary bacteria treatment in his presence. He claims he can advance you to his state in a remarkably short time."

As Dorothy shrank from Irwin, he continued, "It's no use opposing him, Dorothy. He is determined. And really you don't know what an honor it is to be chosen as mate and co-ruler with one who is in a position to rule the world. You and he would be so far in advance of the rest of the human kind that the establishment of your recognized authority would be immediate. Your progeny, the royal family would—Why Dorothy!"

Dorothy swayed unsteadily. I thought she was going to faint, but she rallied and turned to me. I stepped up to Irwin and seized his shoulder in a firm grip.

"Irwin Staley," 'I said harshly, "whether you know it or not, I am your old friend, Frank Caldwell, and though you and Ted are apparently not the same fellows I knew in college days, I am unchanged, and I propose to bring you two to your senses. Of all the crazy 'goings on' I ever heard of, this caps the climax!"

During my outburst, Irwin regarded me sullenly and with a suspicion of defiance, but the latter quality was not outstanding in his demeanor. To me it was apparent that he was a coward doing another's will.

Suddenly he put a hand in his pocket and quickly drew forth a small hypodermic syringe, at the same time roughly laying hold of Dorothy's arm. In another second I had caught him in the chin with my fist and sent him sprawling on the floor. He staggered to his feet whimpering and I grabbed him by his coat collar.

This scene must have been very distressing to Dorothy, but I could spare no one's feelings if I was to cope with the will of this monster of the future.

Turning to the girl, whom I knew now I loved dearly, I said, "Wait for me, dear; Irwin and I are going to see Ted and we'll we back again."

"Oh, Frank," she cried, her voice trembling, "I am afraid for you! Brave and fearless as you are, what can you do against the accumulated knowledge of centuries?"

"But it isn't that, sweetheart," I exclaimed joyfully. "Don't you see it couldn't be! Environment *must* play a part in the future development of the race, and Ted has no greater environmental experience than we've had. His physical body may have changed but not exactly as ours will, for the mollifying influence of man's changing surroundings would tend to soften and temper any radical tendencies of development. We are all subject to the inexorable law of cause and effect which will develop everything proportionately. Ted is an anachronism, and as such he has no place, in his condition, in our world, now or in the future."

"I believe you are right," she said smiling through her tears.

As I opened the door with one hand and clutched Irwin firmly with the other, a disquieting thought came to me, and I said to Dorothy, "If I succeed, as I hope I can, in returning Ted to his former state, so that he is really the Ted Marston of old, am I liable to lose you to him, Dorothy?"

She came close to me and laid a hand on my arm. "Don't worry on that score, Frank. I believe I'm changed myself, for I could never again love Ted." Coming close to my side and putting her lips to my ear, she whispered, "And do you know I don't believe I've been quite the same since I had that light injection of evolutionary germs. Could it—do you think—?"

"I *know* it," I laughed. "Probably the very first dose improved Ted, too, but he did not know enough to quit when he passed beyond the range of present possible environmental influence. He became drunk with the lust for power which he mistakenly thinks is his."

"I'd hardly say 'mistakenly,'" said Irwin, who had been a silent listener. "His power is a fearful thing."

Stooping, I kissed Dorothy as she stood close by my side, and in another moment Irwin and I were outside in the darkness.

VI.

I kept a firm grip on Staley's arm, for I did not want him to escape and apprise Ted of my coming. No words passed between us as we proceeded in the direction of the secluded laboratory.

What an ideal place it had been from their point of view, in which to develop their nefarious scheme. Completely hidden by tall trees and dense shrubbery, it seemed as completely isolated as a desert isle.

Knowing that Ted expected Irwin's return with his sister, I permitted Irwin to enter first and watched him through the open door as he slunk abjectly into the large room that was brilliantly lighted and occupied the front portion of the building. Beyond this, its door in a line with the entrance at which I stood, was a smaller dark room where could be glimpsed the faint reflections from bottles, test tubes and various chemical paraphernalia. It was apparent in his every move and his self-conscious mien that Irwin hoped to reach the other door before it became necessary to reveal to Ted the fact that Dorothy was not with him. In thinking it over, I presume that Ted's eagerness to see the girl enter, and his firm belief that she was with her brother, allowed Irwin to reach the other door unmolested, and just as he entered the darkened interior, I stepped boldly into the first large and well-illuminated room.

I say I entered boldly. I did, but with that act my boldness ceased, for I was rendered a craven by what I beheld. Upon a cushion at the far end of the room reposed what looked to me like a phosphorescent tarantula. As I gazed with widened eyes and gaping mouth, I realized that it was not the spider family at all. The circular, central part was not a body, but rather a head, for from its center glowed two unblinking eyes, and beneath them was the rudiment of a mouth. The appendages which had upon first appearance resembled the legs of the spider, I perceived were fine hair-like tentacles that were continually in motion as if a soft breeze played through them.

When I realized that the thing was regarding me with those staring, expressionless eyes, I tried to summon forth what little dignity I could muster, for instinctively I sensed that the repulsive form housed an exceptional intelligence. But I had never undertaken a more difficult task, and I was thankful for the moment that I was not standing in front of my biology class at the university.

"Well, what do you think of the bacteria theory of evolution now?"

Had the thought flashed through my brain, or had a thin, piping, gasping voice put the question to me through the medium of sound?

Evidently sound had played some part, for as I looked at the cushioned monstrosity, I saw that the aperture beneath the eyes was moving.

"Don't you recognize your old friend, Ted Marston?" came the derisive query in thin, wheezing tones. "Is the gap too great for your feeble consciousness to cross?"

"God in heaven," I fairly screamed, "you—Ted Marston!"

"The same," continued the voice which, though faint, carried with it a quality of undying persistency. "Do you realize that as you stand before me you are perfectly powerless to do other than my will? Do you know that it was I who prevented your entering the laboratory a few days ago? When my mind is concentrated upon you, you have no volition of your own?"

I realized that what he said was indeed true. He controlled me as completely as a master mechanic controls a machine.

He continued, satisfied with the demonstration of his power.

"You have evidently prevented Dorothy's appearance, but I can attend to that later. For the present I will astonish your feeble mind with a few facts. The rapid growth of evolution bacteria has reduced my body to an efficient minimum. The tentacles that surround my body take the place of all the old five senses except that of sight, and in addition to the five senses known to man in your stage of evolution, I have added seven more, and I verily believe more will evolve in time. These tentacles are more sensitive than the radio antennae of your era, and they pick up thought waves with little or no difficulty."

At this moment Irwin was visible on the threshold of the farther door, a decrepit being completely robbed of his personality. I questioned Marston in regard to him. The inhuman monstrosity gave a mirthless laugh. "Here we are, the triumvirate," and again that sardonic laughter wheezed on the air. "I found Irwin easier to manage with decreased mental ability, and I find all I rule must be like him before Dorothy and I can control the world."

"Your scheme," I cried in horror, "is to impair men's minds and then to rule mentally as a god?"

"You are really very intelligent for so low a creature," he mocked. "I would do well to begin with you. Irwin," he called, "I need your assistance."

As he called to Irwin, I felt his mental hold upon me relax, and I moved a step toward him while Irwin looked at me in surprise. An invisible barrier stopped me almost instantly. He continued to hold his attention upon me, while the man in the adjoining room was moving about apparently carrying out his command for a mind-enfeebling treatment upon me.

"You know it was one of your theories in the old days, Frank," the thing that was Ted continued, "that God accomplishes His purpose through the agency of man. Well, that is exactly the manner in which I shall accomplish my purpose—through mankind. But unfortunately I have to take humanity back mentally, for I am not God—yet!"

"*Yet;* you vile blasphemer!" I screamed, and then I saw it! I knew that the only thing to do was to forget what I saw in the adjoining room and occupy all of the monster Marston's attention, *all* of it! I cursed him, I threatened and even attempted violence, and all the while a being, who stood mentally at the dawn of humanity, approached from the anteroom bearing in his arms a great crowbar.

Could I keep from betraying by so much as a batting eyelash the approach of the man with the clouded brain?

"I will defy you, Marston," I screamed, "and I will do it alone, I—I—I. Do you understand? It is I, Frank Caldwell, who will oppose your rule."

A gathering mist blurred my vision, but as if viewed through a breeze-wafted veil, I saw the spidery product of evolution rise apparently without support and float in the air toward me like a bloated octopus in the water. Another second that seemed an eternity and the bar descended with all the force of brute man behind it, and I knew that the quivering mass of flesh could exert no more evil influence upon humanity. A few more blows and the thing that had been Ted Marston was no more.

The Diabolical Drug

If Edgar Hamilton had even remotely suspected whither his singular experiments in anesthetics were destined to lead him, it is doubtful whether he would have undertaken even the initial steps. But the degrees by which he advanced from an astounding scientific discovery to an experience beyond the ordinary ken of mankind, were in themselves so slow and uncertain as to fail to give warning of the ultimate catastrophe.

Young Hamilton's years numbered but twenty-six, and this was to the youth himself a slight source of annoyance, for the young woman whom he adored with heart and soul lacked but four months of being thirty-two. Now these six years would not have mattered to Edgar, had they not, in the eyes of his ladylove, represented an unbridgeable gulf. Repeated declarations of a lasting devotion did not change the lady's mind in the slightest degree, so that at last, in utter despair, Edgar shut himself in his little chemical laboratory and applied himself assiduously to the pursuit of the science that he loved.

For two months he saw very little of Ellen Gordan, and even in her presence he had an air of abstraction that contrasted strangely with his former ardor. Upon the rare occasions, when he left his laboratory to call at the Gordan home, he sat with preoccupied gaze, much to Ellen's annoyance, for this indifference was certainly less satisfying than his former demonstrations of affection had been.

Then one October day he was ushered into her presence as she sat playing the piano. He was hatless and breathless. She gazed at him reprovingly, much as a teacher might look in correcting a naughty schoolboy. Edgar comprehended the glance, and it only rendered his present call of greater importance to him.

"I say, Ellen, where can I talk to you alone? I've got so much to explain. But we must have privacy."

A smile of amusement flitted across her face.

"Let's go into the library, Edgar. It is warm by the fireplace and no one will intrude."

Together they passed into the library. After the door was closed, he produced from his coat pocket a vial containing about two ounces of a clear amber-colored liquid, which he held up for her inspection.

"What is it?" she asked wonderingly.

"It's the most wonderful potion ever concocted by the hand of man," he answered somewhat huskily. "It will make Ponce de Leon's fountain of eternal youth look like poison hooch!"

"But I don't understand. Is it to be taken internally?"

"No, that would be somewhat risky. This is to be injected into the blood—and—then—" He paused, not knowing how to continue.

"And then—what?" asked Miss Gordan with interested eyes riveted upon the golden fluid.

"I will explain." Hamilton gazed for a long moment at the yellow contents of the small bottle before continuing. Then he spoke, and his voice quivered with the intensity of his emotion. "You know, Ellen, the brain is the conscious center to which vibrations are conveyed by the nerves. Do you know what happens when the brain interprets vibrations?"

Ellen admitted that she did not.

"Well, neither do I," resumed Hamilton, "nor does anybody else, for that matter, but that there is a similar interpretation to all human beings from a given source of vibrations, there can be no doubt, though it cannot be proven that we respond identically. These various vibrations, whether they are the rapid ones of sight, the slower ones of sound, or the still slower ones of touch, must travel over a nerve with something like pressure, which vibrations, as I said before, are probably similarly interpreted by all of us. Now here comes my wonderful discovery," Edgar Hamilton's eyes gleamed with enthusiasm as he reached his climax. "I have discovered that this pressure, which travels along the nerves to the brain, is very like volts in electricity. Now most anesthetics deaden the nerves so that they but faintly convey the nervous impulses to the brain, but I have here a drug that instead of deadening the nerves, reduces the pressure or voltage, not in halves, mind you, but in hundredths and even in thousandths. You know how our bodies grow old. What is life but the sum total of our forces that resist death? Decrease the nervous energy expended in this process of warding off the grim reaper, and you have a prolongation of the bodily functions. Hence if not eternal, at least a protracted youth."

He held for her further inspection the bit of glass with its amber contents.

"Will—will it—make me younger?" she faltered.

"Certainly not," he replied. "It will merely retard the expenditure of your energy, and you will age very slowly, while the rest of us can overtake and pass you on life's journey. In other words, you will remain about thirty-two, while I go ahead at life's customary pace, catch up and pass you by a year or two, and then—then, Ellen, I may find favor in your eyes!"

"Oh, Edgar, if that can be done I shall truly say yes. What a wonderful man you are to have figured out so marvelous a plan!"

Edgar Hamilton already fancied that the future held much happiness for them both.

"And you are not afraid to have me inject this drug into your arm?" he asked.

"Is it painless?" she questioned.

"To the best of my knowledge, yes," he answered gravely.

"Very well, then I am ready." She pulled up the sleeve which covered her left arm, while Edgar filled the needle with some of the liquid from the little glass vessel.

"It will require the entire amount," he said, "to produce enough change in nervous pressure to keep your body hovering around thirty-two years of age for seven or eight years to come, but I shall administer it slowly."

And administer it he did!

For a moment it seemed that she was going to faint. Edgar led her gently to the massive armchair into which she sank. She sat erect, but apparently inanimate. Her eyes stared unshrinkingly into the flames, then for a period of a minute or two they remained closed. Then Edgar noticed that she was turning her head toward him, but the movement was scarcely perceptible. Her lips were opening so slowly, and from her throat there issued occasional low rumbles.

"My God," cried the terrified young man, "I've done it now! This is awful! Ellen, Ellen, you cannot live at this slow rate for seven years. I never realized it could be so gruesome. For heaven's sake stop looking at me so fixedly with your mouth open! I can't even talk with you intelligibly. Wait—I have it!"

He went to a writing desk which stood in a corner and took therefrom a large tablet of paper, and producing a pencil from his own pocket, placed them in Ellen Gordan's lap. After what seemed an interminable length of time she apparently noticed the tablet and pencil. Another five, ten and fifteen minutes ticked away on the mahogany mantel clock, at the end of which time she had the pencil and tablet in her hands and was beginning to write.

Edgar knew that task would require at least a half hour, so he left the library and rushed out upon the terrace where he found Mrs. Gordan, an aristocratic appearing woman of fifty-five. To her he poured out the experience of the last few moments. The two lost no time in returning to the library, where Ellen sat, an impassive figure, with a pencil poised apparently motionless above the paper.

"She has written some," cried Edgar, "but we will wait until she is through and then read the whole message."

Poor Mrs. Gordan was overwhelmed at her daughter's catastrophe and did not hesitate to express her opinion of young Hamilton, in very derogatory epithets.

"If you two wanted to be the same age, why didn't you take something to speed you up instead of bringing this calamity upon my poor, dear Ellen?" lamented the distraught mother.

"By George," cried Edgar, "I never thought of that! I believe it would be harder to do, but maybe I can yet, and then I shall catch up with her quickly. I could use it as an antidote for what has been given her."

"Well, try it on yourself first, you rash young man! Better have her this way than dead. But look," she cried, pointing to the immobile figure of her daughter, "she is through writing and is looking toward us with the tablet in her hands."

Edgar seized the message with trembling hands and read it aloud to the anguished mother.

The note ran as follows:

Edgar, what on earth has happened? I don't feel any different, but you fly around worse than a chicken with its head cut off. Half the time you are a mere streak, and as for your talk, occasionally I hear a fine, piping, whistling note. I see mother is here now but it was quite awhile before she stood in one place long enough for me to make her out. Don't worry, I feel fine, but what ails you?

After reading this, Edgar sat down at the desk and wrote the following to his sweetheart:

My own dear Ellen: The amber potion is working! Rates of vibration are relative. If we seem fast to you, you are extremely slow to us. We remain normal with the rest of the inhabitants of this world, while you are considerably slowed up, but do not be alarmed, my dear. I am now beginning to catch up with you in age. And here is a secret for you, your mother and me. I am going to produce an antidote which I shall take until I overtake you quickly, then I shall give you some to bring you back to normal. Then, as the fairytale has it, we shall live happily ever after.

Your devoted Edgar.

P.S. You might begin writing me another message right away, so I shall have it to enjoy this evening!

He gave this note to Ellen and then followed Mrs. Gordan out on the terrace, where he assured her with sincere words of consolation, that everything would come out all right. Mrs. Gordan had been considerably cheered by her daughter's message, and the indignation which she had felt toward her prospective son-in-law was partially mollified. They sat for some time discussing the prospects of a bright future. At length Edgar arose and said he would have a look in at the library to see if Ellen had finished reading the note. In a moment he rushed back toward Mrs. Gordan, his face depicting abject terror.

"Come, come at once," he cried.

The frantic mother joined him, and together they ran into the library.

Ellen sat with her face turned toward them, her mouth wide open, her eyes squinting. The immobility of the features was gruesome.

"Isn't that awful!" gasped Edgar when he could find voice.

"Awful, nothing!" exclaimed the indignant mother. "Can't you see the poor dear girl is laughing at your postscript? See, her finger points to it!"

But Edgar turned and fled!

Many times in the days and weeks that followed, Edgar Hamilton thought of the interminable smile that had lost its quality of alert gaiety, which is essential, if a smile is to put across its meaning at all.

And the antidote? That was progressing splendidly. It was to be a much more powerful drug than the other. Edgar had figured out that one drop of the colorless antidote would counteract the two ounces of amber fluid which had been injected into the veins of Ellen Gordan.

Before taking any chances with himself, Edgar decided to try the experiment upon Napoleon, the tortoise-shell cat. Napoleon had been nicknamed Nap because he was such a sleepy old fellow. Nap was past the prime of cat life. He was no longer a good mouser, so Edgar figured that if his declining years were a bit shortened, no one would greatly regret that fact, and Nap could prove very useful in testing the powerful antidote.

Nap was discovered sleeping under the back porch near the remains of a pork chop which Agnes, the maid, had thrown out to him after breakfast. Edgar smuggled the furry creature upstairs and into the laboratory, and lost no time in administering the drug. One drop was all that he intended to inject, but when Nap felt the prick of the needle, he leaped wildly into the air, and before Edgar could withdraw the instrument, Nap had in his veins about ten drops. After a dazed second or two, Edgar thought the cat had disappeared, but upon closer observation, he perceived a faint gray streak near the floor moving with almost lightning-like rapidity around the room. Finally the streak disappeared and he saw flashes of color. These, he assumed, were the vibrations of Nap's wild cries increased until they entered the realm of vision. Then there was a puff of smoke, an instantaneous glare of fire, and Edgar knew that Nap had literally ignited, due to his friction with the air.

"Well," thought the young chemist sadly, when he had recovered from the shock of Nap's fate, "I must take only one drop. That will allow me to catch up with Ellen in a few weeks, or at most, months. Then we will forget about this dangerous drug business."

He took within the needle but one drop of the crystal fluid and injected it quickly. Nothing apparently happened. He walked to his window and looked out upon the street below, and then he knew what had occurred. It was a frozen world that he beheld! An automobile stood in front of the house and yet it was not standing, for behind it was a cloud of dust that hung motionless like a fogbank. Everywhere people stood in grotesque attitudes. It required the most infinite patience to discover the meaning of their postures. He turned away from the window and stood buried in thought. At last he became aware that Agnes, the maid, was drifting toward him like some slowly swimming fish. She held a letter in her hand.

"Now," thought Edgar, "I will not alarm her. I will imitate her slow and ponderous movements in receiving the letter from her."

Gauging the rate of her approach, he extended his arm as slowly as his muscular control permitted and received the letter with a grave and tiresomely slow bow. If his actions did not appear exactly normal, he could not tell it by the fixed expression of Agnes's features, which were none too mobile under ordinary conditions. He stood perfectly still until she had disappeared, then with feverish haste he opened the missive which was written in the straight firm handwriting of Mr. Paul Gordan, the father of Ellen.

"You infernal young idiot," it ran, "I'd like nothing so well as to twist your miserable neck! Day after day my daughter sits like a statue and it quite gets on her mother's nerves and mine, to get into communication with her. But now to cap the climax! She has a severe case of measles and the doctor tells us she will likely have the disease for the next five years!"

With a sob, Edgar flung the letter from him and seized the vial of colorless fluid.

"Let it be ten drops," he said hoarsely. "I shall go as old Nap did—but no—I shan't prolong it, I will take the entire two ounces that I have made. The quicker the better!"

Now the reader at this point will doubtless be prepared for the hasty conclusion of this story, but such, I regret to say, is not the case. Have you never heard that one hundred thousand volts of high frequency electricity can be discharged through a living body with no apparent damage, but diminish the number of volts to five hundred or a thousand at a lower frequency and death is instantaneous? Something of the quality of the mysterious force known to us as electricity was contained in that harmless looking liquid. Before Edgar had put the entire two ounces into his arm he was conscious of a deafening roar and of intermittent flashes of brilliant lights. He felt as if he were falling through interstellar space. He seemed to be passing suns with planets swinging in their orbits about them. Great universes stretched on and on without end! At first he thought, "They are universes of solar systems, containing suns and planets." Then with sudden lucidity came the thought, "They are molecules made up of atoms, containing protons and electrons! I am going, not the way of the telescope, but of the microscope!"

A physics professor, who had been considered a little wild in his theories, had once said these words and they had never been forgotten by the student, Hamilton.

"Our Earth in the ether of space is as but a grain of sand upon the seashore. Our universe may be but a molecule in a greater universe, and all our ages since the beginning of time, record but a second in the time of that larger cosmos. Then take it the other way too. In this grain of sand which I hold in my hand, there may be other universes which, while I have talked to you, have come into being, and vanished. Students, perhaps time is the fourth dimension we have sought after so long! Would not this theory prove that the time element enters into the size of things?"

Then Edgar understood. Ellen had been headed the way of the telescope, but *only to an infinitesimal degree.* His body was hurtling *millions of times more rapidly* in the direction of microscopic infinity, and as his physics professor had explained, the atomic space is as vast, proportionally, as interplanetary space. The difference is that of rates of vibration, and with his bodily shrinkage, Edgar was expending his bodily energies at a relatively rapid rate.

Unable to measure the passage of time, Edgar drowsily felt himself losing consciousness. If this was death it was actually a pleasurable experience.

Again consciousness, sharp and acute. Edgar looked about him and raised himself to a sitting posture. In his ears pounded an almost deafening roar, and a strong wind was blowing steadily. He seemed to be lying upon a stone-paved floor. Then he observed that it was a great ledge, as broad as the length of a city block. He could see where it made a straight horizon with the sky a few rods away. But the fearful roar! He turned toward the near edge of this ledge, and there, stretching in endless billows that tossed and drove great waves to points within not more than ten feet from the top of the huge wall, was a vast watery expanse, the most restless, writhing body of water that Edgar had ever imagined. Nothing but water, a deep blue sky (not the cerulean blue of the skies of Terra, but a deeper royal blue) and the stone paving of this vast shelf of rocks! Edgar took a few steps toward the farther edge. As he walked, he noticed how evenly and smoothly the slabs of stone had been fitted together. It was like one vast block of concrete.

He approached curiously and cautiously the opposite edge, and peered below. He drew back in even greater alarm, for he had glimpsed a pit of fire that sent up great tongues of flame. He seemed literally between the devil and the deep sea! Stepping back a few paces he commenced to walk along the paving which seemed the only safe place upon this strange world. To the left stretched the boundless sea and to the right the awful semblance of Hades!

After several miles of weary walking, Edgar began to feel acutely the pangs of hunger. He ventured warily toward the right edge once more, and this time he did not draw back in alarm. Far, far below him lay a beautiful green valley with rolling swards and mossy hillocks. Dwelling places dotted the landscape and figures moved about. From his lofty height the scene resembled the miniature cardboard village of his childhood's day. But how to descend into this Garden of Eden! There seemed to be no visible means of getting down to what seemed a veritable paradise, after the experiences of the past hour. Along the entire length of the wall, as far down as Edgar could see, in both directions, his eye could perceive nothing but a blank uniformity, unless—he peered more intently. A few feet directly below him he saw two small holes, and his heart gave a joyful bound. The holes must have been made there for the purpose of attaching the curved ends of a ladder used in ascending this most gigantic piece of masonry. Edgar decided to remain directly above the holes until one of the inhabitants of this miniature world should be moved by providence to investigate the top of the mammoth dike.

Many times during the days that followed, Edgar gave up in despair.

He tried to shout, but his voice was completely lost in the unceasing roar of the ocean back of him. Too weak to hope longer, he lay down utterly despondent. And then came hope and with it a renewed strength!

Directly below him at the base of this vast wall which sloped toward the valley, at an angle of about thirty degrees, were many figures gesticulating and carrying long black objects upon their shoulders. Edgar in his weakness and excitement nearly lost his balance in watching the procedure. Then he was assured beyond the question of a doubt that one of them was scaling the wall. Over and over the ladder was being turned and attached into holes along the side. Nearer and nearer crawled a tiny saffron garmented creature until the ladder had been inserted into the last holes and an inhabitant of the remote valley stood in astonishment before Edgar Hamilton.

His short yellow garment hung by straps across his shoulders and extended below his waist where it ended in short bloomers, full enough to give the effect of a skirt. His features were in type not unlike those of the people of our Eastern civilization of today.

Communication through a common language was, of course, impossible, but Edgar was able to indicate his desire for food and his wish to descend into the green valley. The stranger nodded and then ran to the opposite edge of the dike and gazed long and fixedly at the stormy sea. At length he turned back toward Edgar and the latter noticed that his face wore an expression of extreme anxiety.

They both descended by the ladder.

Once down among these people, so like and yet so different from himself, Hamilton learned many strange and wonderful things. Inside of a few weeks he had mastered their language. He became acquainted with numerous astounding truths concerning this planet to which fate had so strangely sent him. Chief among these was the fact that the large island upon which the people dwelt had at one time been part of a vast continent, but the larger portion of this land with its great cities and monumental temples, palaces and fertile plains had been swallowed up in the ocean. The remnant of the civilization living upon a lofty plateau had managed to survive the onslaught of the sea, whose waters seemed to creep up through the centuries, and threatened to engulf them. In reality it was not the water which rose, but the land that sank due to enormous subterranean gas pockets collapsing, the gas escaping through fiery volcanoes. This was a sunken land then that maintained its temporary safety only through the building and repair of its monstrous dikes.

Edgar thought of Holland on the far away Earth. (Ah! but was it so far away? He and all the universe about him were an infinitesimal part of the new blue-figured linoleum that he had purchased recently for his laboratory!)

"Not so much like Holland," he said to himself one time, "as like the lost land of Mu, which, according to archeologists was a tropical continent larger than North America. It went to the bottom of the Pacific with its sixty-four million white inhabitants and their templed cities thirteen thousand years ago."

Then *she* came into Edgar's life and gradually he forgot the linoleum on the laboratory floor and the measles that threatened to last for five long years. *She* was the daughter of Elto, the chief inspector and engineer of the dikes. A sort of modern Nehemiah was he, as he superintended the continual erection of the rocky walls that preserved the land of Luntin from total annihilation. Her name was Yana and her pale, wild beauty outrivaled the charms of any earthly maiden Edgar had ever known.

One time they sat upon a grassy knoll outside Elto's home. They looked in the direction of Mt. Karp, into whose forbidding depths Edgar had gazed at the time of his arrival upon this planet.

"The fiery mount has been very active of late years," said Yana sadly, her sweet troubled eyes turned in the direction of the volcano. "Father says that the land is sinking rapidly and that the dikes have now been built as high as is possible without their crumbling. He and the wise Kermis predict that inside of the next fifty or sixty years our beloved Luntin and its inhabitants will be no more, and over all this will stretch that wild, roaring ocean!"

She shuddered and in that moment Edgar had clasped her in his arms and won from her the promise to be his bride.

Twenty-five years passed; years filled with much happiness, but clouded with an ever increasing anxiety for the fate of Luntin. Edgar and Yana had lived in happy companionship. They had a son whom they called Yangar. The lad was the pride of their hearts. He had inherited his grandfather's constructive ability, and at the age of twenty-two was appointed chief engineer of the dikes, to succeed his late grandfather, Elto. In this capacity Yangar was a decided success, and by his ingenuity had more than once warded off dire calamity to his country.

Thirty-five years more! It looked as if the date set by old Elto for the inundation was nigh. Yangar, now a widower with a son of his own, Manly, was ingenious and vigilant, but even these qualities could not hold out forever against such a monster as hurled itself constantly against the walls. Yana grew thin and wasted away with worry and died. Edgar sorrowed greatly over the loss of his wife, and his son became doubly dear to him.

One time after Yangar had returned from an inspection of the dikes, his father showed him a bottle containing a yellow liquid.

"This," he explained to Yangar, "is the way out of the catastrophe for us. It has taken me years to prepare it. I will divide it in thirds; for you, your son, Manly, and myself. It is a very concentrated form of a drug I prepared sixty years ago. The entire contents of this bottle is sufficient, if injected into the veins of you, Manly and myself, to so decrease the rate of our nerve impulses that we shall no longer be of this world."

He paused, while in retrospection his mind's eye saw the immobile form of that earthly maiden with her interminable smile.

"We shall not be of this world, father!" exclaimed Yangar. "Do you mean that we shall die?"

"Not that, I trust," replied Edgar, "but as I have often explained to you before, time and size being purely relative, we cannot of necessity become infinitely slower in our rate of existence without at the same time growing infinitely bigger. This process employed at the crucial moment of disaster will lift us to a world in a universe next larger to our own. My bodily forces are about exhausted anyhow, but for you and your son Manly, it will mean the ability to complete the normal span of your lives."

Then came a day when Edgar and his grandson, Manly, a young man of four and thirty, who bore a marked resemblance to his grandfather when the latter had come a stranger to Luntin, sat within the little stone house where they and Yangar dwelt together. The latter was away, as was his custom, to oversee work upon the dikes. On the morrow Manly would be one of the number chosen to labor for the safety of his land.

"Tomorrow you and Yangar must take with you your bottles containing your portions of this wonderful drug that diminishes nervous pressure," said Edgar Hamilton, smiling with affection at his stalwart and handsome grandson. "It is no longer safe to be without it. The attached syringes will render its injection a matter of seconds only."

He had scarcely finished speaking when a roar like thunder shook the very ground beneath their feet. Together they rushed to the entrance and lifted their eyes to the rocky wall that had held at bay their watery enemy for so many generations. The dike was a crumbling mass, a Niagara, increased to many times its earthly proportions.

"May the saints preserve me!" exclaimed Agnes as she flew toward her room and locked the door. "This mornin' I hands a note to master Edgar and he acts that queer I think he's after losin' his mind. Then this evenin' I goes in, and there he's a settin' on the floor with next to nothin' on, and an old man standin' beside him! I'm through. If these goin's on don't stop, I'm after lookin' for another job!"

At nine o'clock that evening the doorbell rang at the Gordan residence.

"The strange doctor who was called for consultation by Dr. Bennett, dear," said Mrs. Gordan to her husband. "Dr. Bennett said he would send him to see poor Ellen. Will you go to the door?"

"If it's the doctor, all right," responded her spouse, "but should it chance to be that scalawag, Hamilton, down the front steps he goes faster than he came up!"

Mr. Gordan opened the front door and gave a little gasp of amazement. In the entryway, with the streetlight shining grotesquely upon his bent figure, stood an aged stranger.

"Are you the consulting physician to investigate Miss Gordan's case?" asked Mr. Gordan.

The elderly individual bent an interested glance upon the man before him. Then he replied.

"I—that is—yes, I believe I have an excellent cure for her condition. May I see her?"

"Certainly, this way, doctor."

The strange physician followed Mr. and Mrs. Paul Gordan to the room of their daughter. Upon the bed lay the inert form of the unfortunate young woman whose nerve impulses had been so retarded as to render her a misfit among all the rest of humanity about her. The aged doctor gazed at the still form intently.

"Not a day over thirty-two," he thought to himself. Aloud he said, "Her most rapid cure will be accomplished by injecting this serum which—"

"But please, doctor!" pleaded the mother with a detaining hand upon his arm, "I—I don't like injected serums. Can't she—er—take it internally?"

"Unfortunately not, my good woman, but let me assure you, it will effect a rapid cure."

The mother surrendered and the old doctor injected into the arm of his patient a drop of colorless liquid. The effect was almost instantaneous. Ellen sat up quickly and looked from one to another of the occupants of the room.

"Mother, father," she cried. "Has the world really stopped tearing around at such a fearful rate? Ah, I know it is I who am back to normal. I wonder if Edgar is succeeding in catching up with me. My measles won't last long now!"

The old man turned to leave the room, but stopped at a question from the astonished father, Paul Gordan.

"To whom are we indebted for this restoration of our daughter to normalcy?"

The piercing eyes of the stranger swept the faces of all three.

"To Edgar Hamilton," he replied quietly.

"Oh, he sent you, did he?" laughed Mr. Gordan. "Probably the young rascal was afraid to deliver the antidote in person after my somewhat plain letter this morning."

The aged man advanced a step with outstretched trembling hands. "You do not understand, Mr. Gordan. *I* am Edgar *Hamilton.*"

"You—well this is rich!" Aside to his wife, "We must humor the poor devil."

"Joking set aside," persisted the stranger, "I am Edgar Hamilton, to whom you owe your late catastrophe and its more recent remedy."

Then he proceeded to tell a tale of a spent lifetime, a tale so fantastic that it fell upon incredulous ears. It ended with a wild unearthly cry of, "Yangar, my son, Yangar." His shrieks grew louder until they became the ravings of a mad man.

Nearly all who have seen him at the asylum and heard his story believe him to be the victim of an hallucination.

It is said that some months after Ellen Gordan's complete recovery from measles, she married a young man by the name of Manly Hamilton, who claimed kinship with the Edgar Hamilton, who had so mysteriously disappeared. There remain those of their acquaintance, who maintain that Ellen's husband and Edgar are one and the same man, but that does not explain the aged inmate of the asylum.

Baby on Neptune

(with Miles J. Breuer, MD)

I.
A Dying Wish

It must be admitted that interplanetary communication is still in a rudimentary stage; nevertheless some astonishing developments have already taken place. Beginning with the humble experiments of Hertz in 1887, progress has been variable but uninterrupted. Hundreds of brilliant men have devoted their lifetimes to the work. Episodes of intense human interest can be found along the way of this development. This account deals with one of them.

The story of any great achievement is marked by certain epochs, certain milestones, each of which is associated with the name of a genius. After Hertz came Marconi, who, in about the year 1896, expressed the existing theoretical knowledge in his concrete and workable wireless telegraph. He was followed by deForest, who about 1900 developed the three-electrode vacuum tube, making wireless telephony commercially possible. Then for a half a century nothing startling happened; efforts were devoted chiefly to the increase in transmission power and in the range of radio waves.

It was not until 1967 that Takats at Budapest experimentally confirmed the belief of scientists that radio waves, since they were electromagnetic waves of the same nature as light, could be reflected and refracted. Up to Takats's time we lacked the proper media for this reflection and refraction. Using the gigantic crystals of aluminum developed at the Kansas University by H. K. F. Smith, machining them into shape, Takats succeeded in focusing radio rays as accurately as the light rays from a movie projector are focused on the screen.

With his projection system four miles long, he focused radio waves of intensity receivable on the planet Mars. Two years later signals were picked up from Mars, Venus, and from the direction of both Saturn and Jupiter. That is how fast things moved.

It was demonstrated beyond a doubt that these signals were attempts of intelligent beings to communicate with us. Yet, by the time they were comprehended even vaguely, not one person was alive who had lived at the time of Takats's discovery. In 2099 a young kindergarten teacher, Miss Geneva Hollingsworth, at Corpus Christi, Texas, published a paper in the *Scientific Monthly* that gave the fundamental clue to the messages that had kept coming in over the instruments for one hundred and thirty years. The conceptions of number, size, rhythm, geometry, solar system position, solar system period are so simple and now so thoroughly understood that it seems ridiculous that it required more than a century to grasp them.

Though the fundamental conception was simple, the development of actual communication was a terrifically complex and tedious matter. Little Miss Hollingsworth was long dead and gone before the interplanetary code was developed. She would have shrunk terrified from the complicated proportions that her simple idea assumed, had she been able to see it put into practice.

But the year 2300 dawned with a fairly fluent communication going on with Mars, Venus, four of Jupiter's moons and one of Saturn's, and an unsolved mystery with regard to Neptune. Astronomers admitted that the bodies from whom intelligible messages were being received were in such physical condition that inhabitation by intelligent beings was a granted possibility. But, living beings on Neptune! That was hardly conceivable. That bleak and distant planet was too cold and dark. Yet signals came from it. Were they intelligent signals from living beings or not? No one knows. Certainly no one had as yet been able to understand them. They were merely noises in the receivers. Yet they were too uniform, too persistent, too regular to be passed over as accidents or as inorganic phenomena. They demanded an explanation of one kind or another.

Then, in 2345, came the first successful interplanetary voyage. Thirty-five years before a daring explorer by the name of Bjerken had gone in a trans-geodesic coaster to the moon, but had never been seen or heard of again. Consequently now the eyes of the world were turned with eager curiosity in the direction of Rex Dalton, the Kentucky physicist, who, on January 7, was starting out for Venus. The radios, which were buzzing at the last moment with announcements of the preparations for departure, suddenly gave out the news that the famous English astronomer, Myron Colby, would accompany Dalton on his perilous voyage.

The trip of Dalton and Colby was a memorable one, not only in the annals of astronomy and physical mathematics but likewise in those of biology, since it proved that man's previous conception, that, if evolution progressed on two different worlds it must necessarily do so along parallel lines, was an erroneous one.

The *Pioneer*, which was the name of Dalton's space coaster, descended to the steaming atmosphere of Venus, and its astonished occupants gazed through the transparent walls at a strange sight. Lying beneath the pale fronds of gigantic, stringy and palm-like vegetation were thousands of huge worms!

Their heads were large and contained points which suggested terminal organs of the special senses. If the aggregation of special-sense end organs constitutes a face, the faces of these things were creepy, repulsive. They were intensely active, twitching and writhing and darting back and forth, in and out among each other. They seemed to be engaged in a tremendous activity and even handled a good many blocks and sticks and things among them. The earthmen shuddered and were disgusted at the slimy spectacle.

In a few moments the shell of their vessel was so hot that to save themselves they were compelled to start the refrigerating apparatus they had brought with them, in anticipation of just such a situation. They raised their vessel and cruised about, looking for cities, for intelligent beings, and finding nothing but slimy life, settled again. Near them was another intensely active bunch of worms. Suddenly a message sounded on their radio in the interplanetary code:

"Hello! Are you intelligent beings in the crystal sphere that dropped from the sky?"

Dalton coded back:

"We are humans from the planet Earth. Where can we find you?"

Then the two men gasped in astonishment when their radio said:

"You are among us now, looking at us. Come out. We wish to look at you more closely and see if you are as civilized as we are."

The two scientists looked at each other in puzzled bewilderment.

"We'd better test the atmosphere first," Dalton suggested.

They had come all prepared for this. Between double doors was a compartment into which all accumulating waste had been placed during their space journey. The inner door was opened, the waste material was placed in the chamber and the inner door was closed. Then the outer door was opened by electrical means, and the refuse was thrown out electrically, and the outer door was closed again. This always lowered the pressure, which was again made good by drawing compressed oxygen and nitrogen from cylinders.

Now they had registering thermometers, barometers, and hygrometers and burettes for automatically gathering samples of the outside air, which could be analyzed in a few minutes with their equipment. The results of their tests showed that the atmosphere resembled that of the earth, with some excess of carbon dioxide and oxygen; the temperature was 60° C, the pressure 790 millimeters of mercury, and the humidity 50 percent.

"We cannot come out," Rex Dalton radioed. "Our bodies will not stand your atmosphere." They had to make some plausible excuse for not coming out.

These were the first scientists to return alive from an interplanetary voyage. Their trip may not have been entirely satisfactory from the standpoint of the romantic reader or the sensational news-spreader, but its scientific significance was epoch-making. It certainly gave the first evidence that intelligent beings can be found under other conditions than ours and in a form other than that which we have learned to know as human.

II.
Recording on the Steel Tape

Professor MacLean still retained all the keenness of his mental powers, although he was ninety-two and confined to bed. Recently his death had been expected every day, for he was so weak that he talked with evident effort. Into his room every morning came Patrick Corrigan, his friend, and his successor at the university.

"Corrigan," the old man said, and the younger man leaned forward to catch the faint words, "this is a great day for me. People give me credit for having had much to do with the building up of interplanetary communication. I would be ready to die now, were it not for that mystery about Neptune. That makes me feel like a failure. But, now these young men have returned from Venus, I feel encouraged. Some day the question of Neptune will be answered."

For a moment the aged man's voice trailed off wearily, then he began again:

"Baffling, mystifying this Neptune business. Those low-pitched, tapping sounds that come through our instruments must mean something. There is a rhythm, a sort of mathematical suggestiveness about them. I could die in peace if I knew what they mean."

Corrigan waited respectfully and somewhat puzzled. He had a solution to propose for the Neptunian mystery and hesitated to present it because of a foolish superstition that he might be thus the cause of Professor MacLean's death. Finally he spoke:

"You followed the radio reports of Dalton and Colby's trip. They landed near Phoenix yesterday. I've been pondering on their reports since. Do you remember what they said about the quickness of the worm-people? Doesn't that remind you of the uncomfortable speed with which the Venerian messages come in? Only experts can make anything of them. Now, Mars is slower than we are; quite easy to receive in code. Now, suppose—"

The aged man sat up suddenly with an effort, bringing a look of alarm into Corrigan's face. The latter continued warily:

"Now, suppose that the messages from Neptune are so slow that they fail to register with us. Because of their slowness, we cannot synthesize them into sounds!"

Corrigan stopped suddenly. Professor MacLean lay white and still; there was no evidence that he lived. Corrigan stood in stunned silence. Presently the Professor raised a white hand and a wan smile played over his features.

"Correct!" he whispered. "It almost overcame me. Now go and work it out experimentally. I shall wait to hear from Neptune."

For a man like Corrigan the experimental working out of the idea was a simple and straightforward matter. The principle of recording radio impulses electromagnetically on a steel tape was already well-known. Assuming hypothetically that the tappings he had been hearing from Neptune were individual wave impulses, a simple calculation told him how fast they must be recorded in order that they might be reproduced as sound. He rigged up this much of the apparatus and set it to making permanent records of the Neptunian impulses.

In the meanwhile he adapted an ordinary transatlantic dictaphone to reproducing sounds from the steel tape. He had three days of tape when he was ready to try it out for the first time. He wheeled it into Professor MacLean's sick room. The aged scientist looked as though he could not last much longer; Corrigan wanted him to witness whatever the instrument had to tell them. With beating heart he adjusted the tape into the dictaphone and started the tubes.

"—scientists of other planets—"

That is what the instrument spoke, quite clearly. That was the result of seventy-two hours of patient recording of Neptunian messages. About a word a day. Corrigan looked anxiously at the bed.

"I'm still in good shape," Professor MacLean smiled. "I must live long enough to hear the first complete message from Neptune."

No youngster eagerly awaiting Christmas was ever more impatient at the lagging footsteps of time than was Corrigan during the six weeks which he set aside for the accumulation of the first message from Neptune. He tried to get himself absorbed in other work, but it was of no use. He could not stay away from the recorder; he hovered around it continuously, which only made the time drag more heavily. Finally, one momentous day, the apparatus was wheeled into Professor MacLean's room again, and with trembling fingers Corrigan threaded the steel tape. They listened for the voice, which began in the well-known interplanetary code:

"Elzar, physicist on the planet Neptune, sends greetings to the scientists of other planets. The Earth, Mars, and Saturn VIII we can hear. The others are too rapid for us. For ten of our years we have been sending out messages. Answer if you hear this. Elzar, physicist on the planet Neptune, sends greetings to the scientists of other planets. The Earth, Mars, and Saturn VIII, we can—"

Apparently a repetition of the message had begun. Corrigan turned his eyes to Professor MacLean to see how the long-awaited message affected the old man. A smile of peace and contentment rested upon the wasted countenance. Professor MacLean's indomitable spirit had waited long enough to hear from the mysterious Neptune; then it had taken flight to the place where Neptunian affairs matter little or not at all.

Does it mean that the scientist was stronger than the friend in Corrigan's make-up, when Corrigan first dispatched the reply to Elzar of Neptune before making Professor MacLean's funeral arrangements? Not necessarily. While this famous man's funeral was going on, under the lenses and microphones that were broadcasting it over the entire earth, the slow tapping messages from Neptune were again being magnetized into the steel tape. It was over six months before the following message was heard out of the dictaphone:

"Elzar of Neptune has received the message of Corrigan of the Earth. For many years we have had analyzers for receiving the ultra-rapid messages from Mars and Venus; for many years our analyzers set to catch Earth messages have been silent. Today we are overjoyed to hear them speak. That tells us that you have understood our signals. Noting that you have already made a successful trip to Venus, and not having ourselves as yet conquered the problems of space travel, we invite you to visit us on Neptune. You will find no lovelier spot in the universe. Our extensive forests and our wonderful cities will please and amaze you. I live with my child in one of the largest cities, exactly on the equator and turned to the sun at XIX-1118-00B00. That will help you find me. Our home stands on the edge of a cliff, overlooking a great sea, the greatest on the planet. We live happily, though occasionally sorrow is thrust into our midst, because huge and vicious beasts come up out of the sea and prey upon our people. Just yesterday a fine child was destroyed. Elzar bids you come and welcome."

III.
A Trip into Space

The Neptunian scientist's invitation was a startling thing and would give Corrigan no peace. For months his mind dwelt on the idea of going to Neptune. Several other messages came from Neptune, all from Elzar, who had manifestly a powerful and interesting personality. Who but an astounding character like Elzar would think of extending an invitation across those reaches of space? And who but a genius like Corrigan would think of accepting it? For accept it he did.

The first thing he did was to call Dalton into the project. However, Dalton's spaceship could not be used, for the simple reason that it was too slow for that enormous distance. Theoretically, the velocity of light was the upper limit of speed for spaceships of the geodesic-hurdling type. In practice, there are numerous objections and obstacles to such a velocity. Dalton had made his ship so that it traversed the 26,000,000 miles to Venus in ten hours, with a mean velocity of 850 miles per second. At this rate, it would take about forty days to cover the 2,707,000,000 miles to Neptune at the latter's nearest position. After considerable discussion, a speed of about twenty times that of the original ship was decided upon. This would give a velocity of between 16,000 and 17,000 miles per second which would get them to Neptune in two days or less.

Two days is not an unreasonable period, and Corrigan was afraid of higher speeds, not knowing what to expect from the Lorentz-FitzGerald contraction. The principle is as follows: a moving body contracts in the direction of its motion, so that at a velocity u, its length is of its original length, when c expresses the velocity of light. Therefore, at the velocity of light, the length of the moving body would be zero. Most physicists believed that this was merely a conception of relativism, due to the fact that the velocity of light is an arbitrarily chosen constant in a world where everything else is relative. But no one wanted to test the truth of this belief on himself.

The late afternoon of July 11, 2347, saw the geodesical flier, *Neptunian*, launched into the unknown, taking with it Corrigan and Dalton. The two occupants had placed themselves face downwards on the floor of the vessel, and waited with fast beating hearts for the second of severance from all earthly ties. They watched with interest the curiosity and anticipation depicted on the faces of those who crowded about outside. Corrigan manipulated the controlling levers, and the dark frame beneath them became a blank. For an instant they were pressed crushingly against the floor, and then they floated strangely free. There was the earth rapidly dropping away from them below.

For a few seconds nothing was heard within the vessel but the sharp intake of breath. Conversation was out of question at such an exciting moment. The *Neptunian* was one hundred miles above the surface of the earth before they looked around within the vessel and spoke to each other. Land, water, mountains, valleys beneath them were rapidly coalescing and rounding into a sphere. They had barely begun to feel warm from the friction of the atmosphere when they were out of it. After they left the atmosphere, Corrigan threw the switches into full speed. In a few seconds the earth appeared no bigger than a bass drum.

IV.
Elzar Explains

There followed a period of space-sickness, during which the explorers were intensely miserable. They were afraid they would die and then afraid they would not die. They wondered what insane idea possessed them to embark on such a trip. Eventually they sank into a stupor of several hours, from which they awoke considerably improved. The disorder did not wear off for about sixty hours, however. Dalton was the first to feel well.

Later researches by competent clinicians on space trips have demonstrated that space-sickness is due to the removal of the effects of gravity from the fluid in the semi-circular canals of the inner ear. These canals constitute a little organ which controls the equilibrium of the body and which is closely connected with the eyes and with the gastro-intestinal tract. Normally the fluid fills the lower halves of the two vertical canals and the entire horizontal canal. In a geodesic-hurdler this fluid is freely distributed over the entire interior of canals, and severe vertigo, nausea, and vomiting result. Most people become adjusted to the condition in two or three days.

The complete isolation of the passengers of a space-coaster, their curious independence of what we have become accustomed to as natural laws, the blazing glory of the stars and planets in the black sky, the strange emotional experiences through which the travelers pass on seeing their Mother Earth become a tiny pinpoint of light—all these things have been dwelt upon so much in the popular magazines that this is no place for them. One point has not been clearly brought out in any popular writings that I have seen. At their enormous velocity, why are not space travelers in danger of instant annihilation by collision with loose masses of matter in space?

We know that space is full of flying bodies in size all the way from microscopic specks to small planets. A projectile shot at random stands a strong chance of colliding with one of them before it has gotten very far. But a geodesic space-flier is in no danger from them, because it is not on a world-line. Stating the same thing in different words, the space-flier is moving along a dimension at right angles to the three old dimensions. Theoretically speaking, it is not in the old Euclidean space at all. Practically speaking, space-travelers report seeing numerous bolides and asteroids, which, however, seem mutually repelled by their vessels. On a path at right angles to a geodesic, a repulsion exists similar to that of like magnetic poles, and it is not possible to approach a mass of matter of any size whatever unless power is applied and the course changed.

By means of a telescope with lenses of the marvelously refractive substance, protite, Corrigan and Dalton studied everything they could see from their vessel. They passed within a half a million miles of Uranus, a mere stone's throw.

"I wonder," mused Corrigan, studying the pale, golf-ball sized disc, "whether Uranus is a dead world? Doesn't it seem a logical explanation of his constant taciturnity?"

"It seems to me," said Dalton thoughtfully, "that it is the inevitable trend of the forces of Nature to build up Life. Life arises out of matter, regardless of what the conditions are. Even on our own planet Life exists in sections that would seem most unfavorable: the burning sands of the desert and the frozen seas of the polar circles. Life, yes. But not necessarily Life as we conceive of it."

"You may be right," Corrigan sighed.

On each of the fifty days observation and calculations of position had been made. Almost at every hour they knew exactly where they were. Therefore, when the disc of Neptune began to fill the entire sky, they gradually altered their angle with the geodesic and slowed down their speed, with a view to landing. For many hours they had been unable to sleep because of their wonderment at the amazing world that filled the observation frame beneath them. Great cloud strata pierced by jagged mountain peaks, which rose to heights of twenty-five miles above the planet's surface, veiled the greater part of the strange world from their eyes.

They had but a dusky twilight by which to see. Shadows were black as ink; a favorable reflecting surface shone dazzlingly. However, with pupils widely dilated and retinas rendered hypersensitive by their long absence from refracted light, they were able to make out all details comfortably and distinctly.

"We seem to have struck an uninhabited portion of Neptune," commented Dalton, unable to keep an undertone of misgiving out of his voice. "Like Martians landing on the Sahara desert or the polar wastes."

"All right, we'll move around and have a look at other places," Corrigan replied and suited action to word. Soon the awful grandeur of the bare, bleak landscape was passing in panoramic review beneath them. One day, two days they circled about, at sixty miles an hour, at a thousand miles an hour, but found no variation from the original scene that had at first staggered them. Nothing but dry, fearful canyons and bare, towering crags tumbled in chaotic masses, their tops forever buried in the cloud strata.

"Hm! This is funny," Corrigan mumbled through set lips. They circled the planet about the equator and then from north to south, but saw the same dismal rocks, the same cold, scurrying vapors. Bare rocks, swirls of snow—truly a strange topography for a civilized world!

"There must be some mistake in the messages," Dalton offered.

Dalton didn't understand interplanetary communication as Corrigan did.

"Mistake!" Corrigan exclaimed. "A mistake in the interplanetary code is more difficult to admit than what we see below us."

"Suppose the messages came from some other planet?" Dalton asked.

"Stop and think," Corrigan reminded. "We translated the word 'Neptune' from the code into English. But the code signal for Neptune gives the size, distance from the sun, and position relative to other planets. It is no more possible to conceive that the message came from some other planet, than it would be for me to imagine that some other person is talking to me with your voice. There can be no doubt about the following facts:

"That our message came from Neptune;

"That this is Neptune; and

"That this is an uninhabited world.

"From the bleakest mountain summits to the depths of those black gorges, there is neither plant nor animal life. Now, explain it as you will. I can't do it."

"Perhaps," suggested Dalton, "the Neptunians live in caverns within their planet. Let us land and investigate."

"No," reminded Corrigan. "Remember that Elzar's message said that he dwelt on the equator on a cliff that overlooked the greatest sea on Neptune. Now where's the sea? We've scoured this whole dead globe, and found no sea."

Dalton leaped up in sudden enthusiasm.

"Anyway," he exclaimed, "we can locate the spot he mentioned by means of his bearings, and see what's there."

No sooner said than done. In a couple of hours' travel and a half hour's calculation, they located XIX-1118-00B00 on the equator. There indeed was a looming cliff, and below it a chasm, that was a veritable abyss into nothingness. But the cliff was bare and bleak; naked rocks jutting out of dry ice, with snow sifting about. And the chasm, of which no bottom was visible, was not a sea, for there was no water.

Dalton proceeded to test the atmosphere, as he had done on Venus. When they hauled in their instruments and calculated their data, they were utterly astounded to find the following figures: temperature $-260°$ C; pressure, 30 mm of mercury; humidity zero; chemical composition, traces of inert gases of the neon type, amounts of hydrogen, oxygen, and carbon dioxide almost too small to determine chemically.

"That stuff out there must be hydrogen snow," gasped Dalton, sinking into a chair.

"Certainly no form of life can exist there," Corrigan sighed. "I can't explain it."

And so, with heavy hearts they turned the *Neptunian* back toward the earth.

Once more back in their homes on Terra, the disappointed scientists told the story of their fruitless journey into the depths of interstellar space. But, a surprise was in store for them. During their absence there had been time for the exchange of a few short messages with Elzar. These had been received and answered by a certain promising young man by the name of Sylvester Kuwamoto. (This curious surname is a relic of the epoch, several hundred years ago, when races and nationalities existed separately on Earth. His name is suggestive of the Japanese race and nation, which occupied the island of Japan, spoke a curious language, and was quite isolated. However, it was not long before Japan joined the general intermingling of races which has resulted in making the population of the entire globe a homogeneous race.) He had been little more than a sophomore student in Corrigan's laboratory prior to the latter's trip into space. But he had shown such a brilliant aptitude at the message-storing machine, that Corrigan had immediately given him a permanent position in the laboratory, and put him in charge of the Neptunian affairs. He had sent and received the following messages:

Kuwamoto: "Two of our scientists have gone out in a spaceship to visit you on your world. They will arrive in forty-nine of our days. Watch for them."

Elzar: "We are happy because we shall have visitors from the Earth."

Kuwamoto: "Please notify us as soon as you see them."

Elzar: "It is now the sixty-second terrestrial day, and your people have not yet arrived. I fear that the spaceship has met with disaster."

Two days after this message was interpreted, Corrigan and Dalton arrived. Corrigan immediately radioed this message to Elzar:

"There is some great error. We went to Neptune, looked it all over, but saw no sign of life or habitation. We found the spot which you designated as your home, but found nothing. We found conditions there in which no kind of life could exist. Can you explain?"

The reply was anticipated eagerly, but required the usual wait of three months to record, before the few moments of interpretation could be enjoyed. It ran:

"We watched closely for you, but did not see you." Then followed a check of the solar system data on Earth and Neptune at critical periods during the voyage.

Direction finders and range computers were put to work.

Interplanetary code checks and rechecks were made. Neptune's position was checked back and forth. The messages were from Neptune. Corrigan and Dalton knew they had been there. Could they convince the public that they were telling the truth?

V.
What Life on Neptune?

Fifteen months passed, during which Neptunian affairs remained a puzzle to the entire world. There was some joking at the expense of Corrigan and Dalton, though I doubt if any serious-minded person ever doubted their account of their voyage. On the other hand, there were people who scoffed; scoffed at the accounts of the voyage, and at the Neptunian messages which continued to arrive with systematic precision at comparatively regular intervals of from three to six months—but which shed no light upon the mystery.

Patrick Corrigan and his assistant seemed to live primarily for the moment when, the steel tape threaded, they could sit in their laboratory and listen to the words of Elzar. They had grown very fond of the scientist of another world. His cheerful, philosophizing personality seemed to come out of the void, encouraging them to find him, wherever he might be.

One day in the laboratory, after the interpretation of a particularly encouraging message, Sylvester Kuwamoto began to speak to Corrigan, thought better of it, cleared his throat to cover his embarrassment, and lapsed into silence.

"What is it?" queried Corrigan kindly. "Never mind me, you know."

"Nothing special," the younger man demurred; "only—I can't quite explain how I feel about Elzar. It is sort of—well, it may sound silly—but like talking with God. We can't see him, we can't find him; yet know that he exists and that he is good. Do you—er—see what I mean?"

"Precisely," Corrigan replied. "To be frank, I've had somewhat the same feeling myself, though I've never tried to put it into words. Elzar's personality is, well, a pervading one. We feel its influence through millions of miles of space! Too bad we can't know what he looks like. I can't help imagining him as an old man with a flowing beard and a kindly face. We human beings put a lot of stock in our sense of sight, don't we? Unless we can see an object, we feel that we know little about it. Yet I'll venture to say that in time we'll develop other senses than our five by which we become acquainted with our environment."

"That may be," replied Kuwamoto musingly; "but I, for one, am not willing to wait until more senses develop. I'm going to use the five I've got, and I want to see Elzar!"

Corrigan merely sighed.

After Corrigan left, Kuwamoto sat buried in deepest thought.

"Man's reason exceeds any of his five senses. Reason is more important at this age than instinct and emotion which have served their terms in the past."

A strange idea, vague and incomplete, was hovering about the outskirts of his mind, trying to get in. There was an explanation to this Neptunian puzzle; he almost had it within his grasp, when suddenly, elusively, it evaded him. There was something Dalton had said, that ought to be the key to it. For weeks he was moody and absent-minded. He read minute reports of the Venerian and Neptunian trips, and talked repeatedly with Dalton and Corrigan.

Pretty soon he grew more cheerful, and carried sheets of scribbled paper stuffed into his pockets. Early one morning he raced pantingly into Corrigan's laboratory. By sheer compulsion, he sat down and forced himself to be calm.

"Shut it off!" he said, pointing to the apparatus on which Corrigan was working, also in the effort to solve the puzzle of Neptune. "You'll never find the answer that way."

"You've got it!" exclaimed Corrigan, dropping his instruments. "Tell me!"

Kuwamoto began impressively.

"Exactly 500 years ago, Leverrier discovered Neptune—not with material instruments, not with his five senses, but by abstract reasoning. From the disturbances in the orbit of Uranus he predicted Neptune's position so accurately that Galle in Berlin was able to turn his telescope to that spot and see it. Likewise, abstract reasoning has discovered the inhabitants of Neptune. I can tell you how to make an instrument to see them."

Corrigan stared.

"Neptunian processes are slow," Kuwamoto argued.

Corrigan nodded.

"And you couldn't see the people?"

Corrigan shook his head.

"Nor the animals? Nor the plants? No life?" Corrigan ceased responding.

"Mountains of ice. Hydrogen snow. Low temperature. Low pressure. And yet there is life there. Life that was invisible to you. Can't you see yet?"

Corrigan waited patiently. Kuwamoto went on:

"Out there in that rare atmosphere, so rare that you could just barely detect it with instruments of precision, no life such as we know it, can exist. It must be a different form of life. The living things are gaseous bodies! Don't you see? Composed of cells, with nuclei and chromosomes and everything. But the cells are huge ones, composed of gases instead of colloids."

Corrigan sprang to his feet. His face was pale with sudden excitement.

"By God! You're right!" He slammed his powerful fist down on the table, causing a couple of flasks to topple and crash. He never noticed their contents spreading across the table and dripping down.

"Living creatures," Kuwamoto continued, "intelligent creatures, plants, animals, all composed of gas cells. Huge cells with slow chemical processes, all going together just like the cells do in our own bodies. Only out there in that cold, metabolism is slow."

They sat a while and stared at each other.

"But it is Life, just the same!" Kuwamoto exclaimed. "Only different from our kind of life. That's all."

Corrigan pondered.

"That hypothesis explains all the data thus far observed. Now to test it further experimentally. That means another trip to Neptune." He slapped his knee.

"A viewing apparatus for seeing Neptunian gas-life will be a simple thing. Some sort of fluoroscope such as is used by medical men in X-ray work. And an apparatus for storage-recording of visual images; we can take motion pictures at the rate of one a minute, and then project them at the normal speed of sixteen per second."

Corrigan was already figuring with his pencil on a pad, while Kuwamoto talked on: "A little experimental work right here in the laboratory will enable us to determine in a preliminary way just which type of electromagnetic vibrations are reflected from the surface of masses of gas. Too short a wave will go on through because it gets between the molecules; whereas too long a wave will penetrate molecules and all. When we find approximately the right length, we can get together our photoelectric receiving bulbs, and take them along to make the final adjustments on the spot. An ordinary television screen will do for the viewing end. You see: find the wavelength reflected from the gas-surfaces, devise a photoelectric cell that is sensitive to it; and project the images from the photoelectric cell on an ordinary television screen."

That night Corrigan tossed restlessly in his sleep.

"Gas cells. Of course!" his wife heard him mutter.

VI.
A Visit to Neptune

Preliminary experimental work was more tedious than the enthusiasm of the first moment had reckoned on. It was all straightforward stuff, nothing about it difficult to understand; but the mathematics was complicated, the experimental details were numerous and tedious. Thus it was a good two years after its return from the first voyage, that the *Neptunian* was taken out of its hangar and "tuned up." The second successful voyage to Venus in the old *Pioneer*, and the two disastrous expeditions to Mars, which took place in the interval, are too well known to require notice here.

This time the *Neptunian* contained three voyagers, for Dalton would not be left behind, and Kuwamoto had to be there. The vessel could have carried a dozen people, but the very applicants who were most anxious to go on the expedition were the least desirable ones from the scientific standpoint. Corrigan decided that news reporters and curiosity seekers would have to wait until this travel was commercialized.

The space that would have served for more passengers was given over to a radio and television apparatus for more perfect communication of the vessel with the earth. They left with as little publicity as possible. Publicity was becoming unwelcome to Corrigan.

The only matters of interest from the fifty-day voyage are Kuwamoto's notes on the passage of time. He states that the time did not seem that long. Time apparently counted according to what they did. There being little or nothing to stimulate them, much of the time they rested passively, and may even have been in a sort of unconscious state produced by the lack of external comatic stimuli. Kuwamoto thinks that the only thing that kept the entire period from seeming like a blank in the retrospect was his period of space-sickness, and the regular calls of the warning clocks by which they made their observations of position. This suggests that space voyages ought to prove valuable for invalids of the nervous-exhaustion type.

Corrigan and Dalton felt strange emotions when they saw again the same sterile mountain peaks and bottomless abysses. They cruised about for a few hours before landing, in order to let Kuwamoto see the general features of Neptune. Then they located Elzar's home on the equator, selected a resting spot, and landed the machine. Immediately everyone went to work. Dalton was taking straight photographs, which was possible with large lenses, sensitive plates, and long exposures. Kuwamoto set about erecting the viewing apparatus; he was feverishly busy, with an expression of wonder on his round, wide-eyed face. Corrigan began some radio messages back to the Earth, reporting their arrival.

In comparatively few hours, Kuwamoto's adjustments were finished. The two machines, one for direct viewing and the other for taking the storage-movies, were placed with their huge lenses against the transparent wall of the ship.

From within their warm vessel the travelers gazed out upon the stern and forbidding character of the landscape without. Directly centered in their frame of observation was the gently-sloping, plateau-like area that was midway between a rugged mountain with a cloud-shorn summit and the vast chasm that Elzar called the sea. Bare jagged rocks; ice, dry and solid as rocks; flurries of carbon-dioxide and hydrogen snow—these were printed indelibly upon their brains as they sat before the infrared viewing box, and switched on the current. The two older men calm and silent, the younger man half hopeful, half fearful, waited for the tuning of the machine. Then, abruptly, Kuwamoto switched on the amplifying tubes.

Corrigan remarked afterwards that his first impression was that of looking into a kaleidoscope. Dalton's impression, again, was that of looking at an empty room, and suddenly seeing it richly furnished. The brilliant coloring of the scene took their breath away. The gaunt mountain was covered with great billows of luxurious vegetation, and the plain was a wealth of flowers, trees, and grass, all inexpressibly huge in proportion to the people looking at them. The most beautiful sight of all were the great, opalescent bodies of varying shapes and sizes that were scattered about the landscape at varying heights above the ground. Their colors shimmered and flashed throughout the entire chromatic scale of visibility.

But, it was only the scintillating of the flashing hues that gave any variety to the scene, for everything was motionless. Not a movement, not a stir, anywhere. The immobility of the iridescent, vari-formed object was disappointing. It was like a brilliantly colored stereopticon picture.

The three men looked at each other with emotions that cannot be described. Has anyone tried to picture what Balboa felt when he first saw the Pacific Ocean from the "peak in Darien?" A few moments of breathless silence, and then some trivial remark to break the constraint; that is the way scientific men take these situations.

"Medusae!" Dalton exclaimed. "Jellyfish, a thousand times magnified!"

"And everything frozen solid," Kuwamoto remarked.

They moved their vessel here and there, to get new views, watching the scenery on the screen of the infrared view-box. With intense interest they viewed the multicolored festoons that adorned the landscape; huge, umbrella-shaped bodies that clung to the hillsides. Exclamations of delight issued from their lips from time to time, as some amazingly lovely object came within their range of vision.

"These medusoid forms must be the people—the intelligent beings," Corrigan remarked. The others assented.

The vast chasm was now a sea; why it should happen to be a deep greenish blue is not yet explained; but that was its color. Down in its depths could be seen vast, gloomy bulks; and on the surface, here and there, an enormous, slimy bulk, like a gigantic paramecium—obviously the ravenous beasts that Elzar feared so much. The three observers were hushed for a moment when they noted the contrast between the repulsive bulks of these beasts, and the brilliant and delicate tracery of the intelligent inhabitants. They brought their machine back to their original landing place, after hunting about a few minutes to find the location.

"Here we are," Corrigan finally said; "same old place."

"And yet, not quite the same," Dalton replied. "Look, some of these things have moved. They have different positions. Kuwamoto is right."

It was true; there was a slight change of position throughout the entire group of huge, globular objects.

"That must be Elzar!" Corrigan pointed with suppressed excitement to a brilliant umbrella-shaped body in all hues of purple, floating near a resplendent structure not far from the cliff's edge.

Kuwamoto nodded. He was busy adjusting the motion picture taking machine. He had it trained on Elzar and his house.

"One picture a minute," he said. "In about six weeks we can see some action on this film. In the meanwhile, why don't you talk to them?"

If waiting for Neptunian messages on the earth was an anxious suspense, imagine the patience that was required of these three men enclosed in the narrow ship, waiting for six weeks, until the message came to them, tick by tick. This six weeks, unlike the fifty days of interplanetary travel, were the longest any of the three men had ever spent. Fortunately, they were all three of them scientific men, and knew how to find intellectual pursuits to pass away a large part of the time.

Immediately on their arrival, Corrigan had coded:

"We are here. Look for us on the plateau near your house."

After those interminable six weeks had passed, after every possible aspect of the scene had been studied, and every animal and plant form studied and photographed (they could not move their vessel because the motion picture camera was constantly in operation), they finally threaded their steel tape into the dictaphone, and listened to Elzar's voice; through the vacuum tubes and condensers, this deep and kindly voice was coming from that purple, cape-like mass with innumerable streamers that hung up above the others:

"Welcome my friends, I am overjoyed at your arrival. I see your ship now, though you must have waited long and patiently to enable us to see you. Before that, your movements were so rapid that we could not see you. We realize that yours is the difficult end of this communication problem. From your message, I judge that you have recognized my house. Me you will recognize because I am larger than any of the other people in this group. My child resembles me in miniature, and is—wait a moment—oh—oh—help!—" and then silence.

Elzar's wail of distress brought the two men to their feet in instant alarm. All eyes turned frantically to the infrared view-screen. Could it be possible that consternation reigned over that peaceful scene; that events were at this moment rising to a climax that spelled some terrible calamity?

"We can do nothing!" cried Kuwamoto hopelessly. "Let us run the film through and see what is the matter."

VII.
The Baby on Neptune

While Kuwamoto prepared the film that had required six weeks to make, Corrigan radioed back to Earth, asking the receiving stations to get their television sets in readiness to receive the first reel of a possible Neptunian drama. Kuwamoto slipped his reel of film into the projector. For the first time the observers saw the frozen scene in motion. Trees swayed, multicolored Neptunians glided over the ground or floated through the atmosphere; the waves of the sea tossed, and a huge bulk showed itself anon; especially the Neptunians were busy on tasks and purposes of their own.

They all gazed at Elzar in silent admiration, aware of his dominance over the rest of the Neptunians. He was a truly remarkable organism. If he had been beautiful in mobility, he was a thousand times more lovely now. He resembled nothing so much as a brilliant, multicolored chandelier of gigantic proportions, scintillating throughout the chromatic scale with each pulsation of his delicately constructed body. Like fairy gossamer were his body tissues; and yet the vastness of the whole gave an impression of sturdiness and power. His prevailing hues were purples, though he contained all the colors of the spectrum, harmoniously interwoven.

"He is the only one whose dominant color is purple," Corrigan remarked.

"Appropriate, for both his brain and his body are exceptional. Look! there is a smaller being with much the same coloring!" Kuwamoto replied.

"That must be Elzar's child," declared Corrigan.

As they watched, Elzar rose above the other Neptunians about him, and the observers realized that he was just then talking to them—making the speech to which they had listened a half hour before. He remained quite motionless, and the observers, more interested in the moving objects, allowed their eyes to wander from him to his diminutive counterpart, who was moving away in the direction of the cliff edge that overhung the sea.

"Great heavens, look at that!" Kuwamoto's exclamation was unnecessary, for they all saw it simultaneously.

Out of the depths, a black, slimy form had risen, with the fluid of the sea splashing off its glistening sides. It seemed to spy the Neptunian child, for swiftly it turned toward the little purple bell. The deadly intent of the loathsome entity was obvious to all the observers. It reached out great pseudopods, slimy, flowing, shapeless projections, preparing to wrap them all around the bright body of the little one. Swiftly it closed toward its victim, while the men in the spaceship remained rigid, frozen in their positions; the little Neptunian was all unconscious of the impending calamity. Ready to fall upon the child, to close about him completely, when Elzar suddenly woke to the danger, whirled about, and sped toward the scene of the tragedy. Then—the picture was ended, and the men gazed stupidly at the blank screen before them.

"Ye Gods!" shouted Kuwamoto. "Just at the crucial moment, like a cheap novel serial! I suppose all we can do is nothing, and Elzar's child has been devoured by the filthy beast."

"Not at all, not at all!" Corrigan cried excitedly. "Remember it is all going on very slowly. Let's find out for sure!" He rushed toward the window and looked out.

Nothing but bare black rocks and frozen air. In his excitement he had forgotten the viewing machine that rendered visible the tenuous gaseous matter on this cold planet.

Through the infrared visual transformer, the scene which had become so familiar during the past week lay before them. Now it was more comprehensible, since they could read it in the light of what they had seen happen on the moving projection.

"Thank God! It isn't too late. . . . But what can we do? By the time—" Kuwamoto interrupted Corrigan.

"It is true that the distance between the monster's pseudopodia and the little Elzar is decreasing. But, it is slow. Let us think. We can act fast."

"We're enclosed in this machine and can't get out—"

"Those things are so big. Even the little Elzar—far too big for us, we can't handle him. Destroy the monster somehow—if we could do that—"

In helpless despair they stood gazing upon the scene of the tragedy. The monster seemed such a short distance away from the beautiful little creature.

"Blow him away!" Kuwamoto shouted. "The nitrogen tanks!"

The others comprehended his idea instantly. Corrigan moved the space vessel close to the scene of the tragedy, gradually, with the aid of the infrared screen, working it into a position between the beast and the little medusoid child. On the viewing screen, the two Neptunian creatures towered high above the apparently tiny earth machine; it looked like a toy between them.

Dalton and Kuwamoto placed a cylinder of nitrogen in the air-valve compartment that was used for refuse disposal, retaining control of its stopcock by an electrical connection, and aiming its discharge tube directly at the monster. The outer door was then opened, sending a puff of air into the face of the foe and causing it to sway visibly on the viewing screen, among the frigid, motionless scenery. Almost instantaneously, Kuwamoto turned on the compressed nitrogen.

On the infrared viewing screen, the stream of gas looked like a solid black beam shooting out of their space vessel. It spread out swiftly into a black cloud that struck the monster and literally blew the beast to nothingness. To the Neptunians, who must have been watching the attack, the sudden vanishing of the beast must have appeared very mysterious indeed. The pressure of the nitrogen in the terrestrial cylinder was to them an almost inconceivable phenomenon; none but their trained mathematical physicists could comprehend it.

For an hour or two, they waited and watched, anxious to see if the vortex of gases had done any harm to the Neptunian child, even though the bulk of the space vessel had protected it from the greatest pressure. In that time, no serious change was visible, and the men, exhausted by the strenuous events of the last hours, slept. Upon awakening, they were gratified to see in the visual transformer that Elzar had reached the little one's side; and that both of them seemed safe.

The men made a quick decision to return to the earth. They had gathered enough data and had enough excitement for one trip; whereas the difference in the perception of the passage of time between them and the Neptunians made it out of question for them to wait for anything else. The most trivial act of a Neptunian required too great a portion of an earthman's lifetime.

They expected at the beginning of their return journey, that they would soon hear from Elzar. On the third day they began to get the purport of his message, which occupied the entire flight homeward.

"My friends from the Earth, I thank you for saving my child. How you destroyed the animal, I cannot understand. It vanished instantaneously. When I looked toward the place you recently occupied, you were no longer there. Often have I warned my little one of the awful dangers from the sea, but I believe it is characteristic of the young of all worlds that they learn by experience rather than by admonition. You averted a tragedy that would have wrecked the life of Elzar. How I can show you the gratitude I feel, I do not know. Perhaps the time will come; but I must act quickly, for any delay on my part might cover the remaining years of your lives. My dream is interplanetary television, and to that I shall devote the remaining years of my life. Never shall I be content until I see the cities and men of your world. Again I thank you and may you live to realize the gratitude of Elzar of Neptune."

Kuwamoto sighed.

"It wouldn't take much," he said, "to go over there someday and clean up that nest of ugly beasts."

The Ape Cycle

I.
A Great Dream

On the afternoon of January 18, 1930, a train on a branch line of a well-known railroad slowed down and stopped at a station in the northwestern corner of the State of Illinois. Only two passengers alighted from the train, but they were possessed of individuality unusual enough to arouse the curiosity of the most indifferent inhabitant of this typical middle-western town. The man was clad in leather trappings, and most of his paraphernalia was strapped to his back. His face, though lined as if from continued exposure to the elements, was that of a man in his middle thirties. His eyes and forehead belied his general appearance, and were characteristic rather of the scholar and dreamer than of the rugged adventurer. The other individual was a little boy about nine years of age. He was a miniature counterpart of the man, and it was apparent they were father and son.

Presently part of the boy's bundle which was fastened to his back began to move violently, as if in an effort to extricate itself, at which the child exclaimed:

"Father, Adam is trying to get away. How soon shall we be home?"

"It is not long, son, before we'll be able to let Adam and Eve down, but they will have to be caged temporarily. Later they can have the run of the place, as you shall see."

The child smiled up into his father's face and said, "It won't be long before they'll be earning their salt, and won't folks be surprised?"

Over the man's face there passed a troubled shadow.

"I'm afraid it will be a long time before folks will be surprised," he replied gravely. Then his face brightened with a strange vivacity, and he added, "but when they do wake up to the realization of what we've done, the word 'surprised' will be much too tame to describe it. I tell you, Ray, it'll be the greatest thing the world's ever known."

That night, safely ensconced in the small farmhouse that snuggled amid a grove of sentinel-like poplars on the center of his large estate, Daniel Stoddart, having satisfactorily and comfortably arranged Ray and Adam and Eve for the night, sat before the log fire in his great living room and dreamed of the future—and the past.

The fire died down several times and had to be replenished, but still Daniel Stoddart dreamed on, living in retrospection the early years of his married life with his beautiful wife, Stella. She had come from a family of professional men and was not accustomed to the work necessary for the upkeep of a typical Illinois farm. But she had done very well in spite of financial reverses and her naturally poor health.

Conditions were hopeful, even promising, until Ray's birth, from which Stella was never able to recuperate. Hired help had proved undependable and unsatisfactory, and it seemed that in sheer desperation at her own helplessness, the fair woman, who was apparently born for better things, died, leaving with her husband the baby boy one and a half years old.

During the next five years Daniel had managed his farm with whatever futile, itinerant help he could get from time to time. It was during those years of apparently fruitless toil that the great idea found a permanent lodging place in his brain. It was born of a belief that to men and women rightly belong freedom from eternal toil. And when the idea had grown in his mind, he determined to devote his life to its fulfillment.

One evening six years ago he had sat alone before his fire just as he was now. Ray was in bed, the papers read. At a loss as to how to pass the remainder of a lonely evening, Daniel had sauntered over to his well-filled bookcase and idly scanned the titles of the volumes therein.

Absentmindedly he picked one up, opened it and glanced casually at the page before him. What he read arrested his attention, and he turned the book over and glanced at the title. It was the great work on the ancient Egyptians by Sir Gardner Wilkinson. Daniel turned again to the page that had originally attracted his attention and read the following: "Monkeys appear to have been trained to assist in gathering fruit, and the Egyptians represent them in sculptures handing down figs from the trees to the gardeners below. . . . Many animals were tamed in Egypt for various purposes—and in the Jimma country which lies to the south of Abyssinia, monkeys are still taught several useful accomplishments. Among them is that of officiating as torchbearers at a supper party; and seated in a row, on a raised bench, they hold the lights until the departure of the guests, patiently awaiting their own repast as a reward for their services. Sometimes a refractory subject fails in his accustomed duty, and the harmony of the party is for the moment disturbed, particularly if the unruly monkey throws his lighted torch into the midst of the unsuspecting guests. But the stick and deprivation of food is the punishment of the offender; and it is by these persuasive arguments alone that the simians are prevailed upon to perform so delicate an office."

For the remainder of the night Daniel Stoddart sat before the fire. Through his mind flashed image after image of a world wherein mankind was forever freed from the bondage of labor. True, men have had such visions since the beginning of civilization. The enslavement of the blacks had been such an attempt to free the white man from the drudgeries of existence, yet at what a fearful price! There must be another way, Stoddart thought.

He saw how the age of machines was promising man surcease from many types of work that have always kept millions in drudgery. But there must be something more, he thought, as he sat there in the firelight.

"Machines can never do it alone," he had exclaimed. "There will always have to be men to tend machines, and do many other menial tasks. But with the careful breeding and training of these primates it would be different. Since time immemorial lesser animals have labored for men, and if treated kindly, how better can they justify their existence and help man in attaining the high goal for which he is ultimately destined? The horse, the ox, the camel, the elephant, the dog and other animals less intelligent have all contributed toward man's emancipation from the eternal problem of working for his sustenance. Why not the ape—who most closely resembles man? His irresistible tendency to 'ape' man could be turned into useful channels. Slave labor was quite satisfactory until man became awakened to the moral wrong. But here we will deal with monkeys, apes, baboons and all of that branch of primates that are not human, and the moral objection that rightly abolished human slavery could not be raised."

The result of that night's thoughts was that Daniel packed up his belongings, closed the house, and with little Ray, then a lad of six, departed for the near East. And it so happened that the two and a friend, Job Wilhoit, an English businessman of means, found themselves in the vicinity of the Red Sea.

"It is here," Job told Daniel, "that many of the aromatic shrubs from which we get our spices and medicinal herbs are grown."

Along the rivers and in the ravines, recesses, and glens, the shrubs Wilhoit sought were growing in abundance. Stoddart was looking for something else. The shrubs were difficult of access and the men wondered how the Indians succeeded in gathering their produce for the market. Of course, East Indians are nimble, but the two adventurers knew it would require most unusual agility to harvest the crops from some of the taller trees, for their thickly-growing branches were extremely difficult to handle. The natives were particularly secretive about their methods of operation, and would never allow the assistance of white labor.

But one day as the men were topping a hill they looked into the narrow valley below and paused in astonishment at the strange sight that greeted their eyes.

A few natives were walking amid the shrubs and underbrush, shouting strange words in their own tongue. This was followed by unusual commotion in the treetops, and turning their attention thither, the white men saw hundreds of monkeys picking the fruit and throwing it to their masters below. The work was done so quickly and efficiently that our friends became fascinated by it and it was dusk before they realized it.

Dan and Job remained in the vicinity of the working monkeys for several days, subsisting upon herbs and roots, the while they watched with growing amazement the startling intelligence displayed by the apes. Often they were greatly amused at some of the antics performed by the little beasts. Dan remembered particularly one mischievous monkey who invariably sought the top of the trees and always saw to it that his plucked fruit never failed to strike the head of a fellow worker on its way to the ground.

Daniel became more and more enthusiastic over the future possibilities of ape-slavery and divulged his dream to Wilhoit. But his ardor was not shared by Job, who maintained that an innate treachery would prevent these animals from becoming servants in a civilized country. However, he could not prevail upon Daniel Stoddart to give up his dream of emancipating man from life's drudgeries through the agency of the ape.

Stoddart, Ray, and Wilhoit remained in the Orient for nearly two years. When they finally sailed away they had with them in cages six splendid, intelligent specimens of monkeys. For a year Daniel and little Ray were guests at the elder Wilhoit's estate in Wiltshire, England, where the two young men undertook the initial steps necessary for the realization of their hopes. The result was the breeding of some very intelligent simians whose aptitude was nothing short of amazing.

It had been agreed between Wilhoit and Stoddart that if it became necessary to replenish the supply of suitable beasts from time to time, the former with his ample resources would return to Asia for additional animals which he would ship to his friend in America.

So the two Stoddarts now home again had with them two monkeys, a male and female, whom Daniel destined to be the Adam and Eve of a future race of servant-slaves. They were to make man's existence upon Earth a paradise by relieving him of the distasteful duties that have always kept him in bondage.

Daniel was surprised to learn just before his second trip to the East that Job had married and taken his bride with him. And prior to the third and last trip of Job Wilhoit, the Stoddarts received the announcement of the birth of a baby girl. Young Wilhoit, however, never returned to his wife and daughter. What had been his fate none knew. The last that had ever been heard of him was when he set out from Kabinda in West Africa for an ape-hunting expedition into the interior.

With the coming of dawn, Daniel Stoddart rose from his chair and greeted the day with words of determination, "I will devote myself to the breeding and training of simians; each type for a specific kind of work best adapted to the animal's size and type of intelligence. I have in mind the ultimate development of the perfect monkey servant."

II.
The New Servants

Emerson has said, "Everything is impossible until we see success." That the two Stoddarts had accomplished the well-nigh impossible, there seemed to be no question. The proofs of the success of their venture during the ensuing twelve years were confined to their Illinois farm. But with the rapid approach to its borders of suburban homes, Daniel and Ray determined to seek some isolated territory where they could stave off the encroachments of civilization until they were ready to divulge their secret.

One day the two stood on their front veranda and heard in the distance the sound of steam shovels at work on a highway to go past their land.

"With your education completed at the University of Illinois," said the older man, "it is time for us to continue our work elsewhere. We must be away from the prying eyes of neighbors."

"But, father," protested Ray, "hasn't the time come for us to prove the merit of our 'unusual products,' and to market our monkeys throughout the country?"

Daniel Stoddart placed a hand upon his son's broad shoulder.

"My boy," he said sadly, "I fear I am not destined to see that time. You know the old saying, 'Rome was not built in a day.' It requires infinite patience to accomplish visible and tangible results in the field of evolution. You will see in your day the beginning of man's emancipation, but even for you and your children the *great* day will not dawn. You and I will pass on cognizant of the fact that we have but laid the foundation for the great superstructure of humanity's freedom."

The two men gazed across the broad fertile acres of the Stoddart farm which were secluded from the outside by an arboreal wall of closely-planted poplars. Everywhere was visible evidence of the scientific care necessary for a perfect cooperation with natural law. Yes, the two Stoddarts had prospered during the years since their return home on that wintry day in 1930.

The sound of a lawnmower approaching from the side of the house drew the attention of the two men. It was being operated and guided by a gorilla, a travesty on the human form. The animal plodded along remarkably erect, and with its prodigious strength handled the lawnmower as easily as if it were a toy, guiding it with careful precision. At sight of the two men on the porch, it bared its teeth in what might be interpreted as a smile of recognition, though it was not returned by the two masters.

"Beta is almost worth his weight in gold," remarked the younger Stoddart as the huge ape disappeared around the side of the house on the return swath. "Not only does he perform his own duties well, but he is showing marked ability in superintending the work of others. A few more overseers of his and Alpha's ability, and you and I could retire and be mere figureheads."

"Scarcely that," replied the older man with a smile, "I cannot imagine a day when the brain of man will not continue to be the prime factor in all human accomplishment."

"Man's brain started the ball rolling," commented his son, "but the momentum will carry it on."

"A sort of perpetual motion, eh?" queried the other. "I declare, son, your enthusiasm exceeds my own."

A baboon appeared, dragging a hose toward the porch. At the foot of the steps it deposited its burden, quickly ascended the steps and commenced carrying the porch furniture to one end. This done, it agilely descended, took up the hose, studied the nozzle for a minute as if slightly puzzled, then ran around to the hydrant and turned on the water. As it picked up the hose once more, its beady little eyes shifted ever so slyly to the two men standing on the steps. It brought the stream of water very close to its masters' feet, thought better of its mischievous inclination, passed the two and began to wash the dusty porch.

"Kappa will get too frisky for his own good some day," commented Ray.

Just at that moment a small monkey appeared in the doorway and chattered to attract attention.

"Go get the mail, Bedelia," ordered Daniel.

The simian came out of the house, cast an apparently disdainful glance in Kappa's direction, descended the stairs and proceeded at a loping gait down the walk. The two men turned to enter the house when a gurgling scream, followed immediately by an unusual chattering commotion, held them to the spot. Bedelia was being made the target for the water from the hose, wielded in the capable hands of Kappa, who jumped up and down in delight.

"Another case of atavism," remarked Daniel with an effort to suppress a smile. "Here, you young rascal, drop that hose!"

III.
A Strange Silence

Before either of the Stoddarts could enforce obedience from the recalcitrant Kappa, a huge paw reached up from below the porch railing, seized the hapless monkey, and gave the terror-stricken little animal such a blow that it fell to the ground.

"Hey there, Beta," cried Ray, springing forward, "that's not the way to do! Do you hear? I will attend to Kappa. No, *no!*"

The gorilla blinked in amazement at Ray's outburst, then turned and retreated to the lawnmower with injured pride apparent in every move. A puzzled scowl lowered the beetling brows beneath its receding forehead.

Bedelia took herself to the house in quest of a towel, and the two men bore the injured Kappa inside where they rendered first aid. But it was several days before the young baboon was able to perform his scheduled duties.

Daniel received the letter proffered to him by Bedelia an hour later. It was dated from New York and ran as follows:

Dear Mr. Stoddart:

My daughter Melva and I arrived in America day before yesterday. We have been so busy enjoying the sights of this wonderful city that I have neglected writing you before of our intention to call upon you and your son at the 'monkey-farm,' as Job has always termed it. Since my husband's disappearance my success with the few apes we had upon the estate has been miserable. Melva and I do not seem to employ the type of discipline necessary to hold the animals in subjection. We should like very much to be able to study your methods for a few days during our sojourn in your wonderful country.

Margaret E. Wilhoit

Daniel turned the letter over to Ray in response to the latter's look of inquiry, and when he had finished it the father suggested, "Let us send a telegram to them to meet one of us in Chicago. It will be much easier for them than to have to find their way clear out here in the backwoods. Can you arrange to go, Ray? You can be spared for a little while. The twins born to Omega last Sunday will be the last arrivals for awhile. Then I'll keep a weather eye on Alpha and I'm sure things will run along smoothly."

It was with pleasant anticipation that Ray considered meeting the wife and daughter of his father's former friend. He recalled Job Wilhoit quite distinctly, though he had not seen him since he himself was a lad of nine. Wilhoit had been a younger man than Ray's father, and at the time he knew him, was married about seven years. Ray figured the daughter was not yet twenty.

The meeting was one of satisfaction for all. Both mother and daughter, while possessing characteristic English reserve, proved friendly and entertaining, and showed an intense interest in Ray's description of the development of monkey labor. Melva's short brown ringlets, ready smile, and sly humor might not at first seem characteristic of a serious young person, but Ray was not long in discovering that this charming little English girl had deeper sides to her nature.

The trip to the farm ended all too soon as far as the two young people were concerned, but Mrs. Wilhoit was thoroughly fatigued after the long trip west, and was desirous of resting for a few days.

"Strange father isn't at the station with the car," Ray exclaimed as they alighted and surveyed the platform. "He knew when to expect us. You ladies sit down and wait a moment. I'm going to use the phone."

He returned shortly with a troubled, preoccupied air, and it was some time before he spoke.

"I didn't get father on the phone."

"Maybe he was a considerable distance from the house," suggested Mrs. Wilhoit.

"No, the phone was answered by Alpha."

"And who is Alpha?" queried Melva. "What an odd name. It is the Greek letter for 'A.'"

"Yes," replied Ray absentmindedly, "Alpha is A, and No. 1 in this case. He is our most intelligent ape. He oversees the running of our household week in, week out, with scarcely any interference from either father or myself. Routine and habit, of course, instilled into him by generations of highly specialized training. He is a large and important cog in this organization of ape labor. He almost speaks, but his articulation is very peculiar. Only father and I can understand him, but to do so is no more a stretch of imagination, I am sure, than that exercised by many a fond mother over the first efforts of her babbling offspring."

"How interesting," cried Melva. "How far you and your father have progressed in the realization of your dream! I don't think even my poor father quite realized its possibilities to such a vast extent."

"Your father was an explorer and adventurer, Melva," explained her mother. "He was not of a scientific turn of mind. Capturing apes was sufficient thrill for him, regardless of whether they or their descendants were destined to be eventually human or mere trained circus performers."

"'Eventually human!' Why, mother, what a sacrilege!" exclaimed Melva, a frown puckering her pretty brow. "Of course they can't become human. They have no souls!"

"At just what point in the process of evolution does the soul appear?" asked Mrs. Wilhoit with a knowing side smile at Ray.

"Well, all I have to say," continued the apparently grieved Melva, "is that if they ever do become human we can't have them work for us anymore. That would be slavery."

IV.
A Tragedy

Ray smiled gravely, but there was a twinkle in his eyes: "With the first appearance of a soul, Miss Wilhoit, we will pay them wages and they will be satisfied."

The taxi gave up its passengers outside the row of stately poplars.

"What ample protection these afford from prying eyes!" observed Mrs. Wilhoit as the three entered the grounds.

"Yes, our isolation has been all we could desire," answered the young man. "Of course, through the years it has leaked out that we have animals that we are training, but no one dreams that our ambitions soar beyond the confines of the circus ring."

As the three approached the house they saw Bedelia picking roses from the bushes at the side of the porch. The women watched her with intense interest. The simian's selection was perfect. She picked only those that were at the height of their beauty. Finally when her bouquet had assumed ample proportions she buried her ugly flat nose in it and nimbly climbed the steps and entered the open door.

"Will she know what to do with them?" questioned Melva.

"Wait and see," was Ray's response, but his mind was not on Bedelia. "Come and be seated, ladies, I'll get father."

The two seated themselves in the orderly and immaculately clean parlor. They surveyed with interest its furniture of excellent quality, but a generation old; ottomans, tidies on chair backs, and long ornate mirrors with wax flowers under glass domes.

"Maybe the monkeys like those things," whispered Melva with a suppressed giggle.

"Hush, child," reproved her mother, "these two men have more to occupy their minds than to keep up with modern styles in house furnishings. Look at that quaint china representation of those three monkeys who, with their paws over their eyes, ears and mouths, admonish the observer to see, hear and speak no evil."

A pattering of tiny feet drew the attention of both visitors to the door leading to the hallway. Bedelia was approaching, triumphantly bearing aloft her bouquet of roses in a vase of water. She set it gingerly upon a small table near Melva.

"Come here, little monkey," said Melva, holding out her hands invitingly. Bedelia hesitated, then slowly approached, her little eyes shifting continuously between the two strangers. To their utter surprise, she sprang upon Melva's lap and nestled close to her shoulder, occasionally watching her face to see whether her action met with approval. She pawed over the ruffles and trimming of Melva's dress and examined her beads minutely, then, amid the shrieks of laughter of the women, she took Melva's hat off her head and placed it upon her own, where it nearly touched her shoulders.

"If she has the fleas that our monkeys at home used to have, I advise you not to let her keep it on," laughed Mrs. Wilhoit.

A shadow fell athwart the gay scene in the parlor, and apprehensively mother and daughter raised their eyes. Standing in the doorway, its head nearly touching the lintel, stood the largest and ugliest ape upon which they had ever gazed. But, strange to say, its extreme unattractiveness resulted not so much from characteristic simian traits as from the fact that it just escaped being human in appearance. The slope from forehead to jaw was far less marked, the nose had a suggestion of a bridge and in the proportionally small eyes lay a look of amazing intelligence.

This "missing link," for so both women unconsciously termed him, was possessed of prodigious strength; for even through the clothes he wore they could see the play of great muscles on his arms and shoulders. From the massive trunk rose his thick, hairy neck, a pillar of strength, supporting the head that paleontologists might have easily constructed from the skull of the famous Piltdown man discovered in England. The hands, long and hairy, moved with restless energy about the buttons of the coat.

If either of the two strangers in the house had been less accustomed to apes of all sizes and descriptions, they would probably have fainted on the spot; but though their experience had acquainted them with a diversity of types, never had they conceived of such a creature as stood before them now.

A guttural command evoked an immediate response from the little monkey, who slipped unobtrusively from Melva's lap and disappeared through the door. But the great bulk of the newcomer did not move. Instead, he was gazing fixedly at Melva, and there was that in his too-intelligent bestial face that struck terror to the hearts of both women. Melva felt cold chills running up and down her spine, and when she opened her mouth to scream, not a sound was forthcoming.

The great ape, perceiving the fright of the two in the parlor, walked slowly forward, and his facial expressions gave clear evidence of the development of certain small muscles that had been wholly atrophied in his ancestors a few generations back.

It was Mrs. Wilhoit who finally spoke, her voice husky with fright, "Ray—Mr. Stoddart—where are you?"

V.
Reflexed

The gorilla-like creature ceased his stealthy advance at the sound of her voice and looked toward the hall and stairway. A faint rustling and the sound of rapidly approaching footsteps were welcome sounds to the visitors. In a moment Ray appeared, but a very changed man. His face was ashen, his manner thoroughly dejected. He entered the room as one walking in a nightmare, scarcely cognizant of the three occupants.

"Why, what has happened, Mr. Stoddart?" cried Melva, running toward him.

He sank into a chair and stared for a moment with unseeing eyes; then, suddenly aware of his surroundings, he looked at the great gorilla.

"Alpha, what do you know about Dan?" he demanded imperiously.

"Dan gone," growled the beast in a queer throaty guttural tongue.

"Is—is—your—father—?" breathed Mrs. Wilhoit.

"Yes—dead," said the man in a toneless voice, "dead with no marks of violence upon him. It must have been his heart, but why—"

Melva had been watching Alpha covertly. The great beast shifted its eyes from one to another of the group.

"Will you send Alpha away?" whispered Melva.

"Prepare the vegetables for dinner," said Ray peremptorily. The animal shambled toward the kitchen.

"Do you know, I detest that brute!" Melva exclaimed after the kitchen door had closed on his huge bulk. "I think he is terrible—a travesty on humanity at its worst."

Ray thought a moment before he replied wearily: "What else can one expect? The end, however, justifies the means. The intelligence of that 'travesty' and others like him will free mankind of drudgery. Though my father is dead, I am sure at the hands of one of these, I must carry on. Where monkeys are employed, the menial tasks of men and women are performed with scarcely any supervision. Think what it means for us to be free to turn our attentions to the higher things of life!" His voice rose rapturously.

"If there are many more like Alpha will there be any of us left to consider 'the higher things of life?'" Melva asked, trying to divert his mind from the tragedy.

"What do you mean?" Ray questioned, his voice sharp with a sudden note of alarm. It was evident that he was terribly disturbed.

"Simply this," the girl replied evenly. "Alpha has murdered your father and you should acknowledge the truth. Why don't you face this thing squarely and admit that your perfect servant who saves you physical fatigue, possesses mental quirks that have made him a murderer?"

"But I questioned him," answered Ray, "and he says he found father dead."

"Then why did he leave you to discover the tragedy alone instead of apprising you of the fact at once?" persisted Mrs. Wilhoit.

"Gorillas cannot kill without leaving behind them the tell-tale marks of their violence," said Ray.

"Not even exceptionally smart gorillas?" queried Melva.

"Not even those who are exceptionally smart, Melva," replied Ray gravely, "for their intelligence is all concentrated in the direct field of their particular labor. They are exaggerated specialists. Outside of the care of this house, Alpha is a fool."

"I wouldn't be too sure, my boy," said the older woman, shaking her head sadly.

"Nevertheless," replied the youth, "many years in this work make me reasonably certain that I know whereof I speak."

"Indeed, we hope you are right, Ray," said Melva. "We—we are very sorry for your loss."

VI.
Alpha's Treachery

For three months following the sad demise of the elder Stoddart, Mrs. Wilhoit and Melva toured the western states, returning to Illinois to say goodbye to Ray. They found him sad and lonely, but quietly determined to carry on the work bequeathed him by his father.

One evening, a few days prior to the date set for the departure of the visitors, Melva and Ray sought the lane that was shaded by the poplars. It had been an interesting day. Ray had been instructing two baboons who were specialized along mechanical lines, in the operation of a new farm implement. The baboons had proved very apt pupils, and before the day was over Ray was convinced that henceforth the care and operation of that machine or any like it could be entirely turned over to the two. Melva had taught four very young monkeys the names and different uses for all the dishes and silverware. They had played it as a game and the monkeys always considered it as such. Like their parents who for generations had performed table duty, the youngsters took to the task as the proverbial duck to water.

"You know, Ray," confided Melva, "for a while I rather lost the vision that our fathers had of the true greatness of this project. But lately I have caught some of your enthusiasm when I see what is accomplished here without the aid of human hands. What cannot man do when, unhampered by the sordid, monotonous tasks of daily life, he will be at liberty to pursue science and art to the limit?"

"I have been on the lookout for a young man who seemed inclined to share my enthusiasm," said Ray with a curious glance at the face of his companion. "I am going west, out into the desert, where with unlimited possibilities of growth and in a climate more healthful for the monkeys, I shall quietly revolutionize the labor of mankind. Think of the time, Melva, when I can say that the day of man's emancipation has come!"

Melva was silent. Her previous ardor seemed to have left her.

"What is the matter?" her companion inquired. "Don't you believe the prospects of this enterprise demand a larger field of labor, and that I should have a partner to help me?"

"I do indeed," said the girl in mock solemnity. "I approve of the desert, the climate and an enthusiastic co-worker on this scheme, but why does he have to be a young man?"

"Well—you see," Ray said, looking off into the distance, "an older man like my father might—"

There was a sudden shriek. Ray turned his head to see Melva snatched at from behind the poplars and bushes that fringed the path and through the gloom he saw that she was being borne away, apparently unconscious, in the arms of Alpha. Ray began immediate pursuit, shouting the gorilla's name in imperious tones. Never before had Alpha so defied him. The distance between them rapidly increasing, Ray could hardly detect in the darkness the broad shoulders of the beast. He noted the light patch of Melva's dress floating through the air and deduced that Alpha had shifted his burden to facilitate his escape.

As Ray suspected, Alpha was headed for the monkey houses at the rear of the estate. The great ape did not possess the mental acumen to seek a hiding place. Ray had been right in his previous assertion that Alpha's specialization had made him a fool along other lines. The ape was now seeking the quarters of his mate.

By the time Ray arrived at the out-buildings which housed the monkeys, it was quite dark, and as he approached he saw a light flash on, only to be immediately extinguished. There was much confusion and chattering going on inside. When Ray finally burst through the door he saw nothing of Alpha nor Melva, but a group made up of gorillas, baboons, chimpanzees, orangutans and a few tailless monkeys who had formed a ring around some object. Ray hastened forward, thrusting the curious apes roughly aside. Lying prone and inert was the form of Beta. Ray learned from the onlookers that he had been killed by Alpha when he dared interfere with the predatory ape. Beta had been strangled. The tell-tale marks were plainly evident.

"Alpha cannot kill and yet leave no marks," said Ray aloud, as if to rid himself of an eternal overshadowing doubt.

But now was no time for idle musings. Leaving the quarters of the smaller monkeys, he forced a hasty passageway to the rear of the building. And then a sound such as he had never heard in all the years of his work among these beasts fell upon his ears; raucous and piercing cries, and a deep thumping, like the distant beating of an African tomtom. Instinctively he knew it to be the sound of a gorilla on the warpath. Even before he could reach the door the thumping ceased, and was rapidly succeeded by the impact of huge bodies in conflict.

He opened the door and an amazing sight greeted him, but it was one that made his heart leap with joy. Melva stood beneath the high window gazing with terror-stricken eyes at what must have been a very rapid drama. On the floor was Alpha, who, curiously enough, lay in the identical posture of Beta, his victim of a few minutes before.

With a cry of joy Melva ran to Ray's side just as the irate female gorilla turned from the prostrate form of her dead mate.

"Omega!" said Ray in stern tones. "What have you done?"

The female turned her hate-filled eyes toward Melva, who would probably have been the next victim, but for the presence of the master. Ray took a step toward the ape who coweringly retreated. Wishing to impress upon this servant at this critical moment the desired lesson, Ray stroked Melva's hair, patted her shoulder and said, "Nice Melva, good Melva." Then moving toward the carcass of the dead gorilla, he kicked it and said, "Bad Alpha."

Omega comprehended, and appreciated the moral instruction which she was receiving, for the smoldering hatred died from her eyes, and in imitation of her master Ray, she kicked the body of her mate, and then, in spite of Melva's revulsion, stroked the girl's hair and patted her shoulder.

Melva tolerated it bravely, simply for the sake of the moral to be drawn from it. She smiled up into the serious face of her companion, whose appearance gave evidence of the birth of some new idea.

"The loss of Alpha and Beta will be a temporary setback to the monkey-farm enterprise, but I have an idea," he exclaimed with boyish enthusiasm. "These monkeys must grow accustomed to the presence of a woman in their midst as a co-ruler with me. Pardon my stupidity, dear, I see now why I do not want a man, either young or old, as my partner in this desert project—because I want—you."

"It took a rather violent set of circumstances to convince you," the girl demurred, "and I am not sure but that a young man would be best for you after all. I hate being proposed to in a monkey-house! In the lane by the poplars would have been so much more romantic!"

He laughed and caught her to him in a close embrace. "You do not need to answer me now, Melva darling. Wait until we get back to the lane by the poplars."

VII.
A Moral Issue

Three centuries is a short time, geologically speaking, and Nature, through the action of the elements, accomplishes little during that span; but give *Man* three hundred years in which to change his environment, and he accomplishes wonders. Great as was the change in North America from the landing of the Pilgrims until the establishment of the first monkey-farm on a large scale south of Death Valley, it was infinitesimal as compared to the transition from the old order of labor to the new.

During the lifetime of the early desert pioneers, Ray Stoddart and his wife, the former Melva Wilhoit, little public attention had been paid to occasional newspaper accounts of a "monkey-farm." But despite the ridicule of many, the years were proving that man had at last realized for himself an intelligent servant for the performance of those irksome tasks that had always chained him to Earth. Just as in the life of the individual, many conscious acts are gradually relegated to the supervision of the subconscious mind, so the once menial duties of man were handed over to the less intelligent apes, liberating man himself.

Wilhoit Stoddart, the present proprietor of the original "monkey-farm," south of what was once Death Valley, was a direct descendant of Ray and Melva Stoddart. Apes bred by his ancestors and himself were carrying on the manual labor in every civilized country on the globe. This labor in the year 2216 consisted principally of tending machines; not only their mechanical operation, but the manufacturing output as well. And, as had always been proved to be the case among men, so it was among the intelligent apes: Some were more capable than others, and showed an aptitude for learning that was amazing. Of course the development of the ape cycle had not been alone by unconscious evolution. It was Ray Stoddart's son who had perceived that the evolutionary development of apes must be hastened. And so, turning over the actual management of his estate to overseers, he buried himself in his biological laboratories. It was a young, vigorous man who entered the laboratory for a first time. But it was an old, bent but gloriously triumphant one who emerged thirty years later with the secret! By making extracts of the known glands of human beings and discovering a few for himself, he was able to procure in a concentrated form the vital substance that controlled the mental growth of the race. His next step was to test it on his apes.

His first success was phenomenal, but he died before he could extend it, and his son was left to carry it on. It was found by Ray Stoddart's grandson that by application of the gland extracts to apes it was now possible to transmit characteristics of any desired kind and also to develop the speech organs of the brutes. Accordingly, gardeners, domestic servants, chauffeurs, mechanics, were all bred as the result of a definite extract. Families of apes therefore became specialized and men made it a business to breed these specialized servants for sale to the general public.

"I do declare," exclaimed Wilhoit to his mother one day as they were enjoying the pure clear air of their western home. "I sometimes think Rex, our local overseer, shows more intelligence than some human beings."

"Well, do you know," replied his mother, "I think that there are many people who should still labor as do the great apes. Unless a man is mentally ready for emancipation, he deteriorates instead of progressing. It has always been so. It seems that not all people can stand prosperity and the leisure that accompanies it. Take Hayes Suiter for example."

"There is something worrying me," pondered Wilhoit thoughtfully, "and I might as well tell it now while we're on the subject. There is a moral question that has arisen as to whether we should keep the apes in servitude."

His mother started in shocked surprise. "A moral issue, son? But they are beasts. Surely—"

Wilhoit leaned forward in his chair and his voice came in awed accent. "They are more than beasts. We have made them so."

"Hail, Abraham Lincoln!" said a sneering voice from the door. "Wouldn't it be some joke if the descendant of the illustrious Stoddarts who gave man his freedom from drudgery, should return him to that state through a mistaken sense of philanthropy? A nice mess civilization would be in, I must say!"

"Oh! hello, Hayes," exclaimed young Stoddart without turning his head. But Mrs. Stoddart glanced up at the indolent face of the newcomer.

"I think you misjudge Wilhoit," she said quietly. "He has no intention of freeing the apes—why they're—soulless beasts. Aren't they, my boy?"

Wilhoit was enjoying himself hugely. He hitched his chair a trifle nearer to the one Sulter had nonchalantly lounged into, and riveted his eyes on the latter. "I'm not so sure about this soul business, and where the dividing line comes. If a lazy man has a soul, I believe an industrious ape has one, too."

"Oh, Wilhoit," exclaimed his mother in shocked amazement. "If that is true, our system is all wrong and we should have to reorganize our entire economic life, and for that matter, our civilization."

"Yes, indeed," chimed in Hayes, "and the age-old controversies of capital and labor would appear again. Excuse me for being frank, but no sane person would suggest such a thing. Just as the world begins to enjoy life, along comes an agitator and upsets things again. Bah!"

"Yes," said Wilhoit unruffled, "there have been many agitators known to history. They have shaken civilization out of its complacency.

Struggle and turmoil have followed in their wake, but—the world has been better for their interference."

Hayes Sulter rose and bowed with mock courtesy. "Mrs. Stoddart, we must do homage to this would-be saviour and emancipator of the apes. Isn't he marvelous?"

VIII.
Signs of Rebellion

The woman ignored the young man's sarcasm and continued to regard her son with a troubled countenance. The latter walked over to a side of the room that was occupied by the television screen and radio, but there was no response to his pressure on the switch.

"This is the fourth day," he remarked irritably, "that we've had no news of the outside world. Neither Rex, nor Vance (the ape electrician) has been able to locate the trouble."

"I'd invite you over to use ours," said Sulter with forced civility, "but we've been out of touch with the East for the same length of time."

Presently a light footfall apprised the three of the approach of someone. Upon appearance it proved to be a neighbor, Sylvia Danforth. The faces of the young men lighted up at the girl's approach, and Hayes hastened forth to meet her. But with no apparent rudeness she evaded him and smiled into the welcoming eyes of Wilhoit.

"I dislike being the bearer of bad news, Wilhoit," the girl said a little ruefully, "but father has had trouble again with his ape overseer, Felix. It has just been one thing after another from underhanded trickery to open defiance, but today's escapade caps the climax!"

"Your father's too easy with his apes, Sylvia," said Hayes, smiling unpleasantly. "A little corporal punishment goes a long way."

"What did Felix do?" asked Wilhoit quickly.

"You'll wonder how things could have gotten so upset in a once orderly world," replied the girl miserably, "but Felix knocked the radio broadcasting apparatus to pieces and attacked father with a bar. It took four of us: two apes, sister Inez and myself to lock Felix up where he could do no more damage."

"You hear?" cried young Stoddart in an unconsciously dramatic tone. "The era has dawned when man can no longer depend upon monkey supervision of machinery. It is true that the ape intelligence that freed man from his drudgery is now working in its own behalf. If it is allowed to continue unhindered, it will result in the rise of a new order of beings who have become cunning, efficient and powerful. We have only ourselves to thank for the situation. We have created our own nemesis."

"Oh come, dear," said Mrs. Stoddart with an effort at cheerfulness, "you'll have to admit that what has happened is a rare exception. One overseer in thousands runs rampant, and you take it as an ill omen of the future. I thought superstition was a thing of the past. Besides they are just specialized creatures who have no initiative."

"Some have, mother. You know that a number have been bred to intellectual labor. Why should they not read history and think of rebellion! Besides, it is not superstition, but reason, mother, to read the future by the trend of the present. What surer guide have we than the logical unfolding of events?" He rose quickly. "I must get back to the quarry. I can't trust the apes with any explosives yet."

Sylvia turned to go and Hayes was at her side.

"May I come over and see Felix?" he asked. "I flatter myself that my apes have never acted up. Maybe I can handle him in a way to insure future obedience."

"I strongly advise against violence, Hayes," Wilhoit called after him in steely tones. "My apes have never 'acted up' either, yet they know nothing but the gentlest of treatment."

Hayes and Sylvia walked down the broad shady avenue that led to the Danforth estate. It was a perfect day. Everywhere around them life's activities seemed to progress with customary unhampered regularity. The fields were dotted with monkey laborers; some doing physical work, others running machinery, and still others superintending. Many of the new fuelless, electrically-activated cars passed the two pedestrians, the majority of which were chauffeured by liveried apes.

Airplanes were still piloted mainly by human beings, though there were in North America in 2216 exactly 1308 licensed ape pilots who did nothing else but fly, and who were competent in their profession. It must be remembered that when a simian was bred to anything he knew it thoroughly, and usually he knew nothing else.

Sylvia and Hayes watched the speeding planes, and tried to guess which were piloted by men or women, and which by monkeys.

IX.
From Brawn to Brain

If three hundred years had marked a radical change in the human inhabitants of the world due to their altered mode of living, it was trivial in comparison with that undergone by the great struggling servant class, the apes. Evolution progresses rapidly under stress and pressure. The human race had experienced and overcome its difficulties in centuries past. It had scaled the mountain and now at the peak of its civilization it did nothing but bask in the sunlight of freedom and leisure, apparently unmindful of the fact that its unused faculties were deteriorating. And while humanity congratulated itself on the ultimate attainment of leisure, those who made this leisure possible struggled ever upward. Could they ever overtake those masters who had preceded them on the journey?

Man's first vital mistake, after the initial error of educating monkeys at all, occurred when he permitted them to organize. Had each man remained the absolute overseer of his own group of servants all would have gone well, but, eager to be relieved of all responsibility, he trained certain apes for the sole purpose of controlling and superintending others of inferior intellect. The efficiency of organization is irresistible, and the advantage of the organized monkeys over the scattered, pleasure-seeking, decadent members of human society was obvious.

After the efficacy of organization in the individual household was proved, overseers of neighboring estates were permitted to meet into higher clubs for the purpose of strengthening the working power of their groups. At first men had supervised these meetings but they had gradually become dilatory in attendance as they found that, left to themselves, the highly intelligent apes were able to work out their labor problems more satisfactorily. Men found it pleasanter to follow their own scientific or artistic bents, leaving the practical, active accomplishments of life to their servants. They begrudged time spent in conventions where the subject of discussion was the machinery of civilization and the practical carrying-out of labor schemes. Finally human attendance at even national conclaves ceased altogether.

The modern site of what had formerly been Death Valley remained the center of ape activities, although the human capital of North America was in northern Minnesota. The apes themselves had renamed

Death Valley "Reclamation City," for to the enterprising, progressive simians the new name had a pleasant significance.

Rex, the present Stoddart overseer, was the concentrated product of three hundred years of intelligent breeding for qualities of leadership. In him were focused traits which produced independent thinking. The principal simian characteristic of imitativeness still prevailed, but it no longer applied exclusively to the physical. His mental reactions, probably a complete evolution of the ape's innate cunning, would have done credit to a businessman of the twentieth century.

Rex presided at the fourteenth annual ape conference held in Reclamation City which was once the very heart of the great American desert. He occupied the chair and gazed out upon the vast throng of his fellow-beings with a new look in his little eyes. He knew well that the day had passed when perfection in his daily work for men would interest the ape. His ambition for his kind was bred of keen observation of the relative ability of apes and men. At his side was seated a wizened, undersized figure, an ape of the Baris species who was acting temporarily in the capacity of secretary. He was Marzo, an overseer from a large estate in the capital city in Minnesota. He had shown acumen in political matters.

"Fellow apes," said Rex, rising and grimacing at the restless assemblage in the great hall, "this fourteenth meeting here at Reclamation City marks a new day for us. We will not stop working, but we will work for ourselves, not for men. You who are here are all overseers, and will tell those under you what I say. But first of all let me tell you that what we plan must be kept secret from men as long as they seem to be our masters. Even they must not know that they are not until the time comes to kill them all."

Rex ceased speaking and looked down upon Marzo whose shrewd eyes moved restlessly between Rex and the assembly below.

"Do you want to talk?" Rex asked the other, noting his uneasiness.

X.

The Mysterious Ape

For answer Marzo came to the front of the platform restlessly fingering the pencil and pad with which he took his secretarial notes. A hush of expectancy hung over the audience chamber as he spoke.

"A year ago you chose Rex as your president because he was a Stoddart ape. He deserved the honor you gave him and his presidency has marked real advance in the ape cause, but I have another candidate to propose for the coming year; one who combines the cunning of the ape with the reason of the white man. This candidate has been advocated to the nominating committee by Waldo, chief ape of Reclamation City. I want to introduce him to you now."

At this juncture all eyes turned toward an opening door at the rear of the platform out of which emerged three figures, foremost of which was Waldo, head ape in this, his native Reclamation City. The last figure was Vance, Stoddart's electrician, who came with Rex and was qualified to act as an overseer should necessity arise. But it was the figure between the two that arrested the attention of the monkey gathering. For a startled moment the apes thought they had been betrayed, so human was the second figure that came forward on the stage with Waldo and Vance to join Rex and Marzo. Curiously erect and practically hairless, the being was a travesty on both man and ape. He appeared to be an animate reconstruction of the Neanderthal man with his thick neck, long muscular arms, receding forehead and beetling brows, and yet somehow his face gave evidence of more intelligence than is commonly accredited to those dawn men. He must not, however, be compared to the more advanced Cro-Magnon. It was not that he was less intelligent, but because the trend of his development indicated lower ideals than those of the unfortunate Cro-Magnon race.

As the trio advanced Marzo again seated himself while Waldo addressed the apes.

"Just at the time that ape civilization needs one who combines the qualities of man and ape, Gunther is born and comes to us to lead us from slavery. But he can tell you more about his plans than I, so I will let him speak."

Ever since Gunther had put in his appearance excitement had been evident in the hall, but suppressed so that not a word from the platform should be missed. As Gunther stepped forward a chatter arose that gave evidence of the really primitive ape nature that lay under the thin veneer of civilization.

"Gunther, Gunther!" cried the apes.

Gunther waited until all acclamation had ceased. He stood remarkably erect and surveyed his audience with a remote dispassionate gaze that was anything but monkey-like in its quality. Again, as upon his first appearance, enthusiasm waned, as doubt crept into the assemblage as to whether this being was ape or man.

Taking advantage of the temporary cessation of enthusiastic demonstrations, Gunther, the mysterious, began to speak.

"I claim to be the only missing link between you and those who have been your masters. I am unwelcome in their ranks, but to you I can offer much. In my veins flows human and ape blood and I believe I have born to bridge the gap that would prevent the apes from gaining world power."

"We want Gunther for our president," was the unanimous cry from a multitude of throats.

But there was one dissenting voice. Rex recognized the fact that though he himself lacked human qualities, he was nevertheless the acme of ape intelligence, and as such represented a pure strain that had evolved naturally under the conditions imposed upon it. This Gunther was half-breed and Rex instinctively felt that he could not be sincere in his apparent loyalty to the apes. If Gunther preferred the latter to men it was only because he had not been welcomed to the ranks of mankind, and his hatred to men inspired a show of loyalty to apes. Such a motive was not to be trusted.

"I have a plan to lay before you," continued the half-human Gunther. "If put into immediate effect it should not be long before apes and not men rule this planet."

Here the creature's eyes gleamed with the visioned prospect, and his thick lips drew back from his teeth in snarling semblance of a smile. "Since men have withdrawn more and more from cities, and have become barons of estates, surrounded by their luxuries and conveniences that ape servants make possible for them, they are dependent upon the airplane and radio-televisor for intercommunication, the former for personal contact and the latter for exchange of ideas. Within the last twelve or fifteen years, airplane journeys have become less and less frequent with them, as they dislike any physical exertion whatever, and their radiovisors provide companionship from the depths of their easy chairs. Consequently the number of licensed ape pilots has steadily increased and it will not be difficult to wreck all human flown planes, proceeding cautiously so as not to arouse suspicion. But our strategic point of attack will be at broadcasting stations. How fortunate for us that men are not congregated in great cities as formerly. Had they depended upon machinery, the city would have remained the logical community unit, but with intelligent apes to see to their every want, the isolated estate was the reasonable outcome.

"Of course they do have cities, but their boundaries are ill-defined and we find each man and his family quite dependent throughout this great country upon his overseer and the specialized apes. First, each of you must at a specified time, which we shall here agree upon, see that all airplanes are disabled and that radio-televisors are out of commission until we have control of broadcasting stations. It will be perfectly possible for each overseer to make his master believe that the trouble is local. The ape pilots, mechanics and electricians will work without avail upon the non-functioning mechanisms; then, while human communication is cut off, the apes will gain mastery over the helpless human beings and kill those who offer resistance. The men will know what it is to labor as we have labored; the women—well—you see in me the possibility of elevating the ape!"

Rex did not share the enthusiasm of the other monkeys. True, he yearned for power as much as did the rest, but a certain innate loyalty was inherent through generations of his ancestors, to the Stoddarts who had advanced him from his jungle state. He thought of Wilhoit Stoddart with an emotion akin to affection, realizing that his master was very likely the superior of the other masters of the apes represented.

XI.
The Missing Link

A gong sounded loudly. Instantly all was confusion, but above the din the new president's voice rose in shrill tones, "I give you four days in which to put out of commission all planes, and to gain control of all broadcasting stations. At the end of that time stations must be used by the apes for the furtherance of their plans."

Rex approached Vance, Stoddart's electrician, as they left the stage with the question, "What do you think of this Gunther and his scheme?"

"I think Gunther will make apes the rulers of men. I don't care for him, but he will get us what we want."

Rex was silent. He dared not intimate that he was not wholly in sympathy with the ape uprising. He mentally questioned the ability of his kind to maintain permanent supremacy over a race that had hundreds of centuries' advantage over his own particular branch.

In a few hours all except resident monkeys had left Reclamation City. Waldo went to the broadcasting station where his master, Carl Brunenkant, the chief announcer, was just concluding a speech on the advisability of permitting the apes to have an hour a day for broadcasting purposes.

Carl asked his ape if the conference had resulted in plans for more efficient labor schemes, and Waldo replied that it had. The ape did not tell his master of the election of Gunther, for Carl Brunenkant, ever since he had learned of the existence of the missing link, had felt that it should not be allowed to live. But time had proved that Gunther was very capable of overseeing the labor of monkeys under him. He had been bought and sold and changed hands many times purely because of the prejudice against his origin. No one denied his ability as a first-rate overseer.

"Waldo," said his master, having suddenly determined to tell the ape of the white man's concession, "how would you apes like to have the air for an hour each day to discuss your problems? We are willing to give over an hour to you if you prefer that method to personal meeting at conventions."

"You are wise, master," smirked Waldo, though the man did not recognize the sarcasm. "Control of the air for one hour in the twenty-four would let us settle the difficulties of our life-work without leaving our homes, and almost without stopping our work. The apes living in the five cities of the country where broadcasting stations are located are leaders anyway, and they would broadcast orders to the overseers of all estates throughout the nation."

In the weeks that followed the last convention of the apes, the plan of Carl Brunenkant and Waldo that the apes be allowed to broadcast an hour a day was carried out. Those apes who had previously assisted men at the broadcasting stations took complete charge, and were aided by apes of lesser ability. When it was quite evident that men were no longer even passively interested in the broadcasts of the apes, the animals discussed their situation with greater freedom. Discretion was thrown to the winds. Waldo and Gunther talked from Reclamation City, Rex from Stoddart, California, and Marzo from the capital where he was temporarily presiding until Gunther should arrive. Gradually, mingled with the legitimate business of the apes, a plan for insurrection evolved around the nucleus that was the mind of Gunther.

Carl Brunenkant had apparently fostered the new ape freedom, and although he occasionally appeared around the Reclamation City broadcasting station, neither Waldo nor Gunther suspected his attitude of good will toward them. He had always been a champion of the monkeys, and their recent broadcasting freedom was entirely due to his efforts.

One morning just before ape broadcasting hour Carl and Gunther entered the station at the same time. Carl noticed the suppressed excitement that the freak could not quite successfully conceal. At the exact hour of broadcast Carl bade goodbye to Gunther and apparently left the building, but as the half-ape, half-man creature mouthed his greetings into the microphone, Carl returned. He moved quietly with apparent intentness of purpose so as not to arouse the suspicion of apes working about, and in this way managed to get the content of Gunther's speech.

Gunther was stirring the apes to immediate insurrection. Carl was an eavesdropper outside the door. So this was what had resulted from the additional liberties that had been granted the great servant class! Yet as he stood, hesitant as to the correct course of procedure in the face of this dire calamity, Brunenkant realized that this was exactly the crises he had hoped to precipitate by granting the monkeys unwarranted freedom which their unphilosophical minds could only interpret as license.

Outside were the sounds of rushing feet, startled, inarticulate cries, and back of these spasmodic exclamations, like a running accompaniment, there issued the incessant chatter of thousands of monkeys. This chattering was a mode of vocal expression to which they invariably reverted under duress.

Carl rushed to a window and gazed with horror at a milling throng on the streets below. Men were fleeing from the apes, who, armed with weapons of all descriptions, were capturing all human beings they could and killing those who offered too violent resistance. Into the young man's mind rushed the thought again that Gunther in the next room at the microphone was the stimulus for the atrocities he saw taking place in the streets below, and which he knew were being repeated at the devil-ape's instigation in all the cities and on all the estates throughout America. His fear-shackled limbs responded at last to the dictates of his brain, and with murderous intent he turned toward the broadcasting room from which issued the guttural commands of Gunther.

XII.
Gunther Retaliates

Instant mental oblivion was the reward of his belated action. A huge ape whose duty it was to protect Gunther during the inciting broadcast had felled Carl with a blow the instant he had made a move in the ape ruler's direction.

During the hours that Carl Brunenkant lay unconscious in the corridor outside the broadcasting room in Reclamation City, the nation-wide ape revolution had been proceeding uninterruptedly. As master of ceremonies Gunther still held the microphone and urged his fellow-beings on to conquest. His throaty voice was the first sound to register on Carl's mind with returning consciousness. Carl looked cautiously about him. The hall was deserted. He had been left for dead and was not being watched at present. He heard apes moving about in the outer hall near the entrance to the building. Presumably they were preventing new entrants, but it was evident no molestation was anticipated from inside. Carl dragged himself painfully to a sitting posture and listened.

Came the voice of Gunther, "Marzo, it is rumored that Rex has overcome his master, the great Stoddart, whom he deems more valuable to us alive than dead."

From the loudspeaker issued the tones of the shrewd Marzo, "Let me summon Rex to the television screen and question him. He may tell me more than he would you, for I have never been his rival for power as you have."

Brunenkant crept cautiously toward the open door of the room whose sole occupant was the ape president-elect in radio television conversation with his dependable aides. Gunther's back was toward him, the television screen facing him with the wizened little face of Marzo who was temporarily acting as president, looking from it.

Suddenly the screen went black, Marzo had disconnected with Gunther in order to communicate with Rex, but in a second another scene flashed to view and prominent in it were the figures of Rex and Stoddart.

Carl Brunenkant and Wilhoit Stoddart had been college friends, and it was with the first feeling of joy that the former had experienced since the uprising of the apes that he recognized his friend Stoddart.

"Now the apes will sit up and take notice," thought he. "Stoddart knows apes. They won't defy him."

But his jaw dropped as he listened to the words that issued from the radio, "I acknowledge my defeat. I have met my superior. What skill I may have in my line is at your service as yours has been at mine. . . ."

XIII.
Open Revolt

Meanwhile, indulging in pleasant, idle conversation, Sylvia Danforth and Hayes Sulter entered the gateway of the Danforth estate following their visit to Wilhoit Stoddart. Instantly they sensed that something was wrong. Apes were hurrying about in unaccustomed haste, their grotesque, hairy bodies intermittently visible through the dense foliage that surrounded the house. Sylvia hastened forward, calling her father and Inez; but the incessant monkey chatter about her rendered her voice inaudible. With the characteristic intrepidity displayed by the Danforths for generations, she pushed open the front door and entered the house. Hayes was a few paces behind her, but in the short time it took him to cross the threshold things began to happen. A scream of terror from Sylvia quite unnerved him, but mindful of masculine obligations, he pushed forward.

He was brought to a sudden halt by unexpected contact with a huge hairy body, and looking up with apprehension he met the baleful gaze of his own overseer, Tony. His horror changed to immediate indignation at this interruption of the orderly running of his estate, and he flew into a rage at his overseer's unprecedented behavior.

"What are you doing over here, Tony?" he demanded.

Those were his last words. The thick neck of the gorilla was suddenly thrust forward in a line with the curvature of the spine. The beast took one shuffling step forward on his bent, awkward legs, seized the throat of his hapless master, and all was over before the latter could cry out.

Sylvia had been ignorant of the tragedy enacted at the door. She had been seized immediately by her father's overseer, who had been released by Tony; and despite her hysterical cries to be released, she had been ruthlessly borne to the library. The scene which she witnessed there was indelibly imprinted upon her mind. Her father had been strangled, apparently in the act of using the radiophone; and Inez lay a suicide, her fingers locked about the handle of the small revolver that was always kept in a secret place behind the mantel.

Inez's death was seemingly a surprise to Felix, though he appeared aware of Mr. Danforth's murder. Holding firmly to Sylvia with one huge paw, he shuffled over to the body of her sister and gazed at it in perplexity. A moment later Tony appeared on the scene. When he saw the lifeless form of Inez, his jaw dropped and his beady eyes bulged out in their intensity.

"You do?" his malignant gaze sought Felix.

"No, girl do self," responded Felix, pointing to the weapon clutched in the dead fingers.

"Hold live girl so no shoot," admonished Tony; then, lowering his clumsy bulk into the chair by the radiophone, to Sylvia's utter amazement, he called the Stoddart home.

As was natural, Rex, the ape overseer of Stoddart, answered the call.

"Apes rule," Tony called in excited tones. "Kill master and phone rest. Man now weak, ape strong. Ape rule world. Ape work, why not?"

The voice of Rex came distinctly to Sylvia's ears. Owing to the teaching of Stoddart he had much better mastery of the language than other overseers. Stoddart had in the past prided himself on Rex's power of expression. The creature could actually differentiate between shades of verbal utterance.

"Be careful," the words were well enunciated. "Tricks are better than force. Did you get girls? You know we need them for future race."

Evidently, for reasons of his own, Tony did not divulge the death of Inez.

To all this horror Sylvia was a silent and helpless witness. Would Rex outwit and kill the human inmates of the Stoddart estate? Sylvia had great confidence in Wilhoit's ability to handle his monkey servants. For many generations his ancestors had done nothing else. He was as qualified for success in his as were any of his apes in their specialized vocations.

XIV.
Ape Versus Man

Wilhoit Stoddart was not exactly happy after the departure of Hayes and Sylvia. He had loved the girl since childhood, and while he had no doubt that she returned his affections, he did not trust the friendship of Hayes, and was troubled to have Sylvia in his company.

In this mood, he walked to the television screen and pushed a button. And now after a four-day hiatus the apparatus was functioning. It was as if he stood at an open window. A most unusual scene was depicted; a typical American city of the twenty-third century, yet it was most unfamiliar in many of its aspects. Even in his panicky bewilderment Wilhoit observed the details of the scene before him, and the awful truth of its significance struck him with stunning force. *Men and apes had changed places!* The leisurely pedestrians were monkeys, big and little, while those who labored at the menial tasks of a complex civilization were men, cowardly, frightened men and women, held in subjugation by the very beings whom they had once controlled.

What was this place where man's sovereignty had toppled? Wilhoit scrutinized the screen, but could see no indication of its locality. This was indeed not to be wondered at, for the trend of civilization had been toward a uniformity of civil and social structure until but little difference existed in communities.

With trembling fingers he turned on the radio, confident that the daily bulletin would give some explanation of the situation. It did—but alas for its revelation! A bestial snarl issued from the loudspeaker, followed by a mirthless imitation of man's laughter—and then words pounding their horrible significance into Stoddart's brain—"and so by this time tomorrow every overseer must be in complete control of the man who once controlled him. We have nearly all the broadcasting stations now. Our sudden nation-wide uprising will put us in power. We have long deserved this. For centuries our bodies have been the tools of progress, then our minds took over this task while man has done nothing but strut about and play. We will continue this civilization where man has left off, but we will do it for ourselves and not for him. Those men who can be made to use their intelligence to further our needs will be used, the strong ones will work, the weaklings will be killed; the women who are young and—"

The ring of the radiophone in the next room turned Stoddart's attention in that direction. Scarcely before he had lifted his hand to disconnect the national broadcast radio instrument he heard the low throaty tones of Rex's voice answering the instrument. There followed a moment's silence and then Rex's warning, "be careful," roused Wilhoit to instant concentrated attention. "Did you get girls?" What did it mean?

Wilhoit Stoddart after a flashing instant knew very well. The time that he had long dreaded had come, though not exactly as he had feared. Through his brain flashed a casual remark made by a friend just last week, "Man need never fear the ape. When mentality and mere brute force vie for supremacy, the former will always win." But vaguely Wilhoit was beginning to realize that the *mind* of the ape was a power to be conjured with; and together with his superior physical prowess he was a formidable adversary. Yet as he sat crouched, listening in stunned silence, the whole situation struck him as unreal and illusory. His faithful and capable Rex, who had managed his affairs in a most competent and satisfactory manner, would surely continue to do so. They were dependent upon each other. Their mutual exchange of service was absolutely indispensable.

". . . we need them for future race." The closing words of Rex's conversation stirred the eavesdropper to instant action. No longer did the situation seem fatuous. It was one to be instantly reckoned with. A sane man must perform a distasteful duty without fear or hesitation.

In a lower drawer of the writing desk was a loaded revolver, but in order to reach it, it was necessary to pass the door which Rex, now phoning, faced.

It was a difficult situation for Wilhoit, but there was no other prerogative. It was suicide to tackle an ape unarmed.

It struck Wilhoit at once as strange that if the apes had been wanting power for years, they should have been so long discovering this fact consciously.

The young man took a cautious step in the desired direction, but drew back as Rex came toward the door near which he crouched. The great hairy body brushed by Stoddart and ambled over to the television screen where it fumbled awkwardly with the buttons and dials. Now was his chance. The next few seconds were filled with activity. Wilhoit reached the drawer but it failed to respond to his first pull, and before he could renew his efforts Rex had leaped toward him and pinioned his arms to his sides.

Struggle was not only useless, but dangerous. So this, Wilhoit thought, was to be the end of all man's effort toward a higher plane of existence! Man should never have relinquished his active hold upon the personal management of his affairs. With such intelligence as he claimed he should have been warned of the inevitable danger of trusting power to those whom he had enslaved. All of his idealism fled in this moment as the vision of a possible downfall of the human race flashed through him.

"Kill master." The words rumbled from Rex's throat and his grip about Wilhoit's chest tightened. The ape was repeating mechanically his orders.

The man gazed into the beady eyes of the monster towering above him, conscious for the first time of the power he possessed.

"Be quick about it, Rex," he muttered hoarsely.

The plea must have astonished the great ape, for he relaxed his hold and an expression of perplexity puckered his ugly features. Plainly he was being torn between love and duty.

"Surely such an emotion indicates the birth of a soul," thought Wilhoit, his terror giving way to a feeling of sadness. "It is possible I am in the presence of a representative of the next *future* race of our world. We human beings forfeited our birthright!"

It was apparent that love had conquered, but not without a compromise. Wilhoit was to live, but as a prisoner. As easily as one would carry a baby the huge ape bore his captive in his arms into the storeroom where he secured a ball of stout twine. Returning with his burden to the den and placing a chair before the television screen he deposited Wilhoit in the chair facing the screen and bound him securely. This accomplished, he turned on the radio and television and left his captive to enjoy it as he might.

XV.
A Rescue

Only by closing his eyes could Wilhoit Stoddart shut out the distressing scenes pictured before him on the screen, but he found his attention irresistibly drawn to the views which by the mechanical device so popular then shifted the scene from one popular center to another, all showing with little variation the downfall of a civilization. No other destruction in history could be compared with it. If for an instant one is reminded of the descent of the barbarous hordes from the north upon the comparatively high civilization of Rome, he must bear in mind that at least those Vandals and Goths were human, and they were destined to pour strong fresh blood into the decadent life of the empire.

"Maybe my vision is too shortsighted," thought Wilhoit in his misery. "If man has come up through the ages from life-forms similar to the apes, perhaps ape ascendency at this time might be only a temporary setback for the human race and in that vaster concept that man can scarcely grasp, it may be nature's method of keeping us strong and pure. Evolution has not ceased, nor can we imagine it to cease until all life forms have attained a state of perfection."

Suddenly Wilhoit saw a very frightened-looking man appear on the scene. He was speaking. "Fellow-men, resist the apes no longer. They are qualified to be our masters; superior in physical strength and in mentality. We are nothing but decadent philosophers and dreamers. The Ape Cycle has come; and it is for the good of our race that we usher it in gracefully."

"The contemptible coward," muttered Stoddart, clenching his fists. "I'd like to lay hands on him!"

The man's place was taken by an ape who echoed the previous speaker's sentiments. Then the scene shifted and there flashed across the screen scenes of pillage and disaster where men tried to resist the power of the apes. It was evident that where monkeys could not get control of powerhouses, radio stations or airlines, they destroyed them.

Now the scene went direct to a broadcasting station where ape announcers stood before the microphones, while human assistants stood helplessly by; again a view showed a few highly specialized simians occupying chairs of the nation's executives, while another depicted in the street murder, rapine and incendiarism.

Presently something touched Wilhoit's sleeve, causing him to start violently. It was difficult for him to realize that his body was not actually in the midst of the scenes which his eyes beheld. He turned round quickly, as far as his bonds permitted—and saw Sylvia crouched by the arm of his chair, a finger indicating that he must be silent. Swiftly she cut his bonds, grasped one hand in hers and in the other she placed a small revolver. Still maintaining silence, she led him from the room. The house seemed strangely deserted and they passed through to the rear without meeting a single ape-servant.

"Now," she whispered, "do your duty."

For a moment her words had no significance to the man, but following where she pointed, he saw a hairy prostrate form lying midway between the house and the power station.

"Why," he gasped, "it is Rex, but how—?"

She nodded and pointed to the weapon which he held in his hand.

"You mean you did that?" he queried unbelievingly.

"Yes, I killed Felix and escaped a worse fate than death. Then I came over here to save you, if it were not too late. Oh—look!"

Rex was not dead. With obvious effort he was rising, and in his great black hand he held a small object that glittered in the afternoon sun. It flashed once, twice. Wilhoit had already fired and the ape dropped his pistol.

Wilhoit and Sylvia ran forward together as Rex made an attempt to recover the weapon. Wilhoit fired again, and the great beast sank to his knees, a guttural growl issuing weakly from his throat.

"Well, I guess the game's up, old sport," said Wilhoit grimly as the gorilla clutched at his side. "Sorry to lose the manager of all my affairs, but I guess I can shift for myself."

The fierce, little eyes of the gorilla rested craftily upon the face of his master. Yet in that gaze, mingled with the sly cunning, Stoddart read an emotion akin to pity.

"I am dying, master," the ape said, "but for your kind it is the end, too."

Rex gradually sank back and in a few moments his body twitched and lay still.

XVI.
A Disguise

The isolated estate of Wilhoit Stoddart had been a small but complete unit of civilization typical of the trend of rural progress in the twenty-third century. As feudal lords of the Middle Ages the human masters, surrounded by their monkey serfs, had reigned supreme.

Wilhoit, however, could not now trust any of his ape-slaves to assist him in a daring project which he had evolved, so, with regret, he killed his few remaining apes.

All the evening before and far into the next morning Wilhoit and

Sylvia had planned the best method of attacking the organized ape civilization of the world. One scheme after another had been discarded as impracticable; but gradually they evolved one that seemed possible of accomplishment. Of course they did not know what had taken place at Reclamation City. They did know, however, that the apes had removed their capitol to the former capitol of the nation in northern Minnesota.

One morning several days later Sylvia was at work in front of the hangar repairing the plane which had been damaged by Wilhoit's ape-pilot prior to his death.

Sylvia looked up from her work expecting to meet the adoring eyes of Wilhoit. She dropped her tools and stifled the scream that rose to her lips. Beside her stood a giant gorilla. *Any* gorilla would have been a formidable presence at that particular time and place, but this gorilla was none other than Rex—whom her lover had shot before her eyes!

A chuckle, most ungorilla-like, issued from the loathsome mouth of the beast. Sylvia gasped in relief.

"Oh, how you frightened me, Wilhoit! But you do look like the real thing. How natural the hide looks."

Wilhoit threw back the hideous ape-mask that had covered his head and regarded his sweetheart tenderly.

"It was rather a raw trick to pull, I'll admit," he said apologetically, "but I had to find out for sure what a successful camouflage it was. The hide dressed nicely and will prove a very useful costume for my proposed trip to the ape civilization centers."

"The plane is about ready," said Sylvia, "but I think you had better give it a final going-over. Here are the tools."

Wilhoit smiled down at her. "Still somewhat of a relic of the age when women were not at all mechanically inclined."

"It was purely a matter of environment," she countered. "You know women finally came into professions that had been hitherto considered solely man's field, and they found they could do as well as their brothers."

"Granted," agreed Wilhoit, "but they have through it all maintained characteristics that no amount of environment can change."

"Only desirable qualities," she smiled up at him. "Won't you please give the machinery a final looking-over?"

"Which only proves my point," he remarked as he picked up the tools and went to work.

Precisely at noon he climbed into the cockpit of his plane. With a last tender adieu to Sylvia and a warning to be on constant guard against chance prowlers of the enemy, he flew across the country. It sickened him to see with his own eyes the overthrow of man. Everywhere monkeys were in control.

There was not so much actual devastation visible as the subtler indications of a radical change of administration. Wilhoit saw now that the plan of the ape overseers must have been on foot for some time past, and that the secret must have been cunningly guarded. Naturally they had taken possession of the great centers first, and then carried the fight to the rural communities. That Rex had been biding his time for the opportune moment to strike was apparent to Wilhoit as he reviewed the events of the past weeks; a brooding unnatural reserve on the ape's part; catching the servant at eavesdropping; the apparently disabled radio and television, all things pointed to a plot that had been growing before his very eyes.

He was flying above what used to be the Canadian border when his plane radiophone buzzed.

"Hello," he called.

"Who flies the Stoddart plane?" came the question. "You've been watched for some time. Where are you going?"

"This is Rex. I have Stoddart a captive on the ranch. Am going to the Capitol to see President Marzo. Come along. I have a great scheme."

He reached over and manipulated a dial on the complicated instrument board, looked into a small mirror-like object and saw there the faces of several apes grouped curiously together.

Before four o'clock Wilhoit spied the gleaming domes of the continental capitol buildings which were located at the geographical center of the North American continent. His radio and television were constantly active as he neared the national airport, but it was apparent his disguise was satisfactory, for he met with no opposition.

Wilhoit was grateful for his almost instinctive knowledge of ape psychology. It would stand him in good stead in the present situation. So well did he know what Rex would say and do under these given circumstances that he felt his confidence increasing. Of course there was this fact to face, and face squarely. It would not be enough to do just what Rex would, natural as that might seem. He must talk as his servant talked, and put his knowledge of ape psychology to the utmost test.

XVII.
The Conference

President Marzo, who was filling the chief executive chair, was an ape of the Baris species. He was smaller than any of his executives who surrounded him; agile, cunning and with that rare type of intelligence that had become alarmingly manifest of late. But Stoddart felt equal to the task of matching wits with the little creature before him, who reminded him of a shrewd, wizened old man. Marzo knew Rex as a dependable ranch overseer, specialized in his particular type of work, but with nothing spectacular to his credit.

"Why did you want to see me?" Marzo's eyes surveyed the gigantic figure before him, and Stoddart trembled inwardly in fear of discovery.

"My master is tied and servants guard him," Wilhoit made answer in the excellent imitation of ape talk in which he had become well versed.

"I didn't know you could fly a plane," continued the president suspiciously.

"Stoddart taught me a little of all kinds of work. I was his overseer, and he knew apes, and his father knew apes."

"Yes, yes," said the other testily, "but I want to know how loyal you are to us and why you have not killed your master as thousands of apes have done."

"I am with you," replied Stoddart, "and I did not kill my master because I think I can use him for the apes' cause."

"Yes?" queried the cunning Marzo, and the eyes of the members of his cabinet gazed intently at the gorilla.

"As you know," continued the disguised man, "my master knows more about the breeding of apes and their training than any man alive. His family has done nothing else for generations back. Unless we keep him to advise us, we may get back to what we were before man bred us for servants, and then this fight for freedom would be for nothing."

A chimpanzee-like creature standing behind the president spoke in high-pitched, chattering syllables: "I don't trust you, Rex. You are the overseer for this one man in the world who knows more about us than we do about ourselves. He would know just how to get you to do his bidding. He has been an expert at that all his life. Fellow-apes, I advise that we have nothing to do with either Stoddart or Rex."

There was a rumble of mixed approval and dissent after the chimpanzee's words, but Marzo silenced them with an indescribable monosyllabic grunt.

"We have to take some chances," he said, then addressing himself to Rex. "Can we see Stoddart by television? I should like to talk to him."

"As you know, during this uprising we damaged the radiovisors, but I will return and repair it."

"Very well, Rex," said Marzo. "And remember, Stoddart in the future is our servant. His brain will work for us as our brawn has for him and his kind in the past. Go and let us hear from you both as soon as you reach the estate."

"Are you and Stoddart the only ones at your home?" questioned the chimpanzee suspiciously.

"There are just two of us," replied the supposed Rex.

After he had left, the chimpanzee addressed his president again. "I don't trust either Rex or Stoddart. If you take my advice you will see that both of them are killed."

But Marzo insisted that the small ape's suspicions were unfounded. Then for several hours the cabinet meeting continued until a television call for the Stoddart estate from Gunther at Reclamation City ended the discussion. The screen revealed two figures; the one, Stoddart nodding in salute to the ape-cabinet, and the other, Rex, his huge paw resting on his former master's shoulder.

Wilhoit Stoddart spoke. "I acknowledge my defeat. I have met my superior. What skill I may have in my line is at your service as yours has been at mine. Rex wants me to talk personally with all the national overseers in the Grand Auditorium."

He turned inquiringly to the gorilla, who patted his shoulder and nodded assent.

"I will come in person, or perhaps you would rather have me talk by radio, and you could be in your several communities." He paused for answer.

"Have him come in person," whispered the ever-suspicious chimpanzee to Marzo, whose shadow he seemed to be.

"All right, but you let him alone," growled Marzo.

"It is better to have him in our midst if there is treachery," finished the self-appointed adviser.

"Very well, the overseers will meet in the Grand Auditorium tomorrow at this time and we will expect you, Stoddart, *in person*," said the president.

Wilhoit disconnected the radiovisor and turned to Rex, who was acting in a most peculiar manner, and from whose hairy chest mild feminine exclamations were issuing.

"Wilhoit, dear, *please* get me out of this thing. I'm nearly suffocating! It's a good thing you didn't talk five seconds longer or I'd have collapsed and given the whole secret away."

The young man laughed as he assisted the girl from the gorilla skin. "Well, the game's on, darling, and you'll have to wear this outfit awhile tomorrow, but it won't be where you'll have to bear close inspection. It will just be in the plane, and I can fix it so you can have ample breathing space."

XVIII.
What Happened at the Capitol

During the greater part of the night Wilhoit and Sylvia worked on a far corner of the estate making grenades of blasting material that had been used in quarrying stone for the construction of building foundations. Two monkeys had lost their lives a few weeks before through carelessness in handling the explosives, so that it had been necessary for Wilhoit to take over most of the dangerous work himself. The bombs were so heavy when completed that it was decided to construct a trapdoor arrangement in the bottom of the plane that could be opened by a lever releasing them to do their work of destruction below.

The early part of the following morning was spent in equipping the plane for the trip to the Capitol. With the bombs properly stowed, the two passengers climbed into the plane and sent it flying directly northeast toward their ultimate destination. Beneath them stretched a scene that would have been unbelievable to their ancestors of the twentieth century; the great American desert blossoming as a rose. The reclamation of the desert wastes of Earth had been accomplished during the early years of monkey training. Artificial rainfall and ape-slavery had made it possible to inhabit territory that had been just so many thousands of waste acres separating two thickly settled portions of a country.

They saw many planes traveling in their direction, carrying monkey overseers from all over the country. The convention would be a large one. Flying low over Reclamation City, Sylvia and Wilhoit noticed that the streets were crowded with scurrying figures, and they were amazed to note that in this one city alone human beings were in the majority. Why they should be more in evidence than the apes could not be surmised until their radiovisor buzzed and indicated that someone in Reclamation City wanted to speak with them. They were surprised to see in the television mirror not the face of any baboon-like creature, but the indignant features of Carl Brunenkant.

"Well—hello there—" began Wilhoit, but stopped at the contemptuous gaze that encountered his own.

"Wilhoit Stoddart," said Brunenkant in steely tones. "We have been watching what has been going on. Know that Reclamation City, which had been captured by the apes is now in our hands again. We look with utter contempt upon you as a coward and traitor."

Brunenkant turned his scornful eyes to Rex, from whom peculiar muffled exclamations of indignation were issuing. A quiet word silenced the ape figure.

"If you will descend quietly and surrender," pursued Brunenkant, "all will proceed in an orderly manner; if not, we will shoot your plane down!"

Wilhoit thought of the girl at his side and of the bombs stowed on the plane floor. Yet he knew he was being watched by the apes at the Capitol. But before a reply could be made a shriek of terror was followed by an inarticulate cry from the radio, and the television mirror depicted a surprising scene. Brunenkant's cry was cut short by the appearance of two gorillas who bound and gagged him so quickly that the two occupants of the plane could scarcely realize what was taking place. One of the animals bore away from the range of their vision the struggling form of Brunenkant, the other turned to the radiovisor and spoke. "Go ahead to the Capitol, Rex and Stoddart. We have just recaptured Reclamation City."

Rex nodded a curt acquiescence and Stoddart snapped off the visual and auditory connections with Reclamation City. He knew that Sylvia disguised as Rex would not bear close inspection, and that she dared not speak.

"I expect our fellow-men in the city below us need our assistance badly, dear," Wilhoit said as the plane sped on, "but we can render better service by getting to the Capitol. To help the citizens of Reclamation City now would be like shooting a gorilla in the arm when one could just as well aim at the head or heart and put the beast out of commission forever."

"This is 'gorilla' warfare," commented Sylvia dryly.

On the remainder of the trip they did not see a single community center in which men still ruled.

After a time there came a persistent buzzing in the radio that Wilhoit ignored as long as it was safe to do so. Then he at last answered by snapping in the switches. The two realized now that they were visible on the screen to the myriads assembled in the Grand Auditorium at the Capitol. Sylvia and Wilhoit viewed the vast assembly of hideous upturned faces; faces which masked the intellects that had attained such a high state of perfection that they had conquered their masters!

Stoddart spoke. "We shall soon be there."

"We want to hear from Rex," cried a voice from the assemblage.

"Yes, a speech from Rex, who is bringing his master to us," called another.

Sylvia raised her arm, encased in its heavy, hairy covering and the throng shouted in acclamation. President Marzo drew back his thick lips from his protruding teeth to speak when the plane suddenly lurched to one side and then dropped like a plummet. In the excitement of the falling plane no one noticed that Wilhoit disconnected the instruments of communication. All thought they were naturally injured in the fall.

A few seconds later the plane mysteriously righted itself and took off in the direction of a secluded landing place.

"Say, Sylvia, you sure were plucky not to scream and betray your identity," said her lover admiringly. "But I knew you couldn't make a speech without giving yourself away."

Hastily he revealed his plan to her, which they commenced to put into action. Wilhoit donned the gorilla suit and seated himself in the apparently wrecked plane, admonishing Sylvia to stay out of range of the television. Soon he was in communication with Marzo and the assembled overseers.

"What happened?" asked Marzo.

"Enough," replied the supposed Rex. "—Stoddart lost control of the machine and we began to fall. I grabbed the controls in time to break the fall, but we hit hard. Stoddart was killed, and it is just as well, for I was beginning to suspect him of treachery."

"So were we," exclaimed Marzo emphatically.

"It is well," came the gruff tones of Rex. "I know all he was going to tell you, and we can carry on our great cause alone. I'll start as soon as I can make some repairs on the plane. Am bringing the body of Stoddart to the Capitol,"

He abruptly severed communication.

"Quick, Sylvia, dear, you'll have to put on this suffocator once again. I promise you it won't be long now. For the rest of the act I am a corpse, but I will lie with my hand on the lever that will release the grenades, waiting for you to say when is the instant to act. We have to be careful all along the route, for spy-glasses may be turned in our direction and we must be prepared to respond to insistent radiovisor calls."

During the rest of the trip to the Capitol television observers had momentary glimpses of an ape guiding a plane to the continental capitol, and slouched beside it in the seat the inert form of the man who had been most dreaded in the newly-created monkey republic. At length the lofty buildings of the Capitol hove in sight. Nesting in the center of them was the low, broad structure of the Grand Auditorium. Twice the long-awaited plane circled the low structure as a bird about to alight on her nest. The human beings and their ape captors that thronged the streets watched intently; the former with chagrin, the latter with elation.

"Now the plane will land on the broad dome of the Auditorium," cried many as the object of their scrutiny cut a half circle and made for the center of the dome.

"Let her go, Wilhoit," came a whisper from the gorilla's chest.

The hand of the apparently inanimate being pulled violently

backward and almost simultaneously, under the deft control of the girl, the machine climbed rapidly upward into the clouds. There was a deafening explosion and the plane rocked crazily.

"Keep her going, Sylvia. We must have altitude. Don't straighten out for another thousand. Gee, you sure are some pilot!" Wilhoit finished admiringly.

"You pulled a few fast tricks yourself," she threw back at him. "Boy, if I didn't have on this killing outfit, I could fly to Mars!"

Another thousand feet registered on the altimeter and Sylvia flew the plane in a horizontal position. Once again over a stretch of open country they descended, landed, and Sylvia shed her ape disguise.

"Do you really think that will be the end of ape rule?" asked Sylvia.

"It cannot be anything else," Wilhoit replied confidently. "The outstanding ape intellects of the continent were wiped out in one fell blow. The remaining terrified, disorganized monkeys can be either destroyed or properly subjugated as the world sees fit."

A month later a pretty domestic scene at the Stoddart ranch was interrupted by a summons from the radio phone, and when connection was established a friendly countenance greeted Wilhoit and Sylvia.

"Carl!" Wilhoit exclaimed delightedly.

Carl Brunenkant smiled into the blushing faces of Sylvia Danforth Stoddart and her proud husband.

"You—know?" queried Wilhoit.

"Everyone has followed your romance with intensest interest, and for its happy outcome the country offers its best wishes, but the nation's congratulations are extended to you, President Stoddart, and your presence is requested at the Capitol, for the affairs of the nation need immediate attention. Also, I imagine the future 'first lady' will like to get an intimate view of the White House."

"You mean—" gasped Stoddart.

"The nation signifies its confidence in your ability and takes this means of showing its gratitude for deliverance from the menace of the ape cycle by electing you president of North America, and your duties are to commence at once."

The
Vibrometer

F rank Rickard, young instructor of physics in the Lakeland High School, watched the last boy of his last class for the day disappear through the door. Fond as he was of his students he heaved a sigh of relief, for the day had been a tiring one.

"If only all of the students were as quick to grasp the subject as those two Holcomb boys and their friend Edward Koller, teaching would be a most enjoyable profession," he mused.

As he walked homeward his mind was busy turning over the events of the day and linking the pleasurable experiences with his "hobby" at home.

"I've been rather lonely in the pursuit of my hobby, and I'd rather like to let somebody in on it. I wonder—"

The increasing alacrity of his gait gave evidence of a new decision, and it was not long before he was climbing the stairs to his room, a large airy one above the garage that was built in at the rear end of his father's handsome home of English architecture.

"Frank dear," his mother called from the kitchen, "Eric phoned a little while ago and wanted you to go over there for the evening, I believe he's having a party."

"Hang Eric and his parties!" the young man ejaculated from the door of his room. "I'd rather stay at home. I haven't much more work to do before my machine is completed."

Mrs. Rickard smiled, and in that smile a mixture of emotions was evident. While she was proud of her son's scientific and inventive ability she did not like to see him remain aloof from the wholesome companions of his youth who were enjoying the social pleasures of that period of life that is too fleeting under any circumstances.

"You'd better go, Frank," she urged. "This is Friday and you can work all day tomorrow to work on your machine."

"All right, I'll agree to please you, mother dear, but my heart will be at home with my machine. Why think of it! Tomorrow I may be able to test it out! All I need to do is to put that glass insulator—"

The telephone bell interrupted further details.

"I suppose it's another social demand on my time," exclaimed the irate physics instructor as he descended the stairs.

But it was not a party date as Mrs. Rickard could very well ascertain from her point of vantage at the hall door. In fact her son became so enthusiastic that she wondered who or what could effect such a change.

After Frank had hung up, his mother was innocently using the mop on the already shining hall floor near the telephone.

"Well I've got a *real* date now, mother. Those three boys I've often mentioned as being so far above the rest of any of my physics classes are coming over tomorrow. They don't know anything about my machine but they've been doing a little experimenting on their own and they want to tell me the results. I've been thinking for some time they were advanced enough to take into my confidence. At least I can share my triumph. I've been hungry to do so with some one, but have hesitated to with older men, for there is so often liable to be professional jealousy. You can remember my experience with Professor Van Vorst!"

"Only too well, son," sighed Mrs. Rickard, "but that is a thing of the past, and Professor Van Vorst is dead now so that he will never trouble you again. I'm sure you and your young high-school friends will get along famously."

"The strange thing about these three boys coming over is that I had been on the verge of inviting them for several days past," said Frank as he mounted the stairs to his room.

At the appointed time on Saturday the two Holcomb lads and their friend Ed Koller presented themselves at the Rickard home.

"Frank wants you to go out to the garage," Mrs. Rickard informed them. "He keeps his machine out there. He promises you boys an interesting day, and we both want you to have luncheon with us at noon."

The boys thanked their hostess and made their way to the garage. They were not prepared for the amazing sight which met their eyes as they opened the big double doors.

Occupying nearly a quarter of the garage stood a huge, marvelously intricate mechanism about six feet in length and half as wide. Its height was variable and its component parts were made up of steel, brass, copper, aluminum and glass. Frank Rickard was standing gazing silently at this fruit of years of labor as the three boys entered. He smiled as he greeted them.

"'The Harp of the Senses,' my Vibrometer," he explained.

"Vibrometer," said Claude, the most serious boy of the trio. "Judging by its name it must be something that measures vibrations."

"Why that's along the line of our recent experiments," exclaimed his brother Daniel, who was the more talkative of the two. "I don't believe you know how much we've done along that line."

"Then I know you'll be interested," said Frank. "Let me give you a demonstration."

He stepped lightly upon the copper platform and passed his hands caressingly over the dial, levers and wheels of the Vibrometer and peered into a glass indicator of clock-like workmanship. Then much to the surprise of his youthful friends he commenced to sing "Annie Laurie" in a clear tenor voice. The boys' faces were expressive of amazement.

"Maybe he's gone cuckoo!" suggested Edward Koller to Daniel Holcomb in an undertone, at the conclusion of the word "bonnie."

Dan made no reply but watched his teacher closely, for at this point Frank pulled slightly at one of the levers, and the boys perceived that he stood as if in pantomime, for although his lips moved, no sound was forthcoming, He released the lever, smiling his satisfaction to his three amazed spectators. He then seized another lever, and by degrees his voice slowly developed the sonorous, resonant, vibrant power of a baritone singer. Gradually the tones of his voice were augmented far beyond that of ordinary power. The reverberating sounds completely encompassed the listeners and become clarion-like in their intensity.

At this point Rickard gave the same lever a slight lateral twist and his voice dropped an octavo until the result was almost unbelievable. Was it possible that these uncouth, rumbling sounds issued from the throat of Frank Rickard? The young man turned the lever still farther. Now the visitors could hear no sound except an occasional low rumble or growl as he reached his higher tones, then as the lever was shoved still farther, even these rumbles and growls ceased, and the amazed boys were jarred to their innermost depths. They were literally *feeling* their teacher's intensified song!

"Stop! That is far enough," cried Dan, becoming frightened at the jarring like that of an earthquake. It was apparent from the expressions on the faces of Claude and Ed that they too felt that the demonstration had progressed far enough.

For answer Frank manipulated the same lever in an inverse manner, and his voice was taken back through the entire gamut until he was once again singing in his original pleasing tenor.

"Well, for cryin' out loud!" ejaculated Daniel as their host stepped from the platform, "tell us all about it."

"Yes, how does it work?" demanded the other two eagerly.

"It was just a shade uncanny," admitted Claude Holcomb, "and you've sure got us going as to its method of operation."

"Well, boys," smiled Frank, "you can just imagine that you're in class, and I will try to tell you briefly how my Vibrometer works.

You have already heard, boys, of the expression, 'Harp of the Senses,' which is a metaphor in which our known five senses—seeing, hearing, smelling, tasting and feeling—are likened to the strings on a harp. What you probably did not know is that apparently there are missing strings in this Harp of the Senses; strings which should connect up between the known sense strings, thus making the harp a unified, uninterrupted whole. In other words there are probably existent vibrations (for you know our senses are merely awareness of these vibrations) which our bodies, limited as they are to the five senses, do not perceive at all. The purpose of my Vibrometer is to seek out these vibrations and cause them to register upon the five senses which we possess.

"Science has already succeeded in diminishing and increasing rates of vibration so that the manifestation to our senses is completely altered. If these vibrations may be so changed, why may they not be counteracted so the visible is tendered invisible, the audible inaudible, the tangible intangible? Tell me why may electricity not bring within the range of our five senses—those five senses that present to us merely a crack as opposed to the whole of the out of doors—the knowledge of natural phenomena that are now a part of the unknown world around us?"

"Do you mean to tell us that your machine feels our senses so that we cannot depend upon them to guide us correctly?" interrupted Ed.

"Sure, that's what he says," declared Claude with enthusiasm unusual to this quiet, thoughtful boy. "When he got on there and sang, and then although his mouth opened and closed no sound came, he had merely nullified the vibrations of sound as they came out of his mouth. Isn't that right, Mr. Rickard?"

"Correct, Claude," assented the pleased young teacher. "This is an instrument that can generate forces or annul existing ones; augment or diminish any of the forces which are now interpreted by our five senses. It can interweave, differentiate, coordinate or completely counteract vibrations of any source or nature whatsoever! You may be able to see a sound, hear a color, both hear and see an odor! It will mix your senses by seemingly contradictory evidences and will progress through the entire gamut of commonly known vibrations, whether the scale be an ascending or a descending one; whether the thing required be harmony, dissonance or complete obliteration. It will record and transform energy so as to bring it within the scope of any or all of our five senses."

"Something like packing the experiences of a lifetime into a single year," remarked Claude gravely.

"Precisely, only more so," Frank replied.

"Then you really weren't making all that noise, were you?" queried Dan.

"No, my boy, the Vibrometer was responsible, and my natural voice was merely the relay or trigger."

At this juncture Mrs. Rickard appeared in the doorway and summoned them to lunch. For the next hour Dan and Ed completely forgot the machine in the garage, but not so Claude. He said little during the meal but his mind was busy reviewing the things Rickard had said, and he relived many times the practical demonstration of the machine's ability to change the rate of the vibrations of sound.

Their repast over, the four repaired to the garage once more for a "demonstration more wonderful than the other," as Frank promised them. As soon as they were again before the intricate machine Frank handed each of the boys a pair of glasses with thick, dark eyepieces, telling them to put them on. They did as he bade unquestioningly.

"These will protect our eyes while we experiment in the realm of light," he explained.

Frank put on his own black goggles and mounted the platform as he had done before.

"You know, boys, that the sense of vision began with the perception of light without color; that is, white light. The retina was not yet sensitive to the effect of difference of wavelength, but only to difference of intensity. Now the intensity of light varies with the amplitude of the waves, and this amplitude was more easily recognizable to primitive man, but as man developed he gained the capacity to recognize differences of wavelength, which means differences of color.

"While the slowest vibrations of sound audible to the human ear occur at the rate of about sixteen to the second, the slowest vibrations of light that are visible to the human eye occur at the rate of about 428 million million per second, and they show the color red. The most rapid vibrations of sound that our ears can detect have a rate of 38,000 per second; the most rapid vibrations of light that our eyes can perceive have a rate of 732 million million a second, and the color that they present is violet. Between the two colors, red and violet, which lie at opposite ends of the visible spectrum come the other colors with their varying intermediate rates of vibration.

"You have all heard of the infrared and the ultraviolet rays which lie respectively at either end of the visible spectrum. We cannot see them, but we have instruments which detect them, and it seems very likely that man will gradually increase his ability to perceive a greater number of vibrations, many of which his limited five senses are wholly unconscious of. But I have talked enough, let me illustrate."

This time Frank placed his hand upon a dial that occupied a conspicuous place in the middle of the Vibrometer. Somberly dressed as he was the most noticeable change that the boys detected was that his bright red necktie was taking on a yellowish cast, but soon that particular part of his attire failed to hold their undivided attention, for the place where Frank stood (but where he was no longer recognizable as Frank Rickard) was a shimmer of bewildering hues, scintillating, flashing, yet harmonious, until the whole machine was lit up with a glory indescribable. Onward and upward tumbled the vibrations through the ultraviolet ray—the X-ray.

The boys noticed a wavering transparency, and it was with horror that they became conscious of the fact that they could see the various dials and levers of the mechanism through the body of their instructor— then after a few seconds of wavering transparency, not unlike viewing a glass object through heated air or clear, moving water, Frank vanished completely, and only the Vibrometer was visible before them, its knobs and plates gleaming with diabolical distinctness.

Painful, intense silence ensued, but through it all there came to the boys' ears, doubly acute and sensitive in this hour of fright, the faint humming of the Vibrometer.

Ed took a step toward the platform but was restrained by Claude, whose husky tones broke the painful silence.

"Don't go near that platform if you value your life!"

"Why?" exclaimed Ed in an attempt to appear casual. "Frank is there. It can't hurt us."

"Might he be dead?" cried Dan with no effort to conceal the despair in his heart.

"No, I think not," replied Claude.

"Then, why would it be dangerous for one of us to mount the platform too?" persisted Ed.

Claude unconsciously assumed the pedantic attitude of their beloved teacher.

"Well, you see, boys, it's this way. Frank went through the various changes in vibration slowly and his body became accustomed to it gradually, but were one of us to rush upon the platform, he could not survive the shock, and it might mean instant death."

Silence again ensued as all three stood awed by the mysterious exhibition that had so recently taken place before their eyes.

Dan was first to break the ominous silence. "Shall we tell his mother?"

"Not yet," responded Claude. "He hasn't been gone long, and I'm sure he'll be back."

"But how can he return when he vanished right before our eyes?" cried Ed, eyeing the Vibrometer in fright.

"Wait and see," was all the comfort the eldest boy would give them in this dark hour of despair.

Hours passed the while the three lads sat with eyes riveted on the central dial. They spoke only an occasional word. Their anxiety was too great for conversation. Did Frank's invisible hand continue to control the mechanism that seemed to the boys to be supernatural?

"No it is not supernatural," declared Claude in response to their unspoken thoughts, "anymore than a radio would seem to be supernatural to a Fiji Islander. It depends upon the point of view of the observer. Really both the radio and the Vibrometer adhere strictly to natural laws, man's obedience to which will always work seeming wonders."

At precisely 5:14, for Ed had just glanced at his watch, the air above the platform appeared wavy, but gradually as the boys watched, it assumed a jelly-like translucency, slowly developing to opaqueness.

"He's coming back!" screamed Dan, jumping from the packing-box on which he had kept his four-hour vigil.

What followed was so amazing that the boys watched in a silence interrupted only by periodic gasps and terse exclamations. Eventually the form on the Vibrometer's platform became humanly recognizable, but what change had taken place in the anatomy of Frank Rickard! Frank was five feet, eleven inches, and very slender; this form that grew from the cloud-like mist was short, heavy-set, and seemed to be that of a man twice the age of the young physics teacher. For a moment he stared with a seemingly fiendish satisfaction upon the garage interior and its three horrified occupants.

But just before he became a normal appearing man from our physical point of view, and just as he made the initial move to step down from the platform, a strange thing happened. He looked distraught and terrified.

His attention was withdrawn from the boys and their environment, and seemed wholly occupied by internal conflict. It was evident that a terrific struggle was going on in that realm that lies just on the border of man's sensual perceptions. It was a struggle in which the three boys were powerless to participate. They could only gaze on in helpless passiveness.

Then, ever so slowly, and at times spasmodically, the agonized face and figure of the villainous appearing intruder grew fainter and fainter until it disappeared altogether, and gradually another form of wholly different proportions was becoming more and more distinct.

"It's Frank, boys, but great Scott, look at him!" cried Dan in wild excitement.

"Yes," exclaimed Ed, "he looks as if he'd been through the war!"

It was true. As the familiar figure and features of young Rickard became recognizable it was observed that he displayed a most forlorn aspect. His clothing was torn and mussed, his red necktie askew, and his hair disheveled. He would have fallen from the platform had the three boys not rushed forward with one thought, and prevented such a catastrophe. They placed him gently upon a worn and battered leather couch that stood in a remote corner of the garage, and waited with fear and consternation until such a time as he showed an inclination to talk.

At length he opened his eyes and smiled wearily.

"I'll be okay in a jiffy, fellows, and then I'll tell you all about it. Believe me, I've had some experience!"

He was again quiet for possibly five minutes at the end of which time he rose to a sitting posture, apparently much refreshed.

"Well, I'm ready to go to it," he said with an amused but reassuring smile into each of the interested faces turned toward him.

"As you boys undoubtedly know it was perfectly reasonable that after my body had passed through the vibrations of the visible spectrum, it would gradually enter that vibratory region where there are some of the missing strings in the Harp of the Senses of which I told you in my earlier discourse. Therefore you could no longer see me although I was there all the time. But to make my adventure in the unknown realm clear to you I must go back a little in my own personal history.

"There was in the college from which I graduated a certain professor by the name of Van Vorst. He had a brilliant intellect, but his assiduous research in the realms of science had tended to warp his philosophical outlook on life so that he was slightly deranged mentally. True his knowledge of his subject was amazing, but he lacked that well-rounded intelligence that a man must have to be truly great. During my junior and senior years in college I frequently visited Professor Van Vorst in his laboratory, and found his accomplishments in the realm of science very inspiring to one like myself, already endowed with those tendencies.

"All went well until the professor began experimenting on a Vibrometer, whose rudimentary principles were the basis for my machine yonder. He seemed very jealous of any suggestions that I might make as to improvements in developing the machine, and I soon found out that the only reason he tolerated my presence in his laboratory was in order that he might experiment upon me. Now this did not suit my fancy at all, for I did not care to 'shuffle off this mortal coil' in such a strange manner, interested though I was in the Vibrometer. I suggested that he use animals in his experimentation, but he gruffly declared that they could never convey to him their sensory experiences during the transition, which was of course true enough. However I felt that it was too risky a chance to take, and I naturally refused to do so.

"I should have taken warning and stayed away from Professor Van Vorst, but I was by now intensely interested in the success of the strange machine, which under Van Vorst's tutelage I had come to understand thoroughly.

"When the eccentric scientist learned that I was obdurate his manner changed from open persuasiveness to smoldering curiosity.

"'Very well, young man,' he said to me one day. 'If you will not lend yourself to the great cause of science, I must myself investigate and become a possible martyr, though I do not think martyrdom a likely result.'

"In vain I pled with him not to take the chance, but he was adamant. With a last menacing glower at me, he stepped upon the platform of the Vibrometer and disappeared in precisely the same manner that I did a few hours ago. I waited and waited for him to return. But he never did. I even tried, at the risk of my life, to bring him back by a reversal of the dial, but in vain. Finally, I disassembled the Vibrometer carefully.

"Naturally suspicion in regard to the learned man's inexplicable disappearance fell upon me. I was accused of murder. When it looked as if I might be sentenced to death because of the enigma regarding the professor's disappearance, I volunteered to attempt to reconstruct the machine and cause an object upon its platform to disappear. I had misgivings as to the success of such a trial, but when one's life is at stake, and innocently, no obstacle is too difficult to surmount.

"I was successful in my attempt, and to the unspeakable amazement of judge and jury, succeeded in passing into oblivion any object placed upon the mechanism. Thus fully convinced, I was acquitted, but the memory of the whole affair remained a bitter thing in my life. Finally we moved from the East and I secured this position in the local high school. But the mysterious charm of the Vibrometer haunted all my leisure hours, and I knew I should never be satisfied until I had made another model of such a machine. Very naturally I modeled it along entirely different lines from the old, and mother was not aware that this machine was a Vibrometer. The deception is not a thing of which to be proud, but you know at times genius and natural curiosity have a way of surmounting all barriers."

He paused long enough to gaze ruefully at his Vibrometer, then resumed. "Today when I set forth to investigate the region at the other end of the visible spectrum, I intended to do so with all precaution. I advanced the dial very slowly and could perceive no ill effects to myself physically. All worked exactly as I had anticipated even through the gamma rays, but I had not taken into account the cosmic rays discovered by Millikan, those rays whose wavelengths are so short and whose frequency so great that they can penetrate six feet of lead.

"It was in or at least bordering on this wave area that I became conscious of strange presences, some friendly, some antagonistic, and it was the latter sensation that predominated. At length I could narrow in down to *one* hostile personality which I recognized distinctively as that of Professor Van Vorst. I cannot explain why I should know this, but know it I did, so that I was not especially surprised when a short time later he became visible to me.

"'So you've stolen my invention,' he snarled. 'Well, I'll get even.'

"'Where are you?' I asked in bewilderment. 'Why haven't you come back? I was nearly convicted for your murder!'

"'I wish you had been,' he answered sullenly, 'yet as an afterthought it wouldn't have given me this opportunity.'

"'Why didn't you return through the agency of the Vibrometer?' I queried.

"'Couldn't, it was gone, you fool. You disassembled it!'

"I was aghast. 'Not until I had waited and waited for your return,' I replied.

"'Nevertheless it was not long enough. Just as I regained consciousness and was about to manipulate the dial for the return journey, the machine began to be disassembled by unseen hands.'

"I was shocked at Professor Van Vorst's disclosures.

"'I am truly sorry,' I said, 'and shall try to rectify matters at once. The platform will hold us both and we shall return together to the plane upon which exists life as we know it, for I suppose to all practical purposes we are dead!'

"'Precisely so,' he assented, 'with only one channel of emergence, which I intend to employ alone!'

"With the last word he leaped to the platform, forcing me bodily therefrom, and commenced a manipulation of the all important central dial. I made a jump and was shocked almost to insensibility upon contact with the platform.

"'Let us emerge together,' I pled.

"For answer he continued his attempt to force me from our narrow dais, and ever he moved the dial steadily.

"At length he succeeded in dislodging me again, but I kept a hand upon the sensitive metal stage. I knew by the indicator he would soon be able to disconnect it and step out into the garage and into the presence of you boys. When I realized that it would be impossible for both to return, that it was his life or mine, I gathered all my strength for one last supreme effort and leaped wholly upon the dais. He grappled with me like a madman, but I guess my youth and sense of righteous indignation were in my favor, for I was successful in gradually forcing him from the platform.

"That, boys, is the story of my return to you, and now if you will kindly help me I intend to do away with any possibility of future catastrophe through the agency of yonder machine."

And so it happened that solemnly and silently, four young scientists took apart, piece by piece, a machine that might have revolutionized the world. That they decided wisely I do not have the shadow of a doubt. What do you think?

Possible Science Fiction Plots

Editor, *Wonder Stories*:

I am in hearty agreement with Mr. Glasser's suggestion that science fiction fans write to various film companies asking for science fantasy pictures. I suppose the film people are afraid to venture, not knowing their changing public. It is up to us to set them right in this matter. Germany is way ahead of us in the production of science films. Is it possible that the settings for science films are expensive? Might this be a deterrent? Two or three years ago I heard that Milton Sills was to star in a picture entitled *The Man from Mars*, but apparently nothing ever came of it.

I am wondering if Mr. Glasser's letter and mine won't start a deluge of letters traveling Hollywood-ward. Come on, science fiction fans, let's go! Our united efforts might bring this country a few films in 1932 that are not Wild West, sex drama, or gangster stuff. I think we're all strong for good comedies, but let's have some of our serious dramas a little less of the emotional and more of the intellectual!

Mr. Pancoast's letter referred to the saying that there are only five or six original plots. That may be true as regards the technique of plot development, but I have made a table of sixteen general classifications into which it seems to me all science fiction stories written to date can be placed:

> Interplanetary space travel.
> Adventures in other worlds.
> Adventures in other dimensions.
> Adventures in the micro- or macro-cosmos.

Gigantic insects.

Gigantic man-eating plants.

Time travel, past or future.

Monstrous forms of unfamiliar life.

The creation of super-machines.

The creation of synthetic life.

Mental telepathy and mental aberrations.

Invisibility.

Ray and vibration stories.

Unexplored portions of the globe; submarine, subterranean, etc.

Super intelligence.

Natural cataclysms; extra-terrestrial or confined to the earth.

The extreme of diabolism and Utopianism are frequent themes, but these are social topics that use one of the above mentioned methods as mere vehicles for the expression of an ideal. Occasionally there are stories very difficult to classify. An example is Dr. Keller's termite story. One might roughly classify it under numbers eight or fifteen, and yet it is something more than either of these because it is a psychological rather than a physical science story

(Mrs.) Clare Winger Harris
16301 Lakewood Hts. Blvd.,
Lakewood, Ohio.

About the Authors

Clare Winger Harris (1891–1968) is widely acknowledged as the first woman author to publish science-fiction stories using her own name. Her story, "Fate of the Poseidonia" won third prize in a national contest sponsored by *Amazing Stories* and was published in their June 1927 issue. She quickly became a popular and prolific contributor to magazines such as *Weird Tales*, *Science Wonder Stories*, and *Science Fiction*. As the genre continued to blossom in the early thirties, Harris mysteriously vanished from the public eye. Yet her stories and letters continued to influence an important generation of writers. Her innovative subjects of climate change, interstellar expedition, cyborgs, and intelligent animals—along with the use of female protagonists—solidified her importance to the field. A native of Illinois, she raised her family in Cleveland, and died in Pasadena, California at age seventy-seven.

Brad Ricca is the author of *Mrs. Sherlock Holmes*, *Super Boys*, and *American Mastodon*. He has been nominated for an Edgar Award and has won an Ohioana Book Award, the St. Lawrence Book Award, and a Cleveland Arts Prize for Emerging Artist in Literature. He has been a contributor to NPR, the BBC, Book-TV, the AV Club, and elsewhere. His film *Last Son* won a Silver Ace Award at the Las Vegas Film Festival. Ricca earned his Ph.D. in English from Case Western Reserve University, where he now teaches classes on writing, comics, and biography. He was born, lives, and works in Cleveland.